AMERIKANERNEST

AMERIKANERNEST

BRIAN MAURICE

Orcas Island Press
First Printing, 2024
First Edition: April 2024
Printed in the United States of America

ISBN: 979-8-9918407-0-5

Book Cover by:
Rejdan/2211404801/Shutterstock.com
Allexxandar/1869785419/Shutterstock.com

For my wife Terry and our beautiful family

Contents

Preface

"Few Germans believed, when the United States declared war upon us in April 1917, that your Nation could raise, equip and train an army of millions to operate more than 3,000 miles from home. But, because of the knowledge of Americans, gained during my life in Spokane, I was not so confident of this. After the Armistice, I realized how it had been done. I saw, in the marvelous manner in which the Americans came into Coblenze and immediately set up a smooth-working administrative machine, the tremendous organizing ability of the United States. Of its fighting ability, I had already had a demonstration.

"The Americans were fine fighters. They executed their attack [in the Argonne] superbly, but, in that thick forest, they made a serious blunder in neglecting to keep close contact with the units on their right and left. Then, too, the conformation of the ground in this vicinity was such that the attacking force was placed in a canyon or ravine. It was poor strategy on the part of the Americans to allow themselves to be drawn into so dangerous a position." [1]

> Oberleutnant Fritz Prinz
> 254th Reserve Infantry Regiment
> 76th Reserve Division
> Imperial German Army

Prinz's characteristically thoughtful assessment of the US Army's logistics and organizational achievements is accurate—building a new military training infrastructure and implementing the US Army's lofty logistics plans were indeed impressive achievements. [2]

Prinz's acknowledgment of the American Expeditionary Force's (AEFs) fighting ability reflect elements of wry humor and a high degree of military professionalism. His reference to the AEF's "poor strategy" in the Argonne Forest is, arguably, correct. However, the aggressive American approach, combined with the depleted state of German units in 1918 and their diminished will to fight after four years of war, resulted in the retreat of the entrenched German Third Army, so Prinz's statement is open to an interesting debate. Who was Fritz Prinz, why do his opinions matter, and what can we learn from his comments?

Prinz was one of a handful of men sent to Washington State by Kaiser Wilhelm II before the outbreak of the Great War. Their mission was to mine tungsten ore, the world's "key war material," [3] from a mountain outside Spokane and ship it to Krupp Steelworks in the Ruhr Vally in Germany. Krupp used the ore to create high-speed steel tools that quintupled metal machining rates. Using high-speed steel, the Imperial German Army would have a five-fold increase in the production of artillery and weaponry, and the Imperial German Navy would have a similar increase in the production of capital ships and U-boats at Krupp's Kiel factory.[4], [5]

When war broke out in 1914, Prinz returned to Germany and served with the 254th Reserve Infantry Regiment. He fought on the Eastern Front against the Russians and the Romanians. In March 1918, after the Eastern Front collapsed, his unit transitioned from Foscani in Romania to Metz on the Western Front, where he fought the French and the Americans.

In 1927, when the *Sunday Star* interviewed Prinz about the Lost Battalion, he was forty-four years of age, lived in Cassel, and was the general manager of a mine. He had previously worked in Spokane for three years and had a firm grasp of American culture, business, and logistics. He had a deep understanding of global strategic resources and the links between tungsten and arms manufacture. Prinz had amassed significant combat experience on two fronts during the Great War. He had been promoted from Private to Lieutenant, was twice wounded, and was the recipient of the Iron Cross for bravery. Notably, he had played a leadership role in the intense battle between the German

254th Infantry Regiment and the American 77th Division's so-called "Lost Battalion". The battle took place in the rugged terrain around Charlevaux Mill in the Argonne Forest—perhaps the most infamous American battle of the Great War.[6] Because of his remarkable combination of strategic, cultural, and military experiences, Prinz's insights on the AEF performance carry exceptional historical authority.

My part of this story started with a hike through the Argonne Forest in 2017, almost a hundred years after belligerents fired their final shots. More than any other battleground I had visited, the forest still bore visible scars of the war and the fight that once consumed it. Its wild terrain and deep ravines were as unforgiving and uncompromising as they were in 1918.

Because I lived in Washington State, I was drawn to Prinz's mining work in Spokane. I also wanted to learn more about the replacement troops from the Western States that joined the American First Army in the Argonne just days before the most significant American operation of the war.

Through that research, another soldier emerged from the past: Private William Henry Martin of the 308th Infantry Regiment, 77th Division, AEF. Martin's war was short but intense. He was one of the many young men drafted into service in mid-1918 who faced a battle-hardened Imperial German Army without appreciable combat training. Like so many other draftees, Martin would be rushed through a series of organizations over ninety days and assigned to a front-line unit as a replacement just days before that combat unit climbed out of its trenches into the largest American operation of the Great War. His ninety-day indoctrination into the profession of arms was consumed by travel from Washington State to California, New York, England, and ultimately to the Argonne Forest in France.

Prinz and Martin both lived in Spokane, Washington, between 1911 and 1914. Prinz was on his mission to supply strategic material to Krupp; a few blocks away, Martin worked for a paint and sash manufacturer. Both men were called to serve their country. Prinz would serve over four years; Martin would serve less than four months. Both men would cross paths again in 1918 on a hillside deep in the Argonne Forest. That small, bloody hillside was simply called "the pocket" by the Americans; the Germans referred to it as the "Amerikanernest" (American nest). Their coincidental encounter would occur as the AEF pressed relentlessly into the Imperial German Army in the war's closing days and as the Germans fought hard for every foot of ground.

The combination of Prinz's and Martin's stories and intertwined experiences provides a glimpse into the human side of war and the tactical actions surrounding the AEF Lost Battalion. However, viewing their stories through a wider lens allows us to explore other aspects of Great War strategy and Great Power competition.[7]

Martin's journey through the Argonne Forest illuminates controversial aspects of AEF strategy. At the operational level, we now know more about the ruthless decisions made by AEF commanders. These decisions resulted in American infantry pushing relentlessly against entrenched German machine guns and coordinated artillery without regard for flank support. This tactical approach exposed doughboys to high losses and risk of envelopment. It was a gamble that American Generals were willing to take and that German commanders were willing to exploit.

The AEF 77th Division Commander would later state: "My orders were quite positive and precise—the objective was to be gained without regard to losses and without regard to the exposed conditions of my flanks. I considered it most important that this advance should be made and accepted the responsibility and the risk involved in the execution of the orders given." [8]

Prinz believed the American approach in the Argonne was a "serious blunder".[9] Many 77th Division doughboys, including Major Charles Whittlesey[10], commander of the men in the pocket, may have agreed with him. Prinz, predictably balanced in his assessment but perhaps unaware of the AEF orders, commented: "I do not mean to blame anyone [for the poor military strategy in the Argonne], for after four years of war, I know how impossible it often is to match an actual advance with an advance planned and plotted on a map. Half of war is made up by mistakes".[11]

Competition between Great Powers provides the backdrop for the Great War and the context we should apply while we trace Prinz's and Martin's lives leading up to, and through, 1918.

At the turn of the 20th century, eight Great Powers were generally recognized: Austria-Hungary, France, Germany, Britain, Italy, Japan, Russia, and the United States. Each had an ability to exert influence on a global scale, although some were more inclined than others. Great Power competition in economic, diplomatic, and military spheres was constant and dynamic. Each Great Power had unique needs, capabilities, and constraints.

Germany was still evolving from national unification in 1871, the turmoil of the "year of three emperors" in 1888, and the influences of titanic statesmen like Bismarck. Its booming population and industrial power outstripped French, Russian, Austria-Hungary, and British competition. However, there were also tensions, as evidenced by the pivot from Bismarck's steady hands and Realpolitik foreign strategy to Weltpolitik (1891) and the erratic approach to diplomacy taken by Wilhelm II.[12] These German political approaches have interesting parallels to US big stick and moral diplomacy. Germany's colonial aspirations in Africa and the Pacific and the rapid development of the Imperial Navy were indicators of a new and expansionist foreign policy. Prinz, born in 1883, would have been acutely aware of Germany's growing Great Power status and its colonial asperations at the dawn of the twentieth century and must have pondered the latent power he witnessed in the US.

We now know that Germany understood the strategic importance of high-speed steel and acted purposefully upon that knowledge ahead of its Great Power competitors.[13] Germany accrued tungsten from as far away as Burma (present-day Myanmar), Portugal, Argentina, China, Australia, Britain, and the United States until 1914. Between 1900 and 1914, no other Great Power leveraged tungsten as a strategic material. On the contrary, the United States and Britain exported their tungsten to Germany. Although the impact of Germany's tungsten program on the war cannot be quantified, it is a logical assumption that tungsten played a direct role in the deaths of myriad Entente soldiers. By 1919, the US Senate, along with the rest of the world, recognized tungsten as the "most essential of all war materials"[14] underscoring a rapid maturation of the US's appreciation for strategic materials between 1914 and the end of the war. Through Prinz's activities at the Germania mine near Spokane, we witness an element of the advanced German military-industrial apparatus (and the corresponding nonexistant US apparatus) in very human terms.

In the United States, an emerging yet hesitant Great Power was evident. Despite the financial crisis of 1907, the U.S. went through rapid economic growth between 1890 and 1910. It pursued global commerce, generally without overt political commitments. Militarily, it was unsure of its place on the global stage and was woefully unprepared for military conflict in 1917. Compared with other Great Powers, it had a frail military infrastructure, and politically, it struggled to balance an urge for strategic isolationism and an imperialistic impulse. President Roosevelt's big stick diplomacy and President Wilson's moral diplomacy reflect these diverse approaches to US foreign policy. Imperial impulses were evident in blatant US maneuvers involving Alaska, Hawaii, Cuba, the Philippines, and Panama.

In 1917, the US took extraordinary shortcuts in mobilizing and training an unprecedented four million troops from a seedling 127,588 military force. The shortcuts were the fallout of a nascent Great Power with a distrust of a large standing army and an innate sense of isolationism.

President Wilson's drive to go to war in 1917 and raise a new army was a significant pivot for Wilson, Congress, and Americans. US participation in the war with millions of troops under American battlefield leadership changed Great Power dynamics and the narrative of the peace that followed. US naval participation alone, nor a small ground army, would not have forced that level of change.

Wilson's Fourteen Points, delivered in January 1918, outlined the principles for which America would fight: self-determination—the concept that nations should have the right to govern themselves—open diplomacy without secret treaties, freedom of the seas, and free trade, among others. The fourteenth point proposed that "a general association of nations must be formed under specific covenants for the purpose of affording mutual guarantees of political independence and territorial integrity to great and small states alike." Wilson's proposals, out of step with other Great Power visions, would be mostly disregarded during the Treaty of Versailles. The proposals, however, forever established a new benchmark for Great Power narrative, resulting in the formation of the League of Nations and the United Nations.

These Wilsonian concepts would have been baseless without the US Army's extensive mobilization effort, the battlefield impact of the new army, and the sacrifice of so many American lives. Although crude and Machiavellian in nature, the shortcuts taken to mobilize and train millions of American soldiers, including Martin, were not without a just cause or long-term positive impact.

Fritz Prinz's and William Martin's stories have been dormant for over a hundred years. The stories have enormous historical value, adding insight and context to our understanding of the Lost Battalion, the Meuse-Argonne Offensive, and the Great War. Viewing their lived experiences in the context of 20th century Great Power competition is equally relevant, perhaps *more* relevant as we witness competition between 21st century nations. Today's Great Powers are once again grappling with evolving global dynamics, regional uncertainty, and shifting roles, as happened between 1900 and 1914.

Mark Twain is credited with saying: "History doesn't repeat itself, but it often rhymes." Ghosts from the Great War would surely recognize the rhyming with the 21st century and plead that we exhaust all instruments of national power before resorting to military solutions.[15] Great Powers of 1914 would have appeared to have found a way to do precisely the opposite.

Prologue

MONDAY, 7 OCTOBER 1918

ARGONNE FOREST, FRANCE

Private William Martin
Company G, 308th Infantry, 77th Division
American Expeditionary Force
The Pocket

William studied the odd stone inches from his face. Since he arrived in this place, he had seen them bounce into the air when German whiz bangs or woolly bears blew the earth apart.[16] The stones were everywhere: on the forest floor he crawled over and in the holes he dug to stay alive.

What a journey, he thought. Until then, he had been too tired, too preoccupied with cold, hunger, and fear to reflect on the past twelve days. He picked up the stone and felt its edges. Despite the madness that surrounded him that morning, he was, for a moment, at ease.

Twelve days ago, he doubted he would survive this attack into the forest. Now, with his 77th Division brothers, he was confident in his ability to prevail as much as the next man. He would "keep the faith," as Sergeant Greally said, no matter what the Hun threw at him. He ran his fingers over the stone's edges and put it in his pocket. He would keep a piece of this hillside with him, something that would remind him in years to come of this place, this time, and these brothers.

He recalled the barrier between the old guard and the new soldiers when he arrived as a replacement in the 308th Infantry in the woods by the crossroads of Croix Gentin. The groups stayed apart in the secluded forest camp, made sideways eye contact, but didn't cross the boundaries that were clearly there. The New Yorkers had been fighting for months. They were comfortable with each other, with their equipment, and in the chaos of war. They had earned their cynicism and swagger in the Baccarat Sector and along the Vesle River. They had no desire to get to know the replacements—men from faraway places like Idaho, Washington, Oregon, Montana, Minnesota, and California. The New Yorkers grumbled about the fight they knew was coming and about so many green replacements that had just joined their unit.

William recalled how Corporal Dolan, Sergeant Greally, Major Whittlesey, and other extraordinary men had forced brotherhood upon all the men in the unit. *Perhaps,* William thought, *in a peculiar way, it was a common enemy or the calamity of war that forced such unusual fraternity among men.*

He thought of that nail on the back of the door at Jones and Dillingham in Spokane, where he had hung his apron three months earlier. Then came the blur of movement: leaving Spokane's Milwaukee Road Depot; eighteen days in Camp Lewis, Washington; twelve days in Camp Kearny, California; two days in Camp Mills, New York; the vast Atlantic; a few blissful days in England; the Channel; and twenty-seven days in the French countryside a hundred miles from the frontlines. Trains, ships, and his well-worn boots brought him to this hillside. He recalled the nagging feeling that it had been too quick, that the Army had rushed his training, and that he needed more time to prepare for combat.

Eighty-seven days after hanging his apron on that nail in Spokane, he arrived at Company G, 308th Infantry, on the front line. *Jesus, they only gave me three days to get to know these fellas, three days before we went over the top in the largest American offensive of the war.*

Early on 26 September, William and over 1.2 million American troops climbed out of their trenches and into the Argonne Forest.[17] William had spent more time on ships and trains than learning the combat skills that would keep him alive in the Argonne. His 6th Depot Brigade Commander in France knew the score and wrote to his superior at the Army's Services of Supply (SOS), highlighting the shortcomings in field training for William's unit and the need for more time to prepare the men.[18] The General's memo changed nothing. The AEF needed millions of combat troops on the frontline, thousands of miles from home bases. Army leadership discounted their sacred responsibility to train the nation's soldiers for combat. They traded time for numbers, quantity for quality, and blood for ground in the Argonne.

William's injured hand throbbed. His hunger and his fear returned. For twelve days, he had clawed and fought through five kilometers of ravines, hills, dense forest, brambles, barbed wire, and hostile fire. He was cold, miserable, hungry, and desperately low on ammunition. But worse than those temporal problems, he was surrounded by battle-hardened Germans determined to kill him.

The fighting had lulled over the past few hours; there was occasional sniper and MG-08 machine gun fire but, thankfully, no German mortars and no misplaced American artillery. The enemy held the high ground to the front, the steep hills to the rear, and both sides of a narrow sliver of ground that the Germans called the "Amerikanernest" (American Nest) and the Americans called "the pocket." William's hope of relief diminished with every round he fired.

Five hundred and fifty-four Americans had dug into the shale hillside five days previously. Over a hundred were now dead, lying unburied in the pocket. More than twice that number were injured. The remaining fighting men, less than two hundred, made a pact to stick together, not surrender, and keep the faith no matter how desperate the battle.

German trench mortars from three sides and concentrated machine guns opened up simultaneously. Bullets buried into trees, flicked through leaves, and kicked up dirt across the pocket. William gripped his Enfield, glanced at the safety, and felt for the remaining full clips in his cartridge belt. He pressed into the cold walls of his funk hole and waited.[19]

Corporal James Dolan from Killargue County Leitrim, Ireland, lay pressed against the dirt beside William.[20] "If we had half the ammunition they have, we'd be in Berlin by now drinking beer in the some gobshite's garden." William didn't respond, but Dolan's whimsical comment was welcome.

The mortars and machine guns stopped abruptly. For a few seconds, there was silence in the pocket. The American Hotchkiss machine guns and Dolan's Chauchat erupted in short bursts, targeting waves of German troops attacking from all sides. William held fire and waited for the feldgrau[21] uniforms to get closer.

* * *

Oberleutnant (Lieutenant) Fritz Prinz
254th Infantry Regiment, 76th Reserve Division
I Reserve Corps, Third Army
Imperial German Army
Amerikanernest

Five hundred meters from the pocket, a deep bunker was the command post for the 254th Regiment of the German 76th Reserve Division. In the dimly lit space, a trim German officer peered over his dog-eared maps on a table in the center of the earthen room. Oberleutnant Fritz Prinz had a calm demeanor, yet the sense of urgency in the bunker was palpable.

Since September 26, the American 77th Division had attacked the 76th Division through the dense forest from the south. The Americans had made remarkable progress despite the layered German defenses. French, American, and German artillery blasted nearby, close enough that dust and dirt from the ceiling fell steadily on the unrolled maps, irritating the Oberleutnant.

Fritz was not concerned with the artillery. He learned many years before to tell the difference between friendly and enemy fire. Fritz understood that only an unlucky shot threatened him and his staff. As a pragmatic man with four years of combat experience, he discounted that possibility altogether. Besides, he had weightier problems than an errant artillery shell right now.

Five days previously, the adjoining 2nd Landwehr Division and his 76th Reserve Division left a sliver of light between them as they maneuvered their forces along the Giselher Stellung (the second main defensive line in the Argonne Forest) under the weight of the aggressive American and French advance. The units were forced to cover simultaneous attacks from the American 307th Infantry on the east side of Hill 198 and from the French Groupement Durand and the American 308th Infantry to their west, around La Palette and Hill 205. The defenders moved machine guns, mortars, and troops to the east and west, so their line had a small weak point on the west side of Hill 198.

A medium-sized American force had audaciously slipped through their line at that weak point and stubbornly held a small area behind German lines. *They got lucky. The weak spot was not large, and it was not there for long, but the Americans were in the right place at the right time.* He begrudgingly admitted that their audacity, raw aggressiveness, and luck had created an opportunity they had leveraged to maximum effect.

There would be hell to pay for that tactical error, but Fritz knew it was a necessary adjustment based on the tactical situation and limited resources along Giselher Stellung. Major Hünicken, Commander of the 254th Infantry Regiment, would debrief that later when there was time. For now, Fritz focused on eliminating the small unit that anchored the AEF north of the main force.

New intelligence reports painted a grim picture for Fritz. The French were advancing on his western flank, and the American 1st Corps and 5th Corps had made significant progress in Montfaucon and Apremont to his east. Both American and French forces were converging behind him, threatening to cut his unit off. This stubborn Amerikanernest that would not surrender was the fulcrum that everything pivoted on and that pinned him in place. Ironically, the German Third Army would have to retreat or they would be surrounded.[22]

Fritz pondered the Supreme Army Command (Oberste Heeresleitung—OHL)[23] assessment of American troops: they were as fit and stubborn as they were untrained and undisciplined. OHL had been confident that inadequate training and shoddy field leadership would be disastrous for the Americans in battle.

Fritz had seen the AEF's inability to coordinate artillery and infantry maneuver, their careless flank management, and their dumbfounding tactic of attacking dug-in machine guns with bayonets, rifles, grenades, and light machine guns. Yet he had witnessed the Americans consistently proving to be more of a problem than anyone had expected. In fact, they seemed to be employing a poorly executed variation of the German infiltration attacks against static defenses, a chaotic version of what the German shock troops had done in the Kaiserschlacht (the Spring Offensive). He was confident that the Kaiser, General von Hindenburg, General Ludendorff, and the entire OHL had underestimated the Americans at strategic and tactical levels.[24]

Another layer of dirt fell from the ceiling. Fritz methodically brushed it off the table. He exhaled, leaned over his maps, and felt the burden of the past six months weigh on him. He had seen Generals von Hindenburg and Ludendorff squander the enormous opportunity gained in March following Russia's capitulation. Fifty Divisions were freed from the Eastern Front and joined the fight on the Western Front. But the subsequent Spring Offensive and the loss of over a million German soldiers was a body blow to the army—the loss lodged like a bullet in his chest. Four years of hard fighting had left a mark, but the Spring Offensive, followed by the complete collapse of the German Army, was almost too heavy a burden to carry.

In his heart, he knew the combination of America's entry to the war, the loss of a million men, the unraveling of the Kaiser, and the caving in of the Army's morale meant that the military situation was almost hopeless. It occurred to him that the tactical problem he studied on his maps was strategically irrelevant to the war's outcome; it was now only relevant in salvaging regimental pride. That was enough.

He went to work and focused on the Amerikanernest as an opportunity to finish the war on a high note for the 254th frontschwein[25] and the Deutsches Heer[26].

Major Hünicken, just returned from leave, entered the bunker briskly. Oberleutnant Prinz and Hauptmann Hansen, who had commanded the 254th Infantry Regiment in Hünicken's absence, snapped upright.

The Major, agitated and frustrated, exclaimed, "I just got my neck twisted by General von Gallwitz for not having control of my line and for allowing this situation to fester long enough for the French on the right and the damn Americans on the left to drive north of our position. Division is under incredible pressure west of Binarville and around Chatel Chehery—here and here—we are at risk of being cut off. We will withdraw to Grandpré at 1700 hours, regroup, and continue the fight there."

He paused and looked into both men's eyes with an unblinking, intense stare.

"Before we leave, you WILL destroy this wretched Amerikanernest! You have them surrounded; for God's sake, finish them off!"

As if in response, another salvo of artillery whistled overhead, the map table rumbled, and a new layer of dirt landed on the Oberleutnant's map. Major Hünicken stormed out before the dust settled. Oberleutnant Prinz and Hauptmann Hansen got back to work with renewed resolve.

1

Setting Sail

THURSDAY, 19 JANUARY 1911

S.S. PENNSYLVANIA, HAMBURG, GERMANY

Twenty-seven-year-old Fritz Prinz left his home and his fiancée, Auguste, in Cassel the night before he sailed. He stayed in Hamburg and was up early the following day to board the steamship *Pennsylvania,* bound for New York.

Fritz paused to admire all thirteen thousand gross tons of the passenger ship on the banks of the Elbe River. Her blue and white flag fluttered, and smoke from her single funnel drifted aft. The low superstructure housing the bridge, first-class saloon, smoking room, and library ran almost one-third of her length. At her stern, an additional two-deck superstructure looked to Fritz like an afterthought. With all the commotion on the dock, *Pennsylvania* seemed more like a hard-working cargo ship than a stately liner, but she was majestic to Fritz, who had never been to sea.

Figure 1: Fritz Prinz, circa 1927, at his home in Cassel [27]

Captain Knuth and the Chief Steward greeted him as he stepped aboard. Following the steward's directions, he entered the lavishly decorated main hall, lined with wooden panels, ornate lighting, and plush carpets. Fritz settled into his stateroom, enjoyed the luxury of his surroundings for a few moments, and wrote a letter to Auguste.

The *Pennsylvania* pushed back from the berth on time, cruised to the mouth of the Elbe, and stopped briefly at Cuxhaven. It then voyaged into the North Sea to Boulogne-sur-Mer and onto Plymouth in the English Channel before heading into the vast Atlantic. Its powerful twin screws would take her to New York in a respectable sixteen days.

For the first four days, Fritz enjoyed leisurely breakfasts in the company of the other passengers. He spent hours reading in the ship's library and listening to the band on the promenade deck. But, the closer Fritz got to New York, the more his mind became preoccupied with his OHL mission. He began to avoid the distractions of the smoking room and the social hall and spent more time studying his notes in his stateroom. When the *Pennsylvania* was almost forty degrees west of Greenwich, Fritz's anxiety ratcheted up. He began to rise early, would finish his breakfast before the other passengers arrived, and then walked the promenade deck alone for hours. His mind wrestled with mine operations, the mining staff, and how he might improve operations.

On day ten, while he enjoyed the tepid sunshine on the upper deck, he found himself completely distracted by the unknowns at the mine. Agitated, he gave up on his stroll and headed with purpose to his room.

He unlocked his leather case, sat at his desk, and opened his journal, flipping to the page headed 'TUNGSTEN'. Underneath, indented and in bulleted form, he read:

> "... *rare metal, found naturally* ... *almost always combined with other elements in chemical compounds* ... *identified as new element (1781), first*

isolated as metal (1783) . . . 1900 Paris Exhibition, Bethlehem Steel Company . . . ores include Tungstenite (Fe, Mn)WO$_4$ and scheelite CaWO$_4$ . . . remarkable robustness, highest melting point of all the elements discovered (3422 °C/6192 °F/3695 K), highest boiling point (5930 °C /10706 °F/6203 K). . . density 19.3 times of water . . . hardness: close to that of diamond... large deposits in Rocky Mountains, China, Burma . . . addition of tungsten materially increases the hardness and heat resistance of steel.

"Military applications: dramatically increased machining rates for cutting tools that make munitions, artillery, and ships.

"High speed lathe tools can operate at 5-6 times the cutting speed of regular carbon steel tools, and at the same time permit a heavier, deeper cut in the machined part being worked on... key war material. [28]

"1905 Carnegie Steel timed high-speed steel drill testing on armor plate: high-speed steel drill, 17 holes; regular steel drill, 1 hole." [29]

The grey sky was visible through the porthole, and the engine's low rumbling filled the room. Fritz paused his reading and recalled how surprised he had been to be summoned by his Commanding Officer, Hauptmann Weiss, six months previously.

Weiss explained he was well-connected at OHL through former military classmates and many years socializing with the Prussians. He was particularly close with Hauptmann Geyer in the OHL Operations II Mobilization Section. The renowned Colonel Max Bauer and General von Moltke led this critical section. OpsII, as he referred to it, was the section of OHL responsible for liaison with industry to ensure the Army and Navy maintained a technology edge in what many senior officers believed was inevitable—a European war, fueled in part by the Kaiser's Weltpolitik policy and underpinned by ambitions for a "place in the sun" for the fledgling German state. [30]

Hauptmann Geyer had talked freely about the OpsII programs. Weiss was amazed at the scope of operations but was stunned by one program, in particular, involving tungsten. While meeting with Krupp engineers, Ludendorff's officers recognized the strategic value of using tungsten to create metal cutting tools as hard as diamond, increasing Krupp production rates fivefold.

Geyer recounted how OpsII set up a program with Krupp to ensure the Army and Navy had all the capital ships and artillery they needed. Teams of German officers were dispersed globally to mine tungsten, process the ore, and ship the concentrate back to Krupp Steelworks in Essen. Using this new material, Krupp would quintuple its output of weapons, capital ships, and U-boats.[31] OHL leadership knew this strategic material would be a decisive advantage in a protracted war. They also knew their Great Power competitors were unaware of tungsten's advantages.

Geyer had asked Weiss if he knew someone who could manage mines, had expert English, and could be discreet. Weiss thought immediately of Fritz. He had mastered military arts and mining technology and spoke English fluently. He also saw in Fritz a resolve and dedication that inspired confidence.

Weiss coordinated a meeting between Fritz and Geyer. He sent Fritz's complete military records and wrote a personal recommendation summarizing Fritz's suitability for the role. The meeting went as he expected. Geyer was impressed with Fritz and enrolled him in the program before they parted.

Fritz had planned to spend his working years in Cassel, continuing his reserve service and raising a family with Auguste. But he could not pass up working with Krupp and so close to men like Bauer and even von Moltke. The mission pulled Fritz with an irresistible gravitational force. He jumped at the chance to serve the Kaiser and the Empire.

Fritz recalled the weeks he spent at Krupp in Essen. He learned about their global logistics and manufacturing processes. He listened intently while Krupp engineers explained the process of using tungsten ore to produce high-speed steel. The Krupp engineers demonstrated the power of high-speed steel on the shop floor, cutting and milling steel at rates that astounded the onlookers. All they needed, they said, was enough ore to make this plan work at scale.

In Berlin, OHL assigned him to a tungsten mine in Spokane, Washington. It was there that he first learned of Hauptmann Wilhelm Scheck[33] and Oberleutnant Rudolph Hacklander. Hacklander[34] had been in Spokane since 1908, Scheck since 1906. Both were responsible for setting up the American company, initiating tungsten production, and shipping the ore overseas. A German lawyer, Weber, moved to Washington in 1910 to help with legal issues.

Principal stockholders and owners of the mine were a curious bunch—German Consul in San Francisco Franz Bopp,[35] German Consul in St. Paul Hilary Brunot, and a Mr. Piepmier from Cassel.[36]

A knock on the cabin door prompted Fritz to close his journal.

"Dinner in thirty minutes, Herr Prinz," announced the steward.

Figure 2: Krupp Steelworks, Essen [32]

Fritz nodded. He locked his journal back in his case and reached for the only book he packed, his dog-eared copy of Clausewitz's *Vom Kriege* (On War).[37] Fritz was unaware of how relevant the book would be in the coming years or the turmoil ahead for him, his family, and his country.

2

New York

SATURDAY, 4 FEBRUARY 1911

HOBOKEN, NEW JERSEY

The S.S. *Pennsylvania* steamed effortlessly into New York harbor. Brooklyn Bridge, with the towering city in the background, was majestic. As distracted as Fritz was by the city, he moved slowly to port, drawn by the elegance of the Statue of Liberty. Something captured Fritz's imagination and left an indelible imprint.

The ship steamed up the Hudson, passing the West Side, then swung sharply to port, gliding to a stop at the Hamburg American Line pier in Hoboken.

Immigration officers cleared first-class passengers onboard and spared them hours of processing in the arrival hall. Pakie Croke, the immigration officer who boarded the ship in New York Harbor, was functional and quick in his work. In response to Croke's questions, Fritz stated he was a clerk, paid his own fare, and had $160 in his pocket. His destination was Spokane, Washington; his status was "tourist, intending to return after six months," and he would stay with his German friend Mr. Scheck in Spokane.[38] Croke had over eighty passengers to document, and he saw no reason to spend more time on the five-foot-five-inch German with perfect English.

By the time stevedores moored the ship and swung gangways into place, the first-class passengers had all cleared immigration. They walked down the gangway and headed to the arrival hall while others onboard watched them with envy and resentment.

A man holding a sign with "MR. PRINZ" in large black letters awaited. The two men made eye contact and extended their hands as they neared each other. "Welcome Fritz. Good to finally meet you. I'm Meyer from the Embassy. Counselor von Schlegel sends his regards."

The two walked out of the building together and casually discussed the voyage. Meyer was agreeable and talkative, and Fritz was excited to be in New York. They turned onto River Street and arrived at Hoboken Terminal within minutes. Meyer and Fritz boarded a Hudson & Manhattan Railroad car and disappeared into the newly built Hudson River Tunnel. In less than ten minutes, the two arrived at the Hudson Terminal building in lower Manhattan and surfaced to the grey February sky on Church Street.

They walked half a block to Cortlandt Street, climbed the stairs to the Interborough Rapid Transit Company (IRT) 6th Avenue Elevated Line, and boarded. Fritz was overwhelmed with the hectic scene below, barely paying attention to Meyer's chatter. Trinity Church sailed past the window, and they got off one stop later at Rector Street. "Come on, almost there," said Meyer.

"We have a few locations in New York. This one is important," Meyer nodded towards the Hamburg American building, an elegant structure with a large arched entranceway. Meyer held the door open. "This is the administration office; the Operations team is just around the corner on Wall Street. Come on."

Meyer led Fritz to the elevator and up to the third floor. Meyer knocked on a glass door and entered, waving Fritz in. "Mr. von

Schlegel, may I introduce Mr. Fritz Prinz, lately of Cassel, bound for Spokane."

Haniel von Schlegel was from the Embassy in Washington, but he spent most of his time in the New York offices. "Ah, welcome Fritz. We're glad you're here. You're the final member of Immergrün (Evergreen), and that work must start producing results. It has been slower than we wanted, thanks to the legalities we got tangled up in. While the Kaiser has no specific timeline, I think it's fair to say that we must be ready as soon as possible.

"So, let's get down to business. I've arranged a few meetings this afternoon with Major von Mücke and Mr. L. E. Reutter from the Embassy—both these gentlemen spend most of their time here in New York and are critical to Immergrün."

After coffee, Fritz met with Meyer, von Mücke, Reutter, and three junior clerks who supported all the US mining programs. He already had a good understanding of the program from his weeks at OHL, but the New York team provided more detail, and he took additional notes.

The Spokane operation was to take control of the tungsten resources in the area, process it, and ship the ore concentrate back to Krupp. The team had legal difficulties that delayed operations for multiple years, but those had been resolved. Tungsten from the mine was first shipped to the St. Louis Exposition in 1894, where industrialists first became aware of its strategic value. Roselle Mining Co., a Canadian Company, began mining the ore in 1904. Between 1904 and 1907, Roselle shipped 1,647 tons of tungsten to the Krupp Steelworks. Krupp analyzed the ore and found it to be exceptionally high-quality.[39]

Scheck established Germania Mining Incorporated in 1906. After a few years of legal proceedings with Roselle, Germania invested in a twenty-four-ton gravity concentration mill, which became operational in October 1909. In March 1910, it shipped fifty-three tons of ore through G. L. Andrews in Springdale, Washington, to Hamburg and finally to Krupp Steelworks in Essen. Germania grew from sixty to one hundred fifty miners to meet the Krupp demand. The remote mine site was nine miles southeast of Fruitland in Stevens County, Washington, about fifty miles northwest of Spokane, at 3,500 feet.

Fritz summarized the information in his journal and was pleased with how well-organized the New York team was. Meyer and Fritz said their goodbyes, left the Hamburg American building, and took the Elevated Line and a series of trolleys through Manhattan. The two men chatted as they walked the last few blocks to get dinner at 112 Central Park South, the *Deutscher Verein* (German Club).[40]

German socialites crowded the Club, switching effortlessly between German and English. It seemed to Fritz that the clientele was neither German nor American but a strange amalgam of the two. The decor was also an odd mixture of German and American emblems; on one wall was Kaiser Wilhelm II, and on the opposing wall was a picture of George Washington. It fascinated him; he knew he was in a different country, but it had the trappings of his homeland.

After dinner and two beers, Meyer accompanied Fritz to the Hotel Astor on West 44th Street, where the Embassy had arranged his room. In the lobby, Meyer chatted easily for a few minutes but noticed Fritz was fading. He decided to let the new arrival get some rest. "Good luck, Fritz. Remember, contact me as soon as you need anything. We are counting on you to make sure Immergrün is successful." They shook hands, and Meyer left.

The noise of the city traffic wafted into his eighth-floor window. Fritz lay on his bed, exhausted. His mind wrestled with Meyer's words, ". . . we are counting on you to make sure Immergrün is successful . . ." *What did that mean?* He wondered at the spectacle that was New York—the majestic buildings, the chaotic crowds, the diverse inhabitants untethered to the old ways. His last thoughts were of Auguste and his home in Cassel before he drifted into a deep sleep.

3

Out West

SUNDAY, 5 FEBRUARY 1911

HOTEL ASTOR, NEW YORK

Fritz woke refreshed and ready for the long day ahead. He walked the short distance to Summit Avenue subway on 33rd Street. He spotted a small café with an inviting sign and a small table inside the front window. A newsboy lingered at the subway entrance with a stack of newspapers under his arm. Fritz could not resist his habit; he bought a *New York Tribune* and sauntered to the café to kill time before his long train journey.

While sipping his coffee, he opened his *Tribune* and read the headlines. The US Army was still having trouble along the Mexican border. Fritz smiled while he reflected on America's foreign policy. *It is so focused on its own hemisphere, happy to keep Europe at arms-length but smart enough to flex imperialistic muscles. American imperial impulses were clear—the purchase of Alaska, the annexation of Hawaii, dislodging the Spanish from Cuba, securing a strategic foothold in the Philippines, and forcing the separation of the new country of Panama from Columbia in return for building the Panama Canal. Our empires are not so different,* he thought, *just different surroundings—you have the Pacific and the Atlantic, we have Russia and France.*

The absurdity of the thought made him smile. It occurred to him that, in the end, America and Germany had the same aspirations of economic, military, and political autonomy. Ever the strategist, Fritz's brain toyed with America's transition from the Monroe Doctrine to President Roosevelt's regional "Big Stick" doctrine and the leveraging of economic power. He sipped his coffee and pondered the parallels with his Empire's transition from Bismarck's Realpolitik to Wilhelm's Weltpolitik and the rise of German global economics. *No wonder Auguste never allowed him to read the newspaper at breakfast,* he mused. He decided to fold the paper, stop thinking, and enjoy New York and his coffee.

Fritz arrived relaxed at the Delaware, Lackawanna, and Western Railroad station in Hoboken to begin the first leg of his westward journey. Guided by a sharply dressed Pullman Porter in a dark blue tunic and peaked hat, he boarded a sleeper car on the New York, Chicago, St Louis Railroad Train #5, commonly called the "Nickel Plate". He found his berth and stowed his case in the compartment above the seat.

The Porter came by, "Welcome aboard the Nickel Plate, Sir. My name is John. If you need anything, just ask."

Fritz looked up, noted the pressed lines in John's uniform, and nodded with a smile.

The Nickel Plate pulled out of Hoboken at the stroke of 2:00 p.m. Moving slowly, it passed through Newark and over the Passaic River. After an hour, they covered fifteen miles of track to the industrial town of Paterson, its tall red-brick factory chimneys looming over the landscape.

After Paterson, Fritz saw the landscape change rapidly. Now, woods, fields, and small towns dotted the expanding countryside. The openness felt good after the compressed architecture of Manhattan. Here, he was not drawn to look upwards but outwards.

By 4:00 p.m., the Nickel Plate crossed sixty more miles of New Jersey countryside, and Fritz had barely blinked. They passed through the three thousand-foot Oxford tunnel, the small town of Oxford Furnace, over the Paulinskill River, and then onto Bridgefield and Delaware. As the light faded, the locomotive found the majestic Delaware River and crossed its span over the iron truss' and concrete footings of the Lackawanna Bridge.

John closed the window blinds in the car and reminded travelers that dinner was at 6:30 p.m. After dinner, the Nickel Plate climbed through the Pocono Mountains, traveled north into New York State, then west, and at 1:45 a.m., screeched to a halt in snowy Buffalo.

In the morning, Fritz sat up and opened the curtains, squinted at the morning light. He picked up his map and realized that he was probably on the banks of Lake Erie. Fritz dressed quickly, took his map and headed to the dining car. He passed John on the way. "Good morning, Mr. Prinz. I trust you slept well despite the noisy stop in Buffalo?"

"Good morning, John," he replied, "don't you ever sleep?"

"I do, Mr. Prinz, just not when you do." [41]

Fritz realized how flawless John was in his bearing and speech, how sharp his uniform always looked.

"Where are we?" he inquired.

"Just a few miles past Rocky River, Ohio, Lake Erie is on your right. The next town is Loraine, Ohio. We're running about ten minutes late due to the weather."

John's meticulousness, manner, and precision were what Fritz needed. He nodded his appreciation and continued to the dining car.

After breakfast, he settled into his habit of scratching off the towns on his map as they passed and writing notes in the margin. He soon ran out of space and continued writing in his journal, scribbling place-names and short paragraphs about the land he passed through—*farm-*

land expansive, as far as the horizon would let it go; little town without hills or forests to hide behind seen miles away from the track; flat land interrupted only by an automobile and horses.

The Nickle Plate stopped at Fort Wayne at 12:30 p.m. The dining car served lunch as soon as the train left the station. Conversations began to spring up between diners, now more comfortable with each other than on the first day.

Fritz shared a table with a middle-aged businessman, Wilhelm Keuffel, who was anxious to talk after a full day of solitude. Wilhelm was President of Keuffel & Esser Company, a manufacturer of surveying, drafting, and calculating tools for architects and engineers. Wilhelm was the son of one of the founders. He was born and raised in Hoboken, although he spent many months of his childhood in Europe with his father's family. As a result, his German was fluent. The two men chatted. Both were well-read and interested in world affairs. Their conversation swung fluidly from the German monarchy to President Taft, from the Spanish-American War to the Triple Entente. They talked about the passing of Bismarck, Zeppelins, the Brooklyn Trolley Dodgers, and a young man from Oklahoma named Jim Thorp, who was taking football, track and field, baseball, basketball, and ballroom dancing by storm.

The conversation turned to Fritz's first impressions of New York as they ate. He discussed the city's pace, the German thread he saw everywhere, and the cross-section of immigrants that mingled throughout the city.

"Ah, there is the very point of it," said Wilhelm. "To understand America, you must recognize that although I see myself as a German-American and I cling to my father's family home with heartfelt affection, although all of that is absolutely true, I am—through and through—an American first."

Something clicked in Fritz's brain that made sense of everything he had seen. The street scenes, guests at the German Club, the people on the subway, and the Pullman Porters made sense once he thought of them all as Americans, an oddly homogeneous group independent of their origins. He nodded and was happy he met Wilhelm.

The Nickle Plate pulled into Chicago's snow-covered La Salle Street Station at 5:45 p.m. Both men bundled up in long coats and stepped into the frigid platform air. John was there to guide them off. "Goodbye, Mr. Prinz and Mr. Keuffel. It's been a pleasure."

Fritz stepped outside the station to find his way to his next train connection, a mile to the north. Cold horses with blankets over their backs lined the street, awaiting passengers. Fritz approached the first carriage and enquired, "Wells Street Depot?"

The driver looked up, happy to get moving, and gestured towards the covered seat behind him. The short trip only took fifteen minutes. Fritz went directly to platform two, where the Oregon-Washington Limited #7-17 was parked. He boarded and had an hour to relax before departure. The Pullman Porter, Gus Alden, introduced himself with a smile and continued to patrol his cars to meet his new passengers.

The train pulled out on time and rolled through western Illinois and half of Iowa before the sun rose on 7 February. Fritz woke, immediately opened the curtains, and squinted when the bright winter sunlight invaded the car. The land was flat as far as he could see, broken up by clumps of bare trees, frozen farmland, and occasional houses scattered randomly through the landscape.

The day blurred for Fritz. Only short conversations with Gus broke up the monotony of the journey through miles of open country. They reached Omaha and continued west into Nebraska, flowing the Platte River and the old Oregon Trail.

Somewhere close to Odessa, Gus and Fritz talked about Fritz's home and where he would work for the next few years. Fritz was amazed that Gus had heard of Cassel and the Kaiser's summer palace there.

"I read a lot, and one of the advantages of this job is that I get to talk to a lot of people from places all over, so it all fits together up here," he said, pointing to his temple. "Doesn't hurt that we get a lot of Germans on the train, French too, British, Spanish, you name it, we get 'em. As a result, my European geography is pretty good."

By evening, the train passed Hershey, Nebraska, and the terrain changed dramatically. The land was dryer and sandier, like a desert. Low mountains and hills filled the horizon, their tops eroded flat and dotted with brown and green sage. The change in terrain shook Fritz into a different mood. As on the boat, he felt his journey coming to an end. He saw in the initial foothills the beginning of Immergrün. His focus on the mission latched onto him relentlessly, and he tightened like a spring with every passing mile. He re-read his notes and sketched a list of things to do once he got to Spokane. He thought about Scheck, Hacklander, and Weber. Which one would be the dynamo? Which one would be the brake?

During the night, #7-17 steamed west through what sixty-three years earlier had been the Mexican territory of Alta California. They crossed over the Continental Divide, through Sweetwater County, past Castle Rock, and across the Green River in darkness. At the small town of Granger, Wyoming, they crossed the shallow Hams Fork River, with only the engineer noting the minor change in the resonance of the wheels on the timber-supported trails. In the small hours of February 8, they crossed the Idaho State line.

By sunrise, #7-17 was five miles east of Pocatello, Idaho. The hills and the Portneuf River, high with mountain runoff, provided a majestic setting that cold morning. The small town, home to a few thousand people, had wide-open dirt streets, a handful of stone buildings signifying the town center, and smaller homes stretching out to the surrounding countryside. Fritz saw what he thought must be a hydroelectric plant on the river and streetlamps on the streets. Horses and buggies traversed the town.

The engine stopped outside the *Pacific Hotel*, doubling as the train depot. Gus passed and asked Fritz if he wanted to stretch his legs in town as they had forty-five minutes to load coal and water and switch engineers. "I won't leave without you, Mr. Prinz." Something in Gus' sincerity made Fritz believe Gus would stand before the train if he had to.

Fritz was out of his seat in a flash, down the steps of the car, and onto the frozen dirt. He walked east for a block and then north on Center Street. He found the plain facades of the red and grey buildings and the wooden planked sidewalks refreshingly simple. The place had an unsophisticated order to it.

Fritz passed the red-bricked Monarch Hotel and, next door, an impressive sandstone-arched building called the Idaho Furniture Company. He paused to walk through the inviting store and noted less furniture and more hats, boots, hardware, and broomsticks. As was his habit, he bought the local paper, the *Semi-Weekly Pocatello Tribune*, and continued his walk down Center Street. Cigar shops, The Toggery clothing shop, and a barbershop with a "U.R. Next" sign made up a commercial town core fueled by mining and the railroad. The worn street was compacted dirt scarred from wagon wheels, automobiles, and horseshoes. Fritz noted a sense of commerce and activity that surprised him in this remote town.

At the intersection of Main and Center, he wandered into the Temple Pharmacy, drawn in by the sign promising "Fancy Ice Creams, Sherbets, Punches." The pharmacy was packed with medicinal compounds, colored glass bottles on open shelving, and an oddly placed ice cream bar attached to the main counter.

A lady behind the counter looked up as the bell above the door chimed and watched him enter with some interest, noting his European clothes, tight haircut, and neat appearance. Fritz was unaware of how out of place he looked, but the lady's lingering look reminded him of his conspicuousness in this small town. He ordered a sherbet and sat on a metal chair close to the window to unfold his *Tribune*. He had just settled into the headlines when he was interrupted by a question from over his shoulder.

"Where you from, Mister?" asked the lady.

"Germany."

"Got a lot of Germans here, ya know. You work for a mine?"

"Not here. I'm traveling to Spokane."

"We got all kinds of mines here: gold, silver, lead, copper. Seems like a little bit of everything. Town is full of miners—rough crowd, but we can't prosper without them. German, Irish, Greek, even have some new ones from Basque country, that's in Spain."

"Yes, I know," responded Fritz curtly, enjoying his newspaper and attempting to put the conversation to rest. He liked the feel of this town, wide-open, well-designed, mining, railroads, and a good local paper—*what else could a man ask for?*

The silence was too much for the server, "So what's that Kaiser fella with the funny mustache been doin' lately?"

Fritz inadvertently raised both eyebrows in reaction to the loose comment about the Crown Prince of the German Empire and the Kingdom of Prussia, as if someone had poked him in the eye. He supposed that was what a meritocracy delivered in some cases. Fritz looked out the window and recovered his composure. He didn't know what to say in response, so he said nothing. The silence lingered and grew awkward. Fritz's paper-reading interlude was disrupted, so he finished his sherbet quickly and left.

Back on the train, Gus served coffee to his passengers. Fritz unfolded the *Pocatello Tribune* and enjoyed the coffee and the ordered atmosphere in the car. In a more relaxed mood, he read the paper fresh from the experience of walking the town.

US Army's first use of an airplane in a military operation, the pilot Harry Harkness flew his Antoinette monoplane thirty-two miles round-trip in fifty-six minutes to deliver a message to commanders in the field on the Mexican border. Pocatello was building a sewer system. George Winter and Fred Cahill published a claim for mining gold, silver, and copper at Belle March Queen Load. Oregon Short Line tracks washed out at Inkom. British Parliament to open on Monday. Hawkins Basin reservoir burst causing damage. Mexican rebels attacked the city of Juarez. Henry Arness, a lo-

cal steelworker jailed for six days for disturbing the peace. Miners Richard Hartlin and James Ward jailed for six days for fighting.

Putting the paper down, Fritz could not shake his affinity for that small mountain town. Over the coming decades, he would often think of its charming setting, wide-open streets, and the opportunity it offered to those willing to live there. He even occasionally thought of the exasperating lady at the Temple Pharmacy.

They hurled through the homesteads of Kimama and Dietrich. The land did not change all day—dry high desert filled the window for hours.

The engine stopped to refuel at Nampa at 3:50 p.m. Fritz got off briefly to stretch his legs. From the platform, he observed the fireman oil the drive rods and the conductor check his pocket watch. His mind raced under his calm demeanor. He knew that within three hours, he would be crossing the border into Oregon State, and within twenty-four hours, after months of preparation, Immergrün would begin in earnest. He stared into the small waiting room fireplace when Gus tapped his shoulder, "Mr. Prinz, we're ready to roll."

The train steamed off and passed quickly through Middleton, Emmett, and Payette. Over dinner, they crossed the old Oregon Trail again and passed one more time over the Snake River, which had intertwined with the train for hundreds of miles. Fritz watched the evening light fade over Huntington, Oregon and barely touched his meal.

At 1:20 a.m. on Thursday, February 9, Gus whispered. "Mr. Prinz, I wanted to let you know your station is coming up in one hour. Would you like a cup of coffee?"

There was no need for the wake-up call; Fritz dressed at 1:00 a.m. At 2:20 a.m., #7-17 steamed into Pendleton, Oregon. Gus stood at the foot of the stairs.

"Herr Prinz, it's been a pleasure having you aboard. I do wish you the very best in your venture in Spokane. Auf Wiedersehen."

"Thank you, Gus. Been a pleasure getting to know you."

Fritz stayed in the station for another thirty minutes while the fireman worked on the Oregon-Washington Railroad and Navigation train #6's boiler. By 3:00 a.m., all passengers were aboard, and the train steamed slowly out of the station. Fritz was cold and tired but could not sleep, knowing how close he was to his destination.

They stopped briefly at Walla Walla, Washington, still cloaked in darkness. When dawn broke, #6 steamed north through Alto, and Fritz watched the landscape unfold in the morning light. The land became rockier, and tall evergreen trees sprouted up in small clumps. *Immergrün,* thought Fritz, *now it made sense.*

The train approached Spokane at 1:30 p.m. and pulled into the impressive Great Northern Railroad Depot on Havermale Island. Fritz stepped off the car onto the platform and followed the crowds into the main hall. A small-framed man in an expensive wool jacket and a felt Derby hat was watching from the side of the room. The crowds cleared, leaving Fritz standing almost alone under the hall's large clock. The man with the derby hat knew a fellow German when he saw one. He walked up to Fritz, "Herr Prinz, I presume?"

"Herr Scheck, I presume?"

4

The Evergreen State

THURSDAY, 9 FEBRUARY 1911

SPOKANE, WASHINGTON

Scheck paid a porter to deliver Fritz's suitcase to his hotel, and the two men walked to the front of the Great Northern Railroad Depot and into the winter air. Scheck flatly enquired about Fritz's trip and von Schlegel's New York office. His raspy voice was unnerving, and he was direct and blunt in his manner, but Fritz understood how to manage the familiar narrative and tone.

Stepping into a carriage, they crossed the magnificent Spokane River, quickly covered the two blocks to Riverside Avenue, and then crossed bustling Main Ave. The carriage stopped outside the six-story Rookery building on the corner of Riverside and Howard. Scheck climbed creaky stairs to the fifth floor and entered the Germania Mines office. The small office was lined with binders, maps, and file cabinets. A conference table, stacked with papers, took up most of the room; behind it hung the Empire's black, white, and red tricolor. Over

Scheck's desk, a painting of the Kaiser in full military regalia watched coldly over the room. *The man does appear to have a fetish for uniforms,* thought Fritz.

Scheck closed the door and motioned to a chair by the window. Apologetically, he rasped, "We're getting new offices. This place is too small for our needs."

He opened a humidor and clipped a cigar without offering one to Fritz. He lit a match and slowly took three long draws before looking at the red embers. He noisily shifted his chair closer to the desk, scraping the floor. A silence lingered that neither man perforated.

Scheck looked at Fritz without uttering a word. He took another long draw of his cigar and rasped, "I've been here on and off since 1908. It's a busy place. We're done with legalities, and our miners are now digging tungsten out of the mountain."

He puffed on his cigar and continued, "River and rail access are at our fingertips. Mining labor, metalworking, and mining suppliers are everywhere. We've established a reasonable logistics channel from the mine back to Essen."

Scheck's tone changed to a lower timbre, and he shifted in his chair again to face Fritz directly, "Prinz, your role is to get tungsten moving more efficiently as we ramp up production. I want you to begin immediately and get concentrate to Essen this month and every month as smoothly as possible. You come with solid qualifications and high recommendations—I expect you will fulfill your role efficiently."

He drew again on his cigar, filling the space between him and Fritz with thick, blueish smoke. "I will coordinate with New York and with OHL. I want you to focus on moving the concentrate through New York, to Hamburg, to Krupp."

Scheck paused and looked out the window. Again, the silence crept in and filled the room. Both men were happy to let it be.

He drew on his cigar, looked at the red embers, remade eye contact with Fritz, and then continued, "One other thing Prinz... We have lawyers, miners, suppliers, and logisticians with whom we work almost daily. Keep your distance from them. Is this clear?"

Years of military experience kicked in. Fritz stared directly into Scheck's eyes and replied curtly, "It is Herr Scheck." From that moment on, he knew Schech would remain aloof and that he would concentrate on his task with the quiet professionalism that was his strong suit.

Scheck nodded and outlined events for the next few days. Fritz would review the mine plans, projections, and logistics plans. The next day, he would meet with Rudolf Hacklander, and they would travel to the mine together.

The conversation dwindled into silence. Fritz stood, recognizing that the meeting was at a close. Scheck walked to the office door.

"We have booked a room at the Pennington Hotel for a few weeks while you settle in. It's a five-minute walk from here. Your trunk should be there already."

"Thank you, Herr Scheck. I'm sure that will be fine."

Scheck opened the door, gave Fritz directions, and the men parted.

Outside, Fritz was relieved to be in the bright sunshine and the fresh air, out of the office, the thick smoke, and the awkward silences. He found Scheck tolerable but recognized that there would be no familiarity between them and that extended silences would likely be part of their regular interactions. He inhaled the thin mountain air. *I think I'm going to like it here.*

He walked south on Howard Street to 1ˢᵗ Ave and turned right. It was less crowded than New York but far larger than any city or town he had seen since leaving Chicago. People crisscrossed the street everywhere, dodging trolleys, automobiles, and horses. It was a scene of prosperity and energy, and he immediately felt like an equal participant in this city of opportunity.

He passed Tull and Gibbs furniture store, pausing to look in the large window, knowing he would need furniture soon. Next door, he looked in the window of Jones and Dillingham. The store had window sashes lined side by side and neatly stacked cans of paint arranged in a giant pyramid. The colored paint cans caught his eye and appealed to his sense of symmetry.

From behind the pyramid of paint cans, a tall young man with broad cheeks and shaggy blond hair appeared and looked up from his can-stacking task. William Henry Martin flashed a toothy smile. Without breaking stride, he went back to his work on the pyramid.

Fritz barely noticed the young man with the broad smile but remembered the pyramid of paint cans for years. He continued his walk towards the Pennington Hotel and noticed it from almost a block away. The hotel's unusual stucco mission-style architecture, the striped awnings, and the clock tower stood out amidst the other redbrick buildings on the street. *This is definitely not Europe*, Fritz noted.

Fritz rose early on 10 February. After breakfast, he walked two frigid blocks to the office and met with Rudolf Hacklander to review the mine plans. Hacklander, a few years younger than Fritz, was born and raised in Cassel. His colleague had an easy way about him, a casual style that radiated from his core. He was well-educated and well-spoken but did not flaunt those privileges, which Fritz greatly appreciated.

After a short discussion about their shared hometown, they got to work. The two Germans studied the plats, mine plans, mill details, and logistics channels. They discussed power supply, road access, and depth mined. Hacklander talked about the miners, the local Industrial Workers of the World (IWW) branch, known as the Wobblies, and the transportation needed to get the concentrate to Germany. They broke for lunch in a café by the office and poked a little fun at their mutual boss. Fritz was confident that Rudolf knew what he was doing, and Rudolf felt the same about Fritz.

Figure 3: Jones and Dillingham, Spokane, circa 1902 [42]

Fritz and Rudolf were on Great Northern Railway train 256 the following day. It was mostly empty, bar a few families and miners aboard headed back north to the small towns that dotted the hills between Spokane and the Canadian border.

"Be warned," said Rudolf, "it's like the 1700s all the way up there on that mountain, but once you get to the mine, it's not that bad—you'll see."

They passed through Deer Park and Loon Lake. At 10:55 a.m., they disembarked at Springdale, thirty-eight miles north of Spokane, a natural center of gravity for the surrounding mining, timber, and farming communities. In 1911, it had four hundred hardy inhabitants, and on the morning Fritz arrived, half that number seemed to be on the streets. The bustling town had a fire engine, three general stores, a bank, a newspaper (the *Springdale Reformer*), two sawmills, two liveries, three churches, two hotels, two restaurants, saloons, a drug store, a harness store, a barber, and a doctor.

Hacklander knew his way around and went directly to the end of town and into the Springdale & Fruitland Stage Line. "Morning, Rich," he said to Rich Bruce, owner of the R. H. Bruce Company.

"Rudolf! Thought I'd see you today. You want lunch?"

"Two, please, Rich, one for my friend Fritz here. He's going to be a regular."

"Welcome, Fritz. Looks like you guys are really going to get things moving this time. You fellas have about twenty minutes; Arlo is hitching up the team. Make yerselves comfortable."

Within a few minutes, the largest man Fritz had ever seen walked into the office with an old bolt action rifle slung over his shoulder. He wore a dirty, wide-brimmed hat and a full-length white fur coat, making him seem even larger. Fritz looked at him with disbelief.

Hacklander noticed Fritz's expression, "I should have mentioned the area we are working in is safe, but there are bears, cougars, snakes, and lots of ways to lose a limb or your life. People up here in the mountains are different than those down in Spokane. It's a rough bunch, but they take care of each other."

Fritz's brain scrambled to take it all in. He realized he was now deep into the rural tapestry of this vast country and about to get even deeper.

They climbed onto Arlo's coach at exactly noon. Arlo arrived like a giant furry animal, munching on an apple. The coach creaked under his weight when the big man climbed into his seat. Inside, the stage was dirty and old. However, it had two stout, cushioned seats and plenty of legroom and storage. A cylindrical metal container in the middle of the coach held a hot charcoal brick, warming the interior comfortably. Fritz remembered what Rudolf had said the day before, "Be warned, it's like the 1700s all the way up there on that mountain, but once you get to the mine, it's not that bad—you'll see." *God, I hope he's right*, he thought.

Arlo drove the team quickly through the flat valley west of Springdale, flush with high grasses and clumped bushes. The dirt road to Fruitland wound through the foothills of the wild Huckleberry range. In the distance, green mountain peaks surrounded the lowland. *Somewhere up there was the tungsten that would help the Kaiser win a war*, thought Fritz.

Soon, the openness disappeared, and the snorting horses began a slow climb. The wooded hills closed in tightly on the stage as they worked their way up the east side of the range. The terrain flattened out beautifully at the summit into a high meadow with clumps of trees and rolling knolls.

At 4:00 p.m., the wagon pulled into a rest station where Fritz and Hacklander ate hot stew served by the owners. Arlo watered and talked to his horses, picked up the mail, and within forty-five minutes, the team was back on the mountain road headed west. He said they would make time up on the last leg; the team knew it was downhill and would be in a hurry to get there.

It was dusk when they drove through Hunter and dark when they pulled into the small town of Fruitland just east of the vast Columbia River. Arlo tipped his large hat and grunted farewell to Fritz and Hacklander before tending to his tired horses. The two men walked across the street to a bleak hotel called Reeder's and checked in.

By 5:00 a.m. the next morning, both men were wide awake. They watched their breath by the yellow oil light and could not spend any more time in the freezing room. Both got dressed and ate a dismal breakfast of fatty bacon and stale bread, which Fritz found particularly difficult to finish. He looked at Hacklander, who simply shrugged and giggled at his companion's discomfort. Still dark, they walked to Wilf Peltier's stable's other end of the one-street town, where they saddled two of the saddest horses Fritz had ever seen. The thrill of the backwoods and mountains wore thin for Fritz that morning.

By 7:00 a.m., they were on the road to Turk Post Office, a short five-mile stretch of gently sloping trail into the Huckleberry mountains. The horses followed the well-worn wagon path that cut through the high grass, requiring no effort from their listless and hungry riders.

The mountain crossroads of Turk had two buildings—a bunkhouse that catered to local miners and a Post Office that doubled as the central administrative building for the Huckleberry region. The travelers tied up their horses, stomped mud off their boots, and took their hats off before they entered the tiny Post Office. Inside, a potbelly stove was fired up and filled the space with heat, the sound of crackling wood, and a pine odor.

The old postmaster, Joel Wesch, nodded at Hacklander, recognizing him as a regular visitor. He looked quizzically at Fritz, noting his foreign clothes and boots. Wesch could not resist a new arrival in the area and sarcastically probed, "Nice boots you got there, cowboy . . ."

He did not see a flinch of a response from Fritz, but he was not a man to be easily discouraged. He decided to push on.

"Who you outlaws running from in them fancy boots?" He grinned, content that the direct question would solicit a response from the stranger.

Hacklander knew how Wesch was. He tilted his head to look at Fritz's boots in an obvious manner and decided to see how Fritz would handle the cranky postmaster.

Fritz recognized Hacklander's hand-off and picked up the challenge, "Generally, us Germans are not inclined to do much running, in or out of our boots."

Joel grinned back, happy to have elicited a spirited response and a little more information from the stranger. His otherwise bleak morning might be entertaining after all.

"Seen that a time or two back in '63, had a bunch of you fellas in my old battery. Stubborn as mules. Scrappy bunch, gave hell to ol' Johnny Reb from ahind our twelve pounders. Sure as heck did, gave them fellas all kinda hell..."

"Well, I doubt if Johnny Reb cared what boots the Yankees wore while hell was being delivered."

Old Wesch nodded, lost in some battle almost fifty years earlier. "...all kinda hell... twelve pounders..." he said softly.

Fritz looked down at his boots and decided to change the mood, which had taken a considerable dip. He rolled his lip in mock sadness, "You have a point about the boots, though; maybe a little too fancy for the Huckleberry this time of year."

Wesh bounced back to life, "Well, that's what I'm sayin'! Can't come on up here wearing that fancy shit, gonna get in a fight with some pick-slinger."

Hacklander laughed and decided Fritz was a good man to have on the team. *God knows*, he thought *the mine could use a little levity.*

After some more banter about miners and the Civil War, both men said goodbye to Wesch and mounted their old horses for the last leg of the journey.

The two rode into Germania camp at 10:00 a.m. from the north. The mine was as neat as Fritz had seen anywhere in Germany. They stopped at the stables, tied up their horses, and slid the saddles off. A stableman appeared to take over feeding and stalling the animals, and the men strolled up the hill toward the office. Fritz studied the camp as they walked. Three large bunkhouses could hold as many as a hundred miners. Just beyond the bunkhouses was Sand Creek, a narrow stream that flowed deep and provided very appealing background noise. Hacklander pointed out a laundry house, a blacksmith shop, and a sawmill. *Good*, thought Fritz, *this place has everything we need.* He knew the evergreen trees provided a plentiful supply of timber for building, mine support beams, and heat at night.

"Is there anything you don't have here?" asked Fritz.

"Frankly, no, besides a good weissbier. And you haven't even seen the best parts."

Germania's tall wooden office building had a clear view of the entire site. Hacklander and Fritz walked into the main office, where Ernst Weber stood to greet them from behind a desk overflowing with folders. Weber was the attorney who arrived at the mine from Cassel the previous year, traveling through New York the day after Christmas. His responsibilities included all legal matters, of which there were many, and corporate administration. He was young and had a noticeable schmisse (dueling scar) on his cheek,[43] a social ritual Fritz never understood.

"Rudolf!" shouted Weber.

The men shook hands warmly.

"Ernst! How are you? May I introduce Fritz Prinz, the latest resident of Germania."

Weber broke into German, asking how things were going at home and how the always-precarious relations were with the French. The discussion wandered from hometowns to national politics and gradually changed to mining operations on the mountain. Weber talked for twenty minutes about the mine and local characters. Midway through, he opened an ornate liquor cabinet with a range of whiskeys that Fritz would have only expected in a well-stocked bar in Berlin. With everyone's glass full, Weber opened sliding doors to a large smoking room with leather chairs, a stone fireplace, a large painting of the Kaiser, and even a grand piano.[44] Wood paneling and Persian rugs completed the luxurious ambiance. Fritz was staggered by the opulence at the office—it seemed so out of place in this remote mountain site, so unexpected at the end of his miserable journey from Springdale. *How is this possible? How is there so much money for this operation? How did this stuff even get here?*

A loud knock on the door stopped the conversation, heads turned, and a stocky man in corduroy pants and a flannel shirt strode into the room. The man was in his late twenties, and Fritz imagined he was more at home in the mine than in the paneled room. He walked directly to Fritz and extended his hand, "Welcome, Mr. Prinz. Hans Köhler, Site Superintendent." Weber poured a drink and handed it to Köhler, and the four men settled into the large leather chairs overlooking the mine.

"So Fritz, what do you know about the mine? I assume you got the usual OHL, Essen, and New York briefings?"

"I did, but I'd imagine you all know more about it than they do, so please assume I know nothing."

Weber started from the beginning. Fritz settled into his plush leather chair and used this opportunity to study the team.

"The mine opened in 1894 and was staked for gold, which didn't work out well. They found tungsten, which was not interesting to the Americans, French, or British back then. We got involved after the 1894 Saint Louis Exposition and, more acutely, after the 1900 Paris Exhibition, where Bethlehem Steel did some interesting demonstrations on high-speed steel.

"Krupp scientists understood the strategic importance of the ore—grenades that used to take three and a half hours to make were being turned in twelve minutes using tungsten carbide.[45] How can you fight a war unless you have such material? Outproducing our adversaries in artillery, munitions, U-boats, and battleships could be the difference in winning or losing a war."[46]

Fritz knew all this from his days at Krupp, but it was good to know that the attorney understood more than just the law.

Köhler, whom Fritz categorized as the pragmatist on the team, concentrated on data and production. "We have a quartz vein with an average width of two feet.[47] It's high grade—far better than what's mined in Colorado. We operate a forty-ton mill and produce five grades of concentrates ranging from fifty-eight to seventy-four percent tungstic acid. Up to the end of December, we mined 1,647 tons of ore, which produced eighty-two tons of concentrate containing seventy percent tungsten oxide. We've been shipping about fifteen tons of concentrate a month in the past few months.[48]

"Power comes from an eighty-horsepower boiler, a compressor and engine, a fifteen-horsepower induction motor, and a small slide-valve engine.[49] The camp and mine have electricity, so we have no problems keeping production going even in the winter."

Köhler sipped his whiskey. "We can walk afterward; I'll show you the whole operation."

Weber addressed the transportation they used to get the concentrate from the mine to the Krupp Steelworks in Essen. "Springdale-Fruitland stage line has two four-horse teams hauling two tons of ore to the Springdale depot a few times a week. I believe you met Rich Bruce already; he's the owner."

Fritz nodded, "I met him yesterday. He seemed like a man you could trust to get the job done."

Weber acknowledged and continued, "Rich is dependable. He passes it off to G. L. Andrews in Springdale. The lower-grade concentrate goes to a smelter at Tacoma and ends up in lamp bulb filaments; it's useless to Krupp. Andrews transports bulk cars of the concentrates by train from Springdale to Spokane and then to New York. Andrews is solid and rarely misses a beat. From there, it goes by ship to Hamburg. Our agent in Cassell transports it by train to the Essen Steelworks.

"The cost of mining and milling is estimated at $2.50 a ton of crude ore. It costs $10 a ton to haul the concentrate to Springdale.[50] We ship in lots of twenty-five to thirty tons per car at a cost of $16-$18 a ton to New York. That means we ship a car every two months at our current production rate. When the concentrate reaches Germany, the net cost of producing and delivering one ton of concentrates is about $200. A great deal for Deutsches Heer."

The group talked more about the production plans for 1912 and the new equipment ordered to keep up with the demand from Krupp. Despite his discomfort with the luxury of the office, Fritz's mind was at ease. The team was professional, and the operation appeared well-managed.

Their glasses drained, Köhler stood and offered Fritz a tour, which Fritz jumped at. The two men walked a few hundred feet west to the mill. It was in full production, and the sounds of water flowing, grinding, crushing, sifting, and grading the ore were music to Fritz's ears. This was his domain, in the mountains, among miners and engineers—not a lawyer or an aristocrat within two hundred feet.

Köhler knew the mill like the back of his hand. "We had this built at the Union Iron Works in Spokane. She's a beauty, can do forty ton a day. The ore goes directly from the bins to a seven-by-ten-inch Blake breaker. The jaws crush the ore to one inch or less, and then it goes to ten by sixteen-inch rolls where it is crushed even smaller."

Köhler pointed as he spoke, proud of his mill's raw power.

"Then onto the revolving screens of eight and four mesh. Ore that passes through the eight-mesh screen goes to a classifier; the sands go to a jig. The overflow goes to another classifier, the first sands going to a four-compartment, three-inch Richards pulsator jig, the second sands to a Card table, and the overflow to a Wilfley table. The material that will not pass the eight-mesh screen passes the four mesh and goes to two jigs, where coarse concentrates and middlings are made. The middlings and the middlings from the first jig are elevated over there, sent to a sixteen-inch re-crushing roll, and sent back through the revolving screens again.[51] Not a bad system."

Fritz was impressed. They had everything they needed: water, electricity, miners, money, and most importantly, good ore. Logistics back to Essen were functional, but he knew he would improve it.

They walked into the mineshaft, stepping aside as muckers pushed carts on tracks past them without paying attention to the two Germans. Fritz kicked the posts, examined the lagging, and found them in great shape. The miners at the face clawed at the ore with their picks and barely stopped to nod at the visitors.

Köhler walked him back to the office, where Weber showed Fritz his boarding room, the large gymnasium for management only, and the camp's kitchen, which was always open and well-stocked.[52] Finally, he showed Fritz his office, looking out onto the mill and the creek. There were files, a large desk, a map table, and a well-stocked whiskey cabinet—everything that Fritz would need to ensure the mine would operate as efficiently as possible.

The days at the mine turned into weeks and then months. Fritz split his time between Spokane and the mountain. Spring turned into long summer days in the mountains, and crisp fall flowed into a bitterly cold winter.

Fritz was happy at the mine. His work was satisfying and meaningful, living conditions were luxurious, and he was well compensated by the deep pockets of Krupp and the Kaiser.

Over the months, Germania hired more miners, the bunkhouse filled, the volume of ore concentrate increased daily, and Krupp produced more advanced arms. Fritz dedicated himself to improving logistics at every point between the mountain and the steelworks in Essen. He spent as much time as possible in the mines and the mill. The miners reminded him of miners he worked with in Germany—a rough bunch prone to laughing, swearing, drinking, and fighting but men who took pride in their ability to extract large quantities of ore from the earth.

Tungsten production increased, and Fritz initiated daily pick-ups by R. H. Bruce and ensured G. L. Andrews moved the ore on time to Spokane, where the ore was loaded onto trains bound for the east coast, across the ocean, onto the port of Hamburg, and finally to the Ruhr Valley. Fritz worked every detail of the ore production and movement until it ran like clockwork.

The other Germania management stayed out of the mine—their world was separate. Besides working hard, which they certainly did, drinking, smoking, and spending time in the gym were their main distractions. Weber played the piano when the mood took him. If he felt more energetic, he would roll out a leather-covered phantom opponent, uncase his schlager, and practice mensur fencing for hours, encouraged by Hacklander and Scheck, who loved to see the old university tradition still practiced.[53]

In Essen, Krupp Steelworks used every ounce of concentrate shipped. Krupp received ore from around the globe, from Spokane, Colorado, and other countries. (Australia, Argentina, and as far away as China). Krupp production surged. The factory produced thousands of new field guns of all calibers ranging from the short-range field guns like the 77mm Feldkanone Model 96, infamous for the signature whiz-bang sound of their shells, to the 42cm Minenwerfer-Gerät (Big Bertha), the siege gun that cracked the Belgian forts at Liège with 1,785-pound shells, and the long-range Paris Gun. Essen also produced thousands of anti-aircraft guns, trench mortars, and grenades. In Kiel, on the Baltic Sea, Krupp Germaniawerft (Germania shipyard) used tungsten to surge the production of capital ships and U-boats for the Imperial German Navy.

Ironically, the Kaiser's and OHL's industrialization plan was working with the help of strong American backs and American tungsten.

5

War Clouds

In October 1911, Auguste, now his wife, joined Fritz at 908 East 9th Avenue, a cozy two-story house on the south side of the Spokane River. Fritz spent his weeks between the mountain mine and working in the office in Spokane.

Auguste loved the city and the surrounding area. Their home, on a quiet residential street, was close to Grant Park and Liberty Park, where Fritz and Auguste would walk in summer and skate on cold winter evenings. The couple would often take day trips over summer weekends and travel south of the city, where the land opened up and the hills rolled in beautiful symmetric arcs. Cheney, Duncan, and Valleyford were regular stops for them during the summers of 1912 and 1913. The scenery gave Fritz the space to think about something other than tungsten.

Auguste often talked about how long they would stay in Spokane—would they be there for years, or would they ever return to Germany? Fritz avoided the discussion on every occasion. He knew that a war in Europe was possible, perhaps even inevitable. The scale of potential war and the catalyst for war were unclear, but competition between the Great Powers had been intense, and the Balkan Wars in 1912 and 1913 were a reminder of how volatile Europe was.

The unification of Germany, the legacy of the Franco-Prussian war, the political void left by Bismarck, the commitment to Weltpolitik, the building of a world-class navy, and the consistent talk of a broader empire all pointed to the possibility of a German war. Then, there was the troublesome temperament of Wilhelm II, which was also a reason for concern.

All these were red flags that Fritz's strategic mind understood. The nail in the coffin was his knowledge of how Krupp and the Kaiser were using tungsten. The scale and purposefulness of the buildup of strategic materials and armaments was an unmistakable indicator that war could be close. A fuse was all that would be required for a sequence of events to kick mobilization into motion. *A few years, three, maybe four. But war was coming.*

As a reserve soldier, he knew what that meant for his family and how it limited any thoughts of long-term life in America. But he owed Hauptmann Weiss more than a glass of schnapps after all the Commander had done for him in arranging this position; it was unthinkable not to show up at his old unit for a war with the old enemy.

On a bright, sunny Monday morning in late June 1914, Fritz woke up, sunburned but refreshed after a long day in the country with Auguste. They had been on a drive through Medical Lake southwest of town and had enjoyed an endless day of swimming and picnicking. He could not have known it would be his last carefree day for over five years.

He looked forward to returning to the mine for a few days and meeting with Bruce and Andrews about minor logistics wrinkles. After breakfast, he said goodbye to Auguste, hugged her, and headed to the train station.

He habitually bought a *Spokesman Review* for the train. That beautiful June morning, he was running late, so he rolled the paper up and hurried to the train without glancing at the headlines. Flustered, he climbed into the car, placed his hat and bag on the rack above him, and settled into an empty row. He felt the burn on his shoulders from the weekend and was content to watch the city and the morning crowds as the train left the station and headed north.

The train slowed as it climbed the hills and left the city behind. Fritz felt more relaxed and remembered his newspaper. He settled into his seat and snapped the paper into a reading position. His eyes scanned the front page and froze. He leaned forward, intensely focused on the headline: *Archduke Franz Ferdinand Killed by Assassin.*

The article provided no information on the German reaction or the strategic implications; it detailed the tragedy of the killing and the background of the Habsburgs. Fritz reread it and tried to put the potential outcomes together in his head. His thoughts spun and multiplied. He knew the tight bonds between the Kaiser and the Austro-Hungarian Emperor Franz Josef. He knew that the Kaiser was a loose cannon and prone to overreact. His mind raced; the permutations multiplied quicker than he could process them.

Austria-Hungary would surely attack Serbia, but could it be a contained regional dispute that would not draw Russia in? The Russo-Serbia relationship centered on Slavic and Orthodox Christian ties went back hundreds of years, and the Russo-French alignment was evident since the Dual Entente in 1894. Fritz tensed up, unable to think about anything other than the worst possible outcome. As much as he resisted the concept of a full European war, he could not think of a German leader with the skills to avoid one, especially given the influence of the German military. *Without Bismarck, the concepts of Realpolitik are long gone, and the current political elite is less capable of navigating these treacherous waters.*

Fritz was confident that Franz Joseph would attack Serbia; how could he not? He was certain that Kaiser Wilhelm II would support Austria-Hungary. The only uncertainty in Fritz's mind was whether

Russia would come to Serbia's defense under these circumstances. Once—if—Russia got involved, France and potentially Britain would be pulled into the fight. *All this over an assassination of an Austrian Archduke by a Bosnian Serb student?*

Fritz's mind imploded. In his calculation, the chance of war was far greater than the chance of avoiding war. He formed the only rational conclusion—if Austria-Hungary did not temper its reaction, this parochial situation could spiral out of control rapidly. Fritz felt a chill and a tightening in his belly. He slumped into his seat and let the paper fall on his lap. Long-term plans in Spokane suddenly seemed far-fetched.

The engine pulled into Springdale. Fritz sat frozen in thought and almost forgot to disembark. He hastily grabbed his bag and hat, then scrambled to the platform before the train moved off.

Fritz watched the townspeople go about their business. Fritz doubted that many of the inhabitants read the paper, or if they did, that they understood the complex ties between Austria-Hungary, Germany, Russia, France, and England. Surely, they must know that if Franz Joseph goes to war with Serbia, Germany will too, and the fuse will be lit. *Probably not*, he thought as a middle-aged man smiled happily at him and said, "Beautiful morning! Enjoy the sunshine!" Fritz nodded stoically in reply.

"Morning, Fritz," said Rich Bruce. "Coffee?"

"Sure, Rich." They talked about the weather while they sipped coffee and eventually addressed the teams. Fritz was happy for the idle chat but was distracted and burdened. Rich noticed Fritz's unusual mood and casually asked if Fritz had seen the morning newspaper.

Fritz nodded.

"So?" probed Rich.

"So what?" replied Fritz.

"So, Franz Joseph going to pull Wilhelm into a fight all over Europe over a regional spat? Are you going to have to go back to Germany?"

Fritz was astounded. The paper had not done any analysis on what may happen next, yet the livery manager in Springdale was putting two and two together like a Prussian diplomat in Berlin.

"I'll honestly tell you I don't know Rich. I hope not."

"I hope not either, Fritz."

The men finished their coffee just as Arlo stuck his giant head into the office.

"All ready, Mr. Prinz?"

For the past year, Bruce's teams went directly to the Germania Camp once a day. Fritz and the other Spokane managers caught rides with the team whenever they needed to get in or out of camp.

Fritz climbed up on the wagon. It was not as comfortable as the stage to Fruitland, but it was quicker.

Arlo hardly ever talked, but that morning, he handed Fritz his rifle and grinned, ". . . case you see some Bosnian Serbs up in them hills," then he laughed raucously and gruffly took his rifle back from his passenger.

Fritz, caught by surprise, joined in Arlo's laughing. Given the absurdity of the moment, it was all he could do.

As they left town together, Fritz was bothered that he may have underestimated Bruce's awareness of European development. Even Arlo's joke about Serbians in the hills was based on a fundamental understanding of the German perspective. *Had I misunderstood the American perspective? Had I incorrectly assumed indifference? Or ignorance?*

Upon arriving at the mine, he immediately went into Weber's office. Weber stood immediately and stepped from behind his desk.

"Fritz, glad you're here. You've heard about Franz Ferdinand, I presume?"

Fritz shook hands and nodded.

"Hacklander and Scheck will be here on Thursday. They have some options to discuss. In the meantime, I've asked Köhler to ramp up production as quickly as possible. I suggest you get a contingency plan together for irregular shipments to Essen."

Fritz agreed and went to his office to see what he could do to get the increased product to Essen.

Scheck, Hacklander, Weber, and Prinz met on-site on Thursday, 2 July. Scheck had contacted OHL and received directions to prepare for two possibilities. Scheck had everyone's attention in the room.

"The first possibility is a limited regional war between Austria-Hungary and Serbia in southern Europe. In this case, the Immergrün team and mission would be unaffected, and we stay in place to continue our mission and serve the Kaiser here."

He paused, drew on his customary cigar, prolonged the tension, and continued in his hoarse voice.

"The second possibility," he paused, "is a major European war involving the Triple Entente and the Triple Alliance. If this were to happen, we would blow the mine so the tungsten could not be used against us, and all reserve officers would return to their home units at once. We'll see if Field Marshal von Schlieffen did his homework correctly." [54]

The men relaxed. Hearing the two clear options broke the tension in the room. They looked at each other for a few seconds, then the questions came.

Hacklander spoke first, "How long before we know which option will be decided?"

"A few weeks, perhaps. The Kaiser is talking with the Austrian Foreign Ministry as we speak. I have not heard anything from OHL, but my money is that the Kaiser will back Franz Joseph to the hilt. The wild card is Tsar Nicholas. He's aligned with the French, but he is a blood relative of the Kaiser. Willy and Nicky (as Kaiser Wilhelm and Tsar Nicholas were often referred to informally) have a close but odd relationship. What they decide—or don't decide—will define the outcome of this ridiculous Bosnia incident."

Scheck stood and looked out the window at the mine. "Here is what we must do . . . First, expect the most disruptive possibility and plan for that. So, anticipate destroying the mill and caving the shafts within two weeks. I need details from each of you for that option by tomorrow. In the meantime, ramp up production."

He turned to face the men. "Second, get your personal affairs in order, pay your debts, prepare to move back home. Lose ten damn pounds so you fit in your uniforms again—Hacklander—twenty pounds for you.

"And above all, remember, not a word to anyone outside this room, including your wives and girlfriends."

The men nodded. Fritz had to give Scheck credit; he did not care for his aloofness, but the man could manage the team.

Hacklander was the first to speak again. Standing on the table, he raised his glass and announced, "I propose a toast to His Imperial and Royal Highness, German Crown Prince, Crown Prince of Prussia, Wilhelm II; good hunting!"

"Good hunting!" the men shouted and tossed back their whiskeys.

The evening devolved into multiple side conversations as the group got drunker and louder. Weber played the piano poorly and brought out his *schlager* saber[55] and leather-covered phantom to everyone's delight. The men were jubilant; all had military training, and all grew up proud of the Kaiser's triumph in the Franco-Prussian war, the taking of Paris, the land gains in the west, and most importantly, the humiliation of the old enemy. They had all worked hard to position Krupp and the Army for success in the next war. Now, it seemed Germany would have an opportunity to break out of its landlocked position and find its place in the sun. They talked of a quick war like the last one—a caving in of the old foes and a glorious victory that would change Germany and Europe forever. Whiskey was served by the bottle, and a haze of cigar smoke filled the room. The miners wondered what could be such good news that the Germans were so sloppy drunk early on a Thursday evening.

The following day, Fritz met with Köhler at the mill. They instructed the miners to increase production and produce as much ore as possible for the coming week. Scheck authorized extra pay for the longer work hours. Fritz was astonished by the miners' adaptability and grit and how they worked through problems that neither Köhler nor he had foreseen. Once they knew the objective, they improvised to make things happen without checking with Köhler or Fritz. Their impact was visible in the sacks of concentrate ready for shipment each day.

Fritz planned the mill's destruction. He knew where he would place the explosives to bring the tunnels down and destroy the posts and beams lining the shafts. In the afternoon, he wrote out a list of supplies. Weber signed the order and gave it to Arlo to put on account at Bruce's. Fritz instructed Köhler to ship all concentrate daily, even if that meant shipping halfloads. He also instructed shipment by rail from Springdale to New York every week, regardless of the tonnage.

* * *

In Germany, on 5 July, the Kaiser met with an envoy from the Austrian Foreign Ministry in Potsdam, a few miles southwest of Berlin. Wilhelm II was a friend to both Franz Joseph and Franz Ferdinand, and he was committed to supporting his sworn ally. On July 6, Wilhelm consulted with a crown council attended by Reich Chancellor Theobald von Bethmann Hollweg, Foreign Secretary Arthur Zimmermann, and War Minister Erich von Falkenhayn. Through Hollweg, Wilhelm sent a telegram to the German Embassy in Vienna, in which he stated that Germany would "faithfully stand by Austria-Hungary, as is required by the obligations of his alliance and his ancient friendship." It was clear to Austria-Hungary that Germany would support them no matter what Franz Joseph decided to do.[56]

With Germany locked in on their side, Austria-Hungary debated how to respond to Serbia. Some wanted an immediate invasion, and some wanted a legal basis for war, thus supporting an ultimatum. On July 23, Austria-Hungary sent Serbia an ultimatum that left no room for the Serbian government to maneuver.

On July 28, Austria-Hungary declared war on Serbia, and on the same day, Russia mobilized. Following a flurry of letters between Willy and Nicky, both pleading to each other to avoid an all-out war, Germany sent Russia an ultimatum on July 30.

* * *

That same day, Scheck sent a message to Weber to execute option two at Germania mine. There was a flurry of activity at the mine. Within twelve hours, the miners were released and told that the operation was shutting down. Scheck paid their wages through the middle of August, so there was no trouble from the workers, who left confused but happy to have some extra money. That night, Fritz and the other Germans burned the mill and blew the mine shafts to pieces. Germania mine was out of commission.

The next morning, as the first rays of light lit up the draw from the east, Fritz, Weber, and Hacklander left the mine for the last time. They looked over their shoulders from horseback on their way out of camp. Black smoke rose slowly above Germania, signifying the end of their mission on the Huckleberry and the beginning of a more dangerous mission in Europe.

Regarding the war, Fritz did not share the unbounded optimism of the others; he had concerns. At home, he studied European maps anew. He studied the Armies and Navies that would oppose each other and the strategies they might pursue. Four problems bothered him, problems that his Clausewitzian mind could not fully resolve.

The first problem was that this would be a two-front war. The vast Empire of Russia was to the east, and to the west was the old enemy, France. The Schlieffen Plan was supposed to address that, but Fritz had doubts. What if the British joined and disrupted the German 'right hook' through Belgium? What if the French were tougher than Schlieffen assumed and did not fold quickly? What if Russia mobilized quicker than expected and pushed from the east before France fell? The Schlieffen plan had strategic and logical gaps and a distinct lack of contingencies.

The second problem was the British Navy. Long the ruler of the seas, the British Navy would put a chokehold on Germany if it joined the war. From the North Sea to the Atlantic to the Mediterranean, the British Navy would seal off Germany from any possible external source of food, munitions, or strategic resources. The new Imperial Navy and fleet of U-boats would attempt to break the chokehold, but the outcome of this inevitable and colossal sea battle was uncertain in Fritz's mind.

The third problem was the reliability and strength of the Triple Alliance. As much as he appreciated the collective size of Germany, Austria-Hungary, and Italy, he worried about the military and political unity of the partners. He especially worried about the commitment of the Italians, whose allegiance seemed tenuous at best.

Fritz concluded the first three problems required Germany to win quickly. If Germany could not win quickly, he calculated the odds of winning a war went down rapidly. He was glad that his role in supplying Krupp with tungsten would help Germany breathe during that strangulation process, but would it be enough?

The fourth problem Fritz considered was weaponry and tactics. The last war was fought with breech-loading rifles and artillery—monumental changes in weaponry for the time. This war would test many new weapons—machine guns, U-boats, poison gas, and aircraft, to mention just a few. These largely untested weapons bothered Fritz; he could not tell which side would gain the advantage through some minor design advance or unique operational usage—a spring, a gasket, an industrial process, or a new tactic.

The fourth problem was a wild card. Even for Fritz, a student of military sciences, there was no way to predict which new weapons would impact the battlefield.

In Spokane, at 9:04 a.m. on August 1, 1918, four minutes behind schedule, Fritz and Auguste left their home and took a cab across town to board the train to New York. Auguste was not only leaving a place she loved, but she knew her beloved Fritz was going to war. She trembled that morning. They watched their house disappear as the cab turned the corner and tightly grasped each other's hands.

On 118 Stone Street, a little over a mile from Fritz's cab, William Martin walked out his front door on his way to work. He also pondered a European war but with a sense of distant curiosity.

* * *

At that same time in Germany, the Kaiser's government delivered a telegram formally declaring war on Russia, and the Kaiser mobilized the Imperial German Army and Navy.

The world pivoted at just that moment. Unbeknownst to William or Fritz, events that would draw them together in a dark French forest were already in motion.

6

Young William

In 1907, William Henry Martin was fifteen and loved life in Spokane. He was born in the small mountain town of Chewelah, fifty miles north of Spokane. His mother, Selma Carlson, was a Swedish immigrant. His father, Samuel Peterson, was an immigrant from Finland. Selma left Samuel when William was young and moved with her children to 42 Front Avenue on the east side of Spokane, south of the roaring Spokane River.

Moving homes was part of young William's life. The young family transitioned from Front Avenue to Main Avenue and then a few blocks to 118 South Stone Street. William's older brother John, younger brother Charlie (Freddie), and younger sister Mary grew up in that area of town where houses were small and packed close together. The young family changed their names from Peterson to Martin after his mother's second husband, Charles Martin, a good man whom William readily adopted as a role model.

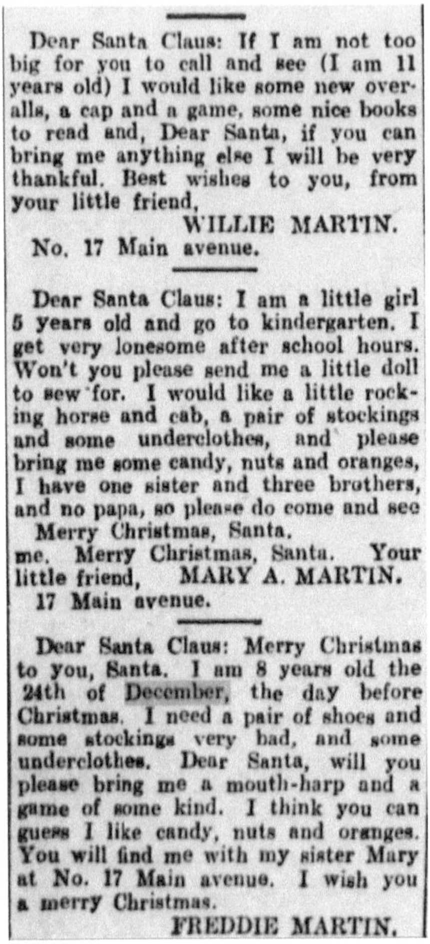

Dear Santa Claus: If I am not too big for you to call and see (I am 11 years old) I would like some new over-alls, a cap and a game, some nice books to read and, Dear Santa, if you can bring me anything else I will be very thankful. Best wishes to you, from your little friend,
WILLIE MARTIN.
No. 17 Main avenue.

Dear Santa Claus: I am a little girl 5 years old and go to kindergarten. I get very lonesome after school hours. Won't you please send me a little doll to sew for. I would like a little rock-ing horse and cab, a pair of stockings and some underclothes, and please bring me some candy, nuts and oranges. I have one sister and three brothers, and no papa, so please do come and see me. Merry Christmas, Santa. Your little friend, MARY A. MARTIN.
17 Main avenue.

Dear Santa Claus: Merry Christmas to you, Santa. I am 8 years old the 24th of December, the day before Christmas. I need a pair of shoes and some stockings very bad, and some underclothes. Dear Santa, will you please bring me a mouth-harp and a game of some kind. I think you can guess I like candy, nuts and oranges. You will find me with my sister Mary at No. 17 Main avenue. I wish you a merry Christmas.
FREDDIE MARTIN.

Figure 4: Martin Children, Christmas 1903 [57]

William left school early and found a job delivering milk and but-ter for the Elgin Dairy Company. He paid rent to support his mother and had enough money for a low-key teenage social life. His friends and brothers sipped beer in parks on summer afternoons and played cards in neighborhood kitchens till late. Selma disapproved when William wandered home later each evening, smelling of beer and cigarettes, but she knew he was growing up and that he would settle down after a few wild summers. She hoped that time would come soon.

After work one evening in 1908, William took the tram from downtown to Mission Street and walked up Jackson Street. The Hughes kids lingered against a red brick wall with their hands stuffed deep in their pockets. Bored, they awaited as William approached, head down, mindlessly watching the cracks in the pavement and avoiding stepping on them.

Daniel, Liam, Ben, and Fiona were the sort of characters his mother would disapprove of most. They always seemed up to some mischief, and Selma blamed them for leading William astray. The group was rarely bored. There was a lot to do in Spokane for kids with a few dollars in their pockets and time on their hands. In the winter, the mountain town was a spectacle. Distant snow-covered peaks provided a beautiful backdrop for the icy Spokane River. The gang would skate at Liberty Park close to their homes, where the ice froze five feet thick. They had old skates, very little skill, and a lot of energy. The teenagers terrorized older couples skating together as they whipped recklessly around the pond.

The highlight of every summer was the Spokane Interstate Fair, held at the fairgrounds just blocks from William's house. It drew over a hundred thousand people from all over the Northwest. For William, it was a place of endless fun and adventure. The friends ate toffee apples and ice cream and watched oddities like Dr. Frank G. Odel, "The Bee Wizard",[58] and the nightly reenactments of "Pioneer Days in the Palouse". They wandered for miles through the crowds, listened to the bands at the grandstand, and lost most of their money betting on harness races. At night, they watched fireworks light up the cloudless sky and smoked cigarettes. Life could not get much better for the five. They had no worries and nothing but opportunity ahead of them.

In 1910, William was eighteen, over six feet tall, and broad-shouldered. He had a perpetual smile and an innate ability to relate to almost everyone he met.

Growing tired of the early mornings at Elgin, his older brother John arranged a job for him as a sash maker with Jones and Dillingham in downtown Spokane. J&D, as locals called it, had a thriving paint business. John worked there for a few years and was known to be dependable and hard-working, so hiring another of the Martin boys was easy for J&D.

William started work at 29 East Desmet Avenue, on the north side of the river, making window sashes. He no longer had to get up at 4:00 a.m.; that alone was a joy. J&D also had a two-story store at 713-715 West 1st Avenue. William moved quickly from production to the retail store and began working as a stocking clerk. For the first time in his life, he took work seriously. He got home earlier at night and spent more time with his family. At eighteen, William had all the optimism of a young man at the turn of the century in a city where anything was possible.

In 1914, William was twenty-two and happy with his life in Spokane. He got ready for work at 8:30 a.m. on Saturday, August 1. He was early, so he made a cup of coffee and read the newspaper that had been in the kitchen for a day. *Austria-Hungary declares war on Serbia, Russia Mobilizes.* He read quietly about the breakdown in Europe that threatened to tear the continent to pieces. He studied the map on page two, looked at the countries, and wondered. He heard stories from his mother about Sweden and knew neighbors from Germany, France, Italy, Belgium, Ireland, Russia, and England. He had heard stories about their homelands and their journeys to America. In a way, he felt like he knew the distant continent already.

The newspaper told of a major war with potentially millions of casualties. William put his jacket on and left the paper on the table. Walking onto Stone Street, he thought briefly about how young men his age all over Europe must feel. *Wouldn't want to be them*, he thought. He stuffed his hands in his pockets and wondered what he should do on Sunday, his day off.

A mile away, the taxi carrying Fritz turned onto Sprague Avenue. Fritz and William were on different journeys, but both were on their way to war. Fritz was leaving directly; William would get there in due course.

7

Call to The Colors

Congress passed the Selective Service Act on 18 May 1917. The Act authorized President Wilson to raise a National Army of millions of men to augment the tiny 127,500-man Regular Army.[59] The Act required all men aged 21 to 45 to register for military service. Approximately twenty-four million men registered. By the end of 1918, the Army had grown to four million men and had trained 200,000 new officers to lead them.[60] Drafting, training, and deploying this new force was a daunting logistics and operational challenge.

On Tuesday, 5 June, William left his small apartment at 126 ½ Second Avenue and got on a jitney downtown. He walked across the bridge, up Monroe Street, and entered the beautifully ornate City Courthouse with a stream of other young men.[61]

His frame had broadened since his teenage years, and his prominent cheeks, deep-set blue eyes, and permanent grin still invited smiles. He was twenty-four years old, unmarried, and had no dependents. In terms of the Army's classification system, this made him "Class I", a perfect fit for what the Army needed. William worried about his skills; he was sure paint store clerking experience was not what the Army needed, and it concerned him that they might not want to enlist him.

Inside the Courthouse, William joined a queue of more than one hundred men lined up for Spokane Division No.2 registration. The board spent a minute with each man, making progress slow for those in line.

William picked up a registration card, filled it in, and then took his place in line. Looking around, he noticed there was not a single soldier, no bunting, and not a wisp of militarism in the room. William felt left down; he was not expecting such an administrative process.

Like most men in line, he had watched the war intensely since 1914. He knew of President Wilson's non-intervention policy. William and his friends were enraged by the sinking of the *Lusitania* in 1915. The murderous battle of the Somme and the insanity of Verdun made the Spokane headlines for months, and William got drawn into the daily, bleak narrative in the newspapers. Finally, the resumption of unrestricted submarine warfare and the notorious Zimmerman telegraph in 1917 removed all doubt from his mind. By the time President Wilson formally declared war on April 6, 1917, William didn't have to think twice; joining the Army was a decision he made quickly.

When William reached the top of the registration line, Mr. Elmer Johnson reached out for his card and read it, "You are twenty-four," he said, looking up at William, "A natural-born citizen. You are unmarried, and nobody is dependent on you, financially or otherwise?"

"That's right."

"Ah, you're a mucker in a mine. Good, used to physical labor!" said Mr. Johnson, smiling. "Let's take a look at you. Two arms, two legs, two eyes, flaxen hair, two light blue eyes, tall, medium build," he said as he filled out the back of the card and signed it. "Thank you, Mr. Martin. You'll hear from us soon. Next."

William turned and left, unimpressed with the process. Registration took ninety minutes, eighty-nine minutes of which was spent shuffling forward. He felt bad that he lied about his work on his card but hoped the board would look more favorably on a mucker than a clerk. There were times to come when William wished he could take that lie back.

The Government held the first selective service lottery on 20 July 1917 in Washington, DC. In a stuffy government room, Secretary of War Baker reached into a large glass bowl and pulled the first capsule to a dull round of applause from the old men who watched the spectacle. A clerk called out, "258". On a ladder, a second clerk wrote the number on a large blackboard behind Secretary Baker. All day and late into the night, 10,500 capsules were pulled out one at a time and recorded on the board. In each district of every State, draft boards matched men's names to numbers on 23 July.

The *Spokane News* offices displayed the list publicly. William ran to get there and scanned the list. His heart sank—his number (1228) was in the bottom quarter of the 10,500 numbers called in Washington DC, and his name was well towards the end of the list in the window. He knew he would not be among the first called to the colors, and his plans to march off to war before Christmas were dashed instantly. He could not have known that he would not be called until eleven months later when life would be so different, so much more complicated. For now, he was devastated.

He skipped work that afternoon and headed to a saloon on 2nd Avenue, where he drank his week's wages as quickly as possible.

Over the coming months, he watched the Hughes boys called up between September and February. The ritual became part of that time—they marched to the station, surrounded by family and friends, bands played, and politicians spoke of the honor and glory of service. Then, one last hug, a kiss, and a small step up to the train. Nervous relatives searched to catch a glimpse of their departing loved ones. Then, the inevitable whistle, a blast of steam, and the metallic sound of couplings engaging. Afterward, the crowd dispersed, the bunting came down, and overwhelmed families went home to await word of training camps.

The going-away parties for William's friends became bitter reminders that he was stuck in a clerk's apron while others started their adventures. Liam Hughes got called up early and was on his way by September. Then Daniel, then Ben, all by February 1918.

William's older brother, John, registered for the draft but did not get called up because he was married with two children. William's younger brother, Freddie, was called up on April 26. William, his mother, brother, sister, and neighbors gathered on Stone Street to see him off. William was devastated to see his younger brother leave. He resented the Army's plodding administrative system that randomly chose his younger brother over him.

On 4 March 1918, William read that the Treaty of Brest-Litovsk had been signed the previous day, formally ending Russia's involvement in the Great War. Over the coming weeks, the newspaper documented OHL's shift of forty-four Divisions from the Eastern front to the Western front and the launch of what the Allies called the *Spring Offensive,* or the *Kaiserschlacht* (Emperor's Battle) by Germany. The enormous operation involved one hundred and ninety-two German Divisions, poised to destroy the English and French armies and break through to Paris. Stoßtruppen (shock troops) crashed through Triple Entente lines, using new infiltration tactics, in movement not seen since the war's opening days. The Germans sent British and French armies hurdling backward. The newspapers reported a new artillery gun that bombarded Paris from distances beyond anything previously thought possible.[62] It seemed inevitable that German momentum would carry them to victory.

By April, William read the paper daily and thought his chance of overseas service was gone. But the unexpected happened. The French, British, and American forces held the line and stopped the German shock troops just forty miles from the French capital. The Spring Offensive had cost nearly a million German lives, and the void left in their ranks and the extended logistics lines made their position untenable. The British and the French regrouped, seized the initiative, and pushed the hollowed German force back almost as far as they had been at Christmas. The tide of war turned, and the need to quickly get American troops to Europe was greater than ever. Newspapers wrote of plans for a three-million-man American army in France, which seemed far-fetched to William, but the Army aimed for just that.

It was during this transition, between near defeat and hopeful victory, that William met Lizzie. Lizzie worked in Tull and Gibbs furniture store next door to J&D. Since Christmas 1917, their work schedules matched, and William shared the 2nd Street streetcar with her each morning and evening. After two months, Lizzie moved in with William to his little apartment on 2nd Street.

William shifted his attention to a life with Lizzie rather than life in the trenches in Europe. He longed for a quick end to the war and a release from his bitter commitment to General Pershing and President Wilson.

In early June 1918, Neil Blaise, one of the clerks in J&D and an occasional drinking friend of Williams, ran into the shop.

"William! They just published a huge list—I'm off! And you may be too, so get over to the *Review*. I'm going home. Screw J&D, I'm going to get a swipe at the Hun!"

William tugged at Neil's sleeve, "How many names? Did you see mine?"

"Don't know how many, and 'course I didn't see yours, didn't even look for it! Just saw mine and ran like the wind. Get over there now, will ya? There are pages of names posted. You're sure to be on it."

William hung his apron on the nail in the door frame and bolted the two blocks to the newspaper office. There were crowds of men trying to see the lists. William knew his name was on there. The big push was bound to round up the last names from the first draft. He walked calmly into the crowd and worked his way to the front. There it was, in black and white, "*1224 - Martin, William H, 126 ½ Second Avenue.*" Muster for the men on the list was at 6:00 p.m., June 28, at Union Station. *Jesus*, William thought, *I'm in.*

William was stunned. He felt clammy and subdued. His mind flooded with Lizzie and how these simple few lines changed everything. He turned with his hands in his pockets and walked slowly back to work. He distracted himself by stocking shelves that afternoon and avoiding customers. He was going through the motions without thinking, moving slowly. At 5:00 p.m., he took off his apron and hung it on the nail he had always used. He left the shop by the front entrance, needing a few extra minutes before meeting Lizzie at Tull and Gibbs's rear.

She was waiting and knew her worst fears were confirmed once she saw him. They turned and walked home together, not interested in the trolly and not speaking a word. The entire week went by slowly and silently for Lizzie and William.

William and Lizzie were emotionally exhausted by the morning of June 28. It was a relief to both of them when the day finally came. That evening, dinner was tense, and talk was strained.

"Chances are I'll be home by Spring. Everyone says Germany can't last much more past Christmas."

"Damn you, William Martin. Don't patronize me with that baloney!" Lizzie sparked.

"I can make my mind up, and I know as much about the end of the war as you do, and those bloody generals! Idiots have been at it for years now, and not a single one of them gives a damn about you or me. So let me manage my life as you have seen fit to manage yours."

William knew what she meant; he knew of men who had life changes after they signed up for selective service. Parents became sick; babies were born; sweethearts became wives. The selective service board was not unreasonable if a man's status changed. But now that the War Department has posted his name, there was no turning back.

William knew that he would not dodge his call to the colors and would not have another man take his place. Lizzie knew that, too.

William went to the Courthouse at 6:00 p.m. on June 28. After signing the register, he left the grand building and walked slowly down the hill to Union Station with his mother, John, Mary, Lizzie, and Fiona. They listened to the band and the bland political speeches with five thousand others.

FIVE THOUSAND SEND MEN TO CAMP

Five thousand people were at the Union station Friday night to say goodby to 700 drafted men who left Spokane for Camp Lewis Mothers, fathers, sisters and sweethearts were present and many could not keep back the tears as they bade goodby to the departing men.

This was the largest single group to leave Spokane, although the July draft will probably be just as large, if it includes the number of transfers which came with the June drafted men.

Figure 5: Draftees leave Spokane 29 June 1918 [63]

When the long-winded speeches ended, William hugged his family, Lizzie last, and stepped into the car with seven hundred local men. He fought through the bodies thrashing about on the train, threw his bag on an empty seat, and stuck his head out the window. He could not see Lizzy or his family amongst the crowds of people waving goodbye. The train's steam whistle blew shrilly, and the locomotive lurched an inch forward. William's journey to France had begun.

The train passed through Fishtrap, Ritzville, Mesa, Pasco, and Kennewick. William fell asleep somewhere west of Kennewick, emotionally drained from weeks of anticipation and the stress of leaving everything he loved behind. He awoke to the sound of air brakes engaging and the men around him chattering excitedly. He stretched and yawned, stiff and sore, as the train pulled into Camp Lewis.

8

Missed Opportunities

SATURDAY, 29 JUNE 1918

BEZONVAUX, FRANCE

While William left Spokane on June 28, five thousand miles away in a trench south of Bezonvaux, France, a tired Fritz Prinz ate cold rations without interest.

The 76th Division had arrived at the camp, sixteen kilometers north of Verdun, the previous week. After bitter fighting around Montdidier and Grivesnes, the unit needed to rest and replace the soldiers they lost.[64] After almost four years at war, the rhythm was well known to Fritz: fight, rest, refit, fight. They had refitted and now rested. Next would be an inevitable fight.

Fritz tilted his face up and closed his eyes. It was a rare moment of peace in a world of constant chaos. He was emotionally drained and physically exhausted by the past four years. Fritz once thought a quick victory in the West was possible. But the Schlieffen Plan failed miserably, and the Western Front became a stalemate, resulting in a two-front war.

He remembered reading about the Battle of Tannenberg in August 1914 and the great victory against the Russians. He recalled February 1915 when the 254th Regiment first marched east, through Prussia towards Moscow, almost reaching Minsk before the Russians stood their ground. That front was vast and wild. For all their numbers, the Russians were poorly equipped and even more poorly led. The "Great Retreat" of the Russian Army gave him hope that the two-front dilemma would not crush his country.

Fritz's optimism was short-lived. In May 1915, Italy resigned from the Triple Alliance and joined the Entente, opening a Southern Front and stretching the Alliance's resources. In August 1916, Romania joined the Entente and added to the complexity of the Eastern Front and the Southern Front. Deutsches Heer's defensive lines were extensive, and it was now fully committed to a prolonged three-front war.

The 254th Regiment fought in the east until 1918. Fritz and his comrades remembered how grateful they were to avoid the meatgrinding Somme and the attritional insanity of Verdun. Their battlegrounds, from Vilna and Divina in northern Europe to Romania in the south, were hard but not as insane as Verdun and the Somme. Fritz's proud frontkämpfers[65] fought until the Russian economy was almost bankrupt and until Nicholas II abdicated.

Signing of the Brest-Litovsk Treaty in March 1918 was the last time Fritz felt optimistic. He thought that maybe there was a possibility of ending this war with territorial gain for the Empire. The Russians ended their Great War and ceded Ukraine, Finland, the Baltic provinces, the Caucasus, and Poland. *Could this be the beginning of the end? Could this mean victory after all? Could peace be pursued now that the Kaiser had gained so much territory?*

But the Kaiser, von Hindenburg, and Ludendorff were not done fighting. Following the Russian treaty, the entire 76th Division moved to the Western Front. Fritz knew then that the Generals had squandered a chance for peace, and his nightmare would continue.

America's arrival in Europe surprised Fritz. Years previously, he was confident it would not join in a European war, but he was mistaken. OHL raised questions about the quality of the American soldiers, but the emerging Great Power supplied vast numbers to the Western Front. Those numbers alone gave Fritz cause for concern.

He recalled the early success of the Kaiserschlacht. The new shock troops (Stoßtruppen) cut through layers of enemy lines using small unit infiltration tactics to find defensive weak points. The shock troops pushed hard to the west; their new tactics and weapons broke the stalemate of four years of trench warfare. Krupp's enormous Paris Gun shelled the French capital from over one hundred and thirty kilometers away. For a short time, Fritz saw a possibility of victory. But the enemy was resilient and smart; they fell back but held their nerve and did not break. The Allies, including the Americans, regrouped, counter-attacked, and wore the over-extended German units down to the nub.

Then came Grivesnes on May 9—long, loud, tough days for the 76th. They fought hard. The fight was hand-to-hand combat in the mud and the dirt. Bayonets and hand grenades flashed through Fritz's mind. They had suffered heavy losses, had 258 men taken prisoner,[66] and withdrew from the line on May 15 to reconstitute.[67] Fritz's brow furrowed when he recalled that desperate fight.

On June 15, while the 76th was rebuilding far behind the front, OHL launched the last desperate phase of the Kaiserschlacht, Operation Marneschutz-Reims.[68] That last gasp effort failed dramatically and quickly, and the tide turned—and *oh, how it had turned,* thought Fritz. It was as if that operation had snuffed out the very soul of the Deutsches Heer.

That Saturday morning in June, Fritz struggled to enjoy his moment of peace in the trench. It would not be long before the 76th moved west to face the French and the Americans again. Perhaps another week, maybe two. The Army would soon draw his men into that cauldron, and more of his frontkämpfers would die. Perhaps, this time, his luck might end also. Fritz chewed listlessly.

His patience for this war and its leadership was at an end. Fritz had given it four years of his life. He had hoped for the best, fought hard, and believed in his men and his leaders. However, time after time, the Kaiser, von Hindenburg, and Ludendorff made critical strategic errors. *Two, then three fronts? The loss of the fickle Italian alliance? Austria-Hungary's hapless campaigns? Needless agitation of the Americans by targeting civilian ships and sending inflammatory telegraphs to the Mexicans? Von Falkenhayn's waste of so much German life at Verdun?*

Fritz was despondent. *This war would not end till we are all dead. An armistice would be a windfall.* He closed his eyes and nodded to sleep.

9

Camp Lewis

SATURDAY, 29 JUNE 1918

CAMP LEWIS, WASHINGTON

The troop train screeched to a halt at 6:15 a.m. Passengers clamored to the windows and looked wide-eyed at the expanse of mythical Camp Lewis rolled out before them. The camp sent a chill through the civilians on the train.

The imposing new camp had an enormous rectangular parade ground at its center and countless new barracks and administrative buildings along the long sides of the rectangle. A cloud of dust hung over the camp, kicked up by construction workers and thousands of new soldiers marching purposely across the landscape. In the background, Mount Rainier shadowed the camp majestically. It was, as the newspapers wrote, a marvel to see.

"Get the hell off my train—NOW!" were the first words William heard from a man in uniform. His first full day in the Army had begun. He fleetingly thought it was strange the soldier called it "his" train. In weeks to come, he would not think twice about such army peculiarities.

Within two minutes, the new arrivals clumped awkwardly in a large group on the platform. Some lined up as best they could, but discipline was impossible given the number of untrained men that spilled from the train. It was chaos.

Sergeant Sean Farrell stood on a makeshift platform and eyed the arrivals with disapproval. He left the mob settle down before he addressed them.

"Welcome to Camp Lewis and the United States Army. You knuckle-draggers are standing on my platform with the fine men from the 166th Depot Brigade. Our job is to get you kitted out and trained for combat in France. Starting this morning, we will begin changing you into US Army soldiers.

"As soldiers, your only job will be to kill as many Hun as you can. If you fail to kill the Hun, he will certainly kill you. He's good at it, and he's had four years of practice. It's as simple as that. Am I making myself clear?"

The new men mumbled incoherently.

"DO YOU UNDERSTAND ME?" He seemed more satisfied with their second response and continued.

"Until further notice, do everything my men tell you to do; do nothing without their permission. Don't think, follow my men's orders, and you might get through this. Now, CLEAR MY PLATFORM!"

The soldiers herded the confused new arrivals off the platform. They moved out onto the street and walked five hundred feet towards a large wooden structure called the "Auditorium." The cavernous white inside was well-lit and smelled of new paint. Half the building was filled with shelves of military equipment.

After more shouting and pushing, the recruits lined up in multiple rows. Wasting no time, soldiers directed the new men to pick up footlockers and move along a line of tables. Quartermaster troops threw uniform items into the boxes. Breeches, tunic, trench coat, cartridge belt, puttees, shelter half, mess kit and canteen, a tin of dubbin,[69] bayonet, and US National Army collar disks all came flying at William in rapid succession. A broad Montana peak campaign hat was handed to him with a degree of reverence, cueing William that this was an item he should take extra care of.

Once the men were back at the open area of the building, a soldier stepped forward to address them.

"LISTEN UP! Quit fussing with your gear. There will be enough time for that later! Pay attention to your name. When you hear your name, pick up your locker, step forward to the person calling you, and line up before him."

Another soldier loudly called fifty names. The line of dazed men followed him out of the building and into the morning.

A soldier called William's name in due course. He picked up his footlocker and stood before a short man with two chevrons on his sleeve.

"I'm Corporal Keckler. You men are now part of the 51st Company, 13th Battalion, 166th Depot Brigade. Grab your gear, put it in the truck outside, then form two lines by me. I'm going to get you to your barracks. MOVE OUT!"

They headed out the door, loaded their gear onto a waiting truck, and formed two lines behind the Corporal. The ragtag mob turned right onto Montana Avenue and then walked for ten minutes through clouds of morning dust. They headed up No. 12 Street past a YMCA Hall to a small storehouse where they collected two blankets and two sheets, then marched back towards Montana Avenue to Barracks No. 31.

"Grab your gear, get upstairs, pick a bunk. Be back here in thirty minutes with your uniforms on," said Keckler.

William hauled his locker and bedding up the stairs, where he found long rows of steel-spring bunk beds, each with a straw-filled mattress and a wall locker for hanging uniforms. He chose the bottom bunk halfway down the room and hastily threw the sheets and blankets on the thick mattress. A friendly voice came from the other side.

"Hi. Olin McFeron. Looks like we're bunkies."

William grinned and shook hands. Olin was from Oregon, and the two depended on each other to get through the tough weeks ahead.

The new members of 51st Company got their breeches on and buttoned up their khaki flannel shirts and cotton tunics. William traded his boots for a pair that fit him better. They fumbled with their puttees. Each put the green hat chord on their Montana Peak hats, signifying trainees.

The door burst open. Sergeant Lars Jensen strode up and down the barracks, shouting at the men in his charge. Jensen herded the entire company from the barracks onto the parade ground, where the men formed four crooked lines and stood to attention as they understood it. Jensen shouted, "Open ranks."

Corporal Keckler shoved the men into position. Sergeant Jensen walked slowly in front of each line, looking at each man with piercing eyes. He said nothing nor showed emotion. After ten painful minutes, he returned to the front of the Company and scanned the formation with disdain.

"One fucking man, one man! is wearing his uniform correctly—ONE! How will you fight the bloody Germans if you can't lace your boots up and get your puttees on? How the heck are we going to win this war with knuckle-draggers like you lot prancing around out of uniform?"

He paused, exhaled deeply, and grimaced while he looked at the new men of the 51st Company.

"I can tell you jokers this—if you are going to make it hard for me, I'm going to make it a living hell for all of you!"

He extended his arm and pointed at a tall man in the front row.

"YOU! Get over here!"

The nervous soldier moved quickly in front of the Sergeant. Jensen continued, "This Private is the ONLY one among you who has correctly put on his boots AND puttees. By chance, he also got his collar disks correctly placed. Private, I want you to demonstrate how soldiers in the 51st wear a uniform."

The soldier froze, not knowing what the Sergeant expected of him.

"Take your puttees off and demonstrate to these clowns how to do it right!"

The private sheepishly demonstrated how he put on his puttees. He nervously completed the task while the sergeant impatiently walked behind him.

Jensen shouted, "US National Army collar disk on your right collar, one inch from the collar edge, centered between the top and bottom of the collar. Now, all you misfits have precisely two minutes to un-fuck yourselves and reform the line."

The men scrambled to fix their puttees, but most only made minor improvements on their first efforts.

"You'd better figure this out quickly, or your miserable lives will be even more miserable. Don't step on my parade ground without having your kit in shape unless you like KP (Kitchen Police) and extra drill," roared the Sergeant.

"Now pay attention, we're going to start to make you ball-busters look like soldiers."

Corporal Keckler instructed the men to line up with one arm-length between each man in line and one arm-length between each row. The Drill Sergeant worked the Company hard on left-face, right-face, and about-face movements. He demonstrated how to salute and explained who to salute. Then, they got their first taste of marching in formation.

By noon, Jensen had the formation back in front of the barracks and conferred with Corporal Keckler. Both looked serious to William, who thought for the first time, perhaps this Army life would not suit him. Sergeant Jensen broke away from the Corporal and addressed the men.

"You lot have a long way to go. I have no friggin' idea how we're going to get you lot ready to face the Hun! I'm sure Uncle Sam made some god-awful mistake in drafting you clowns into my Army!

"That means I have to work on you a lot more than I was planning, and that means you boneheads will get to know my voice and the parade ground pretty well over the next few weeks. Corporal Keckler, get these idiots some chow and then have them make up their beds according to Uncle Sam's standards. Next formation is at 1300. DISMISS."

Keckler led the men to the chow hall on the first floor of their barracks. They filed in and were served beef stew, bread, and coffee by unhappy soldiers assigned to KP that day. The company sat and ate quickly, not realizing how hungry they had been.

After chow, Keckler led the men back upstairs and gathered them around while he stood on a footlocker.

"I'm going to demonstrate making a bed the Army way. You worms better figure out how to all see me do this; I ain't gonna do it more than once. I advise you all to start helping each other quickly; things will go a lot better for you if you do."

He made the bed in two minutes. The gray blankets stretched drum-tight over the straw mattress. The men gathered as close as they could, but still, not everyone could see all the tricks the Corporal used to make the bed so sharp. They started their bed-making and helped each other to ensure all the beds looked somewhat similar. Corporal Keckler liked what he saw and, after ten minutes, stood back on the footlocker and laid out the plan for the next few days.

"Work together, lads. That's the best advice I can give you to survive the next few weeks. Check each other before you show up for formation, and don't forget to shave clean. The drill sergeant has a thing for stray facial hair. Check each other's beds and boots. Sergeant Jensen will back off once he sees you have all your collective gear tight."

The men spent a long afternoon on the parade ground; it seemed to William that they had marched ten miles. His feet were sore in his stiff leather boots, and the afternoon sun made him sweat through his flannel shirt.

Figure 6: Private William H. Martin, 1918 [70]

Sergeant Jensen shouted at them constantly, singling out men who could not keep in step and punishing the entire formation when he found fault. Rumors circulated that Sergeant Jensen had been in the Philippines and had fought in the Spanish-American War. The men disliked him intensely but trusted him to prepare them for combat, and they followed every word he shouted.

By 10:00 p.m., all one thousand new soldiers in Camp Lewis lay in their bunks, most in shock after the past sixteen hours, mentally and physically exhausted after their first day in uniform. None of them felt at home; none of them felt comfortable. When Keckler turned the lights out on the 51ˢᵗ Company, almost all pondered a common thought: *what did I get myself into?*

In what seemed like thirty seconds, the lights were back on, a bugler played reveille outside, and Sergeant Jensen marched loudly up and down the barracks, screaming at the recruits.

"Zero Five Thirty, rise and shine, ladies!"

William's head ached; day two came way too quickly for him.

Sunday morning began with all the men in the unit falling in for calisthenics, which included stretching, jumping jacks, pushups, and running. Following that, the men ate breakfast and afterward headed to the washhouse. There were not enough sinks and showers for everyone, so they shaved and washed in minutes as best they could. They got their uniforms on and inspected each other to ensure there were no stains, loose threads, or missed shaving spots.

Outside, Jensen inspected them in detail, corrected minor items, berated the entire company for their slack appearance, and proceeded to drill the company for two hours.

Because it was Sunday, the men had a shorter training day than usual and were dismissed by noon, giving them what seemed like an eternity of free time.

William's younger brother Freddie shipped out to training the previous April and served on Camp with the 166ᵗʰ Depot Brigade. With all the men milling around Camp, William realized he could easily be there for six months without bumping into his brother. Corporal Keckler suggested William start looking at Brigade HQ. Perhaps they could help.

William marched down Montana Avenue to No. 8 Street and into HQ. He found a young clerk who efficiently looked up Private Charles (Freddie) Martin's file and provided directions to his barracks.

They saw each other from a distance. Something about their frames and gates registered in their brains, and they immediately picked each other out from the thousands of other men in uniform. The two settled into oversized leather chairs at YMCA # 4 (Y-4) and chatted for hours. Then, they ate dinner at Freddie's unit and walked together for miles throughout Camp. Freddie did administrative work for the 166th training staff, but his sergeant promised that he would be promoted to Private First Class soon and maybe even to a non-commissioned officer before Christmas. He was happy to stay safely at Camp Lewis despite feeling envy of the men who rotated out to Europe every week.

Freddie had heard that a big push was coming, and his unit was told to prepare for long days in the office. He warned his brother that the Army was serious about getting new recruits to France sooner than expected. But his older brother was steadfast. As much as he missed Spokane, he was determined to make it to France.

On Monday, July 1, Keckler marched another seventy-five men onto the opposite side of their parade ground. The men carried a footlocker full of uniform items and blankets. They looked stunned and confused as they listened to Corporal Keckler shout, "Grab your gear, get upstairs, pick any bunk. Be back here in thirty minutes with your uniforms on." William and his buddies felt as confused as the men who had just arrived.

Jensen cleared up any confusion quickly: "LISTEN UP! Those men that just walked up here are the second half of the 51st Company. They will join you this afternoon, and you WILL form one indivisible unit. You WILL help them with their kit and their bunks. I guarantee it. Now quit sniveling and gawking, and get on with learning your trade. The Boche is busy learning his. You don't have time to waste on feeling hard done by."

Within thirty minutes, seventy-five new men barged out of the upstairs barracks and ran over to the formation. The original men felt like they had been kicked in the gut as these new recruits joined their ranks with their disheveled uniforms and sloppy puttees.

Sergeant Jensen ordered "Open ranks," and the initial training began again for William and his company. It was as if the past two days had been removed from the Army calendar, and all the men's efforts and progress were erased.

The army attempted to keep the 13ᵗʰ Battalion stocked with men from Washington, Idaho, and Montana. Despite initial resentment between the two groups of men in the 51ˢᵗ Company, there were many cases where men came from the same town or county, which helped knit the unit together. Within a few days, the men got used to marching together, the original men taught the newcomers, and life in the 51ˢᵗ Company stabilized. The men were not at all shocked when, two days later, a further twenty-five men were added to the now fully formed Company. William began to take note of the trend.

By Friday, July 5, William had been on Camp for almost a week, and it seemed to him to be a year since he left Spokane. So much had happened, and he felt different in his uniform. Sweat and marching had creased his boots. His feet hardened, now recovered from the initial blisters, and his face darkened from the sun. His campaign hat had formed to the contour of his head. William felt a bond with strangers he met only a week before. They were united by their common experiences and their shared dislike for Sergeant Jensen.

On Monday, July 8, William had his first training on the M1903 Springfield rifle. Sergeant Jensen set up a table in the shade of the barracks and tacked a large poster to the wall. He handled the Springfield efficiently, demonstrating disassembly, assembly, and weapon cleaning. He taught the men the correct rear sight and front sight alignment using the poster and a pencil. The men learned how to come to attention, parade rest with the weapon, and how to shoulder arms. At the end of the day, Keckler counted the weapons and returned them to the armory. That night, the men retired happy—they felt a little like the soldiers they imagined they would be.

The following day, after roll call, morning calisthenics, showers, and breakfast, the men marched to the armory, where each man drew a weapon. They formed up, shouldered arms, and then marched with a new swagger as a full Company through Camp. The formation marched three miles on logging roads to an open clearing where the grass was worn down to the dried layer of mud beneath. The day was splendid. Mount Rainer loomed high above them, still capped with snow. The men marched as a single entity with noticeable new-found confidence. Even Sergeant Jensen seemed cheerful as he yodeled cadence.

The 91st Division, which had left for Europe in late June, had built a series of trenches and approximately one hundred meters in front of the trenches, a long wooden frame ten feet high from which hung rolls of sticks tied together in torso-size bundles. Keckler instructed the men on the drill: get into the trench, line up along the entire length, fix bayonets, climb out of trenches, charge the bundled sticks, extend the bayonet through the target three times shouting loudly, then move around the target and run into the next trench. After two hours, the men were sweaty and happy with their morning's work.

William smoked regularly now, mostly because he enjoyed the company of smokers. They laughed easily, joked around, and made fun of the Sergeants, Corporals, and each other at every opportunity. They also spoke plainly with each other, sharing personal details, secure in the cone of confidence that surrounded their smoking circles. After a week in camp, William was hardly ever without a pack of cigarettes and took any opportunity to light one up.

They formed up and marched back to camp feeling accomplished and a little dangerous with Springfields on their shoulders and bayonets in their scabbards. At the barracks, they stored their Springfields on gun racks and spent the evening cleaning their uniforms and bursting new blisters.

The following days consisted of more marching, push-ups, boxing, stripping weapons, inspections, KP, more cards, idle time at Y-5, and more listening to Sergeant Jensen cussing them for their lack of military bearing. Marching became as normal as breathing. The men began to move as a unit and could feel the swing and swagger of two hundred men moving in unison.

On Friday, July 12, at 0600, Jensen was happier than usual as he took roll call. William was nervous. He was used to Jensen's emotionless face and his cold stare. This was something new and worrying. The Sergeant inspected the men and found less fault than usual.

After inspection, he centered himself on the formation. He curtly told them to get their cartridge belts and haversacks, including a blanket, ground cloth, canteen, medical kit,[71] and mess kit, and reform in five minutes. The men bolted upstairs and grabbed their loaded haversacks and cartridge belts.

"I guess we're going camping!" Olin said as he slung his kit on.

"Looks like it, buddy. Not sure where, but right now, I'd swap this place for Verdun just to change the scenery."

Falling in again, they all felt a sense of excitement and expectation.

"ALL RIGHT, settle down and quit bellyaching! Time for you soldiers to stretch your legs. We're headed to the field for two days, so I hope you packed everything you needed. If it ain't in your haversack now, it ain't coming.

"We have a twenty-four-kilometer route march today, due east to Camp Berlin. We need to be there no later than 1500, or you dummies won't be eating dinner."

Jensen looked at the formation, "Who here does not have a full canteen?" Scores of men did not, but no one answered.

"Alright, I guess you will have enough water then." Sergeant Jensen knew that lesson would be learned without making a bigger deal of it—there would be some headaches that night.

"Drop your kit. You have thirty minutes to get through mess and back here, ready to roll. Don't make me come find you. Dismiss."

"What the heck is a kilometer?" William quizzed Olin.

"No idea, but twenty-four sounds like a lot of them."

They asked Corporal Keckler, who motioned for a Springfield, held it up, and pointed to the rear sling swivel and then to the end of the muzzle.

"That's one meter. One kilometer is one thousand meters, so twenty-four kilometers is about twenty-four thousand Springfields. If you wingnuts make it to France, everything there is metric, so you'll have to speak a lot of metric as well as a little French. The Army is using French maps, so we are all using metric over there—artillery, infantry, the works—last thing you need is a French artillery shell landing on you coz you didn't know a mile from a kilometer."

"So, how many miles is twenty-four kilometers?"

"Dammit, Martin, don't think in miles. Think like this: the manual says a soldier marches one kilometer in ten minutes, so if I account for a fifteen-minute breather every hour, that means roughly four kilometers every hour is a pretty good estimate for routine route marches. We can push it to six kilometers per hour if needed, but you can't maintain that for too long. Anyways, five and a half to six hours is what I'd expect for twenty-four klicks. Now get yer shit together and quit wasting my time." [72]

The men lined up and marched west for an hour before Jensen left them break to relieve themselves and adjust their haversacks. As Keckler predicted, the formation covered just over four kilometers an hour over the forest roads, including breaks. Gradually, talking in the ranks stopped. The men moved silently with only the sound of rustling uniforms and the crunching of hobnails on stones. Every hour, Sergeant Jensen broke ranks to face the column, raised his arm, and motioned to each side of the road.

At 1:05 p.m., Jensen halted the column, studied his map, and headed off the road through the tree line. He bounded back after a few minutes, "Camp Berlin. Home for the night," and jabbed his thumb over his shoulder.

"So that's what twenty-four kilometers feels like," said William to no one in particular, feeling his feet and lower back ache.

The grass in the open meadow behind the tree line was knee-high and home to thousands of clicking insects. The men cut a swath through the field towards a rise on the far side, where Jensen halted and dropped his pack.

Keckler lost no time posting guards, getting the men to stack rifles, pitch shelter halves, and gather wood for fires. Cheers went up from the soldiers when two Liberty trucks arrived, each towing a rolling field kitchen. Cooks fired up stove tops and started preparing dinner for the entire Company, which the men devoured.

That afternoon, the men dug latrines, posted guard duty, and cleaned their Springfields. Keckler briefed them on field hygiene, map reading, compass navigation, the metric system, and basic first aid.

By 6:00 p.m., William and Olin stretched out in front of their shelter half, smoked, and enjoyed the afternoon sun. They felt alive that afternoon, happy they were together in the field, happy they were in the Army.

Early the next morning, the soldiers brewed hot coffee and ate reserve rations left by the Liberty trucks. They folded their blankets, took their shelter halves down, and rolled up their haversacks.

Jensen checked his trench watch, "It's 0630. Let's see how we do on time and distance. Let's move."

The tired troops arrived back at Camp Lewis at 12:45 p.m. Jensen told them he had paperwork and gave them the rest of the day off. The Company spent the afternoon bursting new blisters and resting swollen feet.

On Saturday morning, July 13, Sergeant Jensen did a perfunctory inspection. Barely pausing, he swept through the lines of men. He centered himself on the formation.

"Men, orders have been prepared for everyone in the Company. With few exceptions, you will join the 40th Division in Camp Kearny, California.[73] Most of you lucky bastards, if not all, will be infantry."

William's head spun. Jensen continued talking, but William heard nothing. He could not believe that they were moving out so quickly. *Camp Kearny, wasn't that Southern California? Infantry???? Will Olin be going as well? Is the 40th deploying soon? Furlough home? Lizzie?*

"Orderly Room is preparing orders," continued Jensen. "Report to them after chow. In the meantime, you are released until mess. I recommend you get your gear squared away; you have some time today to ensure you are ready to move. Plan to be on a train within twenty-four to seventy-two hours. Do NOT share this information with any-one outside this unit. Do NOT write letters to your family disclosing this information. Do NOT go to see your best friends in the joy zone. That would be a big mistake this close to deploying. Your ONLY job for right now is to get your shit together and prepare to move. Don't mess this up. DISMISS!"

The men stood stunned. They hesitated before breaking ranks. Each looked at the man next to him and exchanged brief words of dis-belief.

William needed time alone and headed to Y-5, where he wrote let-ters home and sat alone reading a newspaper article on Belleau Wood. Suddenly, the black and white print from the Western Front seemed real and threatening. According to the reporter, the Germans referred to the Marines as "Teufel Hunden" or Devil Dogs. The article focused on the German deaths and prisoners taken, but it was clear that the Marines and the Army's 7th Infantry Regiment suffered heavily as well. First Sergeant Dan Daly[74] reportedly encouraged his men by shouting, "Come on, you sons of bitches, do you want to live forever?"

The words burned into William's brain, and he wondered if he could make it through a fight like that. He felt a chill, uncertain that he could, and put the paper down. He realized that the camping and marching were not what he was training for; his Springfield and bayo-net were not just for the parade ground and straw dummies. There was a deadly intent to everything he was learning. Until that morning, he assumed he would survive this adventure and make it home to Lizzie. The Belleau Wood story shook his confidence.

On Monday morning, Sergeant Jensen addressed them. "Men. You are leaving tomorrow morning at 0600. Have your crap organized and be here ready to roll at 0400. I want the barracks clean as a pin and your blankets returned to stores before you leave. Don't screw over the new lot that are arriving after you leave.

"Now, get any last-minute details taken care of. Holy Joe is avail-able for anyone who needs to talk to him. Make sure your wills are done, Judge Advocate Generals have the paperwork. If you have foot problems or other ailments, see the pill battery.

"Corporal Keckler has postage labels and clothes bags. Fill those labels out, and we will send your civi clothes back to whatever address you have on that label. You won't be needing them in France.

"One last thing, you have all done well, and I know you will do your duty over there. When you men get the chance, and most of you will, put some hurt on those Germans for me. I'll see you tomorrow morning, fall-in at 0400 sharp. DISMISS."

* * *

While William slept, on July 15 in Germany, Fritz Prinz's revamped 76th Reserve Division was on the move. The 76th broke camp, left the safety of Bezonvaux, and entrained for Soissons one-hundred and sixty kilometers to the west. Their mood was somber. They were headed to the frontlines just thirty-eight kilometers north of Belleau Wood, where the US Marines and the Army 7th Infantry fought with such passion ten days earlier. Talk of that fight had circulated through the ranks, and the indelible image of "Teufel Hunden" disturbed them. They were seasoned soldiers, and they understood the intensity of the British, French, and American counterattacks. Most knew their proud Deutsches Heer was in bad shape.

10

Camp Kearny

TUESDAY, 16 JULY 1918

CAMP LEWIS, WASHINGTON

William, Olin, and the rest of the 51st Company packed their haversacks, completed final uniform and kit inspections, barracks inspections, and civilian clothes turn-in, then marched to the train depot in the dark. Following a few words of encouragement from Sergeant Jensen, they piled into the waiting cars without looking back. Only later would William realize how much the Sergeant had done for them.

Thirteen troop cars, two engines, and two working cars moved slowly from the railroad spur in Camp Lewis into the forests towards California. The trip would take three days. For the men, three full days without drills or the constant oversight of sergeants and corporals was a godsend. The kitchen car served regular hot meals and coffee. Boredom was their biggest enemy.

The train took on water and coal in Portland, Oregon. Just north of Ashland, the soldiers got off to stretch their legs and walk the track for an hour. Over the coming days, they passed through San Francisco, Cuesta Pass, and onto San Luis Obispo, Pasadena, and Escondido. They walked a few kilometers daily, exercising and enjoying the freedom and the sunshine. William reminded himself that although this seemed like being on furlough, he moved further from Spokane and closer to France with each step.

On Friday, July 19, the troop train reached Camp Kearny just north of San Diego. The men flocked to the windows to see their new home—a vast sandy plain dotted with sage and surrounded by bald hills on the north and east. A handful of wooden buildings and a water tower with a flag pole attached formed a central hub, but the predominant feature was hundreds of tiny white tents clustered around the hub. It looked far less impressive than Camp Lewis.

William was in-processed into Company H, 158th Infantry Regiment, 79th Brigade, and assigned to a tent within three hours. They assigned Olin to a different Company, and the two friends only had time to wave at each other as they departed in different directions. Both naively assumed they would have time to meet again.

Two men were already in Tent 443 when William swung the flap open and poked his head inside. Both men got up to introduce themselves. Private Gust Dahlgren was born in southern Sweden and emigrated to America in 1909.[75] He enlisted from Cuyuna, Minnesota, where he had worked as a miner at the Rogers Brown Ore Company. Private Osro Deaderick grew up in Oregon, where he spent his youth farming near the small town of Halfway before joining the Army.

"We've been expecting someone. Didn't think the Army would let us have this palace all to ourselves," said Gust in a thick Swedish accent.

William grinned and shook hands. "William Martin, Spokane. Thanks for sharing your palace."

The flap opened again, and two more soldiers entered. Oscar Potter was a farm laborer from Cheney, a few miles outside Spokane[76];

Sigurd Lima[77] was a blacksmith from Stavanger, Norway, who enlisted in Cooperstown, North Dakota.

The tent-mates discovered they had a lot in common on their Army journeys. Sigurd and Oscar were in Camp Lewis with William, both in the 166th Depot Brigade but in different Companies. Oscar left Spokane on the same train as William on June 28. Sigurd passed through Spokane on the train to Camp Lewis a few days before William left on his journey.

Osro and Gust shared what they knew about army life at Camp Kearny. Corporal Marcus Strachan was their Platoon Corporal, Sergeant Julius Maney was their Platoon Sergeant, and Captain Wickersham was the Company Commander. Reveille was at 0515, assembly at 0530, breakfast at 0545, drill assembly at 0700, dinner at noon, retreat was sounded at 1440 each evening, assembly at 1700, followed by supper, then call to quarters at 2200 and taps at 2230.[78] Saturdays and Sundays were more relaxed, although they still had reveille and assembly.

They had not done any training yet. Strachan told Gust that Sergeant Maney wanted to wait until there were enough men to shout at before they started, but the truth was that Strachan and Maney were buried with paperwork at Division HQ. The entire leadership team had its hands full planning the deployment, receiving new men daily, feeding them, and bedding them down.

Earlier that day, Strachan posted a typed list of training activities that included physical fitness, drill, rifle care and handling, and academics on articles of war, military courtesy, sanitary regulations, and personal hygiene.

"Well sounds like we will be very clean and well-mannered when we meet the Hun," grinned Oscar, "I wouldn't want to offend him."

The men laughed. *This will be alright*, thought William.

They washed and got an early night, happy to be in a bunk after three days of sleeping on the train.

Sergeant Maney marched up to his formation on Saturday, July 20, the first day they fell in for roll call.

"Good morning, men. Welcome to Company H, 158th Regiment. I'm Sergeant Maney. I have only one job: to get you lot to France in one piece.

"You may or may not be aware, but we will be leaving Camp in the next ten days, so that means no screw-ups by you between now and then—I don't have the time for the paperwork. If you fuck up, we'll leave you behind for someone else to deal with, and it won't be pretty."

Maney paused to look at the men, steel-eyed, straight-faced.

"For anyone who is considering taking a long walk home and dodging his duty, I can tell you that the last guy who tried was charged under Article 58 of the Articles of War, otherwise known as 'desertion,' and ended up with a dishonorable discharge and twenty-five years in Alcatraz, courtesy of Uncle Sam.[79] It could have been worse; in wartime, the court could have sentenced him to death. For your information, I'd rather face the Hun any day than a Court Martial during a shooting war.

"Let me be plain—the Army owns you now, and we got a job to do. I'm here to see we get it done. Follow my rules, and we will get along just fine. Bust my balls, and you will hate life at the 158th."

Ten days? What training can possibly happen in ten days? From that moment on, his waking hours focused on getting the training he knew he would need to survive what was coming.

Being Saturday, Company H got released for personal time in the afternoon, and William headed to the library. He found a chair and an empty table by the window and scanned newspapers for every word about the war.

The German Spring Offensive and the Second Battle of the Marne. Twenty-three German Divisions attacked around Reims, just one-hundred and fourth-four kilometers from Paris. Quentin Roosevelt, a Nieuport 28 pilot with the 95th Aero Squadron and the youngest son of President Theodore

Roosevelt, was shot down and killed by German ace Sgt. Karl Thom flying a Fokker D.VIIs over Chamery, southwest of Reims.

William's soul darkened. The newspapers plainly revealed why the Army rushed to get men to the front. The enormous military effort was in black and white at that little library. Stone-cold and motionless, he stared through the dusty library window. As if to reinforce what he had just read, he saw thousands of men milling around camp—their blue infantry hat chords like beacons—a sea of white tents and trains unloading even more men and equipment.

Deep in his core, he knew his training at Camp Lewis was likely all he could expect before going overseas. *What could Sergeant Maney realistically do in ten days?* Marine Corps Sergeant Dan Daly's words from Belleau Wood, printed so often in the press, echoed in William's brain: "Come on, you sons of bitches, do you want to live forever?". Desperation gripped William. He had to find a way to increase his odds of surviving the storm he knew awaited him.

Gradually, William received more accouterments for his trade, issued and signed for part by part—new 158th infantry collar disks, a new light blue infantry hat chord, and an Enfield rifle and bayonet. His external transformation into a doughboy became more evident every day. Internally, he struggled to maintain contact with the version of himself that left Spokane.

On Monday evening, William scanned the duty roster. Their names were scheduled to guard the western perimeter of the camp the following day. They packed their kit and reported to the MPs, who issued instructions, directions, and ten rounds of 30-06 ammunition.

The two friends snapped the clips into their cartridge belts, slung their weapons, and headed off on their first unsupervised Army task. The two walked three kilometers across the flat, dry terrain to their post, relieved the two soldiers occupying the guard shack, and settled in for the night. Both men pushed a clip of ammunition into their magazines and put their Enfields on the rack.

As evening fell, William picked up his rifle and walked outside, noting how heavy it felt with the ammunition loaded. He paced off fifty paces, stacked rocks a foot high, and then walked back to the shack. Sigurd curiously picked up his rifle and followed William outside.

"What the heck you doing?"

Sigurd looked at the stacked stones and watched William walk a few steps then and cock his rifle.

"William, you're funking nuts. You know Maney is going to lose his mind."

William knelt on one knee, flipped up the rear sight, adjusted it for fifty meters, and then laid out flat on the sandy ground. He drew the rifle into his shoulder, flipped the safety off, and put his cheek against the stock. Looking through his sights, he saw the mound of rocks and felt the trigger mechanism tighten. An explosion erupted in his ear. He instinctively closed his eyes, and the rifle lurched upwards.

"Well, aren't you the moron," laughed Sigurd, "no taking it back now."

William unlocked the bolt, saw the brass cartridge eject, rammed another round into the chamber, and settled into his firing position.

"Just one more."

Sigurd rolled his eyes.

This time, William gripped the wooden front stock with his right hand and pulled the butt back into his shoulder. Anticipating the trigger resistance, he felt the trigger action tighten and then applied a little more pressure. The round exploded from the barrel, but this time, he kept the rifle tight in his shoulder, his eyes open.

"Nailed it," called Sigurd, caught up in the moment, "now put the damn thing away before you get us thrown in the stockade."

The men were relieved at 0800 the following day.

"Anything unusual?" asked the replacements.

"Nothing much," said William.

Sigurd and William walked the three kilometers back to the MP station, enjoying the morning air and each other's company. The space was easy to fill. They talked about Spokane, North Dakota, Stavanger, their Army experiences, and their families and girlfriends. As they rounded the corner to camp, Sigurd asked, "What will you tell Sergeant Maney?"

"I don't think he's going to buy a bullshit story. I guess I'll just tell him the truth and hope for the best."

"Great plan, genius. Suggest you think about that one. Either way, best outcome may be reduction in rank and a front-row seat at a war. Oh wait, you're already the lowest rank, and you're already going to war. You got nothing to worry about."

"Well, at least I got two more practice rounds than you. I'd say you're screwed when we get to France."

The men walked into the MP office, and William returned three full clips and one clip with two rounds missing.

"What is this?" said the MP, holding up the short clip.

William looked at Sigurd and said, "I thought I saw something moving around on the perimeter..."

The MP straightened his arms on his desk, looked down at the clip, paused, and then looked back up at William.

"...so let me get this straight: you thought you saw something, and you thought you'd discharge two rounds... inside Camp?"

He screwed up his face, his temple pulsed, his eyes squinted, and he stood up slowly. William and Sigurd backed up.

* * *

At just that moment, forty miles south of Paris, nine older men walked out of a large meeting room in an ornate chateau on the outskirts of a small town named Bombon. There were five senior staff officers and four General officers. Of the Generals, two were French, one was English, and one was a tall American. All were distinguished, all mustachioed, all at the peak of their careers, and all looked exhausted.

The shorter French man with the handlebar mustache was Supreme Allied Commander, General Foch. The other three were British General Haig, French General Pétain, and American General Pershing. Foch had pressed the group to go hard on the offensive now that the enemy's Spring Offensive had been halted. The Allies, he argued, had an opportunity to finish the war if they pressed their advantage. They had superiority in aviation and tanks, a marginal superiority in artillery, and, for once, had an advantage in troop numbers due to the monthly arrival of a quarter of a million Americans.

Foch presented an offensive plan consisting of four coordinated attacks, three to free up strategic railroads and one in northern France to free up coal reserves. The attacks would push the enemy back across the entire front and further attrit the damaged German forces.

The American mission was to take the Paris-Avricourt Railroad by eliminating the St. Mihiel salient. It would be the first independent American operation in the war, the first opportunity to engage the US First Army in battle under US leadership. General Pershing had pressed for this for months, and despite initial rejection by Foch, he had won his case. Now, the Americans would fight as a unified force independent of British and French leadership. The United States had an Army of almost two million men in France, and it would assert itself as a uniquely American force with American strategy and, ultimately, with American ideals to shape the peace Pershing knew was approaching.

Pershing had rejected the concept of trench warfare in favor of an open war of movement.[80] This strategy, along with his unyielding character, had caused fractions in the Entente.

The American left the other Allied Generals to retire for the night. Walking to his quarters, he felt the enormous burden of proving to the Allies and the Germans that the Americans would not fail. His faith in his American soldiers, their rifles and bayonets, open warfare, and maneuver would soon be tested.[81] He recognized both the enormity of the opportunity and the immensity of the risk, but he was committed to the strategy. He would use every ounce of influence to ensure the entire Army, from General Officers down to the newest Privates, was equally committed.

* * *

The MP addressed William over the missing two rounds.

"In six months doing this, I ain't never had to deal with one of these forms. Damn it, Private! You think I got nothing better to do than type this crap for you two knuckleheads."

The MP continued to berate William for five minutes, raising his voice to a roar, causing others to look up and wonder what the poor privates had done to deserve such a lashing. When the MP ran out of ways to reprimand the two privates verbally, William moved to a desk and sheepishly filled out duplicate paperwork describing the incident and the movement he saw on the perimeter. The two left the office with one last barrage from the MP telling them, "Get the hell outa my sight..." and then something about their Company Sergeant. Both Privates scurried out the door.

It only took forty-five minutes till Sergeant Maney stormed into tent 443.

"Everyone out except Lima and Martin!"

The other three bounded out of the tent in two seconds flat. William and Sigurd stood at attention while Sergeant Maney tore into them.

"Don't think for one minute that I believe anything bigger than a jackrabbit was crawling around in the desert in the middle of the night. You jokers thought it was a good idea to start shooting into the desert just coz you heard something moving? Jesus, save me. You got exactly three minutes to convince me not to throw both of you in the brig and let the next poor bastard deal with you after we leave—and I've already used one of those minutes."

William looked at Maney and came clean. He explained that he had not fired his weapon yet and wanted to be sure he could hit a target in France.

Maney bit his cheek to hold back a smile and turned away from the two privates. He was acutely aware that he needed to maintain good order and discipline with these new troops. They needed tempering. He knew he would ask them to do difficult things when they got to France, and he needed men he could trust completely. He also concluded that the soldiers showed a degree of initiative and risk-taking. *These guys would be useful in France.* He would uphold the Articles of War and unit discipline, but he would not squash their inventiveness or their willingness to take a risk.

Turning back, he reset his jaw and barked at both of them.

"Hope you like potatoes and calisthenics. You two dolts will be KP'ing it from now till we leave, and first time I need volunteers for some shitty duty in France, it's you two!

"Also, you trigger-happy tools owe me twenty laps of the parade ground in full battle kit; that's ten laps for each round fired. That starts this evening and lasts till you log twenty. Find Corporal Strachan and apologize to him up front for wasting his time watching you sweat."

He turned and stormed out of the tent, then turned on his heel, exploded back in, and made a beeline for Sigurd, stopping six inches from his face.

"Lesson for you, Lima—and I hope you are paying attention—is that you're as guilty as he is. This is a team sport, and if he fucks up, then you fuck up too. You may as well have fired two rounds too, coz you're going to sweat just as much as him."

"Yes, Sergeant Maney," replied Sigurd.

Outside the tent, Maney smiled and shook his head, happy Martin and Lima were in the unit. *Maybe I got some soldiers here after all*, he thought.

William and Sigurd exhaled, looked at each other, and smiled. The two found Corporal Strachan that evening and reported in for their punishment.

"He wants you to do what?" said Strachan in horror at the thought of the time he would have to watch the two men circle the parade ground.

"Tell you what, start now, and come back and tell me when you're done," he said, annoyed, and disappeared back inside his tent.

The two headed off and started their long march with full kit. Together, they peeled thousands of potatoes in the chow hall. "Worth every potato," William would later say.

On Saturday, July 27, Sergeant Maney gathered his platoon and briefed them on what would happen on Monday and Tuesday. William realized why he had cut their KP time short. It was the same briefing Sergeant Jensen gave, just different trains and destinations. They were going to the firing range on Monday, shipping out to Camp Mills, Long Island, New York, on Tuesday, and from there, to France.

The men fell out and sat on their cots, quietly packing their haversacks. The tent was solemn. The usual banter was missing; only the rustling of equipment punctured the silence.

On Monday, July 29, the Company formed up after breakfast and marched to the firing range five kilometers north. At the range, Sergeant Maney issued them twenty rounds each, and the men took turns getting into position on the firing line—every man qualified. Afterward, Maney marched the men back to their tents, where they stripped and cleaned their weapons.

In the afternoon, the Company marched to the Quartermaster. They drew additional gear: an overseas cap, a slicker, a new first aid packet, a steel helmet, a comb, a toothbrush, soap, an extra pair of trench boots, more dubbin, and an extra pair of laces. Sergeant Maney told them they would soon have to turn in their campaign hats, as they would not be needed in France. They grumbled but understood the practicality of the smaller overseas cap. The men returned to their tents and began to pack their new equipment into their already tight haversacks.

Sigurd looked over to William and Oscar. "Fellas, have a favor to ask once we get through all this."

"What's up," enquired William.

"Well, been on my mind to become a citizen, and there is an opportunity to get it done right quick now that I'm in the Army and all. Plus, it kinda seems like the right thing to do considering we're headed to France tomorrow."

William and Oscar stopped fussing with their kit and looked at Sigurd. "So what do you need?"

"Well, Congress passed a law just last month that allows service members to become naturalized citizens as long as they show proof of enlistment and testimony from two witnesses. Would you guys be willing to bear witness for me?"[82]

"Heck, Sigurd, you sure left it to the last minute. I'm not sure that's very American of you," poked Oscar.

Sigurd smiled, well able to defend himself. He responded, "Based on America joining the war after four years of fighting, I could argue that I'm very well suited."

"Well, heck, I guess he has a point," laughed William. "Least we can do is get you all naturalized before Heinie starts shooting at you. They much prefer to shoot Americans than Vikings. What do you need us to do?"

Sigurd smiled, "I guess it's pretty simple: just witness a form and far as I know, that's all they need."

The two friends accompanied Sigurd to a building with a large canvas banner pinned to the door that read "Naturalization Court, State of California" in red letters. Inside, rows of uniformed men lined up, happy to become citizens of the nation they had already committed to serve. Sigurd filled out a petition, William and Oscar signed it, and he presented it to a Judge who quickly reviewed the paperwork, filed one copy with the court, and approved the petition in less than a minute.

The old Judge looked at Sigurd, stood up, shook his hand, and said, "Congratulations, Private Lima, you are now a Naturalized Citizen of the United States. Thank you for your service."

Sigurd beamed.

William and Oscar hugged the new American. It was the right way to end the day before they left for France.

"Now you're a proper American target for our German friends, much better than that Viking target," joked William.

Back at the tent, all the men recognized that Sigurd had taken an enormous step in his personal journey. He was proud that evening as he took his tunic off, hung it up, and rubbed his thumb over the USNA collar discs.[83] His long journey from Norway and his search for a new life now felt complete in that Army tent. All he had to do was fight this war, then return to North Dakota and his blacksmithing.

On Tuesday, July 30, the men of Company H formed up at 0500, each with their platoon sergeant. Sergeant Maney inspected the line of soldiers.

He stopped opposite William, jammed his fingers into the empty Enfield breech, looked up into William's eyes, and said quietly, "Looks like you're gonna get a chance to shoot some Boche with this thing after all. Don't miss Martin."

"I won't miss, Sergeant Maney."

"I know you won't, Martin."

Captain Wickersham stood ramrod straight at the front of the formation as each unit reported in through a Lieutenant. At the Captain's command, they turned in unison and marched off the parade ground to the rhythm of Sergeant Maney's gravely "Left, left, lefty right, left," just as the sun peaked above the desert horizon.

Camp awoke, and men stopped to watch the large formation pass, knowing where they were going and knowing their turn was coming quickly.

Within fifteen minutes, the formation was at the depot. There were no frills, no bunting, no speeches. Everyone on the platform was there to deploy, so no political rituals were necessary. William was grateful it was pragmatic and functional—fitting for soldiers leaving a soldiers camp for war.

11

Cross-Country

TUESDAY, 30 JULY 1918

CAMP KEARNY, CALIFORNIA

William watched as they passed tent 443, the parade ground, and his library refuge. The troop train left Kearny's fence line within ten minutes, rolled through Linda Vista, and then north towards San Bernardino. Soon, the tired men chatted or sat quietly. Sigurd read a book, which he always had stuffed in his gear. At some point that morning, all the men looked out the window, thought of their families, and wondered what lay ahead.

San Bernardino Station was the largest and newest depot west of the Mississippi River. Sergeant Maney stood at the head of the car when the train slowed to a stop; he steadied himself with both hands on the stowage rails and shouted to his men.

"Quiet down and listen up! Don't wander far and be back on platform ten in forty-five minutes for roll call. We're boarding a new train, so take all your junk. Don't fuck up, get lost, or get arrested! Forty-five minutes!!"

Hundreds of men bounded off the train, roamed the station's tiled halls, chatted, and smoked. William lit a cigarette, got a Red Cross coffee, and found a seat next to Sigurd, who was staring in wonder at the ceiling, ". . . classic mission revival . . ." he mumbled to himself, much to William's confusion.[84]

Gust walked up. He kicked William's boot to have him slide over, looked at Sigurd, and rolled his eyes.

At 08:45 a.m., the men regrouped on platform ten as ordered and boarded a new train on the Santa Fe line. Maney called names, and each man responded and climbed aboard. All the cars had Pullman seats, which delighted the passengers. The Army had transformed the baggage car into a kitchen that housed a full-size range to feed the troops on their trip.[85]

They traveled relentlessly through Arizona, New Mexico, and Texas. The highlight of their day was when they got off to walk the tracks for a few kilometers. There was no formation or cadence called. The men clumped into social groups and strolled along without their packs. Their boots were well worn, and their feet were used to the pounding. Campaign hats, ringed with sweat, formed to their heads perfectly; the wide brim provided much-appreciated shade.

Sergeant Maney studied the men constantly, aware of each man's moods, habits, and social groups. *They were gelling nicely, and I have some leaders in there. They will be fine in France.*

On August 3, they moved through Oklahoma, north across Kansas, and into Kansas City, Missouri. The men were accustomed to the station drill by now. Sergeant Maney stood on a seat at the head of the car and shouted to the soldiers to stay close, stick together, stay in the station, and, whatever happened, do not miss roll call. The soldiers bolted off the train and into Union Station. William and his four friends sprinted through the main hall and left the station immediately. They had seen enough stations, trains, and tracks to last a lifetime. They found jitney cars parked outside and surrounded the first one in line.

"Where are the saloons?" asked William.

"You will want 12th Street, nastiest bars in town, just right for you lot," said the large man driving the Ford Model T.

"Five cents each."

The men gladly paid and were deposited outside O'Donnell's Saloon at the corner of 12th Street and McGee. They rushed across the street and burst through the door. Irish Johnny, the barman, looked up and knew what to expect. Johnny had immigrated to Butte, Montana, in 1905 to work at the Anaconda Cooper Mine. He was used to miners and never met one he didn't like. Soldiers, he thought, were the next best thing.

William dashed to the bar and ordered five beers and five whiskey chasers. *Here we go*, thought Johnny.

"To our newest and our best-read, American!" William toasted Sigurd when the beer arrived. The soldiers drained their glasses in less than a minute. Gust immediately ordered a second round.

Johnny nodded and smiled. "Easy up, lads. No rush. Where are ye off to?"

"Off to see the Kaiser about his dachshunds," Gust burped.

Johnny knew the routine. He had seen soldiers like this for almost a year now. They would scramble into his bar, pile-drive alcohol, and leave in a hurry to catch their trains to the East Coast. He knew they were not supposed to leave the station, but he also understood that this could be their last chance to get a beer in an American bar. The soldiers never caused trouble; they always made it back to the station (as far as he knew) and always paid their bills. Johnny was happy to serve them with all the alcohol they wanted. In fact, he enjoyed their raucous company, and he knew a little about what they were getting into.

When they drained their second glasses, Johnny threw his towel over his shoulder and took a bottle of Paddy Whiskey from the top shelf. He lined up seven shot glasses, one for each soldier, one for himself, and one for his brother.

"This one is on the house, lads. My brother went over in January. He's with the 6th Marine Regiment. They just had a hell of a scrap at Belleau Wood, but he made it through, buíochas le Dia.[86]

"Stay safe over there, boys. May God hold you in the palm of His hand. Slainte!"

He raised his glass to the soldiers, who returned the toast and finished their whiskeys in one swallow. They shook hands with Johnny, thanked him for his generosity of spirit, and piled out of his door in a heap.

Outside, the daylight blinded the friends. William headed to a doorway between Grand Avenue and Walnut Street with "Big River Saloon" above the door. Before the others could stop him, he dashed in and ordered another five beers. They knew they were cutting it close, so they drained the beers and dragged William out before he ordered again. They had fifteen minutes to get back to the station.

Panicked, Sigurd ran into the street and commandeered a jitney, much to the driver's annoyance. The drunken soldiers climbed in, giggling and laughing like schoolboys. Oscar razzed William that Uncle Sam still didn't know he existed; William wrestled with Gust; Sigurd urged the driver to hurry; while Osro reached across the driver to honk the horn at pedestrians, causing the driver to swerve while he swatted Osro's hands away.

The annoyed driver pulled up with three minutes to spare, happy to unload the obnoxious soldiers. The drunks sprinted through the marble halls and onto the platform with one minute to spare before roll call.

Sergeant Maney looked dubiously at the five disheveled men who could hardly stand up straight. He shook his head, decided not to ask questions, and continued checking his list.

The train steamed through Missouri, Iowa, and onto Chicago, arriving on August 4. William and his friends took a quick break in the station, but not long enough to wreak havoc as they did in Missouri.

They got coffee from the Red Cross in the station and re-boarded the train without incident.

Oscar watched a lady walking two long-snout dogs on the platform. "I'd like to get a shot at the Kaiser's little bastard dogs. I bet they're hard to hit, especially with those little pointy helmets."

"Pickelhaube,"[87] said Sigurd, "is the name you're searching for referring to "those little pointy helmets", and the dachshunds' names are Wadl and Hexl."

Sigurd didn't skip a beat. He continued to look out the window, uninterested in impressing the others, just stating the facts as he knew them. Details were important to Sigurd, not so much to the others. William looked at Gust, raised his eyebrows, and smiled. Oscar hit Sigurd with his hat.

The train sped through Indiana and Ohio, then onto Pennsylvania with regularly scheduled walking stops.

On the evening of August 5, the troop train pulled into Grand Central Station in Manhattan. The troops retrieved their weapons from the Quartermaster's car, which took an hour and a lot of shouting by the Sergeants and Corporals. By 6:00 p.m., the Corporals and Sergeants herded their units onto a local train to Camp Mills Long Island. This smaller train had none of the space or legroom they were accustomed to. The troops sat jammed close together with their haversacks on their laps and their rifle butts on the ground between their knees.

The train crossed an enormous suspension bridge, which drew gasps from the passengers, and arrived at Camp Mills by dusk. In-processing was the most efficient William had seen; it even made Camp Kearny seem slow. An advanced team from Camp Kearny had been in camp for a week and had done an excellent job preparing everything for the arrivals. Maney met with a sergeant from the camp and handed over some paperwork. The men formed up and marched to their barracks within forty-five minutes of arrival.

Camp staff had already laid sheets, blankets, and pillows at the foot of each bed. They made up their beds; it is second nature to them now. Rifles were stowed on gun racks, and haversacks were stuffed in bedside lockers.

The soldiers of Company H slept soundly that night, glad to be in a bed that wasn't swaying and clattering its way down a track. The following day, after reveille, they shaved, washed, and dressed, then piled outside their barracks for roll call. Corporal Strachan informed them that Sergeant Maney was busy all day, and they had a free day but restricted them to the camp. Strachan let the excitement die down and then informed them they would leave Camp Mills at 0500 on August 8, just two days away. The men cheered, and some threw their hats in the air. Strachan bristled, then shouted at them to regain their composure. He never understood why his unit lost its bearing so quickly. Back under control, Strachan reminded them to take care of any loose ends they needed to address. He checked his notes and remembered to tell them to leave their campaign hats in the barracks; the doughboys would only take overseas hats with them. He then dismissed the formation and returned to Division headquarters, where he had a full day's paperwork ahead of him.

Those two days were long for William. He chose to spend the time alone, needing time to gather his thoughts. The YMCA and the library were perfect places for him. He wrote to Lizzie and his family and posted the letters at the YMCA. Each night, William went to bed early but could not settle, knowing that he would ship out so soon. He was not afraid, but the unknowns of what lay ahead would not leave him be.

Company H was awake and on the floor before reveille on 8 August. They got their kit together in the pre-dawn darkness, working in pairs to pack their haversacks tightly. Outside the barracks, they quietly formed up and watched the morning light appear with a sense of awe. They knew it was the last dawn they would see in their homeland for quite a while.

At 0500, Sergeant Maney checked roll call and turned to Lieutenant Whipple, "Company H, present and accounted for, Sir."

They marched to the parade ground and joined with 158th Headquarters Company and Company G. Eight hundred and forty-four men of the 158th Infantry sounded off by Company. The deploying unit was presented to the Camp Commander by Captain Wickersham. The officers exchanged salutes, and the Colonel spoke a few words, none of which William heard.

At 0630, Company H tensed up as Sergeant Maney gave the preparatory "Company . . ." then snapped his troops to attention. On command, they shouldered arms, faced left, and marched off the parade ground and out of Camp Mills to the railroad station. There was no chat boarding the train. All the men were focused and withdrawn.

The Long Island Railroad train, carrying the listless 158th, left Camp Mills at 8:00 a.m. Upon arrival in Manhattan, they transferred to ferry boats bound for Jersey City, where the men of Company H formed and marched smartly to Pier 59 in Hoboken. Locals barely noticed the parade of men headed to war. In that part of the city, they saw parades like this daily.

The Navy had lined the large departure hall with ropes, tables, and signs. Pigeons flew in and out at will, perched in the rafters to watch the commotion; William watched back, fascinated with the little birds. More soldiers joined the crowded hall by mid-morning. William would later find out they were part of the 359th Infantry, 88th Division out of Iowa.

The First Sergent told the 158th to fall out and relax, by which the doughboys interpreted that nothing would happen quickly. Strachan instructed them not to leave the cordoned-off area. Osro, Oscar, Gust, and William sat on their haversacks, smoked cigarettes, and watched the proceedings and the pigeons. Sigurd read his book.

The officers and the non-commissioned officers were tense. They talked earnestly with Navy personnel at tall desks stacked with papers. The fussing and checking went on for two hours, by which time the three companies of the 158th had lost interest and either slept, watched pigeons, smoked, or drank coffee.

The Red Cross, who served coffee and bread rolls to all the men from a table in the corner of the building, circulated through the crowds of men handing out "safe-arrival" cards. Each postcard read: "The ship on which I sailed has arrived safely overseas." They instructed the soldiers to take as many as they wanted, address them, and sign them. The Red Cross would mail the cards after they confirmed the ship's arrival in Europe. William signed three: one for his mother, one for Freddie, and one for Lizzie.

* * *

At about the time William tipped his overseas hat over his eyes and tried to get some sleep in Hoboken, the first day of the Battle of Amiens came to an end in France. It started with over two thousand English guns pummeling German positions, followed by an onslaught of twenty-three Entente divisions, supported by over nineteen hundred aircraft and five hundred tanks.

The German Army lost more than thirty thousand soldiers that first day, over half of whom were taken prisoner.

In Hotel Britannique, in the Belgian town of Spa, German General Erich Ludendorff was distressed. He later referred to this day as the "*Schwarzer Tag des Deutschen Heeres*" ("the black day of the German Army"). To General Ludendorff and many others, that day signaled the beginning of the end for the Imperial Army.

* * *

At 11:30 a.m., Sergeant Maney marched with purpose over to Company H and shouted, "Get your shit together and form up. You guys look like a gaggle of hobos!"

The men stood up and quickly got their haversacks on their backs.

"Shut it, Mellick," continued Sergeant Maney to a Private who was about to say something stupid.

The two-hundred and forty-eight men of Company H formed up quickly, aware that Maney meant business—this was as uptight as they had seen their Sergeant. Maney looked at his small notepad and read from his notes.

"You men are entering through gangway seventeen. That's through that opening," he pointed to a large sliding door.

"Once you enter through the door, we will turn to the right and wait. We will call you by name, walk forward, and we'll check you off a roster. You will then receive a billeting slip telling you where your bunk will be. After that, head to the gangway, which will be clearly marked. Not even you buffoons could miss it. The ship, by the way, is the *S.S. Olympic*. For some reason, Uncle Sam has seen fit to transport you maggots on a luxury liner. Beats me."

The men buzzed with excitement. Even though they had been there for hours, they had not seen the enormous ship moored behind the buildings.

Maney continued, "You will be under US Navy control when you get on board. Captain Wickersham, Lieutenant Whipple, First Sergeant Pine, and I still own your lazy asses. The Navy will be responsible for bedding, feeding, keeping you alive, and general law and order on the ship. Do everything they ask you to do; do not argue. Do not make me, the Lieutenant, the good Captain, the proud 158th, or the glorious United States Army look bad, or the Navy will have their way with you first. Then, by God, the Army will have you breaking big rocks into little rocks in Fort Leavenworth.

"As you know, there is a danger of being attacked by those bastard U-boats. Yes, they have torpedoes, which you might see, but they also put down nasty contact mines, which you probably won't see. Last week, the USS San Diego hit a mine just off the coast and sank in twenty-eight minutes. So wake up. This is getting real."[88]

"The Navy will provide training on what to do in that event. Pay close attention to the training. Do NOT play fuck around with the Navy while you're wearing an Army uniform," he looked at Mellick.

"Does everybody understand how this is going to work?"

The soldiers responded in unison. There was no doubt how this would work.

"When you get to the top of the gangway, a sailor will lead you to your berth, and you'll stow your gear. We won't leave today; we leave first thing tomorrow morning, so don't get jumpy. Evening chow is at 1700 hours. I don't know where the chow hall is on a ship, or what they call it in the Navy, but I know you guys will find out where and when to eat. I'm pretty sure none of you will go hungry. That's it, pick up your gear and get ready to move out."

The men did exactly that, and within a few minutes, they marched towards the large door at the end of the building. Turning right, they gasped collectively. The size of the *Olympic* was beyond what they could have ever imagined. It was a classic ocean liner design, with nine decks tall, four giant funnels, and a bizarre paint scheme.

"What the hell is that paint about?" asked Gust.

"Designed to confuse a U-boat about a ship's speed, direction, and size. It's called dazzle camouflage," [89] Sigurd said.

"How the hell does he know that," Gust asked William, who shook his head.

"Maybe you should read a book sometime . . ."

Gust frowned.

First Sergeant Pine called each man by name. The Port Checking Officer and Lieutenant Whipple checked off the names from a roster as the men stepped forward. Next to the checking officer, a sailor handed each man a billeting card that noted the compartment of the ship where the soldier would be quartered and the number of his berth in that compartment. [90]

After being called forward and receiving his billeting card, William walked to the gangway, dropped off his "safe-arrival" postcards in a mail sack, and headed up the narrow ramp. At the top, another sailor handed him a life vest, "Wear it at all times, even while asleep," he said for the thousandth time that day. Petty Officer Peppard took William's billeting card, escorted him through a confusing series of stairs and corridors to his bunk, and informed him, "Stay here until the Captain announces you can come back on deck. Last thing we need is you mud-pounders wandering all over while we're trying to get everyone on board."

Each sleeping quarter housed fifty men but only had twenty-five beds. To the men's surprise, they were told they would share beds to conserve space on the ship, so each man was assigned a bed for twelve hours each day.

"Clearly," William said wryly, "there must be some mistake. This is not the luxury Uncle Sam meant for me to travel in."

Sigurd responded, "He could not care less about Private William Martin, mostly coz he doesn't actually know you even exist."

William ignored the barb, not wanting to encourage his friend's habit of repeating the same joke repeatedly.

The Captain announced that the passengers could leave their quarters, and the men quickly found their way to the main deck. They were once more mesmerized by the ship's scale and the grandeur of Manhattan's imposing skyline across the Hudson.

"You know this is the sister ship to the Titanic. Just three inches shorter than her sister. Not the best omen for us, I'd say," commented Sigurd casually.

"Thanks for the cheery thought. Anything else tragic that you'd like to share with us this evening?" asked Gust.

"Your face is kinda tragic," responded Sigurd, happy to oblige. Everyone laughed except Gust.

They spent an hour leaning over the rails at the stern, smoking and chatting while the dockhands continued to load coal and cargo. They talked about the bars in Kansas City, Sergeant Maney's mood swings, Belleau Wood, the Spring Offensive, the Kaiser's funny mustache, Wadl and Hexl, and their girlfriends. As pointless as their discussions often were, the ritualistic chats helped when they needed to pass the time without focusing on what they were leaving behind or heading into.

William got quiet. His mind struggled to frame how much had happened since he left Spokane on June 28. He faced away from the group and leaned on the railing, drew on his cigarette, and stared over the Hudson. *Forty bloody days!* He had traveled for eleven days from Seattle to San Diego to New York—over four thousand miles. Of the remaining twenty-nine days, he transferred between two different Army units, peeled five hundred potatoes, marched two hundred and fifty miles, bayoneted five straw Huns, shot twenty legal rounds and two illegal rounds of ammunition. He understood KP, how to wear a uniform, salute, metric distances, and how to march and drill.

On that peaceful afternoon at the stern of that magnificent ship, he felt empty and anxious. Perhaps it was true; Uncle Sam really didn't know or care that he existed. He realized that going to war was not the frightening part; knowing how unprepared he was scared him to death.

He turned to his friends and flicked his cigarette into the black water eighty feet below. "Come on," he said, "Let's see what this Navy chow is all about."

12

Across the Pond

FRIDAY, 9 AUGUST 1918

PIER 59, HOBOKEN, NEW JERSEY

Friday morning was a warm seventy degrees. At 8:05 a.m., the S.S. *Olympic*'s steam whistle blew, causing the soldiers on deck to jump. The Captain took the five-minute delay personally.

William's boots vibrated when the coal-fired engine forced the ship to break the state of inertia. The entire hull shook, the deck vibrated, and the pier appeared to move backward. *Olympic*'s propellers turned, and the Hudson churned white. Dockers released the mooring lines, and tugboats pushed the enormous liner away from the pier and into the river.

There were no crowds to see the soldiers off. A few of the longshoremen waved haphazardly. Many of the 6,260 souls on board were on deck enjoying the morning's excitement. They passed Lower Manhattan and Battery Park and steamed past Ellis Island, Governors Island, and the Statue of Liberty. William watched Ellis Island with nostalgia. Selma often talked of the day she arrived there with her mother. *How ironic,* William thought, *that she left Finland in search of a new world, but her son would be drawn back to fight a war that was tearing the old world apart. At least he was doing it unburdened by loyalty to King, Czar, or Kaiser.* As slim a margin as that may have been, he took comfort in it.

Liberty's torch faded from view. The *Olympic* steamed through the narrows between Brooklyn and Staten Island and out to the open ocean. William and his friends stayed on deck long after most of the men drifted below, until the coast was a thin dark line on the horizon.

The *Olympic* had removed most of the luxury fittings she once had, but many features were hard to miss. The troops, if even briefly, forgot they were in uniform while they descended the grand staircase. It seemed to them that the war was still a distant, surreal affair rather than the endpoint of this epic voyage.

Petty Officer Peppard, the skinny sailor who showed William to his quarters, stood on a wooden box. Peppard blew a whistle and, in a booming voice that belied his skinny frame, the sailor announced a long list of rules for all passengers. He hardly took a breath and didn't seem worried if the men around him understood a word he said; his job was to read the list, and that he would do.

"Due to the U-boat threat, there will be no lights visible after dark, no cigarettes on deck after dark, all portholes will be closed after dark, and no throwing garbage overboard. There will be daily life raft drills. The ship only has one escort. Both ships will perform zig-zag maneuvers on the first and last days of the crossing, where the probability of U-boat attacks is highest. A daily roster is posted for guards to watch for U-boats. You will be on guard for two-hour stints. You will not leave your station until you are relieved. Ship's warning system will sound if there is a U-boat threat. If that happens, stay out of the way and let the sailors crew their stations. If you have to abandon ship, do it in a life raft. If you go in the water, survival time in the Atlantic is no more than twenty minutes before hypothermia will kill you."

The soldiers were struggling with the concept of U-boats, abandoning ship, and death in a watery grave, but Peppard inhaled and continued undaunted.

"Chow times will be assigned to ensure the ship's crew can effectively feed all men on board—stick to your chow times. Religious services will be available daily for those wanting to attend."

The sailor finished the list and looked up at the bewildered audience—death, chow times, and religion in the same delivery left them dumbfounded. He was about to step off his box when he remembered one last item not on his list.

"Also, the Captain has instructed us to tell you now that we have left port, you will be getting off at Southampton, England."

The confounded soldiers came back to life and cheered. William doubled over and laughed out loud. Peppard walked off, not understanding the strange Army passengers.

The ship's alarm sounded in the afternoon, and the intercom crackled. "Attention all passengers and crew. This is the Captain. We will be doing defensive maneuvers for the next few hours. There is no imminent threat. I repeat, there is NO imminent threat. Zig-zags will begin now. That is all."

With that, the ship began aggressively switching directions in a zig-zag pattern. William and Gust were on deck chatting when Gust abruptly ran to the railing with his hand over his mouth and threw up violently.

Over the coming days, William, Osro, Sigurd, and Oscar razzed him at every opportunity, teasing him with food at every meal. Gust never found his sea legs and lost ten pounds on the voyage. "Don't care what the Hun has planned; can't be worse than this," he concluded.

The total blackout gave the soldiers unexpected views of the night sky. William walked the deck in total darkness, amazed as he gazed upwards at the thousands of stars that lit up the sky from horizon to horizon. He reached for his cigarettes and then remembered the rule about not smoking after dark. The awe he felt was replaced by panic as he imagined a U-boat maneuvering beneath the waves.

William left the main deck, forgetting the beauty above him. He headed to his quarters and lay wide awake with his life vest on, anticipating a torpedo impact at any moment.

The next day, the friends assembled on the main deck for calisthenics and spent an hour exercising in the sunshine. Afterward, they walked the deck, worried about U-boats, smoked, and talked about obscure things. This pattern continued for days, and the friends got used to the rhythm of the voyage. William stood guard duty on the sixth day, scanning the ocean with binoculars for any sign of a periscope, U-boat, or ship. He felt naked without his rifle but realized this was absurd and resigned himself to the fact that he was at the mercy of the Navy, the U-boats, and the sea.

After eight days, the Captain notified the crew and passengers that the ship would, once more, initiate zig-zag maneuvers as a precaution. The passengers knew they were getting close to England.

First Sergeant Pine gathered the Sergeants and Corporals for an operations briefing. The audience all sat attentively with their notebooks and pencils ready.

"Good morning, men. I'm going to make this short and sweet. We're landing in Southampton in a few hours. Get your men ready to disembark no later than 1400. Lieutenant Whipple will disembark first and scout out the assembly area. He'll return to the ship, and once we get cleared off by our Navy brothers, we'll follow Lieutenant Whipple's lead and assemble as a unit on the main road. A British officer will meet us and direct us to Camp Morn Hill near Winchester. It's about twenty-two kilometers outside of Southampton, so plan on a six-hour march. We'll take plenty of breaks, make sure men have full canteens."

He paused to look around the room; the audience had their heads down, scribbling notes.

"Remember, you and your men represent the United States of America. Stand tall, march tight, and don't fuss with the locals. We'll only be in England for a few days, then we head to France. There will be more on that in due course."

Pine took his notebook from his pocket and read his notes, "Some Camp rules to pass on: Every soldier is confined to camp. Anyone found missing will be charged with desertion. There will be no alcohol in camp. Any man who is found with alcohol will be up on charges and in the brig. Captain Wickersham will take a very dim view of any buffoonery while our British friends are hosting us. I will see that any man lacking discipline will be punished to the full extent of the Articles of War, up to and including death for desertion during wartime or shipping back to Alcatraz or Leavenworth for lesser infractions. Tell the men that the Captain expects everyone to do the 158th proud. Any questions?"

He barely paused, "That's it for now. Get with your men after this and ensure they know the plan. Carry on."

Within a few hours, the southern coast of England was visible. Sergeant Maney ordered the men below to get their gear ready. It took them only a few minutes to gather their things and check their haversacks. William left his life vest on the bed and stood in line in the passageway while the ship docked. He could hear the English dockworkers outside while they prepared to tie off the ship's lines and began rolling out the gangways.

The doughboys stood in line for what seemed like hours. Eventually, Sergeant Maney tapped the front man in the line and told him to follow Lieutenant Whipple. Company H shuffled through the passageways up stairwells, eventually onto the gangway, and into the fresh English air.

The dockers were happy to see them, and the men were equally glad to be on dry land. "Welcome, Yanks," or "Good on ye, Sammy," was repeated a thousand times that first hour on English soil. Sigurd felt that welcome more than most; being called "Yank" or "Sammy" now had a deeper meaning for him.

They exited the pier, passed through a receiving area, and assembled with Company G and HQ troops outside the port entrance. A one-armed British officer leaning on a cane chatted casually with Captain Wickersham at the front of the formation. The British officer pointed and waved his cane, indicating directions, and the two nodded in agreement.

Once the formation was ready, Captain Wickersham turned to face his men and stood ramrod straight as Sergeants reported to Lieutenants, and Lieutenants reported to him. Locals watched the military spectacle with idle curiosity. The entire formation, including the British officer, turned in unison and stepped off together. Hundreds of doughboys marched down Brunswick Street, with its brick houses and ivy-covered walls, to the other side of Southampton.

The British officer guided the formation through town and to the open countryside, where the landscape broadened to beautiful hills. Once outside town, the British officer and Captain Wickersham stepped into a waiting Crosley Tender truck that would take them to Camp Morn Hill ahead of the formation.

The 158th marched through the towns of Chandlers Ford and Otterbourne, along twisted country roads, through woods and low hills. Despite being July, most of the men wore their long coats to keep the thin English air off them. They were used to Texas heat and humidity. Each man shouldered fifty pounds of equipment in their haversacks, but they were all well-conditioned from six weeks of training, and the formation marched effortlessly that day in the English countryside.

After marching for five hours, the 158th reached Camp Morn Hill. Corporal Strachan conferred with Captain Wickersham and then led them to their wooden barracks, where they stowed their gear and went immediately to the chow hall. William got his first taste of British Army chow that evening, and it left him wondering if all the cooks in the British Army were in France.

Gust ate everything he could—the long march on solid ground revived him. He had lost so much weight on the voyage that he returned for seconds, much to the surprise of the English servers.

Camp Morn Hill was just east of the small town of Winchester. It was beautifully set in low rolling hills with clusters of trees as far as one could see. The barracks were simple but clean and well-used by British, Canadian, and, most recently, American forces.

A Red Cross Station offered tea and food, and a YMCA Hall held regular shows. Posters from the previous month advertised Rudyard Kipling. Sigurd was gutted to have missed him, leaving the others confused and wondering who Mr. Kipling was and why Sigurd was upset.

"Shere Khan, Baloo... Nobel Prize for Literature?" said Sigurd, losing patience with his company.[91] They stared back at him vacantly.

The 158th continued conditioning the troops on route marches and provided ongoing operational briefings. On August 17, following breakfast, assembly, and inspection, the men marched into the surrounding countryside for four hours. William was happy and embraced the chance to wander across the English countryside. All five tent-mates from Camp Kearny reverted to their clowning around, as they had done walking the railroad tracks throughout the States. They took a break every hour, sprawling out wherever they could find space, and broke out cigarettes. They had run out of their American Lucky Strikes, Chesterfields, and Bull Durhams, and converted quickly to the English Woodbines, Gold Flakes, and Player's Navy Cuts. That day, they sat back, inhaled their Woodbines, and enjoyed the cloudy English sunshine.

Maney checked in with all his men; he had watched them for weeks and was aware of the characters and the informal groups. Though he showed no overt favoritism, William felt Maney enjoyed talking with the five friends. "How are you, ladies?"

"All good, Sergeant Maney."

"You lot ready for another few hours of this?"

"Sure, Sergeant, easy peasy. Can't march the Hun to death, though. Any idea on when we are heading over?"

"Soon enough, fellas, don't worry, soon enough. Then you'll want to be back here, believe me."

The Sergeant left the men to finish their cigarettes. They drank from their canteens and moved out within ten minutes to finish the day's march. William now thought in terms of kilometers and pace; parts of him had turned into a soldier.

Company G and H assembled in a large theater with hundreds of folding chairs that afternoon. Captain Wickersham walked onto the stage to exaggerated applause and cat-whistles. The Sergeants seethed at the men's lack of bearing.

Wickersham recognized the humor in the moment and allowed the audience to blow off steam, then held his hand up to signify quiet.

"Good evening, men. I have asked intelligence to provide an update from France so we all understand what's happening at the front. Lieutenant Finch, over to you."

Finch stood in front of a large map of France with a wooden pointer and sketched in the main events of the past few months.

"As you know, approximately fifty German Divisions moved from the Eastern to the Western Front in late March due to the Russian collapse. In what we now call the Spring Offensive, or the Kaiserschlacht (Kaiser's Battle), the strengthened German Western Army launched a major offensive that broke through the Allied lines on the Somme, here."

The men booed as if they were at a baseball game; Sergeant Maney flashed a vicious look and shouted, "Quieeett!"

The men giggled but understood the risk of further angering the Sergeant.

Finch continued, "The Germans pushed the Brits back to here," he pointed to the strategically important rail city of Amiens, "only one hundred and twenty-eight kilometers northwest of Paris. Von Hindenburg continued with four more major offensives intended to divert our attention away from this main thrust to Amiens. These efforts continued till about a month ago.

"Ultimately, the Germans failed to take Amiens, and they paid an enormous price in casualties and prisoners. We estimate about thirty thousand in total. As you fellas know, during May and June, we have been fighting here and here, at Belleau Wood and Chateau Thierry."

Another cheer from the men and another glare from Maney.

"The enemy now has longer logistics lines, fewer large guns, demoralized troops, and a longer frontline to hold. In short, we have absorbed the best the Germans had to offer, and we are now massing our armies to hit back hard while they are vulnerable. That's where the 158th comes into the story."

Maney stood up in anticipation of the reaction, looked threateningly at the men, and successfully subverted the cheer.

"We could not have timed our arrival better—we can expect to be part of a counterattack to push the enemy east and hopefully break their back in Germany. That's all I have to say for now. Clearly, there are a lot of things going on, but I thought a general overview of the strategic situation would be helpful. Are there any questions?"

Private Mellick raised his hand before Sergeant Maney could stop him. Maney visibly tensed.

"Sir, will the war be over by Christmas? Got a girl in Wyoming that I've made some tentative commitments to."

The men laughed, and Mellick grinned, happy with his disruption.

"I don't think that's a likely outcome, Private. Germans still have a lot of fight in them. I'd plan to be here in 1919."

Sergeant Maney glared at Mellick, who appeared to want to continue the discussion with the Lieutenant. Mellick saw the threat from Maney and retreated to his chair. Maney made a mental note to find a special place for Mellick once they got to France, somewhere far away from him, HQ, and anything important.

Captain Wickersham stood up again. "Thank you, Lieutenant Finch. I want to share another significant event with you."

Wickersham walked across the stage, "A week ago, General Pershing announced the formation of an independent American army that combined American corps and American divisions into a unified fighting force. Instead of being attached in bits and pieces to the British or French, we will fight for the first time under the American flag and under American command."

The soldiers in the room burst into an instantaneous cheer, including Maney, who jumped from his seat and held both clenched fists in front of him.

Captain Wickersham smiled broadly, allowing the crowd to finish cheering before continuing. "General Pershing is First Army Commander, Col Hugh Drum is Chief of Staff, HQ was established here, at La Ferte-sous-Jouarre, sixty-four kilometers east of Paris on the banks of the Marne River. The First Army initiated operations on August 10, and we have just heard that HQ is on the move to Neufchateau, here, just sixty-four kilometers from this nasty German salient at Saint-Mihiel."

He paused and looked into the crowded room. The men focused on him, and the room went quiet as a graveyard.

"So, I'm not a betting man, but I'd put a month's pay that the 40th Division will be in combat somewhere in this area," he pointed to the southern part of the Western Front around Saint-Mihiel. The room exploded; men cheered, stomped their boots on the floor, and shouted obscenities.

Wickersham waited patiently for the bedlam to reside of its own accord. He walked across the stage and scanned the five hundred faces following his every move.

"One last thing," he continued, "we are headed into combat at a critical time in this war. You have trained hard, but don't be fooled; we face a determined and resourceful enemy. Even if they have been stopped in their tracks, the Germans are not out of this fight. There will be tough days ahead, lads. But I am confident that we will prevail, and God willing, we will be home soon.

"Tomorrow morning, we leave for France. I ask that you each do your duty as United States soldiers, maintain discipline under fire, and follow your officers' orders. With luck and help from above, we will all return safely to our homes and families."

There was total silence in the room as the Captain's words sank in. Then, like a delayed fuse, an enormous cheer shattered the room—men jumped in the air, flung their hats to the rafters, hugged each other, and screamed at the top of their lungs.

After years of anticipation, they were twenty-four hours from setting foot on French soil. Captain Wickersham and his Lieutenants walked off the stage through the chaos. Sergeants and Corporals realized it was pointless to subdue the men and joined the celebration. William and his friends were elated; they felt lucky to be on the threshold of the world stage, about to engage in an epic battle. Their naivety was a blessing.

Sunday, August 18, was overcast and breezy. Company H assembled outside their quarters, and Maney inspected kits. It was the most informal of inspections. Maney tugged on belts, checked snaps, and inspected chambers, but he was just going through the motions, not looking for fault.

For every man, he had a few quiet words and looked each one in the eyes before moving to the next. The Company marched to the parade ground, where they fell in with the other eight hundred and thirty-eight men gathering there. They knew the routine by now: report in, a facing movement, and the inevitable gravelly voice of Sergeant Maney calling cadence.

They left Camp and marched through Winchester, Compton, Otterbourne, and Chandler's Ford. Locals on their way to service stopped to watch the Americans. After four years of war, they knew more about the Americans' fate than any men marching.

They entered Southampton at 2:00 p.m., hundreds of hobnail boots echoing off the rowed stone houses. The 158th arrived at berth forty-one at 3:00 p.m. They broke ranks and lit cigarettes while the officers and non-commissioned officers met with the Navy. They had been through this routine before; it was going to be a while.

The docks were busy despite being Sunday. Two battle-damaged ships were under noisy repair, each with large torpedo holes torn into their hulls. Bent metal and shards of splintered wood deck pointed at odd angles around the gaping holes in their hulls. The violence that must have caused the damage shocked William. Somehow, he had not previously comprehended the raw destructive power of the weapons that would soon target him. He broke his stare and looked at his friends. They were all transfixed with the ship's damage—all thinking the same thing.

At 4:00 p.m., the 158th walked up the gangway to the steamship *Arbroath*. She was nothing like the *Olympic*; the battered old hull was two hundred and eighty feet long, thirty-six feet wide, with a single funnel. *Doesn't look like she was going to break any speed records*, thought William, who was no longer rushed to get to France.

A tiny British sailor who looked no older than fifteen handed each man a life jacket and grimly repeated, "Only slightly used; won't save your life, but you'll be easier to find afterward." The sailor directed the men to stay on deck; they would sail at night to reduce the chance of being spotted by a U-boat. The doughboys removed their gear and laid on the deck, trying to get comfortable. The little sailor walked up and down the vessel's length to remind the passengers that there would be no lights, cigarettes, or food during the crossing. The trip would be quick—more due to Cherbourg's proximity than the ship's speed, which was only sixteen knots.

The steamer's engines started at 9:00 p.m., vibrating through William's bones. Within fifteen minutes, the ship left the safety of the harbor, past the Isle of Wight, and through the cold English Channel in total darkness. William spent the night sleepless, smokeless, and cold. The impulse to talk was soon extinguished; it was a miserable voyage for all the soldiers.

The *Arbroath* arrived in Cherbourg early on August 19, still cloaked in darkness. The docks were chaotic. Everywhere William looked, he saw men that looked stressed, uncomfortable, tired, and ill-humored. For William, it was an uninspiring and anticlimactic arrival on French soil. He had not known exactly what to expect, but it was not this.

13

French Soil

MONDAY, 19 AUGUST 1918

CHERBOURG, FRANCE

Sergeant Maney formed his troops in a staging area and marched them quickly east of town and out of the turmoil of the port. They marched through the old city, across four kilometers of gorse-covered hills, beyond the village of Tourlaville, and on to a location posted as Rest Camp No.1.

The Camp was tiny, approximately four hundred meters square, and hectic. Tattered tents, flimsy wooden huts, a canteen, and a postal facility filled the small field.

Upon arrival, Maney checked with the administration hut while the men sat on the roadside amongst the hedgerows. The tired soldiers were assigned to tattered, twelve-man circular tents within thirty minutes. There were no beds or cots; they slept on the ground with their feet in the center and their heads towards the walls. At night, William and the others folded their greatcoats in two to give their bones a small cushion to lay on.

The chow hall was a disaster. Food was neither plentiful nor appetizing, and the men barely ate. In truth, it was not the cook's fault. Fresh fruit and vegetables were non-existent. Even Gust, who found something redeeming in the Morn Hill mess hall, struggled at Rest Camp No. 1.

No training was conducted at the camp, although the sergeants inspected the troops daily. William slept as much as he could between August 19 and 21, but the hard ground and the cramped conditions ensured he woke up cold and stiff each morning.

"Ironic that these are called Rest Camps when it's impossible to sleep here," William said wryly on the first morning and every morning afterward. The others only laughed on the first morning.

When Maney told them late on the evening of August 21 that they were moving out the following day, the men were ecstatic. In their inexperienced opinions, the frontline could not have been more uncomfortable than Rest Camp No. 1.

On Thursday, August 22, the 158th marched downhill to the train station in Cherbourg. After picking up rations, they waited for hours soaking in the sun and sleeping. The train arrived, but it was not what they expected—small wooden boxcars without seats or benches, labeled "40 Hommes/8 Chevaux" (40 men/8 horses). The grumbling soldiers climbed on board.

"Get on with it!" Sergeants all along the platform shouted, as impatient and tired as their troops. William, his four tent-mates from Kearny, and thirty-five other soldiers climbed into the little wooden box.

Inside the car, the light dimmed to a dull, dust-filled space. It was dirty and bare, but everyone had floor space. The men sat on their haversacks and leaned against each other and the walls. William got comfortable on his rolled-up coat. *This may not be too bad.* Then the train lurched forward, and he felt each wheel hit every gap in the tracks, making it impossible to get comfortable.

"The devil's own gift to transportation," said Osro.

The troop train moved out of Cherbourg through Sainte-Mère-Église and the beautiful French countryside. William watched through the slats. He marveled at the fields and the villages; almost all the buildings were carved stone, and even the smallest villages had town squares, town halls, fountains, and steepled churches. He wondered if the town's size was proportional to the size of the steeple and tested that theory to pass the time in the uncomfortable car.

The train wound slowly through Caen into a large rail yard, where it screeched to a halt. By then, William was sure his steeple theory was valid and shared it with his comrades, who ignored him completely. Even Sigurd was too bored and miserable to give it any thought.

The doors slammed open, and the men poured onto the platform. French soldiers—Poilus[92]—were everywhere. The distinctive light blue coats and Adrian helmets of the French dominated the station. In their crisp white and blue uniforms, the Red Cross, so much a part of every stop along the way, served sweetened coffee to all the soldiers who swarmed their tables. The 158th men smoked, drank, and watched the colorful chaos.

Sigurd surprised no one when he announced he spoke some French and left to see if he could trade cigarettes for food. He gathered some Woodbines from his friends and hurried off, his overseas hat tilted back on his head. He soon returned triumphantly with a loaf of French bread, holding it high above his head as he grinned and pointed at his prize. He tore the loaf in five and handed each their share. That meal of sweet coffee, French bread, and cigarettes was the best William had in weeks. Everything was right with the world for a few moments in that chaotic corner of Caen Station.

The train reloaded and moved through the countryside for the rest of the evening, stopping sixteen kilometers north of Alencon to take on coal and water. The men got out to stretch their legs and enjoyed the last rays of sunshine before the light disappeared and dusk filtered in. One adventurous soul climbed on top of the car to get a better view of the rolling hills and was helping others up when Sergeant Maney arrived.

"Private! What the fuck are you doing up there? Get your worthless butt down here on the double."

The man climbed down and faced the angry sergeant. After much shouting and cursing, Maney turned to the rest of the men and addressed them in a surprisingly parental tone.

"In the past month, three American soldiers died riding on top of these very trains. All thought they could lay flat enough to get through tunnels, and all died a wasteful and painful death.[93] I don't want to write letters to your mothers and fathers telling them you died because I let you do something stupid on my watch. Smarten up, lads. This shit is getting real."

The engineer blew the steam whistle, and the subdued men climbed back into the cars.

"Looks like we messed up," said William.

"Yeah, all the balling out we've had so far has been for crap that doesn't ultimately matter. We ought to get our war faces on," Sigurd responded.

William nodded solemnly in agreement.

It was cold, and the vibrations from the wheels on the tracks transferred directly to the car frame and into the men's bones. They shifted position all night, grumbled, and tried to stay warm. Few slept at all; those that did slept badly. By first light, most were standing to lessen the vibrations through their bodies and smoked cigarettes to pass the time.

The train passed through Le Mans with only a short stop. The troops continued their uncomfortable journey and, by evening, arrived at Remount Depot No. 22, just a mile east of Gievres.[94] William detrained and was bewildered at the scale of the Quartermaster's operation. The depot had hundreds of vehicles of all sizes, storage hangers, oil tanks, and even airplane parts within view from where he stood. Sigurd heard the familiar tones of hammers and anvils and inhaled deeply.

"Oh God, I miss that sound and the smell of those horses. I think I'd rather be in a smithy that just about anywhere else on earth. Especially now, no offense fellas."

The air in the depot made all the men perk up; besides the distinctive smell of horses, it also carried the enticing aroma of coffee and baked bread. William later learned that the Quartermaster had a coffee roasting plant, a bakery, and Europe's largest ice-making and refrigeration plant.[95] He briefly wondered if he made the right choice in putting "mucker" on his draft form back in Spokane. Perhaps he would not have ended up in the infantry if he had written "clerk," perhaps his war might have been spent in a coffee roasting plant outside this pretty French town.

Sergeant Maney directed his men to a large mess hall, where they ate their first hot meal in two days. Services of Supply troops served freshly baked bread, real beef, potatoes, and even cake for dessert. The Company had been starving for fresh food with taste and texture. The friends returned for seconds, and when they could eat no more, Maney gave them more good news.

"You men have four hours before the train leaves again. There are some casual billets around the corner. Follow me and get some sleep before the Captain changes his mind."

They piled into an empty barracks. Each bloated man crashed into a bunk and fell asleep on the soft mattresses before their Sergeant left the room. William's last thoughts were of Lizzie and his family back in Spokane, a million miles and a hundred years away from this happy depot in the middle of France.

Corporal Strachan shook them awake in the middle of the night, and they stumbled out of the barracks, back across the depot yard, and into their wooden boxcars. Most went straight back to sleep. William could not and stayed posted by the slats to watch the dawn west of Bourges. He saw the sun break the horizon and light up the dust in the shabby car. It was a magical moment. His 158th brothers were strewn in heaps across the car in deep slumber, their sleepy forms lit by shards of morning light.

At mid-morning on August 24, the train pulled into the tiny station of Nerondes. The wheels screeched to a halt, voices shouted, and a hundred boxcar doors slid open with a series of thuds. The station master watched with interest as the eight hundred and fifty-five men of the 158th Infantry detained and moved to the open area across from the station on the Rue des Tilleuls. The men grouped slowly, stiff and tired from two and a half days of traveling. They looked around at the surrounding buildings and wondered where exactly they were. After gruff encouragement from corporals, they formed up for roll call, replaying the ancient soldierly ritual now so familiar to the unit.

The two-hundred and fifty-five men in Company H moved off to one side. The Army would billet each company in a different small town in the area. Company H marched off first, turned left at the end of the street, and marched north on Rue de la Gare towards the small town of Garigny, their new home, eleven kilometers away.

They left the quaint train station, marched past rustic stone houses, past old ladies and men who watched vacantly as the Americans passed. The people of Nerondes had been at war since 1914; they had sent their sons, husbands, and neighbors to war years before. They knew that the Americans were marching into a war that would consume many of them, as it had done with their friends and loved ones.

At Mornay-Berry, a small village six kilometers from Nerondes, the men stopped for a rest in the center of the village. William leaned against the wall of a low sandstone storehouse with a meticulous red tile roof. He sipped from his canteen, tilted his head towards the sun, and closed his eyes. His thoughts drifted thousands of miles away to Spokane, his apartment on Second Avenue overlooking town, his kitchen table, and Lizzie. He was completely immersed in the moment. He could smell the coffee and see Lizzie's eyes sparkle.

His daydream was interrupted by Sigurd's banal request. "Got any monkey meat?"

William resented the intrusion and tried to get back to the imaginary kitchen table.

Sergeant Maney circulated through the men, his boots clicking on the stone pavement, "more than halfway home, ladies." William gave up. *This is not going to work.* He opened his eyes and squinted, scanning the crossroad where the unit sprawled out.

Osro and Oscar sat beside each other and took turns throwing pebbles at a stick a few feet from Osro's long legs.

"Potter, you can't hit shit. What's wrong with you?"

Oscar snapped back, "Nickel for the closest pebble . . ."

The two laughed and joked as the tally went up and down. Twenty minutes into the pebble throwing, Sergeant Maney broke up the gambling ring and formed the men up.

The company continued to its destination village. They marched through a wooded area, past a small pond signed "Etang de Doys", and into the small town of Garigny. Maney halted the unit in the town center beside the church. He released the men and instructed them to stay in the town square while they arranged billets. Lieutenant Whipple sent runners to find the mayor, who duly arrived to meet the new arrivals.

The mayor and the Lieutenant chatted for fifteen minutes and appeared to enjoy each other's company. The mayor turned to the soldiers and clapped, then saluted and departed the square. The Lieutenant addressed the men and reminded them that all bars in town were off limits, alcohol was banned, and there was a curfew at 2130 each evening.[96] The formation grumbled, and the Sergeants glared. Whipple dismissed the formation and instructed the men to stay in the village center while billets were assigned. Maney directed corporals to groups of men sitting around in groups. Locals took small groups of men to their billets—houses, barns, and schools throughout the small town. The Company clerks meticulously recorded the names and addresses of the billets and the number of lodgers for payment by the Army.

William, Gust, Sigurd, Osro, Oscar, and four others were grouped together. Corporal Strachan scribbled their names in his notebook, and a local led them to the north end of the village. The local introduced the soldiers to an older lady, who led them to an old stone barn and swung the doors open.

The friends cautiously looked inside. It was dark and smelled of cattle and manure. Tentatively, they stepped into their new home, squishing soft mud under their boots. The old lady pointed to a ladder in the corner, leading through a hole in the wooden ceiling. William climbed up and poked his head into a dusty, dry loft. William whistled to his buddies, and they scrambled upstairs. The loft had a high-pitched tile roof, rough-cut stone walls, old wooden rafters, and a hoist door overlooking the yard and Madame Lemaire's house. Sigurd pushed on the hoist door; hinges creaked, and daylight spilled in.

Oscar spoke first. "Well, don't know about you guys, but I've slept in worse places."

They all agreed. Their new abode even had a handpump for water and a stone trough outside. The loft would be a vast improvement over Rest Camp No. 1 and the boxcar. Each put their gear against the wall and explored their surroundings. William's main concern was finding something to sleep on; his back had been stiff since he left Rest Camp No. 1, and the train journey had done nothing to help.

Madam Theresa Lemaire waived the men down into the yard. She had a kind face and was dressed in black from head to toe. She spoke no English but greeted each man and smiled while she presented the soldiers with dark bread and strong-smelling cheese.

Sigurd took over as translator between the soldiers and the landlady. A bond grew between the woman and the young soldier, and she spoiled the men in the barn from then on. By evening, they had extra blankets, a broom, a lantern, towels, soap, and a wash basin. Osro found a rope to tie between the rafters to keep their uniforms off the dusty floor, and Madam Theresa showed them where they could get straw to sleep on.

Corporal Strachan checked in on them later in the evening.

"Fuck me, you lot did okay! You should see how the rest of them are living. Not all so lucky."

"God watches out for children, drunks, and fools," joked Osro. The men grinned at their good fortune. Strachan giggled.

"Assembly is 1700. Don't be late, fools," he said as he left the loft.

That evening in the town center, Lieutenant Whipple addressed the formation and informed them that training would commence the following morning at 0800, later than usual as it was Sunday morning. The men groaned.

Sergeant Maney made it simple, "0745 show-time, full kit. Quit grumbling; we're going back to work. There's a war on."

14

Garigny

SUNDAY, 25 AUGUST 1918

GARIGNY, FRANCE

The soldiers woke at 0500 on Sunday. William recalled how he hated early deliveries with the Elgin Dairy Company, but now the Army made an early rise normal.

By 0745, they had washed, shaved, dressed, and walked to the church steeple. They learned that all two-hundred and fifty-five men were bedded down somewhere in the small village, in attics, lofts, barns, and every available spare room. The Lieutenant was billeted in a large house with the town mayor on the main road opposite the church. Sergeant Maney stayed next door to him. Some men had drawn short straws and stayed in open stables with little shelter from the chilly nights. None received the treatment that Madam Lemaire piled on her guests.

At 0755, Lieutenant Whipple strode out of his quarters, and Sergeant Pine called the formation to attention. They moved as one unit now, smooth and coordinated. The Sergeants reported in "all present and accounted for," and the Lieutenant ordered the men back at ease. Whipple jumped onto a low wall. He looked serious and uncomfortable that morning. William braced. *Nothing good could come from this*, he thought.

"Good morning, men. I trust you are comfortable in your new quarters, and I'm sure you are as happy as I am to be off that damn train."

"A quick update for you—we are two hundred and seventeen kilometers south of Paris, pretty much as close to the middle of France as we could be, and we are about two hundred and forty kilometers from the closest German, somewhere in that direction," he pointed northeast.

"Our role here in Garigny is to continue to train and to be ready to move to the front at a moment's notice. We start that training today, and we'll continue until we leave, which could be days or weeks." He paused somberly, tugged his uniform straight, and looked straight into the massed men before him.

Here we go, thought William.

"I have some news from Captain Wickersham and Colonel Grinstead. It's not the sort of news we relish but important news for all of us." He paused and cleared his throat.

"We learned yesterday that the 40th Sunshine Division has been redesignated the 6th Depot Division. This means that we will not enter the line as our own Division. As a Depot Division, we will provide replacement troops to frontline Divisions when needed."

There were gasps, and the mass of men visibly wavered as if hit by a giant sledgehammer. Sigurd looked like he had been punched in the stomach and leaned forward, staring at the ground, hands on his knees. William could not absorb what he heard; he could only shake his head. He never understood why the Army dropped change on them so abruptly—like a bag of hammers—did they just not care, or was it that the Army was moving at a pace they could not control?

Lieutenant Whipple let the men grumble. He knew they needed to make that statement while they absorbed the news. He and his brother officers did the same and worse.

In a firm, restrained voice, Sergeant Maney shouted, "Alright, keep it down."

The Lieutenant continued. "Men, I know this is not what we wanted, but make no mistake, this is what we will do. The US First Army is getting ready to strike a blow at the heart of the German Army, and General Pershing has seen it fit to use the 40th Division to bring frontline units up to full strength.

"We WILL embrace this order with everything we have. Our personal preferences have no bearing on what must happen now. General Strong, Colonel Grinstead, and Captain Wickersham will provide more information as it becomes available. We'll post reassignment orders as soon as we receive them. In the meantime, our job as soldiers has not changed; we are in France to kill the Hun, and that is what we will do whether we are part of the 40th or another Division."

He looked solemnly at the men. "Today, we continue training to complete that mission. We will use every moment to prepare for the battles ahead."

The men shuffled and grumbled but now held their military bearing. The non-comms kept an eye on them, and when the Lieutenant finished, they broke the men into Companies and continued the day's training as if the 40th still existed. Behind the façade, every man in the unit, from Captain to Private, was deflated and stunned.[97]

Over the coming days, they marched for kilometers and practiced advancing in line and bayonet charges. They pitched shelter-halves and lived in the pastoral French countryside around Garigny. The Division received various supplies and equipment, distributed them as best they could, and prepared to send men to the front.[98] The orderly room placed a notice board in the village center and posted administrative information there. It provided a place for smokers to gather and share their gripes, rumors, and stories.

Sigurd and William grew tighter, opting to share shelter halves in the field and covering each other on maneuvers through the Garigny forest. Osro and Oscar teamed up as a comic duo, never missing an opportunity to poke fun or compete, no matter how trivial the topic. Gust gravitated to any group he was close to. He floated effortlessly between everyone in the Company, serving as messenger and rumor control.

Companies E and F arrived in Garigny on Tuesday, August 27, doubling the number of Americans in town to over a thousand men. The town was full before, but now every closet housed a doughboy. William's barn absorbed sixteen more men on the ground floor. Madam Lemaire continued to offer what she could to keep the men comfortable, but there were too many troops for her means. She regularly ushered the original nine lodgers into her kitchen for cheese, bread, and occasionally wine—against the Division regulations but welcomed by the young men.

On September 8, Sergeant Maney marched his men to Mornay-Berry, where engineers had built rifle ranges in a quarry half a kilometer south of the village.[99] The men were issued twenty rounds each and spent the day on the firing line.

Over the coming days, groups of men transferred out of the 6th Deport Brigade. On September 11, the Brigade transferred fifteen hundred men to frontline units. Major General Strong, Commander 6th Depot Brigade, was concerned; some of his men had preliminary rifle training, some had gas training, but none had any "appreciable amount of field training."[100] He requested ten days to provide intensive training to bring his men to a "reasonably suitable level of training" before movement to the frontlines.[101]

The officers and non-comms worked the men hard over the next ten days, knowing there was not enough time to get everything done but hoping they could instill the basic combat skills they needed to survive the front.

On September 12, after a day of field training, Lieutenant Whipple gathered Company H in the woods south of the village. The Lieutenant stood facing the semi-circular crowd in front of a large map of Europe, a stick resting under his overlapped hands.

"Men, there are major developments at the front. You already know that the American First Army was formed under General Pershing. Today, several attacks took place along the entire front. I want to draw your attention to here," he turned and pointed his stick to Saint-Mihiel.

"To the southeast of Verdun, Saint-Mihiel salient, this little triangle here, has been in German hands since 1914. The French tried to take it back several times. Today, the American First Army attacked the salient, three American Divisions, one French, all under American command." The crowd cheered and clapped.

"There was also a major push, here, by the British. They attacked towards Belgium around Havrincourt. Both attacks appear to have gone well."

The men could not have known that planning was already underway for a more significant push into the German lines. The American First Army, while still engaged in Saint-Mihiel, was planning to pull the entire force west to support a larger attack, thrusting north, deep into German-held territory. The logistics were planned and directed by Colonel George C. Marshall, who would establish himself as one of the most capable logistics officers in the AEF.

* * *

On September 15, three hundred and twenty kilometers north of Garigny, Lieutenant Prinz and the 76th Reserve Division crossed the Aisne River that wound through Soissons and dug in nine kilometers to the north, close to the small village of Sorny.

Fritz studied maps and intelligence reports. Their position was un-ambiguous: the unit would clearly meet the full force of the pursuing French Army.

Fritz and his fellow officers met with the Commander that morning. Afterward, he met with his non-comms and passed on the clear message that they would meet the French square on, they would stand their ground, and there would be no retreat from this position. Then, they waited patiently for the inevitable drumfire[102] artillery that would signal the beginning of the fight.

Fritz opened his tattered copy of Clausewitz's *Vom Kriege*—the same copy he took to Spokane all those years ago. Folded neatly at the back of the book was the front page of the *Pocatello Tribune*. He usually read Clausewitz to calm his nerves when the war seemed too much to manage; he read the *Pocatello Tribune* to give him hope for the future. That day in Sorny, he read both.

Over the coming days, the 76th Division engaged in what they later called the "grosskampf" (the "big fight").[103] They fought for the first time against embedded Americans under French command. The French and Americans were tough and determined. They attacked relentlessly despite the German machine guns, the artillery, the rifles, and the mortars. Although the 76th made them pay for every inch of ground, the enemy prevailed, and the 76th Division's companies shrunk to twenty-five to thirty men each.[104]

The grosskampf was a hard, dirty fight that shook Fritz and his men to their cores. They staggered backward and understood their bleak tactical and strategic position at a primitive level.

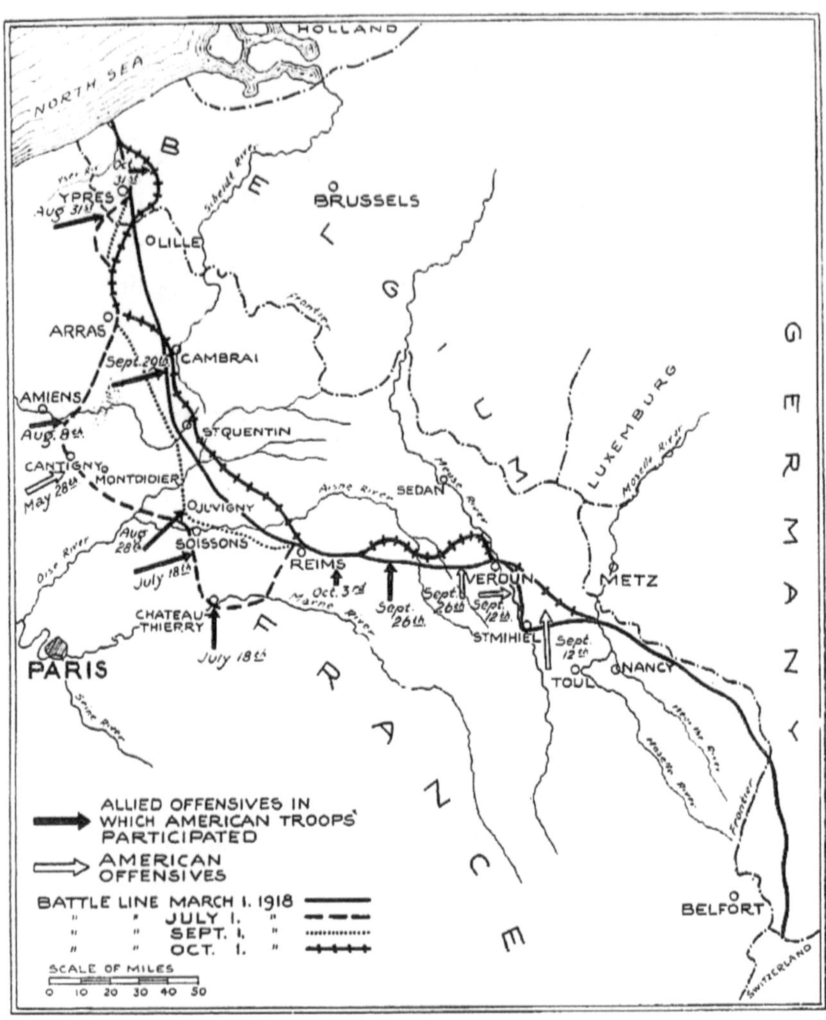

Figure 7: AEF Western Front Engagements, 1918 [105]

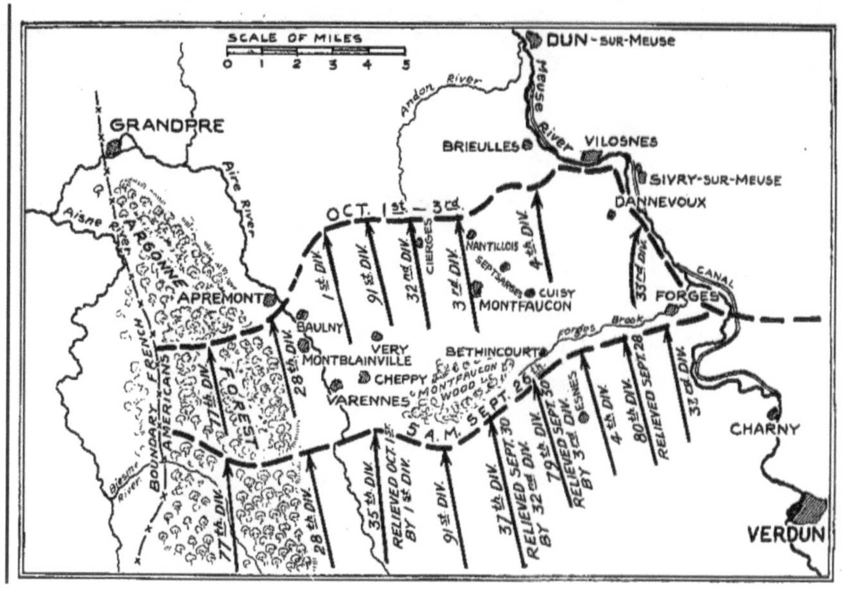

Figure 8: Meuse-Argonne Offensive, 1918 [106]

15

Into the Line

FRIDAY, 20 SEPTEMBER 1918

GARIGNY, FRANCE

On Friday evening, the soldiers gathered in the village center for retreat. Stray cats roamed the churchyard, and locals sat on windowsills to watch the Americans go through their evening formation. In a firm voice, Sergeant Maney read Special Order Number 26, detailing that one thousand men from across the 158th would be moving back to Neronds the following morning. From there, they would board a train and be transferred to a unit codenamed "DOLLY" on the frontline. The formation visibly shifted.

"All right, knock it off," bellowed Maney, annoyed that the men lost their bearing yet again. Other than the reference to DOLLY, there was no information about where they would be going or what unit they would join. That information would be disclosed once they were close to their destination.

Maney read the list of Company H men on the list: ". . . Dahlgren . . . Deaderick . . . Lima . . . Martin . . . Potter . . ."

Walking quickly back to the barn, the friends peppered Sigurd, their reference for all strategy, with questions. Sigurd thought the most likely move was to Saint-Mihiel, where they would advance east towards Metz, a natural logistics center, and only a few days' march from the German border. The group seemed happy with that answer. In the absence of formal briefings by the army, Sigurd's assessment made sense and gave them something to cling to.

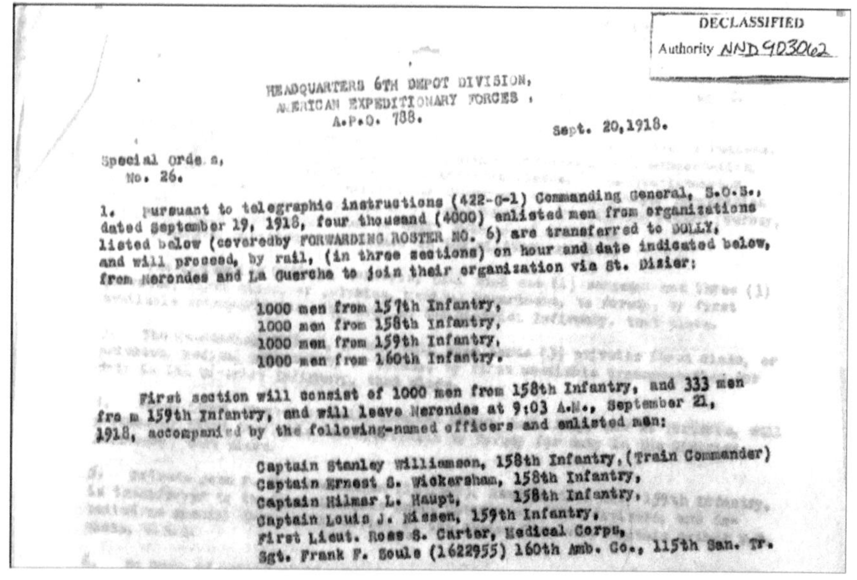

DECLASSIFIED
Authority NND 903062

HEADQUARTERS 6TH DEPOT DIVISION,
AMERICAN EXPEDITIONARY FORCES,
A.P.O. 788.

Sept. 20,1918.

Special Orders,
No. 26.

1.   Pursuant to telegraphic instructions (422-G-1) Commanding General, S.O.S., dated September 19, 1918, four thousand (4000) enlisted men from organizations listed below (coveredby FORWARDING ROSTER NO. 6) are transferred to DOLLY, and will proceed, by rail, (in three sections) on hour and date indicated below, from Nerondes and La Guerche to join their organization via St. Dizier:

1000 men from 157th Infantry,
1000 men from 158th Infantry,
1000 men from 159th Infantry,
1000 men from 160th Infantry.

First section will consist of 1000 men from 158th Infantry, and 333 men from 159th Infantry, and will leave Nerondes at 9:03 A.M., September 21, 1918, accompanied by the following-named officers and enlisted men:

Captain Stanley Williamson, 158th Infantry,(Train Commander)
Captain Ernest S. Wickersham, 158th Infantry,
Captain Hilmar L. Haupt,   158th Infantry,
Captain Louis J. Niesen, 159th Infantry,
First Lieut. Ross S. Carter, Medical Corps,
Sgt. Frank F. Soule (1622955) 160th Amb. Co., 115th San. Tr.

Figure 9: 6th Depot Division, Special Order No. 26 [107]

That night, they moved slowly and methodically, preparing their kits and cleaning their Enfields. There was none of the usual levity or the idle chatter. Madam Theresa's lamp provided a calming yellow hue to the solemn scene. William looked around with an unexpected sense of calm. His temporary home reminded him more of a monastery than a barn. He finished his work and put his head on his straw pillow. His mind released all anxiety and worry, and he fell into a peaceful sleep.

William awoke at 0300, hearing his comrades already moving. He washed, shaved, folded the blankets for Madam Lemaire, and tidied up the loft. The men left a note of thanks on the blankets under the extinguished lamp. They climbed down the ladder and walked in silence to the church.

At 0345 on September 21, more than five hundred men stood in the pitch-black town square. They smoked, chatted in hoarse morning voices, and shifted weight from one foot to another to warm up while officers huddled underneath the church spire.[108]

A Liberty truck pulled into the square and turned on its kerosene lights to provide an eerie half-light across the area. Sergeant Maney marched smartly to the formation and called them to attention.

"I wanted to let you know that it's been a privilege to serve with you. You have performed magnificently as a unit and as individuals.

"I wish I were moving out with you this morning, but that's not happening. Unfortunately, the Army has other plans for me. But I know that each of you will do his duty and will do the 158th proud. Stay safe, remember what you've learned here, take care of one another, and by God's grace, we will meet again after all this passes."

He paused as if to say more but then turned sharply and marched into the semi-darkness.

Sergeant Soule approached the formation. He moved quickly up and down the rows of men, checking only that each man had a rifle and a haversack, tapping each item as he went. Then, he returned to the front of the formation and reported to Captain Wickersham. The Captain bellowed the command, and four hundred ninety-eight men swiveled left and marched forward.

Sergeant Maney positioned himself at the edge of the village and stood to attention as his men filed past, indistinguishable in the morning dark. The formation filed past and disappeared into the darkness, leaving the village and Sergeant Julius Maney in silence.

Colonel Grinstead, Commander of the 158th Infantry Regiment, unable to shake a hollow guilty feeling, sat down and wrote to the Commanding General, 6th Depot Division:

"... *The majority of these men were received by the 158th Infantry after the middle of July. They had been drafted, sent to American Lake [i.e., Camp Lewis] for examination, classification, etc. and then sent to the 40th Division with only a little elementary instruction ...*

... A month on train and transport had not added to the training of these troops, but excellent discipline was maintained ...

... Taking into consideration the time spent in equipping, classifying, traveling, and billeting, these men made remarkable progress. They were not a finished product. The CC 158th Infantry sees great difficulty in turning out a finished soldier under such circumstances. A few weeks more training would have added immensely in their value." [109] [110]

The Colonel paused to re-read the memo. He wondered if it was the correct thing to do at this point in his career but quickly determined that he owed his men an honest assessment. The Commander signed the memo and put it in distribution to the General.

In the early morning, no cadence was called. The men gaggled rather than marched. By 0530, they passed through Mornay-Berry, still asleep in the darkness, and the firing range. Wickersham ordered a ten-minute break. Oscar bummed a smoke from William and sat silently by him. Both men pensively watched dawn crack across the eastern sky.

They arrived in Nerondes at 0700, two hours before their scheduled departure time, and joined a few hundred other men from the 158th. The old station master arrived at 0800, lunch box under his arm, and unlocked his office without paying attention to the thousand men lounging around his tiny platform.

At 0855, a long train of forty-and-eights pulled in. William and his friends stood up, gathered their gear, and climbed aboard. "Devil's gift indeed," William said to himself as he braced for the uncomfortable ride.

They stopped at La Guerche for thirty minutes, collected two days rations, then traveled northeast through the small towns of Clamecy and Auxerre. Questions, doubts, and fears filled William's head. *How would I react under fire? How prepared am I to face the Hun? Will I fight alongside my buddies or be alone in a new unit?* He looked around the car at men he had come to know as his family. Anxiety and uncertainty consumed him.

They stopped occasionally so the men could stretch their legs. As the day progressed, the men heard distant artillery rumbling and realized that their journey was coming to a close. Whatever lay ahead would soon be clear.

Rolling slowly through light rain into St. Dizier, the soldiers flocked to the slats to see the wet city. Once stopped at the station, Captain Wickersham went to each car and told them they had an hour to eat and draw rations. William jumped onto the drenched platform and walked off with purpose into the chaos. It was a confused scene. There was no order or civility, the opposite of the Caen, Le Mans, and Tours stations. William got a cup of sweetened tea from the Red Cross and found a low wall where he sipped the strong brew, smoked, and chatted to Sigurd.

"Rations over there, by them Poilus," announced Osro, pointing at a mass of blue uniforms. The others jumped at the possibility of new exotic rations, maybe something French. They were sadly let down.

"Does the Army do anything else except canned beef?" asked Oscar.

"They do death and confusion very well," Sigurd grinned. The men laughed for the first time that day, and the collective angst disappeared. The jovial mood lasted until they climbed like prisoners back into the dark cars, then gloom descended on them again, weighing them down as they slid the door shut.

Captain Wickersham banged on the door and stuck his head in, "Men, you are going to the 77th Division, code name 'Dolly,' moving into position in the Argonne. We only have about sixty kilometers left.

We'll be going to Sainte Menehould first, then onto a village called Les Islettes, where someone from the 308th Infantry will meet you. I don't have details on what specific Company you will be joining. They will let you know once we get there."

He ducked his head out of the car and slammed the door closed before the men asked any questions, leaving them stunned.

William and his friends sat speechless. They had expected to go to Saint-Mihiel. Most had never heard of the Argonne. Some knew a little about the 77th Division, remembering posters about the division from their brief stay at Camp Mills.

The men in the car descended on Sigurd—Why not Metz? Where was the Argonne? What was the plan if not Metz? Who were the 77th?

"Jesus, I don't know, fellas, I'm a blacksmith from North Dakota! My best guess is that if we are not headed into Metz and from there into Germany, based on what the Captain told us, the main push will be through the Argonne Forest west of Verdun. The frontline there is east-west. So I assume we will be fighting through a forest heading north."

His friends were confused; "fighting through a forest heading north" only inspired more questions.

Sigurd attempted to clarify, "The Metz route would be a sprint into Germany to unhinge the homeland but bypassing most of the heavy combat units in Belgium, France, and Luxembourg. Cutting combat units off from their sources of power, their heads of government, and separating them from their supply lines." He paused, wondering how to pitch the alternative.

"If we are pulling back west of Verdun and heading north, I'd say the intent is to engage with the main combat forces and destroy them in the field—a battle of attrition. Now you have a blacksmith's view. Fuck off and ask a Captain—they get paid to figure this shit out. You'll probably get a completely different answer."

William ignored Sigurd's parry and asked, "So what do you know about the 77th?"

"New York City Division, lots of immigrants. I know there are a bunch of Norwegians in it, probably Swedes, Irish, Italians. I think they go by the 'Liberty Division' because of Lady Libert or the 'Metropolitan Division.' Remember when we were in New York, that blue poster with a golden Statue of Liberty posted everywhere? It was all over the subway stations."

The men looked blankly back at him. Sigurd rolled his eyes and wondered how they consistently managed to miss the obvious.

"That's all I can tell you," he said, aggravated that he was the one who had to explain what the army was thinking when it hardly made sense to him most of the time.

William pressed him with one more question. "Wait, what's a war of attrition?"

Sigurd looked at William and paused while considering the best way to phrase what he had to say.

"It's where the point in a fight is destroying the other army, even if it means your army takes it on the chin. It's not about cutting them off, moving around them, or gaining ground. The theory is that after all the killing is done, you have more men left than the enemy, so you win.

"Remember what General Grant said during the Civil War?" Blank stares. "Well, he said something like, 'The art of war is simple enough. Find out where your enemy is. Get at him as soon as you can. Strike at him as hard as you can and as often as you can, and keep moving on.' Anyway, that's what Grant did, and that's what I think we're headed into."

"Dang," said William, "nice to know. Glad I asked."

Sigurd's audience fell back in unison. They now had a picture in their heads that they needed to absorb, each in his own way.

The train steamed north. Within two hours, they passed through a busy depot called Sainte-Menehould, then rolled slowly west on a minor track through thick forest. They passed by a small hamlet with a spire surrounded by orchards—La Grange Aux Bois—future home of Army Mobile Hospital No. 4. A few kilometers further, the train slowed from walking speed to a complete stop still concealed by the forest, just as dusk settled. They would disembark under full cover of darkness, which would take twenty more agonizing minutes. The men remained transfixed, wound tight as springs.

Darkness closed in. The train lurched out of the forest, rolling slowly along the track. It stopped a kilometer ahead at a bombed-out, deserted village. There was no platform, just a crumbled station house with a faded green sign that read "Les Islettes."

An anonymous soldier walked the train length, hammered on the doors, and ordered the men to stay inside until he opened the door for them. The boxcar doors duly slid open one by one along the length of the train. Each car released a batch of forty tense men into the night. William listened as the commotion approached him, sliding doors, boots stomping on wood, crushed gravel under hobnails. He waited, coiled anxiously by the door, gripped his Enfield, checked his kit, and played nervously with his chinstrap.

Captain Wickersham slid the door open and told them to jump one by one and follow the man in front. The Captain slapped each man on the shoulder as they landed. "Good luck," he said sincerely a thousand times that night. Like Sergeant Maney, he desperately wanted to go with them to the frontline—returning to the Depot Brigade was not how he wanted to serve in this war.

William jumped onto the ballast at 2010 hours on Sunday, September 22. "Good luck, soldier," said the Captain. William nodded in response and strode after Sigurd. He crouched and half-ran a few hundred meters across a soggy field to a tree line. William had taken his first steps in the Meuse Argonne. Squatting on the wet grass under the trees outside the bombed-out village, he thought of working in the coffee roasting plant in Gièvres. It seemed to him that roasting coffee would have been an easier way to fight the Hun.

Sergeant Michael Greally, from County Longford, Ireland, appeared out of the darkness.[111] Greally had left New York in April and had been in the fight since June. He was over six feet tall and lean. His darting eyes moved constantly, taking in everything about the new troops.

"Company H, 158th?" he said. They nodded, intimidated by Greally's imposing presence. He read off a roster of forty-two names, including William, Osro, Gust, Oscar, and Sigurd. The men stood in a loose line, and Greally walked the line, counting each man before continuing.

"I'm Sergeant Greally, Company G, 308th Infantry, Second Battalion, 77th Division, otherwise known as the Metropolitans, otherwise known as your new home. Sorry, it's a shite way to meet.

"You lads may or may not know it, but your timing is perfect. We'll get into that in due course." He smiled at the men briefly.

"Just so's ya know, that direction—north—bad people; that direction—south—good people. Don't get that fucked up in your noggin. End of your tactical awareness briefing.

"Tonight, we march northwest for six klicks, where we'll join the rest of G Company. Roads are shite, and traffic is heavy, weather is not going to get better. No smokin', no talkin', no fuckin' around, no getting lost. Stay in visual contact with the fella in front of you. I don't have time to waste finding stragglers. 'Tis up to you to stay attached. Tighten up your gear; don't let me hear any clattering about."

He looked around at the raw material facing him, hanging on every word, eyes wide with fear. He remembered his first night at the front and how new they were to war. He softened his tone and slowed his pace, realizing that his accent and his fast delivery were probably not helping the new men.

"There's an ammo dump in town. Grab what you can; you're goin' to need it. Field rations, too. There is not much food where you're going, so now's yer chance. That's it, lads. Questions later when we have time. Follow me, single file."

William liked the Seargeant's simple communication, cramming information into as few breaths as possible as if words were scarce. His mind latched onto everything Greally said, but he had to think about every word because of Greally's accent and the rate at which he talked. He clung to each word as if they were scripture, dissecting and storing them for later reference.

Greally moved quickly through the streets and led the men into a barn with stacked ammunition crates. They filled their bandoleers with sixty rounds and loaded another six into their Enfields.

Osro and Oscar, true to form, stuffed extra clips into their pockets as if it were a competition. They picked up two days' rations, more hardtack, and canned beef, and then Greally stood.

"Alright, let's get the hell outa here. We got places to be." Greally left the barn without waiting or looking over his shoulder. All forty-two new men were right behind him.[112]

The rain fell in large drops. Within five minutes, the men were wet from head to toe, water running off their helmets onto their slickers. French and American troops, horses, and trucks of all shapes packed the muddy roads. There were no cigarettes, no truck lights; everything was pitch black and wet.

Greally's pace was quicker than they were used to, like he was in a rush. His speed on the march matched the way he talked. Everything about Greally seemed like it was late and needed to catch up.

The soaked troops arrived at the tiny crossroads of Le Claon, a collection of tired farmhouses, some blasted apart, remnants of the homes they once were. The distant skyline lit up, and seconds later, a roar of artillery cracked through the night. William hunched over and thought, *I'm in it now, no mistake.*

The forty-five men swung left at the crossroads and marched for another kilometer up a windy hill to the small town of Florent-en-Argonne, largely abandoned like all the towns this close to the front. Greally met with another sergeant who pointed down the street, jutted his hand to the left, then nodded. Greally returned and led them to three empty houses.

"Don't get comfortable. This place will do for a bit till we get the rest of the Battalion sorted out. Later on, we'll move a little further tonight."

William and his comrades sat exhausted by the days on the train, the rain, and the nervous energy of the past few hours. Many fell asleep within minutes. William listened to the distant artillery rumble and the rain hitting the side of the broken building, unable to shake the fear and loneliness that gripped him.

Greally returned at 2345. He tapped a few replacements, and they all got to their feet, slung their kits in the darkness, and left the relative comfort of the building. Greally marched the tired men north on a muddy forest road into Bois des Hauts Bâtis. After forty-five minutes of unhappiness, the formation halted at a desolate opening in the woods called La Croix Gentin. Sergeant Greally scouted ahead.

The men sat silently on their helmets in the dark woods. Their slickers pulled over their heads—like ghosts awaiting their final resting places. Their Sergeant returned, formed them up into a straggly line, and led them six hundred meters down the slippery forest road, then into the woods and up a slope to the backside of a low hill.

William could barely see ten feet, but he could sense men in the woods around him moving and murmuring in low tones. Greally walked the length of the line, telling the new men to keep the noise down, find a spot, and settle in for the night. It was 0300.

William laid his trench coat on the ground to stay off the soaked earth and pulled his shelter half, blanket, and slicker over him. Curled up to keep what warmth he could under his covers, he tried to get comfortable, but it was impossible. It was a miserable night for all the new men of the 308th Infantry.

Monday, September 23, William woke up sore and wet, where rain dripped through his makeshift shelter to his uniform. He threw his slicker off and reminded himself to pitch a proper shelter if they stayed the night. Rolling forward, his wet uniform stuck to his skin, and he moaned, then cursed. Sigurd stirred next to him, equally un-happy and miserable.

"What do you say we pitch our shelters together tonight."

William nodded. "What I wouldn't give for a barn and some straw..."

Corporal James Dolan walked over. "Welcome, lads, glad you're here. Sorry about the mess getting in late last night, but that's the way we go."

Dolan, from Glencar, County Leitrim, Ireland, was promoted in the field on August 21. He had a thick brogue, piercing blue eyes, and a happy disposition, even in the miserable forest. *Jesus*, William thought, *is everyone in this unit from somewhere else? Where are the Americans?* Dolan was about to say something but saw a group of men behind William about to light a fire to brew coffee. His happy disposition dis-appeared in a flash.

"Goddammit, Delgrasso, why do you always make me wanna shoot you? Put that fukin' fire out, or you'll have every bloody German gun this side of Berlin on our asses!"

Dolan stormed off shouting abuse at Delgrasso, who stood with arms outstretched and his shoulders hunched in defense. Dolan kicked the fire out and continued to ball Delgrasso out as William watched. Out of earshot, Delgrasso pointed at the small fire and the thick canopy of leaves, putting up a defense that seemed to enrage Corporal Dolan even more.

Osro walked up, kicked William's boot and nodded at Sigurd. "Shitty night." They all nodded. The three men stood in a circle, smok-ing their first cigarette of the day and chatting hoarsely. Dolan re-joined the group.

"Sorry lads, we have some proper feckin' eejits here, don't know what to tell ya . . . Welcome to the 308th. We're still rebuilding from our scraps in Baccarat and the Vesle Sector. We lost some good men back there and have some gaps to fill in the company. You lot look fit and keen, and we're happy to have ye join us.

"The lads," he nodded over his shoulder at the other 308th troops, "are a good bunch, but it'll take them a while to adjust to you new fellas. Give them a break while they get used to you. You'll be countin' on each other soon enough."

The men nodded.

"Anyway, wanted to get you updated on what's goin' on. You know a big stunt is coming up, and we'll be right in the middle of it. Nothing official, but lookin' around, I'd say it's in the next few days, and it'll be a right show. Officers always disappear to some dark cave for a few days right before the shit happens. Takes 'em a while to hatch some clever new way to get us killed. Never seen this much gear stuffed into woods just waiting to attack. So it'll be a grand show."

William and the others bobbed their heads in unison, not knowing what to say about the casual and stunning update.

Dolan continued, "Here's the deal—we're not moving out today or tonight, maybe tomorrow night. No one knows for sure. Major Whittlesey will let us know when the brass lets him know. Either way, for now, we lay low during the day, stay outa sight, rest up. Hun aircraft are up there daily trying to see what we're up to. We move around at night. No fires-ever. Cigarettes are okay during the day.

"Get yourselves ready for a fight; eat, rest, write yer letters home, tell yer mothers you love 'em, and the war is great, make sure ye have ammo, make sure yur shit is tight."

He paused to look at the new men—wet, miserable, pale, lost—and wondered what they must be thinking. "Any questions for me?"

William asked, "When is chow, Corporal?"

"Good question, should have told you . . . you're fucked. Best we have are the iron rations. I don't expect hot chow, so you shouldn't either. Haven't seen a rolling kitchen in a week. Sergeant Freeman is trying to get more field rations tonight."

William nodded.

"Oh, another thing..." Dolan decided there was no time like the present for some teaching, and besides, he wanted to get the new guys focused on anything but their dismal morning. "You'll have problems first time the Boche tries to shove a Whiz Bang up yer arse. First battle is a bit nerve-racking. Not much I can help you with there. But I suggest you get familiar with things that will help you survive, that means grenades, automatic rifles, and semi-automatic pistols. After you get familiar with those little beauties, you can move on to getting handy with Stokes mortars and Hotchkiss guns.

"Yeah, I know it's not in the manuals, but believe me, you'll be glad you learned, and so will we. I assume you know how to use your Enfield, but there's no guarantee that you'll have it when you need it most. Besides, we need every man in the line able to fill in for his battle buddy."

Dolan drew his sidearm and asked if the group used one before. They all shook their heads, which Dolan expected.

"Right, here you go—Colt Model M1911, semi-automatic pistol. If you can't hit your target with a stone, don't waste your time with this."

Dolan dropped the magazine, racked the slide, ejected the round in the chamber, and handed the magazine to William.

"Seven rounds, 45 caliber, just push them down in there to load."

He took the magazine back, added the ejected round, rammed the magazine back into the pistol butt, and re-racked the slide.

"Now you're ready to fire. Safety on the left; up safe, down fire. You don't have to recock anything; as long as there are rounds in the pistol, you just keep pulling the trigger. She'll tell you when she's empty. Push the button to drop the mag, slam in another one, rack it, and you're ready to go."

The men were captivated and forgot about the cold and dampness. Dolan depressed the magazine release button, dropped the magazine, emptied the chamber, and handed the pistol to Osro in one smooth motion.

"Get the hang of it. You won't have one on you at the start of the fight, but they tend to find their way into everyone's hands at some point in a scrap. It might save your life or mine."

Each man took turns handling the weapon, loading it, and racking the slide. When they finished, Dolan reloaded and shoved it back in his holster.

"Delgrasso! Quit looking pitiful and get over here with a grenade."

The tall soldier came over and looked at the Corporal. "What's up, Corp?"

"That's Corporal to you, gobshite. Show these new lads the Mills."

Delgrasso looked hurt. "Mills grenade, simple." He held one up, happy to demonstrate.

"Make sure you have this spoon held down, pull the pin, and throw it. Four seconds later, it goes bang; Hans ends up with a few of these metal chunks in his noggin. Simple."

"Thank you. Now fuck off," said Dolan.

"Good luck, boys. Get to know the natives," he said, nodding over his shoulder to the remnants of the old 308th. "They're all the same as you, good lads, and you're all on the same team now." Dolan looked at the new arrivals as if to imprint their faces, nodded curtly, and walked off to find Sergeant Greally.

William and his gang looked at each other. Corporal Dolan had been right; they needed to forget about the dismal morning and get their heads in the game. They just had five intense minutes of training on grenades and a 1911 pistol. That was five minutes more than they ever got at Camp Lewis or Camp Kearny. They all felt that the Army had forgotten some essential steps in their training, and all were glad Corporal Dolan took the time to give them something tangible to latch onto.

"I'm hungry," said Osro, breaking the awkward silence and heading off to open his rations. Oscar ran behind him and jumped to knock his cap off his head as he passed.

"Quit dropping your shit all over," he laughed.

Sigurd and William got their shelter half up and pushed their haversacks out of the weather. Inside, they laid out their equipment, counted their rounds, and re-filled their bandoleers. They smoked, ate canned beef, rested, and pondered what was now almost upon them.

The drone of an aircraft brought them outside. Above them, an American SPAD[113] aircraft patrolled up and down the frontline, providing reconnaissance reports on German movements and keeping German aircraft away from American movements. William and Sigurd watched the aircraft circle and probe for twenty minutes before they crawled back into their shelter.

Boredom soon got the best of them, so they walked the camp's perimeter, staying in the tree line. They could see artillery units deeper in the woods, setting and sighting their guns. Artillerymen cut into tree trunks along the gun-target lines but wedged them before they cut entirely through to ensure the trees would not fall until the time was right. They could not take the chance that felled trees would give their position away before H-hour. Other troops unloaded ammunition and stacked the boxes waist high, a safe distance from the guns.

"75mm guns," said Sigurd, "French design but made in the US. We used to call them 3-inch guns, but we changed to the 75mm to standardize and to be able to use French ammunition. It's that metric thing we learned about."

William stopped and stared blankly at Sigurd. "What, Private Lima, are you doing in the infantry, or for that matter, in the Army?"

Sigurd paused. "So I'm guessing you don't want to know about recuperator advancements and the impact on accuracy?"

"You're right."

The men laughed and walked back to their shelter half.

On Tuesday, September 24, William and Sigurd slept most of the day. They did not see Sergeant Greally or Corporal Dolan all day. The New Yorkers grumbled that D-Day was coming. "They always disappear right before we go over the top—they'll come out of their holes soon and give us the gory details," they told Sigurd.

The Battalion leadership did, in fact, spend the day studying the plan of attack at Headquarters. The officers laid out the maps on field tables and peered at the terrain and the enemy order of battle. They reviewed each company's strength, readiness of the new replacements, relative balance between veteran soldiers and new arrivals, artillery placement, the terrain, logistics support to ensure they could keep fighting, medical facilities and ambulance operations, and an intelligence assessment of the enemy strong points. The officers discussed the lateral boundaries between the units and the phases the units would gain each day. Divisional leadership wanted more time to make a perfect plan, but they knew the element of surprise dwindled with each passing day.

At 1800, September 25, Sergeant Greally gathered Company G. They all knew what was coming. He cleared a ten-foot square area of the forest floor and told the men to circle around.

"Alright, settle down. Take a knee in front, make sure everyone can see." The crowd shuffled; some stood on logs or rocks, and some crouched low, but everyone ensured they could see the sergeant. He paused and looked around at his men. *Everyone is focused. Its time.*

"We're moving into the line tonight. Break camp at 2000 hours. Full packs. Double-check ammo, canteens, and rations."

He took his bayonet, placed it flat on the ground, and called out, "North," pointing with a large stick in the direction of the blade. He then scraped a line in the dirt and placed a small rock on the line.

"The frontline, and here—the small village of La Harazée, about five klicks north of here. That's our kickoff point. The American First Army is pushing from here, right through to Sedan about sixty-four kilometers to the north."

Sergeant Greally picked up a large rock and walked it three meters from the first rock. "That's Sedan." The soldiers shifted balance and murmured—*sixty-four kilometers*, every soul in that group shivered.

"There are rail lines in Sedan that we must capture that'll cut the German supply lines to France." Souls shivered again. *The Germans would defend those rail lines with everything they got if they were that critical.*

He drew two parallel lines from the frontline in the direction of the North arrow.

"These are the Division boundaries. 77th Division is on the extreme left of the First Army formation, with the French Fourth Army to our west and the 28th Division to our east. The French Groupement Durand is a combined US-French force led by the French; the 368th Infantry and 92nd Division are our boys in there. The 77th will cover about six klicks of the frontline, right here," he pointed between the two parallel lines with his stick and then pointed north to the Sedan rock.

"We're going over the top at 0550 hours Friday morning.

"Remember, standard doctrine. Stay in contact with your left and right flank. Note we have an entirely different Army on our left flank. That gets tricky. Bad enough doing it with our own doughboys on the right."

Sergeant Greally paused, looking around at the soldiers. Not a breath could be heard.

Greally continued slowly, wanting every man to hear every word, "1st Battalion under Major Whittlesey is leading the attack, 2nd Battalion is support, 3rd Battalion is in reserve, lucky bastards." A few men smiled. He drove trench knives into the ground, representing the three battalions.

Pointing to the lead knife, he continued, "1st Battalion—Company D on the left, followed by Company C. Company A on the right, followed by Company B." He placed rocks representing the Companies behind the knife.

"First Battalion will have engineers and artillery liaisons with them." Greally paused; he knew the men were taking mental stock of all this. Unlike many briefings, these details placed every one of them in a particular spot on the battlefield.

Pointing to the second trench knife, he continued, "2nd Battalion, under Captain Budd, in support five hundred meters in trail of 1st Battalion. Company H on the left, Company E on the right. Behind H is Company G—us—behind E is Company F."

Greally paused again. He saw some quizzical looks and reiterated the line-up in a slightly different format. He pointed to a rock he had placed for Company G, "So we're on the left in the second wave behind Company H. We will also have the 306th Machine Gun Battalion with us. Good?" Nods all around.

"Engineers will take on clearing any major obstacle like wire that has not already been torn up with high explosive arty; artillery liaisons will direct fire as needed from the big guns in the rear.

"Bigger picture, the First Army, three full Corps, goes from the 77th Division anchored here," he pointed to the stone representing La Harazée, "all the way east to the Meuse River, here, and we are all pushing north in line. Nine Divisions lads, over a million doughboys, the largest engagement in American history.[114]

"Brits will be pushing east from their positions way up north, French pushing north beside us to our left.

"Our first objective is about sixteen klicks at the north end of the forest. We expect we can cover that ground in two days." Greally looked around at the men, all focused intently on his words. There was more shifting of weight and more uncomfortable murmurs from the soldiers.

"So make no mistake, lads, this is the push that will break the Hun's back, and us lucky bastards will be part of it. I need every man to pull their weight and then some. It's going to be a scrap of epic proportions. I'm counting on you, and so is Captain Budd."

Again, Greally paused and looked into the eyes of the young men gathered before him. They met his gaze, not verbalizing their doubts or fears but committing to each other in silent solidarity.

Greally nodded once and continued, "Redlegs[115] will start the show, French will open up first at 1130 on the 25th as a diversion, our lads will begin at 0230 on the 26th. Standard fare, 75s and 155s. First Army will be going in right behind the rolling barrage, starting at 0530. H-hour is 0550 hours. That's 0550 hours.

"G2 (intelligence) tells us we're facing off against the Kaiser's Third Army's Group with the 2nd Landwehr Division right in front of us. Tough old bastards, especially when they are dug in. And dug in, they surely are. Major Whittlesey has been to the front, and the French have decent trenches; they have been there for years. That means for the slower amongst you—I'm looking at you, Regan—that the Boche will be well dug in. They have been there for years as well, so expect interlocking fields of MG fire, with artillery and mortars dialed in fuckin' tight for good measure.

"Infantry, MG 08s, snipers, potato mashers,[116] whiz bangs, woolly bears, moaning minnies. We can expect the full treatment lads—lead, high explosives, shrapnel, smoke, gas, and kitchen sinks. Some G2 will tell you they are on the retreat and don't have the metal for a hard fight. I don't believe a friggin' word of it.

"I've looked at the charts. Our area is heavily wooded, and it's tough terrain. Contours are tight as bark on a tree in many places, really steep ravines. The terrain will force us into natural avenues of advance—be careful not to be too predictable. The Hun reads terrain better than most of you read books, and he will use it to his best advantage, so watch you don't get railroaded into kill zones if there are suspicious gaps in the wire. Easiest way is not always the best way. Keep thinkin', even when it gets hot. We're in the Hun's backyard, and he won't make it easy on us.

"Expect overcast, cold, and rain for the next few days. After that, we just don't know. We'll be advancing with light packs, so leave the rest of your gear in the trench at La Harazée. It'll catch up.

"Men, this is going to be one colossal hooley. I need your very best; you'll get mine." He paused and looked around at every face in the crowd.

"Be ready to move out at 2000 hours. Remember, ammo, canteens, rations." Another long pause.

"Questions?"

No one had a word to say; they knew their roles, and they knew this would be a tough one.

"Alright, get your shit together. Keep the faith."

William and Sigurd scurried to their shelter half, broke it down and rolled their blankets, slickers, loaded entrenching tools, and equipment. They got their coats, cartridge belts, bandoleers, canteens, first aid kits, trench knives, bayonets, and gas masks in place.

With time to spare, they sat down against a large tree and silently lit cigarettes. Oscar, Osro, and Gust joined them. The men kept to themselves, except for Osro and Oscar, who chatted and threw sticks at a rock that cropped out of the ancient Argonne ground. "How you gonna hit a German if you can't hit that rock?" said Osro.

"How you gonna get out of the trench if you're only four foot two?" responded Oscar. The banter helped the others relax. William dug a small hole in the forest floor with his trench knife, flipping out stones as he dug.

"I'd say Sigurd nailed it," said Gust, "looks a lot like sixteen klicks of attrition to me." No one answered. They made brief eye contact and then went back to their own worlds.

At 2000, Greally mustered the men, and the company slung their heavy packs on, formed up, and moved out to the north led by Lieutenant Buhler. The rain that lingered all day got heavier. They moved north for forty-five minutes to La Placardell, where Buhler wheeled right into a clearing behind the village. The long line entered the forest again and marched to the crest of a hill, then headed down a steep back slope into a broad river valley. It would have been a grand view on a summer day, but that night, loaded with fifty pounds of gear and ammunition, the men of the 308th were not thinking of views or summer days.

Hundreds of boots worked the rain, leaves, and mud into a slippery sludge. A few soldiers slipped and fell hard under the weight of their equipment, cursing in multiple languages. The terrain flattened out at the base of the hill, and the forest disappeared. Outside the cover of the trees, the wind picked up, and the rain fell heavier. The unit crossed over a small stream (the Biesme) that snaked its way through the valley. They climbed up to a road running east-west and swung left. A kilometer further, they passed a shell of a church and a few houses that marked the village of La Harazée—the small rock Sergeant Greally had placed on the French line back at camp. The troops left the road and headed into the canopy of the dark Argonne Forest.

Multiple French companies were pulling out. They looked at the newly arriving Americans with curiosity, and William thought, a degree of sadness in their tired eyes. "Good luck, doughboy," William heard from someone who spoke passable English. "Merci poilu," he responded quietly. The French had held that area of the line for years and knew their German counterparts well. They knew there would be hell to pay once the Americans left their trenches and advanced into the Argonne. Many made eye contact and nodded in appreciation. Some could not, knowing that many of the men they passed would be dead within hours.

Company G moved a kilometer into the forest, up an incline, and into deep, soggy trenches. Companies D, C, and H were already there. The French left a case of wine, which the new occupants greatly appreciated. William sat between Sigurd and Gust, nervously watching the time. Sergeants Healey and Freeman walked the trench, checking and encouraging the men.

At 2330, the French artillery began their diversionary barrage. The new men from the 40th Division got their first taste of frontline drum-fire artillery, and it chilled each of them.

At 0230, American artillery joined all along the front. Two thousand seven hundred M1916 75mm guns and M1917 155mm howitzers fired continuously, pulverizing the German frontlines. *Thank God those shells are not meant for us.*

At 0530, the artillery started a twenty-five-minute standing barrage on the German positions in front of the 308th. The flash from the explosions lit up William's trench. Dirt fell from the sky, the ground shook, and noise filled every crack and crevice. Even the veterans of the 308th were shook; the new arrivals were terrified.

At 0545, Lieutenant Buhler hurried along the trench, shouting, "Five minutes! Five minutes! Remember, you are the second wave! Short packs ONLY! No blankets or shelter halves. Stay light!"

William heard whistles all along the trench, and the men of the 1st Battalion under Major Whittlesey climbed over the top and into the dark morning. William heard a confusing flood of new noises. He would soon be able to distinguish the Hotchkiss from the Chauchat and the MG-08, the Mauser from an Enfield, and the closeness of a bullet from its sound, but that first insane morning, the noises all ran together.

The shooting continued until it was one continuous sound. William checked his cartridge belt, gas mask, canteen, mess kit, entrenching tool, trench knife, rations, and first aid pouch. His mind raced; what was he forgetting? How would his pack catch up with him? When did he refill his canteen? "Shit!" said William out loud, *I'm not ready for this.*

"Supporting Battalion, fix bayonets! Company G and H stand-to!" bellowed Lieutenant Buhler.

William looked to his right. Sigurd was wide-eyed and tense, looking out over the trench. Gust leaned into the trench wall to his left, eyes closed tight, trying to focus his strength and willpower. A whistle blew, William's mind flashed. Without thought, he hauled his body up the trench ladder and onto the mud of the Argonne Forest.

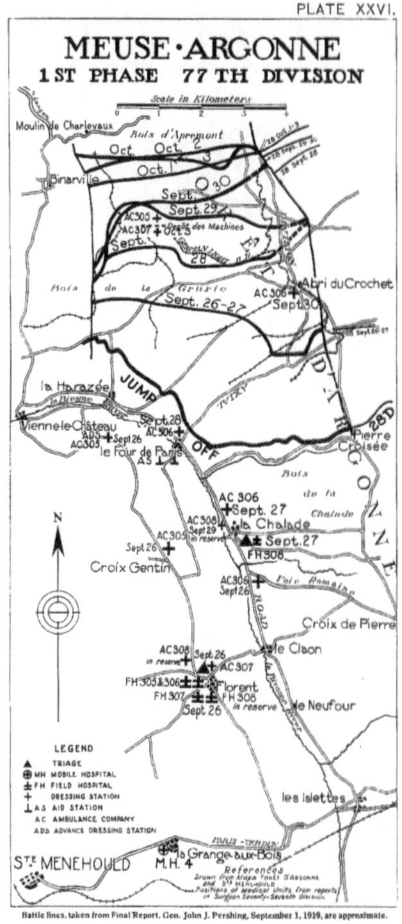

Figure 10: 77th Division Phase Lines, Medical Facilities [117]

16

Argonne Forest Day 1

THURSDAY, 26 SEPTEMBER 1918

LA HARAZÉE [118]

American 75mm guns targeted five hundred meters in front of the advancing men into what the French maps labeled *Bois De La Gruerie*. The twelve-pound shells whistled above the doughboys and exploded with flickering yellow and white flashes in the mist. The guns pounded the impact area for five minutes, then advanced another hundred meters, allowing the soldiers to advance behind a wall of artillery cover. The 155mm howitzers battered the area one hundred meters ahead of the 75mm shells. However, German Commanders had withdrawn most of their troops north of the barrage. They would patiently wait their turn to strike the advancing Americans.

Metal pigtails now pointed at odd angles, rusting barbed wire blown apart in places, smoking shell holes, and tree stumps filled the hillside. With mist and fog making visual references hard, William relied on feeling the force of the forest pushing through his boots to guide him uphill. He crouched behind a small boulder to catch his breath, and a wave of relief washed over him. *Thank God, I'm out of the trench and still alive.*

Corporal Dolan approached, "Let's go, soldier, keep moving." William nodded, wide-eyed, and left his sanctuary.

Without warning, the ground opened and William disappeared into the earth, falling like a rock into an abyss. Before he understood what had happened, he was at the bottom of a dank hole covered with mud, barbed wire, and drenched wet. He thought he had been hit with artillery and checked his chest, arms, and legs. *Jesus, still in one piece!* Gasping with fear, he scrambled out of the hole, dragging barbed wire with him—disoriented, wet, and scratched up. He rolled on the ground, got himself untangled with some difficulty, and then jumped to his feet, afraid he would be left behind. He saw some doughboy uniforms close by and scampered over to them.

Within five minutes, William reached the first German trench and passed through without stopping. It was well constructed, lined with wooden duckboards and firing parapets. A dead German, likely hit with the initial artillery salvo, slumped forward in a sitting position, almost as if he was asleep. The German's stahlhelm (distinctive German bucket helmet)[119] was gashed open, and his gray uniform was shredded at the shoulder. The side of the soldier's face was missing, exposing bone and teeth. William stared in shock. The thought of the man's last violent moments lodged in William's brain.

Twenty feet past the trench, William heard the crack of German bullets for the first time. He threw himself on the ground and brought his rifle to his shoulder. There was nothing to shoot at, nothing to see in the mist but vague outlines of trees. Corporal Dolan came up behind him again.

"Come on, Martin, get your arse moving. They're not shooting at you—you'll know when they are!"

He grabbed William by his cartridge belt and hauled him to his feet. In a moment of clarity, quickly replaced by bewilderment, William realized Corporal Dolan called him by his name. Dolan was moving ahead rapidly, pistol drawn. William followed him without thinking.

Enemy fire erupted ahead of them. For the first time, William felt what it was like to come under targeted fire.

"Machine gun nest, fifty meters, half-left. Santini, Regan covering fire. Mele flank left, Clemons flank right!" roared Dolan.

Company G lay flat and poured fire into where they thought the nest was. The Chauchats and the Hotchkiss guns got into the fight and the fire on the nest area intensified. Stokes mortar teams set up their three-inch tubes and began adjusting the elevation. Dolan moved forward, leading the way. He got within a hundred meters of the MG-08 and saw the stubby nose of the gun as it fired down the slope. He dove to the ground behind a tree. William lined up to his left and flipped his safety off. He saw the nest clearly now, the nose of the gun, the shadows moving inside the thin slit opening, and the doughboys jumping and crawling around to the sides. William rammed his bolt shut and fired a clip in quick succession. Dirt kicked up all over the nest. He could not tell where his rounds hit due to the hail of bullets impacting the target. He saw a doughboy with a musette bag crawl close and lob two grenades quickly into the nest. There was a muffled "thump" and a puff of smoke, then silence from the MG-08.[120]

Now, the men's attention focused on the trench. The Stokes mortars joined in the fight and, combined with the Hotchkiss guns and Chauchats, smothered the relatively light rifle fire. Within five minutes, the lightly defended trench went quiet, and the 308th slowly stood and continued the advance.

Doughboys helped three injured men back through the advancing troops, field bandages soaked through with bright red blood. William passed five American bodies laid out in a line. Comrades had stuck their five rifles bayonet-first into the ground and hung their helmets on the rifle butts. One of the fallen was hit multiple times, his face pushed in, deforming every aspect of his humanity. William could not look away. How could this happen to a man who had walked just minutes before, that left the same trench as William had climbed out of a few hours previously?

He passed close to the machine gun nest, close enough to see twisted bodies, grey uniforms slumped over the twisted barrel of an MG-08, still smoking. The sight of death and the twisted bodies that now scattered the hillside chilled him to his bones. That first morning in the Argonne, something formed in his being that was not there before and was now as palpable as it was anonymous.

It was close to 0800. The 1st Battalion pushed further into the forest, followed by the 2nd Battalion and the support Companies. The distance between the attacking and supporting companies shortened, forced by the terrain and enemy action. A single wave of soldiers several hundred meters deep formed, rather than distinct waves.

Gaps on the right flank opened between the 308th and the 307th as both 77th Regiments fought their way forward. On the left flank, the Franco-American unit (Groupement Durand), under the control of the French Fourth Army, had its own challenges to deal with, and both units struggled to maintain contact across that boundary. Major Whittlesey and the other officers realized that the 308th had both flanks "in the air" and they were at risk of being cut off if they did not rectify the situation.

Morning fog disappeared, and light rain returned, falling in a constant mist that soaked everything in the gloomy forest. The place smelled of smoke and decay to William; it melded with the scenes of death he witnessed and left him hollow that morning.

The slope leveled off past the crest, and the ground turned to soft marsh, torn to pieces by the morning's shelling and covered with watery carters. Trees, thinner on the hilltop and charred from the barrage, offered less cover to the advancing troops.

A shot split the air to the front, followed by another, and then a heavy volley. The trench line ahead, later identified as "Tranchée de la Baltique," ran many kilometers in an east-west direction. Metal pigtails and wooden obstacles laced with layers of barbed wire slowed the American progress. The parapets were seemingly untouched by the shelling, and a small force of Germans had rushed forward to man their positions as soon as the barrage stopped. German command needed time to move troops and artillery further north into better defensive positions. The soldiers in Tranchée de la Baltique were the blood sacrifice for that time; they would slow the Americans, not stop them.

Whittlesey's Battalion paused briefly and studied the barbed wire, the terrain, and the direction of the fire. The tall Major crouched down with the officers and sergeants and planned the attack quickly.

There were no enemy artillery or mortars yet—just rifle fire and machine guns. The Major concluded this was an understrength enemy force, not a serious defensive position. Company D would maneuver to the left, Company A to the right, grenade-throwers would be in front with B and C companies. Chauchats would be in the middle, advancing with B and C, Hotchkiss guns would deploy on the flanks to avoid shooting over the heads of the main force, engineers would be with each group to clear wire. Stokes mortars were to stay in the rear and concentrate fire on the machine guns. The plan was simple to the men of the 308th. There were no shortcuts or easy outs despite the assumed understrength force opposing them. They all knew men would die taking the objective.

Lieutenants and sergeants took charge of the teams without hesitation. The Hotchkiss teams opened up on the machine gun nests, and the Stokes lopped their initial ranging shells moments later. William learned the distinctive signatures of each weapon. The bombers crept forward following the path cleared by the engineers, followed closely by the Chauchat teams and riflemen. One of the MG-08 nests took a direct hit from a lucky mortar and billowed black smoke, unbalancing the defensive position and enabling the doughboys to get close enough to the trench to lob grenades effectively. Once they breached the trench, vicious hand-to-hand fighting ensued. The defenders recognized the fight was lost; they disengaged and scrambled north to deeper positions in the forest.

The 308th took twenty-two prisoners and escorted them back to Brigade for interrogation. It turned out that the German defenders were a surprise unit to the Americans—the 76th Reserve Brigade had fought at Sorny and arrived in the Argonne only twenty-four hours previously. Interrogation also revealed that the American artillery had cut the barbed wire defense, and the defenders did not have time to repair it. The G2 staff concluded that the 308th had been lucky. This trench was not heavily defended, and the German defensive obstacles were damaged, allowing the doughboys to advance without excessive losses.

The tall Major who orchestrated the attack, Charles Whittlesey, a lawyer from New York, knew he needed to push the attack forward to meet Division objectives for the day. He was exhausted but did not want to let the men settle in. Regaining momentum from tired soldiers was a challenge he did not need that morning, especially after the Division Commander's briefing two days previously emphasizing forward movement at all costs. The support battalion entered the trench, and Whittlesey's battalion moved out immediately.

William leaned against the trench wall and gulped from his canteen, unaware of how thirsty he was after the effort and stress of the morning. To his left, dead Germans lay on the duckboards, blood stained their tunics, and ran into the trench sump pit.

A wounded German sat under guard next to the bodies, too injured to march back to battalion. He looked wide-eyed and pale-faced at the enemy in his trench. William studied him. He was in his late forties, slight in frame, and his thinning gray hair made him look harmless. Blood oozed down his hand from a shoulder wound; his leg, badly mangled from a grenade blast or a mortar fragment, jutted at an unnatural angle. He was nothing like what William imagined the Hun would look like. While William scrutinized him, the German looked up, and the men's eyes met awkwardly. Both men broke the human contact almost immediately; neither wanted to look the enemy in the eye.

It was 0915, and the men in Company G had been on the move and under fire for over three hours. The trench provided relative safety and a place to focus after the morning's madness. William sat staring into space, struggling to absorb everything that had happened. Sergeant Greally's approach broke the silence. He came down the trench with three musette bags of grenades, talking rapidly, barely slowing down as he passed.

"Martin, Deaderick, Dahlgren one bag each. Remember, pull the pin, and then you have four seconds. Don't fuck up. Potter, Lima, extra bandoleers and rations from the wounded. Sling 'em, we may need 'em later. Don't get comfortable. We're going over the top in five minutes."

William lit a cigarette, lit one for Sigurd, and drew in a heavy breath. Sigurd turned and said quietly, "We made it, Will."

"So far, buddy," said William, still shaking. *Jesus, we haven't even started!*

Lieutenant Buhler blew his whistle, and Company G climbed out of Tranchée de la Baltique. Ahead, the 1st Battalion immediately encountered another trench no more than two hundred meters to their front. Two German machine guns fired from nests four hundred meters apart with intersecting arcs of fire. Artillery and mortar fire joined with trench rifle fire, causing chaos amongst the Americans. The 308th was pinned down tightly while they organized into small attack groups.

Realizing what was needed, Buhler shouted to Greally, "Get those grenades forward."

Sergeant Greally was already moving before the Lieutenant finished his sentence.

"Martin, Dahlgren, grenades to the left; Deaderick, grenades to the right!"

The men instinctively jumped up and moved forward. William thought, *I might get shot just coz Greally asked for something. Why is that?*

His mind played with that thought as he looked down to pick his way through the rough ground. His mind processed as he ran forward, crouched over, looking directly at the ground rushing by before him. *That treacherous bastard only learned our names so he can tell us what he needs done when the shit happens.*

In a surreal moment, William knelt in a shell hole, scanned his front to re-find the men from 1st Battalion to his left, felt the wet mud seep through his britches to his knee, and a drop of rainfall from his helmet onto the tip of his nose. He swept the musette bag to his back and grunted as his brain processed the subtle treachery of Sergeant Greally. Every fiber in William's body was synchronized for one fraction of a second, and he was aware of everything in his universe.

He climbed out of the small crater and looked down at his boots while he covered five more meters of dirt. He only knew his breath, the sounds of gunfire, and the sound of Gust's footsteps to his left.

William and Gust had less than fifty meters to reach the closest men on the left. Machine gun bullets kicked up dirt to their front, and both men jumped into a large shell hole. The machine gunners shifted fire to another sector, and both men immediately bounded forward to the next hole. Half running, half falling, they made it to the men attacking the gun.

William and Gust found the officer driving the group. "Grenades, Sir."

"McDevitt, Balstad—grenades!" William and Gust realized they would not be crawling forward to lob the grenades.

The officer distributed the musette bags, and McDevitt and Balstad bounded out of the hole, headed in different directions.

"Get fire on that nest!" yelled the Lieutenant.

William and Gust threw themselves on the ground to the front of the hole and fired on the bunker. Concrete chips exploded off it, and chunks of wood flew off the wooden trench blocks. William was unaware of anything except the bunker, his sights, and his brass shells flipping from his breech.

The Chauchats and the Hotchkiss guns hammered away to his left. William saw McDevitt, and then Balstad slowly creep toward their target from different sides. Balstad got into position first and lobbed a grenade toward the gun; it fell short but caused the weapon to swing in his direction. William fired his fifth clip into the machine gun nest and, from the corner of his eye, saw McDevitt come waste deep out of his hole to throw three grenades baseball-style at the bunker. A series of explosions obscured the target, chunks of debris flew in the air, and smoke billowed from inside the nest. Almost immediately, the second machine gun exploded far to William's right.

With the machine guns out of action, the rifle fire and the mortars from the trench died down, and the men bounded forward, staying low and dipping into shell holes as they moved. German light artillery continued but fell long due to the movement of the Americans and had little effect.

A soldier ahead of William collapsed where he stood; the back of his head was an empty shell. A second distinct shot echoed in the forest, ricocheting off a second doughboy's helmet close to William. They recognized the direction of incoming fire was not from the trench ahead but off to the east.

"Sniper, left, hill, 100," shouted Dolan. They took cover immediately and concentrated fire on a hilltop one hundred meters to the left while the rest of the company pressed the attack on the trench home. There was no clear target, but the men fired every weapon they had on that hilltop where they thought the sniper might be hidden. Chunks of tree bark exploded, and the earth kicked up dirt and leaves where the American rounds had impacted.

Amid the chaos, no one noticed a camouflaged figure on the mud moving slowly backward off the adjoining knoll and disappearing into the tree line. Obergefreiter (Corporal) Leopold Kuchler was satisfied with his two hits, and one definite kill, and decided it was getting too hot to stay in position.

"Let's go, move out," called Greally, assuming the sniper was likely not hit but probably forced to relocate—that was good enough for now.

The men got up, bent low, and pushed forward, still under sporadic light fire from the trench but happier to face an enemy they could see. The engineers worked their way through tangles of barbed wire and trench blocks. Potato masher grenades flipped out of the trench but landed short and exploded harmlessly in the mud. Company A crept through the gaps in the wire and lobbed Mills grenades into the trench.

The forward men charged into the trench but found it was abandoned. A wooden placard informed them they were in "Tranchée de Courlande." Scrawled below the trench name was a hastily scribbled "Willkommen in der Hölle Amerikaner" ("Welcome to Hell Americans"). It was 1025 on September 26, not quite five hours since they climbed out of the French trench, and the men were physically and emotionally exhausted.

The 1st Battalion moved forward again, covering approximately sixty meters, while the 2nd Battalion remained in Courlande. The Germans withdrew to trenches further north, willing to concede ground for now. At the same time, their commanders looked for the weak spots and tactical gaps between units, gaps they knew would show in the American lines sooner or later.

The 1st Battalion found a new trench, Karlplatz, an extravagant structure that offered Major Whittlesey an excellent place to pause before pushing forward.

In Tranchée de Courlande, the lightly wounded were cared for with first aid kits, and stretcher-bearers carried the more seriously wounded to regimental aid stations in the rear. Those who needed further care were moved back to Field Hospitals or Mobile Hospitals. The men who died taking Courlande were cared for by their comrades in burial details. Officers recorded the shallow burial locations and reported these as soon as possible to the Chaplin, who would, in turn, notify the newly formed Graves Registration Service (GRS).[121]

1st Battalion had not moved forward from Karlplatz, so Major Budd, not knowing the plan, went forward to discuss the situation with Major Whittlesey. Whittlesey's scouts probed forward but found a solid wall of German resistance at two hundred meters. It was clear to both officers that the Germans had regrouped, and the defenses just to the north were far more substantial than those they had engaged so far. As bad as that first day had been, Whittlesey and Budd knew there were far more challenging days ahead. They knew that the trenches they had taken that day were lightly defended. The German 76th Reserve Division knew what they were doing, and they would make every foot of Argonne ground costly for the Americans.

By 1630, light was fading. Whittlesey decided that movement for the day was done. Corporals posted a picket line and lined the trench with lookouts. In a well-constructed dugout, the two officers lit candles and huddled over maps to plan the next day's advance.

The first day was not what they had planned; they had only gained a little over one kilometer. The officers discussed how to handle the lack of contact on both flanks with the 307th Regiment and the Groupement Durand. Whittlesey decided to move the support battalion in line with the attacking battalion and stretch the line east-west to make better contact with both flanks.

Lieutenants followed standing orders and sent a runner back to the 154th Brigade to report progress, position, enemy status, and the grim numbers provided by the burial details.

At 1730, the 2nd Battalion in Courlande Trench received orders to settle in for the night. Company G moved to the western end of the trench to protect the exposed left flank.[122]

William, Sigurd, Gust, Osro, and Oscar huddled in a dugout. They smoked their cigarettes rapidly, each inhaling a lungful of nicotine. William got some half-hearted ribbing—Osro had seen him fall into the hole and come out pulling a ball of barbed wire behind him.

The friends smiled weakly and appreciated the attempt to lighten the mood.

In a somber tone, Gust offered, "We should keep an eye out for each other tomorrow. There were times today that I didn't know where you fellas were." They all agreed to stick closer together and watch for each other in the coming days.

Private William Baxter, from the US Army Medical Department, patrolled the trenches to care for those with minor injuries. He used iodine swabs on William's cuts, picked up during the tussle with the barbed wire. Then he covered the cuts with zinc oxide adhesive plasters, leaving him looking far worse than he felt.

"Don't want these to get infected. Uncle Sam needs you to go to work tomorrow," Baxter said flatly.

"Can't wait," said William.

Osro had an open wound on his side. A shell fragment had torn through his tunic and nicked his waist, leaving a three-inch gash.

Baxter inspected the wound. "Lucky break, a few inches to the left, and you might have gone west even from that little zinger. Seen it happen too often.

"You'll need anti-tetanus serum and a few stitches, can't do that here. I'll get some iodine and gauze on it, but you need to get back to the regimental aid station. They'll fix you up, and you'll get back to duty tonight. I'm forming up a bunch that's going back there. Best come with me."

"You know I stay as close to him as possible coz who's going to aim for the short guy when they have a six-foot two-inch target like this to aim at," Oscar said, pointing at Osro. "It's my fool-proof plan to make it through this mess."

"You need a fool-proof plan, fucking useless soldier," responded Osro dryly as he left with Baxter.

Sergeant Greally checked in with the group at 2100, "All good lads?" he asked. "First day is the worst; after this it gets a little easier.

You saw a lot today, maybe not the worst, but a lot for one day. Ye all did well, boys. Good on ye."

William could understand most of what the Sergeant said, but once in a while, he really had to work at it, especially if Greally was in a rush and spoke fast. But Greally's praise hit home with all the men and made things momentarily better.

"So ye saw how we do things, right? MG-08s are a bitch, we gang up on them and sort them out first, or they'll ruin your day. Mostly, we get at them with Mills. Machine guns and infantry movement distract them, but it's all about getting them grenades in there. We get lucky with mortars every once in a while, like today, but more often than not, we have to go in and take them out from up close. It gets messy.

"The Whiz Bangs[123] and the Five-Nines[124] are bastards. They are accurate, and seems like every German has one in his pocket. They pop up all over the friggin place. Can't do too much about them; just have to move through the field of fire or dig in and hope for the best. Sometimes, our red legs get them, but rarely. Our artillery liaisons just don't have the means to get them big guns onto targets quick enough. We didn't really see too many minenwerfers[125] today, which tells me that these were not high-value trenches.

"You'll meet moaning minnie soon enough, and you won't like her. No one does. She's a friggin' nightmare.

"So... what ye'll see is we keep the Hotchkiss, Chauchats, and the Stokes on the MGs. Infantry encircle them and bomb them as quickly as possible. If we can't eliminate them, we'll never get into the trenches. Secondary targets are infantry. Snipers are after that, not much you can do against a sniper. With any luck, you can flush them out if you can't kill them—that's what happened earlier today. Don't think we got that one, but we pushed him back. Bastards normally get a few free shots off at us first, and those guys are really good."

Greally lit a cigarette and offered one to each of the new men.

"You boys will start out lugging grenades and extra munitions for the Sho-Shos, but one of these fights, you'll be the lads that have to press it home."

He looked around at the new guys; they looked scared and shook, and he realized he may have given them too much information on their first night in the line.

"You guys will be fine, I seen you in action today, you'll be grand. Get some sleep. Tomorrow, we'll do it again. Keep the faith."

With that, he left and walked down the duckboards. *What the heck does "keep the faith" mean?*

Corporal Dolan swung by and nudged William and Sigurd. "Need two spanners on guard duty, two-hour stints, follow me."

The two stood guard, watching over the trench line towards the Germans and hoping nothing would happen on their first night at the front. German flares lit the night randomly, and artillery harassed the trench line. For William and Sigurd, every sight and sound was new, and neither one relaxed for a moment.

After guard duty, William tried to get some sleep. The cold night, the flares, the artillery, and the perpetual rain would give him no peace. That night, he learned to hate the 77mm guns[126] that delivered the Whiz Bangs all over the forest. They were nerve-racking, plentiful, and accurate. William's brain would not shut down. It was a rough end to a long day.

17

Argonne Forest Day 2

FRIDAY, 27 SEPTEMBER 1918

TRANCHÉE DE COURLANDE

The 154th Brigade planned to attack at 0530 following a thirty-minute rolling barrage, but the orders never reached the 308th. At 0730, after equipment and ammo checks, Lieutenant Buhler's whistle sounded shrilly, and William and Sigurd climbed out of the trench with Gust, Osro, and Oscar ten meters in trail. The ground was marshy and soaked with rain. Shell holes half-filled with muddy water offered miserable cover as the men advanced.

At 0735, 254th Infantry Regiment machine guns from multiple positions raked the advancing men. The 308th adopted the same strategy as the previous day, but now the newcomers knew what must be done. Chauchats rattled in short bursts, Hotchkiss guns opened up with their higher rate of fire, and Stokes mortars thumped into the German positions in the trench line. William could see stahlhelms pop up and down in the trench. He could tell, even based on one day's fighting, that today would be a longer, more frightening day.

Overnight, I Reserve Corps, commanded by General Wellmann, maneuvered forces and repositioned artillery across their section of the front to meet the American and French attacks. Whiz bangs, woolly bears[127], and five-nines blunted the 77th Division attack and devastated the 308th doughboys that day. Movement for the troops was slow, one shell hole at a time. They inched forward on their bellies between holes and behind trees and slithered into divots before pitching forward again. The Stokes were workhorses. William learned to appreciate their simplicity and their murderous effect on indirect targets. Sigurd and he fired over a hundred rounds in the first thirty minutes of the engagement. Neither man could have claimed to hit a single target—firing was rapid and rushed, with little more than a few seconds between rushed shots.

The sounds of battle became routine for William. He learned to only pay attention to the bullets that cracked by him or tore into the mud around him and began to understand artillery reports.

The 254th Infantry machine guns continued to punish Company G despite the relentless progress the men made on their bellies. There were occasional breaks in the fire. William assumed either the gunners were wounded or the barrels overheated. He and Sigurd used the breaks to move between shell holes.

After forty-five minutes of intense fighting, they had moved close enough to see detail in the trench, the MG nest, the pigtails, and the rows of tangled barbed wire. Engineers crept forward and snipped wires one by one despite the fire that raked across them and tore them apart. The formidable defenses and the closeness of death terrified William. *They are not going to give this one up.* He was unsure if he would survive an encounter in the trench, even if he got that far.

The machine gun that William inched towards fired continuously, but then it overheated and went quiet while the crew switched barrels. William listened intently for ten seconds, then perched at the front of his hole. He fired repeatedly into the nest, aiming for the thin slit where the muzzle poked through.

Ahead, he saw three soldiers break cover, crouch as low as they could, and run through gaps in the barbed wire. The three disappeared into a shell hole just as the machine gun opened up again, sending rounds directly over their heads. William thought they must be in grenade range that close to the nest. Three small objects flew from the hole, and within seconds, a cloud of dust and dirt erupted in front of the enemy position. But all three grenades had fallen short.

Two Chauchat gunners jumped into the hole beside William. They propped their gun at the edge of the hole and fired into the MG slit and along the parapet at the bobbing stahlhelms. The three bombers recognized the opportunity and jumped forward to within ten meters of the gun, throwing grenades at the slit. The nest erupted with a massive explosion, sending smoke and dirt high above the trench. Company A and D braced themselves, then charged from their muddy holes all along the line, firing as they weaved through the wire.

The defenders fired point-blank into the advancing Americans. They thinned the ranks but could not stop the momentum. The battered 308th fell into Tranchée de la Tringle.

The ensuing trench fight was vicious—bayonets, trench knives, pistols, grenades, boots, and rifle butts all used in a desperate struggle for survival. When it ended, there were no cheers from the doughboys. The 308th was exhausted and drained, almost broken by the viciousness and intensity of the fight.

Only the bloody aftermath was visible when William crossed the barbed wire and slid into the trench. American dead and wounded were cared for by their buddies. Medics triaged the worst cases and organized men to carry the immobile back to brigade facilities.

Broken enemy bodies lined the trench. Prisoners were searched roughly and moved out of the trench quickly. Men filtered through maps and documents for intelligence, while others scavenged for food or souvenirs. The scene was unholy and chaotic. William felt sick and lay in a heap on the duckboards, unable to process the day's events.

Later, Corporal Dolan stuck his head in the small dugout the men squeezed into.

"Drink water, ye don't realize it, but ye need it. I want you lads fit to fight all day."

Osro, who didn't smoke, puffed cigarettes like a chimney. None of them could eat.

Sergeant Greally entered the dugout with a bag of grenades.

"Martin, Lima, take half of these each. Deaderick, Potter, and Dahlgren, I need you to carry ammunition for the So-Shites and the Hotchkiss'. Come with me."

The men never saw Greally shaken. It seemed to them that he operated above the chaos. He always thought ahead to the next fight, and he always had a plan ready for his men.

Lieutenant Buhler and Sergeant Hagerman occupied an adjoining dugout. William saw them point at a map and heard them reference "Depot des Machines" and "L'homme Mort." The two studied the approaches and the best way to attack. A deep cleft in the earth formed an L-shaped valley; contour lines on the map were so close together that they almost formed one thick line. Several draws cut from the valley up into the steep hills. Both men knew this terrain favored the defense heavily.

The 308th stayed in the trench long enough for the 307th to align on their right. The Germans, as if to warn the Americans of the fight to come, shelled and mortared the trenches.

Sergeant Greally roamed the line. "Get ready, lads. Five minutes till the whistle. We are moving out with the lead Battalion, so it will be plenty hot. Drink water now whether you want to or not. Check weapons, ammo, gas mask, and first aid kits. Keep the Faith."

William looked at Sigurd, who looked pale and began to shake. "Chin up, Sigurd. We'll be okay."

Sigurd looked up, smiled, realized he was shaking, and began pacing to shake off whatever had taken him over. Osro, Oscar, and Gust returned with Chauchat ammunition.

"Trade ya," quipped William, pointing to his musette bag of grenades.

"No thanks," said Osro. "Those little beauties are not good for my health."

William looked around at his army brothers and was grateful for their company.

The Lieutenant blew his whistle, and the advance started. Almost immediately, fire opened up all across their front. Four machine guns blasted away, along with hundreds of rifles, artillery, and mortars. The 254th Infantry Regiment brought a new level of battle intensity to the men of the 308th.

Eighteen men dropped dead in the first three minutes, with seventy wounded. The scramble forward became chaotic and panicked. The Hotchkiss teams set up covering fire, but even that was difficult due to the terrain and the trouble spotting enemy nests. Despite the constant complaining about the Chauchat that William heard, it was light and maneuverable and served the men well that day. Jamming and overheating frustrated the crews, but any weapon that could hit the enemy hard was a welcome ally that day.

Osro, Gust, and Oscar followed the Chauchat team, hauling ammunition from hole to hole.

"Stokes, get your shit together—range that gun," Major Budd yelled, pointing to one exposed machine gun nest. The Stokes team went to work from a deep shell crater. The woods were thick but offered enough open sky for the mortars to be effective. It didn't take long before the shells found their range. The devastating fire forced the defenders to keep their heads down and allowed the advancing men to make progress.

William and Sigurd stayed close to the non-comms. It took forty-five minutes for them to cover the first bloody fifty meters. The Stokes continued to rain down on the trench and the machine gun nests for thirty minutes. Then, they had to cease fire for fear of killing their own advancing men. By then, William and Sigurd were close enough to hear the frantic shouts from the German trench. This defensive position had thick layers of barbed wire. The simple defensive measure slowed progress and cost countless doughboy lives that day.

Private Baxter darted into shell holes to treat the wounded during the battle. His medical belt pouches contained a range of first aid supplies: a spool of zinc oxide plasters, iodine swabs, gauze, and compresses. He covered more ground that day than most of the attacking troops, carrying or leading wounded men back to the regimental aid station before returning to treat and evacuate more wounded.

It was after 1500 when the 308th was within grenade distance. William and Sigurd were on their bellies in shallow dips in the terrain, enough to keep them out of direct fire but not deep enough for either man to feel safe, even for a second. They slung their gas masks to their backs to get closer to the dirt. Potato mashers lobbed from the trench landed close enough to leave their ears ringing.

Simultaneously, the two reached for their grenades, pulled the pins and pitched the bombs toward the enemy. The grenades landed short, and the men knew they had to get closer.

William stuck his head above the ground for two seconds. Ahead, he saw a dead engineer, his hand draped over the barbed wire as if to point the way forward. William ducked below the surface again, his mind braced for what he planned to do. He lunged forward behind the dead body and rolled the man on his side to provide more cover. His rifle was of little use at this range. He took the six grenades out of his musette bag and placed them in a line beside him. German voices no more than six meters away triggered him into action. William picked up the first grenade, pulled the pin and counted.

It took twenty seconds to lob all six Mills grenades. He could hear panicked voices, then screams as the six grenades detonated in quick succession. A man ran from behind and snipped the barbed wire before being shot in the head and falling over the wire. More men followed, and through sheer mass and momentum, they reached the enemy trench.

William could not move forward despite hearing the death struggles only meters from where he lay. Screams, shots, explosions, and shouts filled the space while William lay paralyzed in fear. In what seemed like an hour, hordes of men ran past him. The firing slowed, the noise died down, then disappeared altogether.

Sigurd ran over and knelt by William, "Come on buddy, let's get you safe." He helped William up, and together, they stumbled into Tranchée de Tirpitz.

Scores of dead and wounded from both sides lay inside the trench. The bodies testified to the deadliness of the Stokes mortars—large shrapnel wounds were evident in five bodies close to William. The shells delivered crushing blows to the defenders in an unmistakable and gruesome manner. Others were victims of gunshot wounds; many looked as though they were still alive except for entry wounds from small-caliber rounds. Some unfortunate soldiers stopped some of the larger caliber 8mm Lebel rounds from the Chauchats, leaving terrible, gaping wounds. Prisoners were herded into groups under guard, searched, and moved quickly to the rear.

The doughboys took care of each other as soon as the fighting ceased. They put their Enfields, Chauchats, Stokes, and Hotchkiss' aside and ripped open their first aid kits to apply compresses with bandages and safety pins, providing what comfort they could. Soldiers and medics used stretchers to get the wounded back to the rear, at least as far as the regimental aid station, for further care. From there, the worst cases moved further back to dressing stations at le Four de Paris, or Le Chalade, and ultimately via Model T ambulances to field hospitals and mobile hospitals as far back as Le Grange-aux-Bois. Those that could be fixed up and returned to the fight were back in the trenches within a few hours.

William sat in a dugout that night. The rain, which never seemed to leave the forest, could not reach him in his subterranean shelter. His buddies stayed with him, not talking much. The day was too much for the new soldiers to think about. Private Baxter came by to check the men out. He looked at William, slapped his shoulder, and moved on. Nothing in his pouches could help.

"Rough day," Sigurd said when he saw William flicker to life.

"Could have been worse," replied William weakly, "was for some."

Sigurd nodded, "Could have been."

They smoked and drank cold coffee silently. The five had been on the go for almost two days. Despite the cold, hunger, and nightmare flashbacks, they closed their eyes and slept like the dead.

18

Argonne Forest Day 3

SATURDAY, 28 SEPTEMBER 1918

TRANCHÉE TIRPITZ

William woke up to the sound of 75mm artillery from the south, probably to cover the 153rd Brigade to his east, he assumed.

The others in the dugout got up by candlelight. They began their morning rituals—cigarettes, cold rations, water, and ammunition checks.

Corporal Dolan stuck his head in the musty space.

"Special delivery from Sergeant Greally—two bags of grenades and ammo for the So-Shites. Sling 'em and stand-to."

Osro and Oscar grabbed the musettes containing the grenades, leaving the automatic rifle ammo on the dirt floor. Sigurd, Gust, and William divvied up the ammunition without comment. They knew that their short and tall friends took the less desirable grenades to reduce the burden on them. It was a welcome reprieve that morning.

Fully loaded, they moved into the trench. The usual characters were preparing for the day. Lieutenant Buhler bustled by, repeating,

"Check your water, ammo, grenades, first aid—we're headed to Dead Man's Mill in fifteen minutes," as he moved down the line and disappeared beyond the bend in the trench.

Sergeant Greally followed, "Good work yesterday, boys, ye did yer jobs. Everyone okay?" Greally made eye contact with each man, looking deep into their souls for a fraction of a second. "Keep the Faith. I'll see you on the field."

William was finally decoding Sergeant Greally's thick accent and picked up most of what he was saying. *Now, if only I knew what 'keep the faith' meant.*

The men left Tirpitz at 0700 and moved north. There was no sign of the enemy, and they made headway for several hundred meters across the flat, wooded terrain. At 0730, William heard the familiar whizz-bangs. *Bastards.* The rounds were on target, and men scattered to any cover they could find.

The whizz-bangs devastated everything in their path. Shards of metal whirred through the air and covered vast areas. Doughboys dove behind trees or dug shallow holes to get below the surface as quickly as possible. The bombardment lasted for fifteen minutes, wounding five and leaving two soldiers dead. Company G reappeared like gophers from their holes and moved cautiously north.

By 0900, they crossed a narrow-gauge railway line and saw the terrain fall off to the north, exposing a deep cleft in the earth. William knew enough of the plan to assume this led to Dead Man's Mill and Depot de Machines, the objective for the day. The men pushed on, unaware that German observers watched every move as the Americans approached the kill zone.

Moaning minnies from the 76th Reserve arrived from the ravine and sent the men scattering for cover. William, Osro, Oscar, Sigurd, and Gust dove into a shallow ditch, barely deep and wide enough to fit them. The Minnie's giant shells were now familiar to William. He remembered Sergeant Greally's words: "You'll meet moaning minnie soon enough, and you won't like her. No one does. She's a friggin' nightmare." How right he was.

The intense German bombardment terrified William, but that morning, it triggered new, surprising emotions. He felt frustrated and angry at being unable to fight back against the enemy. His best protection was to burrow into the earth like an animal and wait for the shelling to stop. Woolly bears joined in, making the position untenable for the 308th.

Major Budd shouted to the non-comms to get the men moving out of the kill zone before it was too late. The men rose from their sanctuaries, crouched north, and moved as fast as possible.

Almost immediately, machine gun and rifle fire hit the advancing wave from the crest of the slope that led to Depot des Machines. The men dove for cover again, into any depression on the ground or behind any tree, however small. Company G went into a reactionary tactical response. 76th Reserve Field Artillery ranged the doughboys' position and began blanketing the area.

William, Sigurd, and Gust scanned for the Chauchat's report and ran to the gunners. Gust realized they had all converged on the same gun crew, so he took off to the left with his ammunition and left William and Sigurd in place. The loader looked at William and nodded for more ammunition. William threw his musette bag and got into firing position with his Enfield. The game of cat and mouse with the machine guns began while the troops concentrated fire on the nests, and grenade teams worked their way around the sides. This time, the 308th did not have the advantage of the Stokes mortars due to the thick canopy, but the Hotchkiss', the Chauchats, and hundreds of Enfields provided an intense concentration of fire on the German positions.

William could not see Osro or Oscar. He assumed they were crawling forward with grenades, so he continued firing on the nest closest to him to protect his friends. Four soldiers got within grenade range and lobbed their bombs in quick succession. One rolled through the nest slit and landed inside the confined space. The explosion lifted the concrete roof, and smoke and flames billowed from the gun port. The grenade team rushed the nest and mopped up the hillside around it. From their new vantage point, they opened fire on a group of German troops to their right and began clearing to the east.

Within fifteen minutes, the west side of the crestline was entirely under 308th control. The German infantry continued firing from further east, but the second machine gun withdrew down the steep, wooded slope into the Depot des Machines valley.

William continued to pick out distinctive sounds in the barrage of noises. The whiz bangs, Mausers, and potato mashers registered differently with him now. A few days earlier, a veteran 308th soldier shared his theory on bullet noises with one of the new arrivals, and his story spread like wildfire amongst the new men, giving them something tangible to hold onto in the chaos.

"When a bullet whistles or sings past, it is a comfortable distance clear; when it goes hiss or swish, it is too close for safety; and when it says whutt very sharply and viciously, it is merely a matter of being a few inches out either way."[128]

William remembered this trench logic. It helped him make sense of the chaos. Whether it was true or not, he had no idea. Perhaps because he was more attuned to the variety of noises during the fight, he also discerned the sharp crack of a singular rifle in the noise of battle, remote from other rifles, coming from odd azimuth. William knew this was a sniper doing his lonely work as the Germans retreated down the slope.

The 308th pursued cautiously to the slope's edge and peered into the valley through the trees. William noticed no trench or defensive works besides the fortified machine gun nests where the attackers had been. He looked nervously at Sigurd while they moved north down the slope.

"Not liking this very much, William," said Sigurd. "If that wasn't their main defensive line, then where the heck is it?"

William ignored the troubling question as he peered into the thick forest ahead of him with a sinking feeling in his stomach.

The line moved forward. Ahead, the leading wave took a knee and cautiously approached something man-made and out of place in the dense forest. They found a German cemetery surrounded by a low wooden fence. Both battalions paused cautiously around the structure and dug shallow holes while they awaited the next movement.

William and Sigurd hollowed out a hole large enough for both to get below the surface and curled up in their makeshift home. William unscrewed the cap to his canteen and tipped it upside down to drain the last of his water. "Shit," he said.

Sigurd threw his canteen at him. "Leave me a bit," he said.

William turned on his back and looked up at the sky. He needed to leave the dank, death-filled forest for a few seconds. He looked up at the grey, overcast sky through the trees.

For a minute, he closed his eyes and was back in Spokane, so very far away right then. He realized that he had not thought of home in a week since sometime after he left Garigny. He knew it was just a thought—not a reality or even, for now, a real place—just a thought. He knew he had to pull himself together—he didn't want to leave his brothers down by not being with them now. He reached into his tunic pocket and pulled out two twisted Woodbines that looked as ragged as William felt. He tapped Sigurd on the arm and handed him the smoke.

"Thanks, I think. I'm sure this tastes better than it looks," said Sigurd.

"Last one I got."

William flipped on his stomach, back into the moment, the cold, and the fear. He decided he could not let his mind wander like that.

Major Whittlesey and Major Budd huddled behind a large rock thirty meters south of the cemetery. They unfolded a map onto the ground, knelt, and restudied the terrain contours ahead. Both officers knew rail lines and logistics facilities were in the ravine below. They knew several artillery batteries and major defensive works were just beyond their position in Moulin l'Homme Mort.

Neither officer wanted to push infantry into the Ravine d'Argonne without artillery support. Whittlesey called an artillery liaison and sent a message to the 152nd Field Artillery Brigade requesting fire support. The officers agreed that once the artillery barrage finished, the 308th would advance in two columns; one would enter the ravine to the northeast of the cemetery, and the other would continue north to Moulin l'Homme Mort.

At 1130, the 305th Artillery Regiment unleashed a torrent of 155mm shells targeted just north of Whittlesey's position. The 308th hunkered down and watched as the shells disappeared over the trees and impacted moments later, hurling dust and smoke high above the ravine. Doughboys sat in funk holes, knowing what their counterparts were enduring. This was time for retribution. Every 95-pound high explosive or shrapnel shell that landed meant less fighting and less dying for the doughboys. At 1245, the shelling abruptly stopped, and the infantry prepared to move out.

William and Sigurd moved down the slope through the thick forest and undergrowth to the ravine below. To their east, perhaps two kilometers away, they heard an intense fight with the signature sounds of MG-08s, minenwerfers,[129] Chauchats, and Hotchkiss guns buried among hundreds of rifles. They knew their brothers in the 307th had found a fight.

A section of Company G probed northwest down the wooded slope, crouched over, inching forward nervously as if walking on thin ice. William heard a metallic click in the undergrowth ahead and immediately dropped to one knee. Sigurd followed suit, and the rest of the men a fraction of a second later. The underbrush in front of them erupted, and hundreds of rounds sliced through the wet leaves. A soldier on William's left slumped lifelessly to the ground, shot in the chest and head. The men laid flat and edged backward through the thick brush while Germans on two sides fired in a deadly crossfire. The underbrush that hid the Germans from sight now gave the Americans their only cover. They retreated up the hill in disarray and rallied at the cemetery, breathless and rushed.

Sergeant Greally decided it was not a strong enough defensive position and moved the men back a further two hundred meters to the crest of the hill, where a narrow gauge rail track offered some limited protection and the troops had better fields of fire. The soldiers lined the track and immediately began to scrape shallow holes. Greally ran behind the men, counting as he passed.

"Fuck, eight down," he said, scribbling in his notebook. "Alright, Stokes! Up here now. So-shites one hundred meters apart, Hotchkiss' at each end. Get yer selves un-fucked and move out."

Men scrambled. William, Sigurd, and Gust split to get close to the Chauchats. William felt rage for the second time that day. He was enraged that the Germans caught them so flat-footed, that the artillery had not been effective, that eight men had just died, and that they walked straight into a trap. Fueled by anger and fatigue, he ran fifty meters down the track without crouching, moving with an exhilarating fluidity not felt since he entered the forest. The Chauchat team looked amused at the new guy delivering their ammo with apparent disregard for his own life. They found a moment to smile while William slipped off his musette bag and lay in the prone position behind the tracks.

"Thanks, Westie. Not the smartest Army way to deliver things in a battle, but we appreciate your style."

William grinned. He adjusted his sights and scanned the trees for something to shoot at.

Lieutenant Buhler, Sergeant Greally, and Sergeant Todisco lay in a shallow funk hole in deep discussion. The Lieutenant folded his map into a neat square and held it down on the dirt with his trench knife. They pointed repeatedly to the map. William was learning to watch the officers and the non-comms. He could tell something was brewing, and he assumed it had to do with Major Whittlesey and Major Budd, who had headed north towards l'Homme Mort. They all nodded, then talked some more. Sergeant Greally traced a line on the map with his finger. Then, they seemed to nod in unison. Greally returned to the railroad tracks.

"Martin, Lima—rifles, bayonets, grenades, and trench knives only. Drop everything else. Follow me."

He hurried to the next section and picked two more soldiers.

Greally gathered the men around. He threw a small rock a few feet away—"l'homme Mort." He scraped away the earth to one side of the rock with a stick. "The ravine." Then, he laid a stick at his feet, across the tops of his boots, "the railroad track." A small shale stone marked the cemetery.

"Here's the draw coming up from the ravine's base, got it?" They all nodded. "We're going to head north from our position. Four hundred meters, that's as far as we scout. That's about halfway to the mill. Stay out of the draw and the ravine on your right. I will have a compass. Magnetic North is about ten degrees West." He paused. "Lima, what's magnetic North?"

"Ten degrees West, Sergeant."

"Good. So on the way out, we'll track 010, and on the way back, we'll track 190." He pointed forward with his stick and said "010," then pointed behind him and said "190."

"Single file. No shooting unless you have to. Knives are better, best of all is no contact. Leave all your kit besides weapons here. Nothing that rattles or makes noise comes with you. Make sure your shit is tight. All we want out of this is to see if our boche friends have any plans for us out there. Best case scenario, we run into Major Whittlesey. We leave at dusk. Questions?"

Sigurd had one. "What's the story with our flanks?"

Greally looked at him and said, "That's a problem. The French are back to our rear left—for now, we have an exposed western flank. Haven't seen the eastern flank in a while, although I heard 'em a while ago out there somewhere. Don't worry about it for now, but be aware, those flanks are in the air."

"One last thing: if we get in a tight spot, we're all alone out there. So, our defensive position will be a tight circle. Make best choices on the spot, but typically lead man faces forward, trail man faces backward, and the middle three cover both flanks."

William and Sigurd returned to the railroad track, dug their funk hole a little deeper, then broke out rations and nibbled, preoccupied and nervous.

At dusk, the scouting team gathered. Greally went forward to talk to the Hotchkiss crew.

"So we'll be back this way in a few hours. For fuck's sake, try not to shoot us."

They waited silently till the light faded, then crawled across the tracks and into the forest. After twenty meters, they slowly got to their feet and moved in single file, pausing occasionally behind trees, crouching down to listen. William could hear every breath he took and swore they were too loud. The rain stopped, and a light breeze blew. The trees made a low rustling noise that masked the men's movement.

William was third in line, Sigurd to his front. They were two hundred meters into the wood when Greally and Sigurd heard low murmurs from ahead. The men froze and sank to the ground.

Greally motioned with his closed fist, which only half the men saw, but the others knew what had happened. The men lay prone, one facing backward, William and one other facing the flanks, Sigurd and Sergeant Greally facing forward, pointed at the source of the noise. They lay motionless for what seemed like forever before Greally looked at Sigurd and motioned him to stay in place. Greally inched forward in knee-high foliage. It took him ten minutes to move ten meters. His chin was on the ground, and he tilted his head to listen for even the slightest noise. Nothing stirred except the tops of the trees rustling in the light wind; occasionally, branches creaked. Then Michael Greally's brain froze.

"Hans, prüfe den wasserstand," (Hans, check the water level) said a low voice from bushes fifteen meters ahead.

"Ich habe es bereits überprüft, es ist voll," (I've already checked it, it's full) said another low voice, barely audible.

Greally could see through the low bushes the faint outline of a Maschinengewehr 08 and bucket helmets in a shallow hole. He stayed in place until a light wind picked up, and the branches rustled again. In as much synchronization as he could manage, he crawled backward in line with Sigurd. He jabbed his thumb over his shoulder, signaling the withdrawal. It took them twenty minutes to crawl back fifty meters, then they got to their feet and carefully picked their way home. Greally stopped every twenty steps to check his heading. Little by little, the knot in William's stomach unwound.

When they got within a hundred meters of the rail line, they got back on their stomachs and crawled. At twenty meters, Sergeant Greally whispered, "Greally, 308th". Greally heard the sound of a bolt locking forward.

"Greally—308th," this time louder than anyone was comfortable with.

"Sergeant Greally?" came a low, questioning response.

"Yes fuckin' Sergeant Greally, you great big idiot—I told you not to fuckin' shoot me!"

"Come on back," replied the sheepish voice.

The men clambered over the train tracks and laid on their backs, mentally exhausted. Sergeant Greally gathered them.

"Nice work, lads. Let's go see the Lieutenant."

They found Lieutenant Buhler. "Machine gun nest, about three hundred meters out right about here," Greally said, pointing to the map. "Thing is, they were pointed north." The Lieutenant's looked confused.

Greally continued, "We must have got lucky and slipped through their pickets, but these guys were definitely looking to fire into something from the rear."

"I want two squads ready to move out at first light. I guess they have infiltrated from the west and swung around behind Major Whittlesey. Hopefully, it's just a light advance force, and they don't know we're here yet. We need to find out and get to our guys before it gets any worse," said the Lieutenant.

"Yes, Sir," said Greally.

William and Sigurd crawled into their damp hole. They sipped from their canteens, shared cigarettes, and picked at their rations, uninterested but hungry. They leaned against each other and tried to sleep but could not shake the cold. By first light, they were frozen, hungry, tired, and feeling as low as either had felt in days.

19

Argonne Forest Day 4 and 5

SUNDAY-MONDAY, 29-30 SEPTEMBER 1918

SOUTH OF L'HOMME MORT

The rain returned to add to their misery. Sergeant Greally walked the line early and saw the cratered look on William's and Sigurd's faces. He knew they had been on the line since September 26. He knew they fought hard, had been on patrol, and had not slept. More than all that, he knew the hollow look and blank stare. Greally could not change their roles, but he knew Martin and Lima needed to get off the line, even for a few hours.

"Martin, Lima, come with me."

"Jesus," said Sigurd, "the Infantry just can't get enough of us."

The men drug themselves behind the Sergeant, resigned to the fact that they were headed out on another thankless mission.

"Lieutenant Buhler, got your runners."

The Lieutenant looked up, confused when he saw the two men, and said, "I only have one message, Sergeant."

"They're twins, Sir, only have half a brain each."

The Lieutenant smiled, then warned, "Make it quick. We're going to need every man we can get later on."

Greally gave the note to William.

"Top pocket, Martin, button it. Don't mess around; deliver it to Regimental HQ back in Tranchée de Tirpitz, await a response if one is imminent, and get back here as soon as you get something to eat."

William and Sigurd took off running before anything happened to change the situation. They jogged through the woods and soon felt comfortable enough to sling their Enfields on their backs. Tirpitz was about one thousand meters to the rear but felt like another universe. Artillery, mortars, and machine guns could still range them, but neither felt threatened after what they had been through.

The Command Post was not hard to find. The clerk took the message and told the scruffy soldiers to wait for a reply.

"Want some coffee while you wait?" asked the clerk, noticing the runner's fixation on the pot brewing beside his desk.

Both men jumped up, filled mugs, and held them in their cupped hands. Neither felt that warm since they left Garigny. They inhaled the aroma and gulped the strong, black liquid. The clerk returned with a written note for Lieutenant Buhler and noticed his empty pot.

"That's for the LT. I guess I'll brew more coffee."

William buttoned the note in his pocket, and both men left the Command Port feeling invigorated.

"You heard the Sergeant—don't leave until you get something to eat," grinned William.

The men found rations and Woodbines and sat on ammo boxes while they devoured canned salmon and crackers. They talked about Irish Johnny, the barman in Kansas City, and laughed at how much they drank in fifteen minutes. They wondered how Sergeant Maney was and how far away Camp Lewis was. When they stubbed the cigarettes out, they knew their time was up. They filled their canteens and grabbed spare rations and cigarettes for their buddies.

"Thanks, lads," said Greally when his runners returned. He checked their faces and saw what he was hoping for.

"Thank you, Sergeant Greally," both men replied with sincerity as they turned and left for their funk hole.

"Sometimes I think you have favorites, Sergeant Greally," said the Lieutenant.

"That would not be appropriate, Sir," said Greally straight-faced, "But if I did, they would be two of the boys that earned it honestly."

William and Sigurd returned to their hole, rejuvenated and feeling alive again after what had been the darkest morning of their short Army careers. They shared the rations with the others, spirits rose, and old jokes surfaced among the friends.

They dug deeper into the stone and earth along the rail track. Knowing Germans were within a few hundred meters, and their flank was exposed, was motivation enough for them. William learned from Gust that the second patrol was not as lucky as the first; they yielded nothing but cost two men their lives and five others serious wounds.

There was random shelling and mortar fire, along with sniper and occasional machinegun fire. Still, it was clear that the 76th Reserve was not in a serious offensive mood, preferring to have the Americans attack them where they were strongest—drawing them further into the forest where their second main line of defense awaited.

The moaning minnies continued to haunt William. He sometimes saw the slower indirect fire shells fall to earth. The devastation they caused terrorized him. The German troops that used these highly mobile weapons were well-trained and could pound an area hard once they ranged it, and they ranged a target quickly.

Just before noon, the Germans introduced a new threat. The first shell landed with a dull thud rather than the usual high explosive sound. Private Begley was the first to call "Gas, Gas!". The rounds fell with a puff of smoke, and a light wind blew towards the tracks.

The doughboys scrambled to get their masks on. William and the new troops never practiced using the masks; most had looked curiously at the contraption and did not practice donning it. William fumbled with his helmet and tried to get the mask on over it. Gust and Osro got theirs on quickly, reached over, knocked William's helmet off, and helped him.

"Jesus, Martin, how do you make it through a day?" Sigurd quipped.

William's mask was crooked, but he dared not move it for fear of causing a leak. He looked through the glass and lay prone, watching for a wave of German infantry that never came. The men kept the masks on for an hour before cautiously removing them.

At 1400, Sergeant Greally skipped from hole to hole along the line.

"We're attacking at 1450; that's 50 minutes from now, going right to Dead Man's Mill. Get yer shit together, full battle load out. Ye know what to do."

By 1430, the men were fully prepared to cross the open ground in front of the tracks. William double-checked his bandolier, worked his bolt, tapped his gas mask and rations. This time, he drew the short straw and carried the dreaded musette bag of grenades.

William shivered, remembering his last encounter as a bomber. He was unsure if he could move that close to the enemy again, crawl in the dirt close enough to hear their voices and pull the pins on the Mills. Unsure if he would freeze up again and endanger the lives of his friends.

The men left the tracks, crouched low, and moved quickly into the woods leading to the Mill. It didn't take the 76th Reserve long to react. Heavy field howitzers began first, and then the mortars. Rifles and machine guns fired from their right by the cemetery. The men dodged from tree to tree, but cover was scarce. William moved steadily, not pausing for more than a few seconds behind each trunk. Rounds cracked through the woods, sunk into trees, and snapped small branches clean off. Explosions from the artillery and the mortars blasted throughout the forest.

Two men on William's left fell to rifle fire. Those nearby dropped to the ground and scanned the woods for a target. William crawled forward to get behind a tree trunk. A Chauchat leveled the foliage around the slight rise where the fire seemed to come from, and the men concentrated their rifle fire on the knoll. William crawled to the next tree, which was stouter and offered more cover.

Five hundred meters away, a 25cm trench mortar crew muzzle-loaded an enormous 97-kilogram high explosive shell. The shell launched from the stubby barrel and plowed through the air toward the doughboys. It exploded with devastating power, sending shards of shrapnel over a hundred meters in each direction.

William heard the minnie and buried his face in the earth, waiting for the shattering impact. The air split around him, and the earth erupted. William's helmet rattled, his ears filled with pain, and his vision blurred. The tree in front of William shuttered; a metal shard six inches long and two inches wide pierced the trunk.

Boots ran past him while he tried to get up. He dropped his Enfield, using both hands to push the ground away, then bent forward to pick his rifle up. Deep red blood ran down his fingers onto his rifle. He realized he would fall, so he buckled his knees and collapsed on the ground. Then, he tried to get up on all fours and gradually stood using the tree for support. His senses returned slowly, and the sounds of the battle came back.

Private Baxter appeared out of nowhere. He looked at William's hand, put gauze on it, bandaged it, then looked into William's eyes and said, "Follow me; you're back to Battalion to get fixed up." William followed without argument.

Baxter led a group of five back through the woods. At Battalion, they entered a dugout where an orderly quickly checked them and labeled them one through five. William was number five, which the medic assured him was a good thing, "You really don't want to be number one in this line."

Doctor Josiah Powless,[130] a member of the Oneida Tribe, examined William carefully. The doctor gave him a tetanus shot, took a nickel-sized chunk of metal from the back of his hand, and stitched up the wound. What worried Dr. Powless more was the concussion that he suspected William had.

"You got ringing in your ears?"

William nodded. Dr. Powless looked into his ears.

"Drums are still good, bruised but good. I'd say you got lucky. You may not hear well for a week or two, and your balance may be off, but I think you'll be fine. Check back with me once this push is over, and I'll take another look. Your ears will likely heal on their own, and you'll be right as rain."

He checked his eyes and turned to the orderly, "Make sure he gets something to eat, a short rest, and get him back to his unit."

Powless squeezed William's shoulder as they stood, "Be careful back there, Private Martin. A lot of iron is flying around, and you got a little too close for comfort today. I'd call it a warning shot."

William nodded and left the dugout and the Oneida doctor. The orderly bandaged William's hand and handed him his helmet.

"Nice souvenir. I think Uncle Sam owes you a new one. This one won't keep the rain out anymore."

William looked at his helmet and, for the first time, saw the large gash torn from the top of the helmet to the rear. *Well, that explains why I could hardly stand up after the minnie.*

He found a rolling kitchen and ate a hot meal for the first time in ten days. His head still hurt, and his hearing was muffled, but considering the gash in his helmet, he felt like he had a good day. By nightfall, he was back on the frontlines with extra rations and a few blankets for his friends.

Osro, Oscar, Gust, and Sigurd were giddy to see him. They saw William on his knees but moved past him in the fight and had no idea what happened to him after that. As it turned out, it had been a short engagement that resulted in four dead Germans and four dead doughboys. Sigurd recounted how two men from the unit had to be taken off the line due to mustard gas burns. William inherited one of their helmets, complete with a blue patch and yellow stenciled Statue of Liberty, and tossed his old one out of the funk hole. There was no contact with Major Whittlesey or his group.

The night was thankfully dry but colder than usual. Summer was long gone in the Argonne. The friends slept in their shallow hole, waking every ten or twenty minutes when they repositioned to get warm under their new blankets.

On Monday, September 30, William's entire funk hole was up early, frustrated by their efforts to sleep.

"Think I'm going to walk out there and pick up a gammy wound and see if I can get a hot meal," was how Sigurd started the day.

William's headache still throbbed, and although he smiled, he knew he was not fully functional.

The entire line watched for signs of German movement. The harassing fire continued, as did the random artillery and mortar fire up and down the frontline. American machine gun fire was distinguishable to their front, which they assumed was Major Whittlesey's group.

In the midafternoon, Lieutenant Arthur McKeogh and two enlisted men from Major Whittlesey's isolated unit broke through the lines from the north and rejoined Buhler, Greally, and the others. McKeogh pinpointed where Whittlesey and Budd were dug in. The two Majors had taken their force of four hundred men through German lines and had established a Command Post in a fortified German bunker at Moulin l'Homme Mort. German machine gunners and snipers from the 254th Infantry Regiment had slipped in behind the advancing Americans, cutting the runner line that Whittlesey had left in place. Whittlesey's isolated men were tightly clustered around the command post, cut off from their east and west flanks and the rest of the 308th. The surrounded men took continuous mortar, sniper, and machine gun fire.

At 1830, Lieutenant Buhler, Sergeant Greally, and the rest of the Company loaded up and moved from the railroad tracks toward l'Homme Mort. They swept through the woods and the heavy undergrowth. Resistance was light; most Germans had pulled out and moved north. Within forty minutes, Buhler's unit had captured one German machine gun crew and broke through to the other men of the 308th.

Whittlesey's unit was almost out of ammunition, water, and food, but their spirits were high once their brothers joined them.

The tall Major, whom William had only seen in the distance, walked up and down lines of new troops, shook hands, and thanked them for getting there.

"Thought we were in for a long fight. Sure glad you fellas showed up!"

William watched him as he strode through the men. All he knew about the Major was that he was a New York lawyer and was first out of the trenches every time. He seemed rock steady in combat from what William had seen. *What an odd thing: a blue blood lawyer in the middle of a fight in the Argonne*, William thought.

The 308th took the Moulin de l'Homme Mort but at a high price in American blood. The 307th Infantry on Whittlesey's eastern flank pulled up into line, as did the French on the western flank. Major Budd, who had been with Major Whittlesey for the past few days, left the area without fanfare and returned to Division. Captain McMurtry, a short, stocky lawyer from New York, replaced him. McMurtry was a Rough Rider as a younger man in the Spanish-American war.[131] Officer replacements happened constantly on the line, and William paid no more attention to the new stumpy Captain.

William, Gust, Osro, Sigurd, and Oscar dug a deep funk hole in a sharp draw southwest of the mill. The ground was soft from the continuous rain that shrouded the forest, making digging easy.

Sergeant Greally checked on the men that afternoon and ensured they had ammo. He dropped a bag of Lebel 8mm cartridges in the funk hole "for good measure."

"Martin and Lima, So-Shite rounds. In the morning, stay close to the gunners with this stuff. The rest of you will have grenades. You know where you'll need to be when the fireworks go off. Also, I want all of you, Potter, Deaderick, Dahlgren included, to get yer butts over to the Chauchat squad. I need every man to be able to do multiple things, and that means loading and firing that pile of French shite."

The New Yorkers looked over their shoulders at the five new guys approaching. Private Robert Gafanowitz spoke up.

"Evening, guys. Hey, you're the ammo guy who likes to run around and dare Fritz to shoot you, right?"

The men laughed and shoved William playfully.

"Sergeant Greally told us to get some training on loading and firing the Chauchat," said Osro.

"Well, God damn. I guess if you guys are loading and firing, it means that me and Fitzgerald here are truly fucked."

"I guess that would be right," said William, "probably well AND truly fucked." They all smiled.

Gafanowitz continued, "Well, now that we have that fun detail all sorted out. Here's the deal in five minutes or less. She weighs about twenty pounds, and she kicks like a mule. You'll have to grow a new cheekbone after you fire this bitch. She's not too accurate on semi-automatic, and she's horrible on automatic.

"This lever is how you switch between safe, automatic, and semi-automatic. Forward is safe, rear is semi-automatic—where you need to operate— and middle is automatic, where you don't want to be. Here's your mag. It holds twenty rounds. Never, NEVER, put twenty rounds in there; she'll jam up, and you'll be dead. Eighteen rounds only—that's important.

"Put your finger in here through this slot in the mag and pull this spring back, slip in your rounds like this. When you're done, the mag goes in front first, like this, and then snap it to the rear. You'll hear a click when it sets. You'll want four, maybe six mags ready to go in a fight. Gunner will go through these pretty quickly when the Boche is jumpy. Stay on the gunner's right so you can watch how much ammo is left.

"Being on this side, you'll catch plenty of hot brass, so watch out. I got one down my shirt, and it burned like a bitch. Now, I always keep my tunic buttoned; sometimes, I wear a scarf. Also, these slots in the mag will get clogged up with mud if you don't watch it, especially out in the boonies."

Fitzgerald took over the lesson. "Cock the bolt, insert the mag, set the lever to the rear for semi-auto, and you're in business. She will knock your block off, so be warned. She can sometimes overheat, kinda like Corporal Dolan in an uproar," Fitzgerald flashed a grin, and Gafanowitz laughed on cue, "so stay in semi.

"Slow, deliberate fire—one round at a time—two rounds per second is about right." He snapped his fingers in a steady rhythm to make sure they understood.

"When you need to switch mags, push this lever forward, and the mag will jump right out."

Private Fitzgerald looked around at the men, "Any questions?"

"Let's get two shots off each so you Westies can get the feel of things." Fitzgerald tossed a magazine at each of the men.

"Right, load the mag and shoot off two slow rounds."

William was first up. He laid behind the gun and snapped the magazine in place, slipped the selector to the rear, and looked down the offset sights. The tripod was high, and William had to arch his back to see the front sight. His face was tight against the stock when he squeezed the trigger. The gun recoiled and hit William's cheek viscously. Fitzgerald and Gafanowitz roared with laughter.

"Every time!" said Fitzgerald. "And another thing, not only is your flippin' weapon trying to kill you, but every Hun on the battlefield is looking for you. When they open up with machine guns and snipers, they will be looking for you and the Hotchkiss squads right after the officers. Don't get any extra pay, but we sure get a lot of extra attention from Herr Kraut. Lost a lot of good Chauchat brothers along the trail. All gone west. Welcome to an exclusive club.

"Gaff and me clean her every evening; ain't getting back into that tonight, but we'll do it tomorrow. We'll show you guys then."

"Thanks, Gaff, Fitz. We'll see ya tomorrow," said Osro as the men slumped back to their funk holes.

Major Whittlesey and Captain McMurtry huddled with five sergeants for an hour before the light faded. The men bent over maps, pointed, and gestured with their hands. Whittlesey rubbed his chin and listened. Every man in the Company watched them, knowing the leaders were making decisions that impacted each of them.

20

Argonne Forest Day 6

TUESDAY, 1 OCTOBER 1918

L'HOMME MORT

William nestled with his four friends, tucked under their blankets to keep the cold off them. Frost coated the ravine's mill, rail tracks, and bunkers, and the nearby pond had a layer of mist. William looked at the scene with disinterest, thinking of food and fire.

Sergeant Greally moved from hole to hole to talk to the men in small groups.

"Lads. We're movin' north this morning. So's ya know, we're sitting here in this ravine that runs north-south. About two klicks ahead, this ravine runs right into an east-west ravine with a small creek along its base. Both ravines are massive, and they intersect like a giant T. We won't mistake where they intersect; it's as big as Staten Island."

He put sticks on the ground to illustrate the T-junction.

"There's a road there on the east-west ravine called Charlevaux Mill Road. That's our objective. The French have taken Binarville, about one and a half kilometers west of here, so we have the western flank nailed down for once. The 307th, to our east, is in line as well. So by evening, the entire First Corps and the French are goin' to align along that latitude. Simple enough, what could possibly go wrong." Greally flashed a rare smile.

"Major Whittlesey will lead with 1st Battalion at 0600; 2nd Battalion will follow three hundred meters in trail. After the past few day's shenanigans, you can expect the 2nd Battalion will not be losing sight of the 1st any time soon. We don't want to leave any light between us again; that could have been bad. Ye can also expect more MG's, woolly bears, and every other chunk of metal our Teutonic friends have. And in case you're wondering, we won't be marching right up the middle of the north-south ravine. I'm pretty sure the bad guys will have that dialed in. We will favor the west slope up toward a Hill called 205." He looked at his men and let the plan sink in.

"Ye know what ye have to do. Any questions?"

No one had anything to say. William thought two kilometers sounded like a long way for one day's fighting. He also didn't like that Greally said "simple." Nothing so far had been simple. He glanced at Sigurd and saw the same thought run through his mind. The troops got up and prepared to move out. William carried three extra musette bags of 8mm for the Chauchats, which added considerable weight to his load.

At 0600, Whittlesey and his men stepped into the woods on the western slope of l'Homme Mort ravine. As Greally had relayed, they stayed out of the ravine floor and moved up the westward slope of Hill 205. The hillside was steep, and the undergrowth was thick—it slowed progress and caused men to cluster as they avoided impassable areas.

William, Gust, and Sigurd stayed close to the Chauchat squad but kept a respectful distance, conscious of Fitzgerald's warning about being metal magnets for snipers. They paused every few minutes, stopping behind large trees and watching the forest before moving on. There were occasional artillery reports elsewhere in the forest, but the 308th advance was suspiciously unchallenged.

Oscar and Osro were shoulder to shoulder; William, Sigurd, and Gust were in their triangle. Both elements were always in sight of each other. This pattern was as natural a movement as scratching an itch. It fitted what they needed: a sense of order and comradery while they fought through the dank forest and their fears.

The air split open without warning with a cascade of noise and explosions. Company A walked straight into an eruption of fire and faced a series of trenches[132] with multiple MGs, trench mortars, and dug-in infantry. The initial wave of fire killed and mutilated scores of doughboys. The remaining men dropped to cover while they recovered from the shock of the onslaught. 1st Battalion was spread along a line a few hundred meters down the hill towards the ravine. 2nd Battalion, with Captain McMurtry leading the charge, closed the few hundred meters between the groups in a minute. There was no way the units would be separated again as had happened at l'Homme Mort.

William and his triangle got into position close to Fitzgerald and Gafanowitz. The gunner and loader lay behind a fallen tree, ideal cover for the fight. Fitz loaded mags and watched the rounds disappear from the magazine as Gaff fired into the thick forest. William was in tune with the gun and what the two men were doing. Gaff fired in semi-automatic, rattling off two rounds per second, emptying the magazine in ten to fifteen seconds. Fitz loaded as quickly as he could but lost the fight to keep up with Gaff. He had five fully loaded magazines ready, but he knew he needed help and threw a stick, hitting William with more force than he meant to. William scooted over to Fitz and noticed immediately how many incoming rounds were sinking into the tree in front of them and whizzing past them, kicking up dirt and stones that showered the gunners consistently. The intensity of the fire converging on the Chauchat was frightening.

He worked his finger into the slot, pulled it back against the spring, and slotted in the 8mm cartridges. On the first magazine, he forgot to count the eighteen stressed by Fitzgerald and loaded it with a full twenty rounds. He fumbled to remove two rounds, which he stuck in his pocket, and handed over the first mag. Fitzgerald threw another to him. This time, William opened the cardboard box with twenty rounds, extracted two, stuffed them in his pocket, and loaded the remainder. Fitz watched Gaff's rate of fire and reloaded quickly once each magazine emptied. The three-man team kept up a steady rate of fire on the nests to the left of the line.

During twenty minutes of chaos, the Americans tried to push forward but were repeatedly beaten back as the two sides fought to a stalemate. The Stokes mortars had not fazed the German line, and the Hotchkiss guns seemed ineffective against this trench's well-built and well-concealed defenses.

William checked for Sigurd and Gust. They were to his right, prone and firing rapidly. He had no idea where Osro and Oscar were. Knowing they carried grenades, he figured they were working their way to the sides and the front. He worried for them. This defensive line was unlike the others; there was no give, no weak point, and no respite from the onslaught of fire.[133] He realized the best way to help his brothers was to load up magazines quickly. He redoubled his efforts, loaded rapidly, and checked the holes in the magazine sides to ensure no dirt or debris in the spring mechanism.

After forty-five minutes, the 46th Reserve Division had repositioned their trench mortars and began lobbing enormous 97-kilogram shells into the American lines. The entire area the 308th occupied erupted into huge geysers of earth, and the doughboys lost the ability to fight back. Major Whittlesey gave the order to withdraw.

"Fall back beyond that last draw a few hundred meters back and dig in. Rifles and Hotchkiss first, then leapfrog."

The 308th broke contact and scrambled down the draw and up the other side. It would serve as a natural mote should the Germans pursue them. Small teams dug funk holes with the adrenaline of battle while the corporals and sergeants assessed the damage inflicted by the enemy.

The men were shaken up but not beaten. Company A bore the worst of the engagement and lost nine killed, twelve wounded, and two missing. The Company had no officers left, and it was now down to about fifty percent strength from when it left the trenches in La Harazée six days previously.

The officers tallied the losses, made a quick tactical assessment, and sent runners to the rear to keep the Regiment up to date. The report contained the German trench location, the direction of German artillery fire, a request for counter-battery fire, artillery fire on the trench, and the company's need for more rations and ammunition.

Private Baxter and his fellow medics had a busy afternoon. They triaged what they could with the scant supplies they had at the company level. They moved the walking wounded to the regimental aid station and enlisted the remaining men from Company A to carry the more seriously wounded to the rear. Burial details performed their grim duty for those bodies that were recovered; many bodies from that fight were lost forever.

William and his crew were all okay. Osro's leg had some shrapnel, but it was not serious. Private Baxter removed the metal shard and applied iodine swabs and zinc oxide plasters.

"Not sure that beats Martin's gammy hand-wound," Oscar said. "On the bright side, I think I've proved my theory that a compact man next to a very large man is not a desirable target."

"The word 'compact' does not describe how ridiculously small you actually are," replied Osro.

"Perhaps solid is the word you're searching for."

"No, small, in so many ways." And so it went on. William and the others lost interest. They turned their attention to the front and wondered if the Germans would press an attack or simply wait for the 308th to regroup and try again.

Fitz and Gaff found William dug in on the hillside. They nodded and crouched down beside him.

"Great work today, Will. Never had to take my finger off the trigger for a moment," said Gaff, punching him on the arm. Fitz said they'd ask Corporal Dolan if he and Sigurd could be designated as the ammo guys and backup gunners for their team, if they wanted. William jumped at the offer. He felt for the first time that his actions on the battlefield had an impact, despite the fact that the well-positioned enemy had just chewed up the 308th.

It was clear to William that the first few days of the advance were relatively easy. He also knew that the German defenses were getting tougher; the Germans were deadly serious about holding onto the line they encountered that day. William had witnessed an enemy that still had a lot of fight left in them; they were not the retreating, broken force that some assumed.

His gloomy thoughts were interrupted by Sigurd, who tapped him on the arm, knowing he was in a bad place, and pushed him a Bull Durham to take his mind off whatever he was thinking of.

"What the fuck, you been holding out on me?"

"Just waiting for the right time, Will."

The 76th did not counterattack that evening; they fired woolly bears and lobbed minnies but did not have a good fix on the 308th position, so the shelling was not a concern for the exhausted men.

The friends gathered with Gaff and Fitz late in the evening to strip the Chauchat. Field cleaning and reassembly only took fifteen minutes, including instruction and banter. William was happy to be part of the ammo team despite the weapon's shortcoming as a metal magnet and its bad kicking habit. He returned to his funk hole in the twilight, confident that he could operate the weapon if he had to.

21

Argonne Forest Day 7

WEDNESDAY, 2 OCTOBER 1918

RAVINE D'ARGONNE

William was awake by first light. His night had been another fitful series of catnaps and vivid dreams. He relived the terror of bullets drilled into tree trunks above his head, knocking chunks of bark and wood onto his helmet. His new role on the Chauchat team had made death more personal; the Germans were actively hunting him now. He relived the earth erupting around him in slow motion, men torn apart by the violence of the blasts or disappearing into red mist and shreds of cloth. He was glad to be awake, away from the nightmares that tormented him.

Unable to stand the cold any longer, he walked to relieve himself and passed the Major and the Captain huddled over a map, pointing and talking in depth. Whatever there was to discuss, the two men were deep in deliberation and unhappy. *Can't be good*, he thought.

* * *

The previous evening, Major Whittlesey's frustration had spilled over. He and Captain McMurtry had trekked back to Headquarters to discuss the tactical situation face-to-face with the Regimental Commander, Colonel Cromwell Stacey. Whittlesey pressed home the reality of the rock-solid German defenses he faced on Hill 205, his mounting losses, and his need for more artillery support, food, and water. Whittlesey pounded Stacey's desk to drive home the events in l'Homme Mort and the near-elimination of his four hundred men due to lack of flank support. He was managing fear, combat stress, and lack of sleep, but Whittlesey's concern for the well-being of his men pushed him to the edge with Stacey.

Colonel Stacey had already argued the case with 154th Infantry Brigade Commander General Evan Johnson. The Brigade Commander rejected any idea of slowing progress, regardless of losses, enemy defenses, artillery support, or flank support. Johnson had unambiguous orders from the 77th Division Commander General Alexander, who would later write:

"My orders were quite positive and precise; the objective was to be gained without regard to losses and without regard to the exposed conditions of my flanks. I considered it most important that this advance should be made and accepted the responsibility and the risk involved in the execution of the orders given."[134]

The pressure above Alexander, from General Liggett and his Chief of Staff Craig at I Corps, was enormous—there would be no letting up on the fight for any reason. This mandate came directly from General Pershing at First Army, who was adamant that this offensive could not fail—would not fail.

General Alexander was acutely aware of the consequences should he falter or show reluctance. Pershing would "not hesitate to relieve, on the spot, any officer of whatever rank, who fails to show in this emergency those qualities of leadership required to accomplish the task which confronts us."[135]

The desk-pounding meeting at Regiment HQ was direct and tense. The entire US First Army, to I Corps, to the 77th Division, and down to Regiment Command, were locked in: there was no latitude to discuss delays or hesitations with Whittlesey, McMurtry, or anybody else. Whittlesey's orders remained to continue north until he reached Charlevaux Mill Road and to hold it regardless of losses or status of flank support.[136] Stacey committed to getting artillery support the next day, but that was all Major Whittlesey could expect. The rest was up to him.

* * *

William got back to his funk hole as the others were waking. "Morning, my beauties," he said in a deadpan attempt to raise their spirits. The others groaned. "Too early, I presume."

They looked ragged. None had shaved for days, dirt caked into their faces, and their uniforms were torn and bloodstained. William lit his first cigarette of the day.

Corporal Dolan bounced between the men, full of enthusiasm for some reason.

"Lads. Rations and ammo back over the crest to the left. Don't all go together; need the line intact, two at a time. Okay?"

William and Gust took the first turn. They grabbed two days' iron rations, topped up their canteens from a large water barrel, refilled bandoliers, and stashed handfuls of 8mm cartridges into their bags.

By 0630, Major Whittlesey had briefed his leaders on the day's objective. Greally rotated through funk holes and updated his men in small groups, using sticks and stones to ensure everything was clear to each man.

"Artillery is on the way. We're going in right after. Just like yesterday, orders are that we need to reach that Charlevaux Mill Road. The entire First Corps on the right and the French on our left flank are goin' to align with us there.

"Today, we're goin' to leave a small force in place to pin down that trench system on Hill 205. We don't want those bastards to close in behind us. The main force, including G Company, will work the east side of the ravine toward Hill 198. Seemed like there was not as much fire coming from that side of the ravine yesterday. We may get lucky, find a weak spot, or bypass defenses altogether."

"Bypass is my new favorite word," said Gust. "I'm going to use it all day."

"Please don't," said Osro. "Can't your favorite word be 'friggin' idiot'? I can use that right now."

"That's two words, tosser. I'd like to bypass your suggestion."

"Lads, for fucks sake, pay attention," snapped Greally, short on patience that morning after only two hours of sleep. The loss of so many men the previous day, men he had served with and knew well, had taken a toll on the sergeant. He steadied himself and found his composure.

"Like I said, Lieutenant Knight will take Companies D and F back up Hill 205 and hold that German force in place. The rest of us will move up the ravine, favoring the west side of Hill 198. We might find a way through, or we might end up going over Hill 198. Knight's job is to pin that force in place, protect our flank, and keep that force from slipping in behind us while we move north. Been there, done that, not a lot of fun.

"Company A got hit hard yesterday, so whatever is left is now serving as runners, stretcher-bearers, and augmentees for other companies. You'll probably see a few of them in with us." Greally paused and looked at his men.

"Martin, Lima, Dahlgren—you got the extra 8mm?" They nodded.

"Potter, Deaderick, you got grenades?" More nods.

"Alright, lads, lefty-right-left at 12:30. Make sure you're squared away." Greally slapped shoulders and left.

Major Whittlesey's hard-won artillery barrage streaked overhead, and the 308th relished the sound of the 75mm rounds impacting German positions. At 12:30 sharp, Major Whittlesey moved out with Companies B, C, E, G, and H. The remainder of Company A accompanied them, along with machine gunners from the 306th Machine Gun Battalion.

The men headed north on the east side of the ravine against Hill 198. Advance scouts probed every feature. The Germans had placed obstacles and barbed wire across the ravine floor and up the side of Hill 198, slowing progress. It was, as Whittlesey expected, a tough, unyielding fight. German snipers and machine guns from both Hills 168 and 205 slowed progress and took their deadly toll on the advancing doughboys. German artillery from La Palette, high ground behind Hill 205 on Whittlesey's left flank, also tore into the advancing men in the ravine. Fire from the ravine floor was unyielding. Whittlesey knew he had to change his approach.

He sent a patrol higher on Hill 198 on their right flank. The patrol captured thirty German Hessians, who gave up the fight quickly. Scouts, further up the hill, got even luckier and walked into abandoned trenches. Whittlesey did not hesitate. He did not understand why, but he had found a way through the German defensive lines. He moved his men up the slope and into position on the north slope of Hill 198.

At 17:15, on top of Hill 198, Whittlesey paused and considered his situation. Head counts indicated he had lost ninety casualties from flanking artillery, machine guns, and sniper fire.[137] That meant he still had a reasonable-sized force that could defend itself. He could see Charlevaux Mill Road, his objective, below him on the other side of a steep valley. Whittlesey knew he was further north than his left flank, and Lieutenant Knight was engaged somewhere to his left rear to hold that part of the German line in place and protect that open flank. He had no contact with his right flank, where the 307th was supposed to be. He crouched down and absorbed everything he knew. General

Alexander's clear orders repeated in his head, "The objective was to be gained *without regard to losses* and *without regard to the exposed condition of the flanks.*" Despite what his experience and his gut told him would likely happen, he knew what to do.

Whittlesey's men began climbing down the steep slope towards the roadway, now only three hundred meters away, across the steep V-shaped ravine. The Major left runners every few hundred meters to maintain communication to the rear, not wanting to become detached, as had happened in l'Homme Mort.

William and his buddies were exhausted, but the sight of the roadway and the unhindered progress north gave them the momentum they needed to drive forward. The grade down the slope was dangerously steep, and footing was treacherous. William, Gust, and Sigurd were forced into a single file to work through the thick brambles. Osro and Oscar were only a few meters away from them to their right, but they were invisible.

Gust broke the tense silence. "I wish I could bypass these brambles."

"You're a complete dolt Dahlgren," whispered Sigurd.

By 17:30, the ragtag group of more than five hundred doughboys reached Charlevaux Brook at the northern base of Hill 198. The terrain pitched up again at the far side, as steep as the hillside they just descended but with fewer brambles and more trees.

The Charlevaux Mill Road was only meters away. *I can't believe we made it,* William thought, leaning against a tree halfway up the slope. He opened his canteen and drank generously. The relief of reaching their objective lulled William into a sense of safety. He felt the need for rest, to recoup, shave, wash, eat, and sleep. He sat on the steep hillside and leaned against a tree.

Sergeant Greally appeared out of nowhere.

"Martin, what the hell are you doing? Start thinking like a soldier. About fifty things will kill you within a hundred meters, and you've got seventy-five things to do before you get to take a breather."

The look in Greally's eye was not one of anger but fear, and it sparked panic in William. He remembered what Sergeant Maney said, balling them out on the train to Garigny. *"Smarten up, this shit is getting real."* William was ashamed. He had left his guard down, and he knew Greally was right. He should be digging in, counting ammo, checking left and right to ensure he was close to Gaff and Fitz. They were, after all, chin-deep in German territory and all alone. Suddenly, the wooded hillside looked dark and threatening. The objective looked anything but secure.

Major Whittlesey established an oval-shaped defensive bubble and a make-shift command post just below the roadway. The rationale for staying below the roadway was that the steep reverse slope of the hill below the road offered natural cover from German artillery fired from the north. From left to right, Whittlesey arrayed 308th Companies H, B, C, G, and E with machine guns from 306th and automatic rifles on each flank. The men dug in and waited for their flanks to align.

22

Argonne Forest Day 8

THURSDAY, 3 OCTOBER 1918

THE POCKET

William and Sigurd suspected they were farther north than any other unit in the sector. *Farther north than many Germans*, supposed William.

Major Whittlesey sent scouts to the crest of the hill above them and to both flanks to search for the 307th or the Groupement Durand. They returned with news of an occupied German trench just past the crest of the hill, a few hundred meters from their position. There was no contact on either flank.

Whittlesey worried; he knew he was exposed. He sat in the command post hole and unfolded his map. His legal brain considered his position. Whittlesey knew there was no point in pushing forward; that was further than Stacey ordered, and it would put them at risk of being hit with their own artillery. Falling back was unthinkable after all they had done to reach the objective and the stark orders Alexander or Stacey had given. The Major knew they had to hold their nerve and wait for their flanks to arrive. Alternatively, he pondered, he could try to punch through to Lieutenant Knight on Hill 205 and pull him forward.

At 0600, Major Whittlesey sent Lieutenant James Leak and fifty-one men from Company E to re-establish contact with Knight and Companies D and F—the two companies they had left in place to pin the German forces the previous day. Leak's force would head a little west, then south over Hill 205 to meet up with Companies D and F or attack the rear of the machine guns holding up Companies D and F.[138]

Sigurd watched them check their gear and commented as the men departed. "Glad it's not us, fellas."

"They'll be fine. They'll be back by noon with the others," replied William, although inside, he was as uncomfortable as Sigurd. He worried for Company E but was also concerned that their departure left the hillside vulnerable—a lot of firepower left along with them.

At 0630, the men from the 308th had something to celebrate. Captain Nelson Holderman and Company K, 307th Infantry, emerged from the creek to the south and walked into the pocket.[139] Whittlesey greeted them with relief and had them take over Company E's funk holes, close to William on the west side of the pocket. They added seventy-nine men to the number already entrenched on the hill. Holderman and Company K had followed almost the same route as the 308th: over Hill 198, past the abandoned trench, and down the hill into the pocket.

One of the scouting patrols captured a German prisoner. He disclosed he was part of a seventy-man unit brought up during the night to engage what he called the "Amerikanernest". The prisoner confirmed that neither the 307th nor the French had lined up with the 308th. Whittlesey was uneasy. The new German force was significant, large enough to cut them off.

By 0800, new patrols reported Germans on both flanks, not dug in but moving south through the forest. Private Robert Pou and Private Frederick Evermann stumbled into the pocket. They had been part of the runner post connecting the pocket with brigade to the south. Both reported that the Germans had overrun the running posts. Whittlesey needed to validate that his route to the read was, in fact, sealed off and not just lightly manned.

Whittlesey sent Captain Holderman and Company K, along with twenty scouts from McMurtry's battalion, back over Hill 198 to contact the rest of the 307th. The reinforced Company, he hoped, could punch through the newly arrived Germans.

Sigurd nodded toward the constant churn of captains and lieutenants reporting to the Major. "Everyone's getting twitchy. Not liking this very much, Will."

Sergeant Greally hopped from hole to hole, checking on the men, their ammo, their rations, and their fire zones. Corporal Dolan counted the Chauchat magazines in his squad, the remaining 8mm ammunition, and then recounted the magazines. Whittlesey and McMurtry stalked cautiously through the area, conferring with the junior officers.

At 0825, Greally jumped in the hole with William, Gust, and Sigurd and announced, "Kaiser sends his best and will be around shortly for tea." Then his face got serious, and he asked about the grenades and the ammo.

"We'll be in it soon, lads. We think they have slipped in behind us. We're trying to figure out how strong they are now. Keep yer wits about ye. Your coverage zone is right here," he said, pointing with both arms extended at forty-five degrees.

"Make every shot count when you see them, and for God's sake, stay in yer holes. It's a lot safer in here than it is out there, and we need every trigger-pulling body we've got. Get ready to fight."

At 0840, 76th Reserve 77mm guns targeted the pocket from the northwest. As Major Whittlesey anticipated, the steep reverse slope made it a tough target. The shells had little effect, falling long and out of effective range. Nevertheless, Whittlesey sent a pigeon requesting counter-battery fire and estimating the German artillery position.[140] Taking out that battery could make it easier for Brigade to break through.

A German trench mortar on Hill 205 began firing on the doughboys. This weapon, probably a light 7.58cm Minenwerfer, had a clear view of the pocket and caused severe damage. The 4.6-kilogram shells shook the earth, split trees, and severed branches with each impact. Shrapnel ranging from tiny fragments to large chunks whizzed and tumbled through the air, creating their own sound effects. William jammed his fingers into his ears and pressed his face against the earth in his funk hole to escape the terror.

As soon as the mortar barrage ended, the doughboys reappeared above ground. William, Sigurd, and Gust watched every tree in their sector, looking for any movement. Thankfully, the attack never came. *Maybe that mortar was just ranging us for later reference*, William supposed.

Lieutenant Leak returned to the pocket with only eighteen remaining men from Company E. They had taken twenty casualties and did not make it over Hill 205.[141] Instead, they ran into a well-coordinated German ambush that split their force and drove the Americans off the hill.

Captain Holderman from Company K, 307th Infantry, returned soon after Lieutenant Leak. They found the trench that had been empty on top of Hill 198, but it was now stocked with machine guns and infantry. There was no way through that defensive barrier, laced with machine guns shooting downhill and grenade-throwing infantry.

Both men reported to Major Whittlesey, pointing to the hills and the map they all crouched over.

"I'm no genius, but I'd say the Hun has us snookered, fellas," said Sigurd.

"For once, I'd say you're right: You're no genius," responded Gust.

"Jesus, it's going to get hot in here," William said, ignoring the banter. All three men sunk to the bottom of the hole and stared into space.

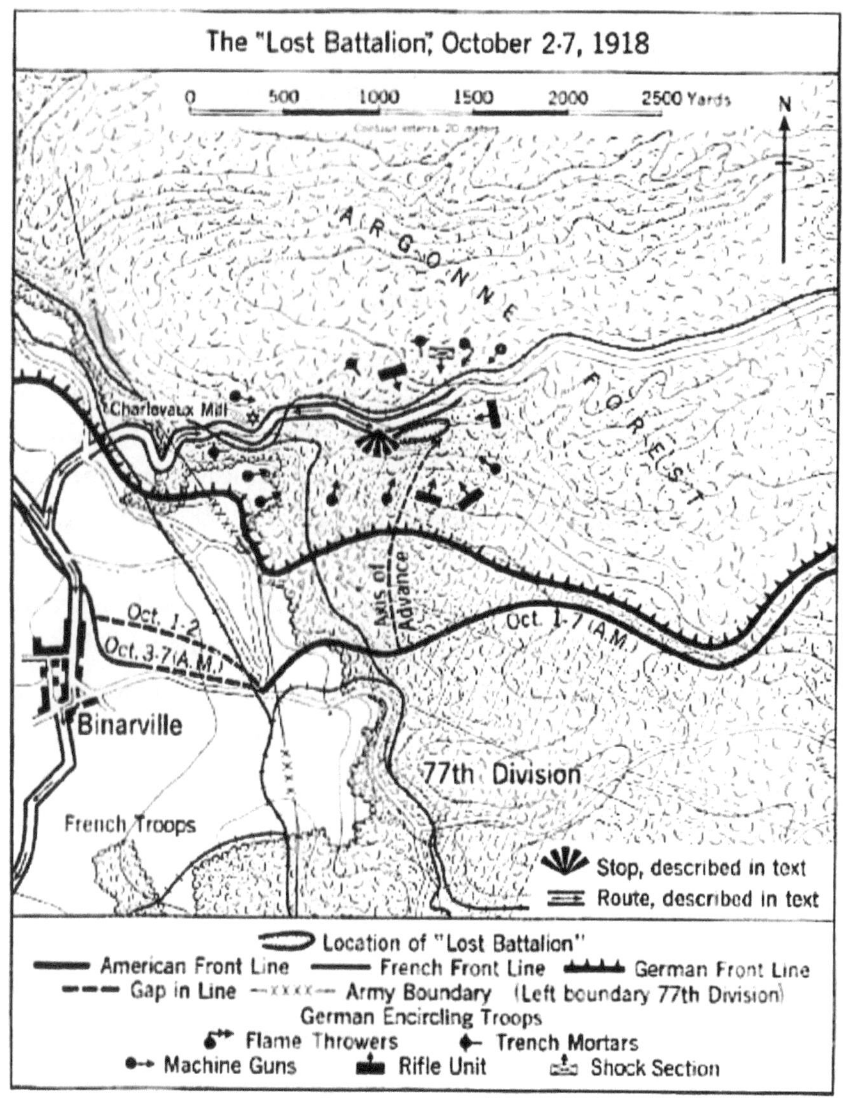

Figure 11: The Pocket [142]

Sergeant Greally landed in the hole. "Alright, boys, here's the deal. Every hole gets four grenades, which means you lot owe me. How many you got?"

The men had six between them, so they handed over two.

While Greally worked the distribution of the grenades, Corporal Dolan came to each funk hole and reiterated the same message to every man in Company G: "It's official. Those lads we sent out bumped into lots of Boche. The Germans got in behind us in pretty good numbers, and they are armed to the teeth.[143] Boss says to tell everyone we're gonna hold this position at all costs. No falling back. Stand firm no matter what happens. The rest of the US Army will catch up with us. Ye lads got it?" [144]

Both hillsides south of the creek erupted with MG-08 machine gun fire. William hugged the side of the hole while rounds zipped through the air, cracked into trees, and bounced leaves and rocks on the ground throughout the pocket. Two rounds thumped into the north wall of his hole, inches from his head, disappearing into the clay and showering his legs with dirt and stone. William used his trench knife to dig into the rocky soil and gain another inch of cover.

Sigurd looked at William and asked calmly, "Got any crackers?"

William reached into his pocket and handed one over.

"Thanks, Will," said Sigurd calmly and started nibbling. The absurdity of the moment put William momentarily at ease.

The MG-08 fire from the southern hills became a secondary concern when mortar rounds arrived simultaneously from Hill 205 and Hill 198. It was a crushing blow for the men; the mortars were far more accurate than the artillery, and although the trees offered some protection, it was not enough. The three men knew their funk hole was their only chance of survival. They dug deeper.

The mortars stopped in the late afternoon. William could not tell how long the bombardment had gone on; time in his funk hole had stopped. Unaccustomed to the sudden silence, the men stuck their heads up like gophers.

Gust was the first to see the movement. "On the crest!" he shouted.

William and Sigurd swung their Enfields into position and flipped the safeties off. In unison, they fired uphill into the grey uniforms. For the first time, William fought the enemy from a defensive position, and perhaps because of their fully visible frames and movement, he saw the enemy as men and not animated shadows or bobbing helmets. He could see faces, hands, expressions, and details on their uniforms that were never part of his previous experiences.

Potato mashers flew into the pocket from the flanks and the north. Machine guns from the south raked the area again. To complete the chaos, German snipers fired into the pocket from all sides.

In a surreal moment, William felt terror, fear, and simultaneously an unexpected feeling of exhilaration in being able to fight back. He was not digging into the earth like an animal while artillery shells tried to kill him; he was not waking up from night terrors, not dreading the prospect of the next fight. He was in the fight and fighting back.

In the next hole, he heard Fitz and Gaff firing in semi-automatic mode, the action of the bolt traveling back and forth in a slow, steady rhythm. The Hotchkiss crew hammered away in short bursts, their distinguishable rate of fire ten times that of the Chauchat. The entire attack only lasted twenty minutes. For William, it felt like hours.

When the 76th Reserve retreated over the crest, William sank into his hole, looked to his left and right at his two friends to ensure they were okay, and put his head on the stock of his upright rifle. He felt a huge wave of relief, as if a massive weight was taken off his shoulders. The entire attack, from MG-08s to mortars, grenades, snipers, and gray-uniformed troops, left him emotionally, mentally, and physically drained. His eyes closed, and thoughts of Spokane and his tiny apartment flooded his brain: *the creaky stairs and the view from the kitchen window overlooking downtown. God, I want to be back there right now.* Sigurd talked to him, but William refused to open his eyes or leave the apartment in his head for a few more seconds.

The wounded in the pocket moaned. Gaff had multiple minor shrapnel wounds. Fitz picked out metal chunks with his knife while Gaff grimaced.

A man on the other side of William had a gunshot wound in the shoulder, and another had a stomach wound. Greally went from position to position, checking on the men. "Wounded? How's your ammo"? He wrote in his notebook and moved quickly through the holes.

At 1605, William looked along the pocket and saw Major Whittlesey writing another message for Division and handing it to Private Theodore Tollefson, who was responsible for the carrier pigeons. The Major had tallied the wounded and the dead. He estimated the effective strength of the men in the pocket as two hundred and forty-five.[145] He also requested eight thousand rounds of rifle ammunition, seventy-five thousand rounds of 8mm, twenty-three boxes of machine gun ammunition, and two hundred fifty grenades. Tollefson rolled up the message tightly, placed it in a small tube, reached into his wooden crate, and gently extracted a pigeon.

Sergeant Greally crept from hole to hole with updates.

"Ammo count, lads. How many rounds and how many grenades?"

The men sounded off. Greally scratched in his notebook.

"It goes without sayin', but in case there is any confusion—shoot slow and steady, we don't know how long we're going to be here, but nobody's going to suddenly show up with beer and ammo—what you got is what you got. Same for the grenades. You good?"

They knew what Greally was saying and nodded. Greally nodded curtly in return and bounded out of the hole. Darkness drifted in. Men settled into their holes, exhausted after their first full day in the pocket.

At 0030, artillery from the south whistled through the air. William could tell they were 75mm shells from American guns. He wondered if the redlegs knew where they were and fired with pinpoint accuracy around their perimeter or if the rounds were more haphazard. Either way, the shelling was uncomfortably close.

23

Argonne Forest Day 9

FRIDAY, 4 OCTOBER 1918

THE POCKET

The American shelling and random German mortars ensured no one in the pocket got any sleep. William smoked his last cigarette at 0500 and prepared for the day's fight. He counted his rounds and checked his breech, receiver, and bolt. He found the 8mm Chauchat rounds from the fight on Hill 205 two days previously. There were about twenty rounds, so a full magazine plus two. He made a mental note to get with Fitz and Gaff.

By first light, Captain McMurtry gathered the Company Sergeants. They nodded in agreement and split along the line. Sergeant Greally picked non-wounded men to scout east of the pocket to establish enemy numbers and activity. He selected William, Sigurd, Gust, Private Begley, and Private Miller.

"Begley, you got this squad. Boss wants you to scout out fifty meters. Don't pick a fight, but you may find one, so stay on your toes. If nothing else, we want to keep those bastards pushed back. Need to know what's out there—nests, infantry, mortars, gaps—whatever you can find out. You'll only have rifles and two 45s. Here's mine and one other. Full clips. I want that fucker back, Martin.

"Begley, I don't care about that one—it's Dolan's, and he never used it, still clean as the day Colt made it," he said, laughing as he handed the pistols to William and Begley.

"Begley, you know what to do. Fifty meters out, circle back, and report. Don't shoot unless you have to. That's it. Fuck off, and don't come back empty-handed."

Begley took over as squad leader. He was a small-framed New Yorker with a permanent, mischievous smile.

"Drop whatever you don't need. Get rid of everything that jingles, jangles, makes noise, or gets caught up on anything. Twenty rounds each in your pockets, no more.

"I've been on these goose chases before, and here's what works: We crawl out on our bellies, then low crouch. I'll be in the middle, two men on each side, line abreast, about three-meter spacing. Check in front—every twig—check left and right to your buddies. Stay in line until you can't or shouldn't. If anyone is on one knee, he sees something and is not moving forward. Stay in place until that man makes the call as to what to do next. It sounds complicated, but it works. Good?"

William, Gust, and Sigurd returned to their hole and dropped canteens, cartridge belts, gas masks, and bandoliers. William slipped the safety off the 45 and slung his Enfield over his back. He took thirty rounds, feeling Begley's twenty was a recommendation, not an order.

Lining up behind Gaff and Fitz, Begley said, "You two pillocks are the last two I'd choose to watch out for us; we'll be back in about thirty minutes."

The Chauchat team shrugged dismissively. "Maybe we'll see you, maybe we won't." Gaff snorted a laugh at Fitz's comment.

Begley ignored the two gunners and turned to his squad.

"In case there is any misunderstanding, as soon as we bump into the Hun out there, I'm counting helmets and heading back. If they see us, I'm firing a full clip and running like hell. This is not about winning the war; this is about figuring out how many Boche are in the woods and letting them know we're still here. I happen to know there are plenty already here, so I'm not so big on counting every last one individually. All clear?"

Makes sense to me, thought William.

As dawn lit the woods to a pale green-grey, the five men got on the ground and slithered outside the safe perimeter of the pocket. William moved quickly over the first ten meters, breathless. He felt the safety of the pocket slip off him like a blanket and crawled to a large tree trunk.

The scouts paused and peered through the trees, watching every brown leaf on the ground, every rock, bump, and branch as far as they could see through the dense forest in the dawn light. The ground sloped steeply down to the creek and smelled of decay and dampness.

Begley looked to his left and right, making eye contact with each of the men, and motioned with his finger to move forward. He slowly stood to a low crouch and moved like a nervous cat. The others followed his lead. Begley paused every five steps, took a knee, and watched every feature in his view before moving on.

Thirty meters out, Sigurd froze. It was the briefest of movements, perhaps fifteen or twenty meters ahead. He slowly lowered to one knee, and within seconds, every man in the squad was on the ground watching Sigurd. William lay flat, his 45 to his front. He studied every feature visible from his position—nothing. Sigurd remained motionless, like a deer listening for a predator's sound. He saw movement again: a camouflaged stahlhelm almost perfectly blended into the background, visible only due to its movement. Sigurd lay flat and watched intently. The others held their breath.

Sigurd pointed to his eyes and then pointed forward. He held up two fingers and sliced the air with his hand in a vertical motion.

William looked up in time to see four Germans crossing the road heading south thirty meters from their position. He caught Begley's eye, motioned four fingers, and sliced the air in the direction he saw them. Begley nodded, then waved the men back; he'd pushed his luck as far as he wanted to.

It took thirty minutes for the men to make it back to the perimeter of the pocket, crawling backward inch by inch, pausing regularly to listen. Begley picked up a stone twenty meters from the pocket and threw it at Fitzgerald. The gunner's head spun around. He peered over the edge of his hole and saw Begley's grinning face. There was no messing about. Fitzgerald tapped Gaff, whispered to the men along the line, and waved Begley in.

Once inside the perimeter, the men gathered in a funk hole. "Good work, Lima. Two Hun, right?"

"Yup, rifles only."

"How about you, Martin?"

"Four, crossing the road at a run, infantry. Thirty meters from where I was, heading south into the woods."

"Great work, fellas. Five men out, five men in; all our important parts are still attached. That's the way to do it," he said as he grabbed his crotch. Begley crouched off to find Sergeant Greally. William and the others hurried back to their holes.

"Well, that's me about tapped out for the day, taking the rest of the day off," said William, getting his gear on again just as mortars started. The three men pressed themselves into the earth one more time, resenting the helplessness of their situation. William gripped his Enfield and hoped the German infantry would attack soon so he could fight back.

"Crackers?" asked Sigurd.

William looked for his rations. He was down to a few crackers and a can of peaches. He broke the crackers in half and shared them with his bunkies.

The mortars peppered the area, reducing Whittlesey's force by five. There were screams, curses, moans, and the sounds of the shells bursting apart and slicing everything beneath them.

The aerial attack stopped after forty-five minutes, and William peered up the hill. To his front, Germans cautiously approached from tree to tree in bounding movements. William opened fire, rapidly at first, then recalling Greally's instructions, more deliberately, taking time with each valuable round. Stick grenades flipped end-over-end, exploding in front of him, scattering stone and earth along with deadly metal fragments.

The battle developed, each side fully engaged and committed to exploiting weaknesses and opportunities. Then something unexpected happened. American artillery from the south fired 155mm shells into the stream, sending gushes of water high into the air. Then the shells crept towards the pocket, one shell in front of the other, rhythmically tearing the earth apart. Trees split in two; foliage ripped from branches, craters erupted, and the air split with flying metal.

The 76th Reserve attack dissipated immediately. The grey uniforms scurried back over the hill to the safety of their trenches, confused about what had just happened. The American artillery tore the hillside apart in the pocket for over an hour. The destructive power of the 155mm high explosive shells shredded everything in their impact zone. Some funk holes took direct hits, leaving nothing of the men huddled inside. Shock waves alone killed many. William's mind told him to run, but he fought the instinct. He could only hug the hole with outstretched palms, clench his teeth, and wait.

Major Whittlesey and Private Omer Richards frantically got another message ready from the Command Post using Richards' last pigeon.[146] He released the bird called Cher Ami. It fluttered and then landed on a tree nearby. Richards threw sticks and shouted at it before it flapped off into the woods.

After ninety minutes of devastation, the American barrage stopped. The bewildered soldiers were nearly broken and tried desperately to regain their senses. The artillery hollowed the men out, leaving them emotionally vacant. It killed thirty doughboys and wounded eighty.[147]

The distinct sound of Chauchat fire came from south of the ravine. The unmistakable slow fire was music to the shattered men's ears. Sigurd and Gust looked at each other and leaned forward in their hole, unable to speak. *Maybe we're going to get through this.*

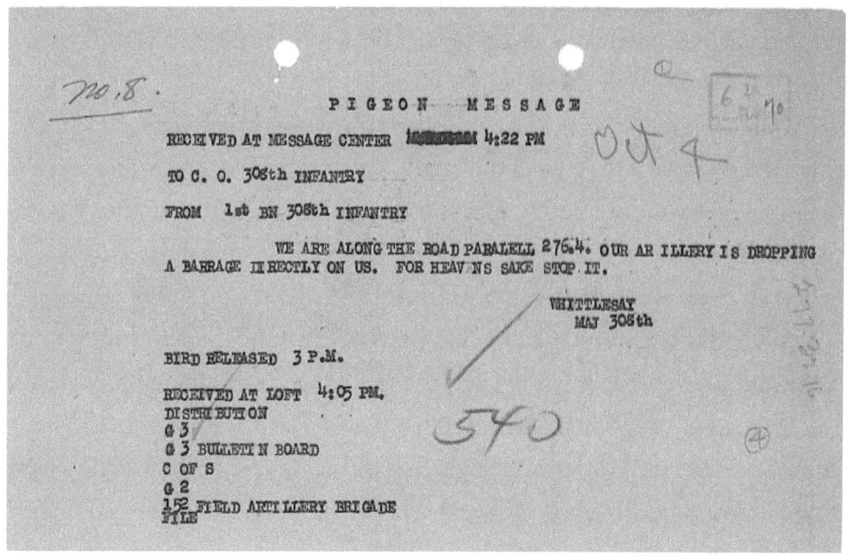

Figure 12: Cher Ami Message [148]

William found the strength to crawl out of his hole, hoping to help men before they forever slipped away from the hillside. The first soldier he found had been struck in the neck and shoulder by a large shard of metal that exposed bone, ligament, and muscle. No bandage or medical help could change the outcome. William pulled the body into a crater and pushed leaves and earth over the corpse, offering the thinnest layer of dignity for the soldier.

He moved to a man hit by shrapnel. The soldier sat immobilized by shock, bleeding from wounds that covered his entire torso. William bandaged what he could. He noticed blood coming from both ears, so he assumed the soldier could not hear. The man reached out his hand uncertainly, grabbed William's arm, and squeezed it. William understood the gesture and talked to the man about getting him out of there, though he knew they were empty words.

Sergeant Greally moved into the hole. William barely looked at him, still trying to bandage the wounded soldier.

"Martin, I need you over here," he said, pulling William away. "There are so many others."

William spent the next two hours splinting, bandaging, and moving men to cover. He noticed Greally was wounded, but not severely. Part of a tree had pierced Captain McMurtry's shoulder, and Corporal Dolan's arm bled. It seemed that there were more men injured and killed than those that were fit to fight.

While darkness fell, he crawled back to his hole, feeling lucky to be alive and unwounded. He lay against the stony wall of the hole, closed his eyes, and in an instant, his body went limp. He dropped into a deep, uninterrupted sleep, unaware of the cold, the noise, or the death that surrounded him.

Early the following day, Major Whittlesey used the cover of darkness to check in with his battered doughboys.

"How are you, men? Holding up okay?"

All three brightened up to see the Major.

"Doing well, Sir. Not gone west yet," replied Gust without a trace of emotion.[149]

"Well, don't go west. There is plenty of work to do before any of us do that," responded Whittlesey. "We'll get through this together. I promise."

24

Argonne Forest Day 10

SATURDAY, 5 OCTOBER 1918

THE POCKET

William, Sigurd, and Gust shared their last can of peaches and huddled together just before a light rain blew across the pocket. William was exhausted from stress and lack of nutrition, but he had the presence of mind to take his helmet off and place it upside down on the edge of his earthen home to catch the rain. After thirty minutes, he had a half-cup of the precious liquid, which he carefully poured into his canteen. *I hope we get reinforcements today; not sure how much more of this hillside I can take.* He dared not share his thoughts with Gust or Sigurd, who looked equally distraught.

Sergeant Greally did his usual rounds but looked tired, weary, and a little old that morning. He asked about water, rations, ammo, and wounds, tabulated responses in his little green book, and moved on with barely an extra word for the men.

By 0700, the pocket erupted with German machine gun fire from four different directions. The soldiers dove for cover, and rounds of "morning hate" tore through the area. The intensity of the fire was greater than previous attacks; the Germans had obviously moved more men and weapons into the area. Thousands of rounds buried into the soil or ricocheted off rocks, dead leaves skipped off the surface and chunks of bark flew off trees. William covered his ears. It helped keep the fear outside his head. American guns did not return fire; the German gunners were too far away for effective Enfield fire. The Hotchkiss rounds, which could range the enemy, were too valuable to waste on an unseen target.

The machine guns stopped in unison, and William immediately prepared for the infantry attack. It came immediately. Hundreds of Germans ran with abandon down the hillside, tossing grenades and firing wildly on the run. William looked down his sights. He fired consistently, with a composed resoluteness—bolt, grip, trigger, sight, breathe, squeeze, bolt—the rhythm calmed him. As frayed as he was, fighting that morning was a welcome physical and mental relief.

The grey uniforms kept coming, wave after wave. The Chauchat and the Hotchkiss gunners kept a steady stream of short-burst fire, clearing out lines of attackers. William could see their faces, their expressions, their fingers. He reached for a grenade, pulled the pin, and threw it forward. The mills exploded under an attacking soldier, tossing him three feet in the air and severing one of his hands. He landed in a heap and sat up in shock, looking at his club wrist, then he slumped over.

The leading wave was now inside ten meters and closing rapidly, shouting and grimacing with the emotion and physical effort of their attack. William stood up, fired a chambered round from the hip, and stepped out over the top of his cover. The first German was so close and moving so quickly that he practically impaled himself on William's bayonet. He could not stop his momentum and was surprised William moved forward to close the gap so quickly.

The Chauchat and Hotchkiss teams continued to fire into the men streaming down the hill, devastating their lines. William re-cocked his rifle and shot again on the move. To his right, he was aware of Sigurd and Gust coming out of their hole and moving forward. Rounds flew past him as he instinctively reloaded another round and fired. He pulled the bolt back and recocked. The action felt wrong and empty. *Fuck*, he thought. He sank to one knee, reached for his cartridge belt with his right hand, and fumbled. *Empty!* In a fraction of a second, he reached to the left side of the belt and found a clip, awkwardly extracted it across his body, inserted it, and cocked the rifle.

It seemed that time slowed down for everything but the attacking uniforms. Looking up, William saw a German barreling toward him—he knew the German was going to reach him before he could raise the gun and fire. He froze, still on one knee, and raised his bayonet in the only defense he could muster. Over his shoulder, three rounds of 8mm snapped through the air and hit the German in the chest and neck. His uniform tore open in an explosion of red. The enemy was dead before he hit the ground, two meters from William. The remaining Germans turned and retreated up the hill, realizing they had lost momentum. Not knowing how long he had held his breath, William exhaled and quickly ducked back into his funk hole.

Gust had a bloodstain on his arm; Sigurd looked intact but shook. The men sank into the hole, hearts racing and bodies twitching, eyes wide. Dead bodies from both sides lay all along the road and the hillside.

The fight seemed to rattle the 76th Reserve, and for a few hours, the hillside was quiet. In the lull, a de Havilland DH-4 Liberty plane flew down the ravine.[150] The German machine guns from both hillsides fired—the aircraft was flying so low through the ravine that the guns were firing downwards at it as it passed. The blue Dutch Girl insignia was clearly visible to the men on the ground.

Private Jim Larney, in charge of battalion airplane signal panels, used most of his panels as bandages but laid out what he had left on the ground. Others waved whatever they could find to attract attention, but the airmen showed no sign of spotting them.

Sigurd wondered out loud, "How can they NOT see us? I could practically see their freckles!" He slumped back into the earth, looking momentarily a broken man.

William put his hand on Sigurd's shoulder, "Don't worry, brother, we'll get the next train right outa here. I'm still planning to be home by Christmas, so I can't mess around here much longer."

Sigurd smiled weakly and closed his eyes momentarily, and when he opened them, he looked like the old Sigurd—balanced and in control.

* * *

First Lieutenant Harold Ernest Goettler (pilot) and Second Lieutenant Erwin Russell Bleckley (observer), both with the 50th Aero Squadron, had taken off that morning searching for Major Whittlesey and his men. Despite flying at just three hundred feet, they saw nothing on the ground on that sortie. They returned to the 1st Corps Observation Group based at Remicourt Aerodrome with their aircraft full of bullet holes. Both agreed that the intensity of fire received from the hillsides around the Mill indicated a solid German force just east of the millpond. They switched planes and headed back out to recheck that ground for visible signs of what was now being called (by everyone but the 308th Infantry and the Germans) the "Lost Battalion".

The DH-4 made another pass down the valley's center, taking intense fire from the hills again. They turned back from the valley's far end and prepared to drop supplies where they thought they had seen some movement on the hillside. The men on the ground waved whatever they could find on both passes, but to their horror, the packages dropped outside the pocket. The German machine guns found their target on that second pass, raking the powerful Liberty V-12 engine, shattering the windshield and the instrument panel, and hitting Lieutenant Goettler in the head. The pilot's last act was to point the damaged aircraft south, where he hoped they could somehow make it to safety. He judged well. The Liberty limped south and crashed behind American lines. Goettler was dead when troops reached the wreck, and Bleckley would die before he reached an aid station.[151]

* * *

After the aircraft disappeared over the hills, William, Gust, and Sigurd leaned on each other throughout the rest of the day. They recognized when one needed a word or a look and when they were best left alone.

Artillery shells from the south, clearly American fire, again impacted the ravine's southern hillsides and began walking toward the pocket. William watched in dread as the shells pounded closer and closer. He clenched his teeth and hugged the ground, waiting for the inevitable hell that was walking towards him. As the shells hit the creek, they abruptly stopped, skipped over the pocket, and pounded the hillside above them, north of the road and beyond.

"Alleluia!" screamed Sigurd, his face breaking into a smile that William had not seen in weeks.

Buoyed by the adrenalin of not being shelled by their own guns, William rolled into Gaff and Fitz's hole. "Howdy fellas."

"Howdy yerself, ya daft cowboy," said Fitz. "Who the heck says, 'Howdy'?"

"Well, have it your way," William replied. "I just found these 8 mm in my pocket. I guess I'll throw them at the Hun next time they come over the hill."

"Why, oh fucking why, didn't you lead with that? Now you have my full attention, and I feel bad for calling you a cowboy. How many you got."

"A full mag."

"Jesus, we only have a few hundred rounds left—another mag is aces."

William handed over the cartridges. As he rolled out of the hole, he looked back at them, "Thanks for saving my ass back there; I thought I was a goner."

"No worries, Will, you'd have done it for us."

25

Argonne Forest Day 11

SUNDAY, 6 OCTOBER 1918

THE POCKET

Sergeant Greally checked in. "How are ye lads? All good?"

He held each man's gaze for a few moments. They nodded and grumbled. He was back to his usual upbeat mood, darting eyes, and rapid speech.

"Word has it, you lads got personal with the Boche yesterday. Earned yer pay, fair play."

Words from Sergeant Greally were welcome any day, but especially that day.

"That last pigeon must have got through.[152] Redlegs and division know where we are now; they got us dialed in. And that Chauchat gets closer every hour. Things are looking up, boys."

Greally paused and inhaled his stubby cigarette.

"Oh, I got some extra ammo." He tossed rounds at each man.

"Where did this come from?" asked Sigurd, amazed. He no sooner uttered the words than realized what it meant.

Sergeant Greally didn't answer. Ignoring Sigurd, he continued.

"Major Whittlesey says we're here, and we ain't movin', so don't friggin' budge, fight those bastards for every inch. We didn't come all this way to roll over now. Every fuckin' square inch, got it?

"We're almost there, boys. It won't be long now. Keep the Faith."

Corporal Dolan jumped in as soon as Greally left.

"Need two of you scouting, working with Reid and Boden. Begley is squad leader. Ten minutes depart time. Drop your shit and get ready."

William didn't ask the others. He unclipped his belt and stripped down to his tunic. The other two looked at each other. Gust reached for a twig, broke it in two, ensuring one was shorter than the other, then held them up to Sigurd.

"Short stick goes out."

Sigurd smiled, delighted with the distraction and the element of chance. He picked a stick.

"Say hello to our Teutonic cousins for me," Sigurd grinned as Gust dropped his gear and looked confused.

"Who the heck are they?" he snarled.

Gust and William returned to the funk hole in under an hour. Germans still boxed in their eastern flank and maintained access and support to Hill 198, which had guns pointed both north and south.

The 76th MG-08s continued to fire randomly into the pocket. They harassed the men constantly and occasionally added to the list of the wounded and dead. Mortars, the most feared weapon in the pocket, lobbed 7.58 shells from Hills 205 and 198, wreaking more random havoc.

To add to the men's misery, a large 25cm trench mortar ranged the pocket from the northwest by Charlevaux Mill and sent enormous mortars into the Americans. William watched in horror as shards of metal ripped into the dead bodies that were now stacked high in rows in the middle of the pocket. The corpses shuttered under the attack as if still alive. The surviving members of the unit were too weak to bury their comrades, and the risk of being caught in the open was too great, leaving all with an enormous burden of guilt that even in death their brothers could not be protected.

Most men in the pocket had not eaten in a few days and drank only what water they could capture from the rain. Sergeant Greally distributed a few more rounds of ammunition per man in the afternoon along with a few words of encouragement. He looked old, his whiskers grey, his eyes hollowed and dark.

The men had hardly snapped their rounds into their belts before the 76th began another attack from the hill to the north. They came in force, running recklessly, not stopping to fire or to take momentary cover, as though immune to the fire from the dug-in Americans. The ferocity and speed of the attack were shocking. William wondered at their bravery, attacking headlong into defensive positions, showing no fear. The Germans closed rapidly to the edge of the road, crossed it without breaking stride, and crashed into the north perimeter of the pocket.

Gaff and Fitz fired on full automatic, a sound that alarmed William. He knew they never fired in that mode, and he understood how low they were on ammunition. William stood half out of his hole and fired as rapidly as he could work his bolt, releasing rapid rounds into the attacking masses.

A young German ran straight for William and seemed to single him out from the others. The man fired from the hip and sprinted recklessly into the American line. William stepped out of his hole and moved to his left to avoid the thrust of the bayonet tip that lunged toward him. The German recovered quickly and turned sharply to re-attack. William was exposed, his weapon was on the wrong side of his body, and the German was turning fast—faster than he was. In a spontaneous movement, William dropped his rifle and drew his trench knife. He reached into the space between them, where a rifle was useless, and a trench knife had an advantage. The terrified German realized he was now the hunted. William's knife pierced deeply into his arm. Momentum carried the young combatant towards William. His face grimaced in shock. William grabbed his attacker's leather shoulder strap and pulled him closer. His eyes latched onto the soldier's enormous cuffs, apple green collar, and epaulets with "76" stitched in red. The trench knife sunk into the German's chest.

William dropped the lifeless body and crawled away in horror. On his hands and knees, he tried to stand up, staggered, picked up his Enfield, and mechanically worked his bolt but did not raise his rifle despite the fighting going on all around him.

A potato masher flipped end over end and landed three meters away in the mud. William watched it, unable to react. For a moment, he thought perhaps it was not going to explode. A blast of air and heat blew him back into his funk hole, and a layer of soil and rock landed on his face. He looked straight up at the trees, branches, and the steel-grey sky above. There was no sound, and time stalled. William drifted into black oblivion.

"Martin, Martin, wake up!" Dolan was above him, shaking his shoulder. William moved. His head and back hurt, and something was wrong with his arm. He tried to sit upright. Sigurd and Dolan helped him as he came back to the world.

Sigurd smiled. "Hey Will, you had us worried."

William was unable to answer, but he smiled weakly. Inside William's head, he replayed the fight, the terror, the apple-green collar, the horror of the struggle, and the sadness that engulfed him. The men around him gave him something human to latch onto, and he embraced that with every fiber in his being, but for now, he needed to stay inside himself.

An hour later, he turned to Sigurd. "Hey," he said weakly.

"Hey yourself," said Sigurd.

William was weak from hunger, shook up, but functional. Looking around, he knew he was doing better than many others. Wounded and dead bodies were strewn all around. Mostly German, but many of

William's clan as well. Fitz and Gaff were not in their funk hole; Corporal Dolan lay on his belly beside the Chauchat.

"Martin—need a loader. You want a new job?" William nodded and crawled slowly over to the adjoining hole. There were five magazines left, none full. All held the eighteen rounds that Gaff suggested.

William turned to Dolan. "About a hundred rounds, no more full automatic."

Dolan nodded. "I'll go easy."

"Where are Gaff and Fitz?"

"They took a grenade, both alive but out of action."

William was relieved. Wounded was not dead.

He noticed his thigh and shoulder were injured but not badly. There was no point in seeing the medic; supplies were long gone, and a superficial frag wound was not significant when there were so many other men to care for. He took out his trench knife, looked at it in terror as his mind froze remembering the fight he just survived, then pushed through that feeling and probed a small piece of metal out of his thigh.

Sigurd poked his head over the hole. "I'm going to see about ammo—I'm down to fifteen rounds."

"Good luck with that," William said dryly. He had only twenty rounds left. After that, there was nothing he could do other than fight hand-to-hand. That was a fight he was sure he would lose next time. He watched Sigurd creep off.

In the late afternoon, the MG-08s raked the area again as if to remind William that he was not in control of his fate and that his foes could torment him at will. He saw Sigurd hopping from hole to hole between bursts to make it back. That large 25cm trench mortar from the northwest joined in the destruction, spraying the men with shards from above. Men all over the pocket braced for the sustained onslaught they knew would punish them. 76th artillery fired from further away, sending larger five-nines and woolly bears screeching into the pocket, most impacted to the south by the creek but contributed to the doughboys' terror. The combined effect was difficult to endure, even for the most battle-hardened men.

William poked his head up after the attack lulled. There were more groans and more screams from the newly wounded. The Germans launched one last solitary mortar, but given what they had just endured, the lone report seemed little threat. The shell whistled closer, and William ducked down deep into his hole. The massive 25cm high explosive shell detonated five meters away with an incredible shock wave. The ground shook. Rocks and chunks of Argonne dirt fell from the sides of his funk hole and rolled on top of him.

William's head pounded with pain. He lost all sense of sound and instinctively looked over his shoulder to check on his friends. Gust lay flat on his back, moaning but eyes wide open, looking at the sky.

Sigurd lay crumpled in a heap, his head a mass of blood. William stood, not knowing what to do. In shock, he climbed out of the hole and shuffled aimlessly, then fell to his knees to steady himself. His head throbbed, but his hearing and his senses returned gradually, and he crawled back to his funk hole, aware he needed cover. William saw Gust holding Sigurd's lifeless body. He knelt, disbelieving his friend could be gone, and straightened Sigurd's hair. Corporal Dolan slid into the hole and checked Sigurd for signs of life. He looked at Gust and William and shook his head.

William and Gust paused, unsure what to do, then, as if ordered, they mechanically picked up Sigurd's body and carried it toward the pile of other corpses. They laid Sigurd's body on the ground next to the others, straightened his arms and legs, and adjusted his tunic buttons to line up correctly on his uniform. William rubbed the USNA and 40th Division collar discs that he knew were important to his friend. They slowly rose, looked at the soulless body on the ground one last time, and walked carelessly back to their hole.

A new source of terror arrived on the battlefield, causing Gust to tap William on the shoulder.

"William, I need you. Look," Gust said, pointing.

"Fuck," gasped William flatly, not ready to fight again. German flamethrowers broached the hillside and ran down the slope with hundreds of infantry. The flames spat sixty feet, scorching trees below the roadway and causing new terror and mayhem in the pocket.

William and the rest of the embattled force focused every round on the men with the canisters, paying less attention to the attackers with rifles and grenades. As a result, most of the flamethrowers were mowed down by the time they made it halfway down the hill, some exploding into human fireballs. However, as a result, the other German infantry made it closer to the pocket that in previous attacks.

William swung his Enfield to the left towards the flamethrowers and fired three rounds quickly.

From William's right, Dolan shouted, "Martin, need a loader!"

William climbed quickly out of his hole and rolled in beside Dolan, who was firing conservative single shots. William checked the mags, tapped them on his helmet as he had seen Fitz do to ensure the spring was not clogged, and reloaded as soon as Dolan emptied his mag.

Despite the terror of the flamethrower attack, it provoked a visceral reaction from the men in the pocket that the Germans nor the Americans expected. William, Gust, and Dolan were enraged enough to climb out of their holes. They were exhausted and starved, and their nerves were shredded—the flamethrowers pushed many of them over the edge. They ran headlong into the remaining attackers, meeting them with momentum well outside their perimeter. Bayonets, rifles, pistols, light machine guns, trench knives, and boots were all employed in a wild counterattack. William fired while he ran, knelt, reloaded, and fired from his hunkers until the last Germans disappeared over the hilltop. Gust picked up a 45 automatic from a wounded doughboy and shot at close range as he moved through the Germans, chasing them far up the hill. He lost the ability to think and act rationally—his reaction was that of a man who had given up hope and the most basic human expectations. He was committed to the moment and the need to strike back at the attackers rather than take more punishment.

After the fight died down, the men in the pocket gathered the wounded and the dead and regrouped in their filthy holes. For William, that day was unthinkable. His head pounded. The war had reached into their trusted inner sanctum, and it had stolen one of them. He had also stolen the life of that young soldier with the apple-green collar. It was the worst day since he arrived on that retched hill-side, the worst day of his life.

26

Argonne Forest Day 12

MONDAY, 7 OCTOBER 1918

THE POCKET

Giselher Stellung, the German's second main defensive line in the Argonne, ran along Hill 198 and Hill 205 for miles to the east and west. Oberleutnant Fritz Prinz, on Hill 198 in a deep command post, was tired and frustrated. Major Hünicken had left thirty minutes earlier, angry that Fritz and Hauptmann Hansen had not wiped out the Amerikanernest. His task was to finish this battle, deny the Americans a propaganda victory, and then withdraw to the French village of Grandpré and the Kriemhilde Stellung (the Hindenburg Line). He stared at his maps and began planning.

Prinz and Hansen had tried everything to dislodge the Amerikanernest for five days, but they were dug in like ancient tree roots on that hillside. The Americans proved to be an effective fighting force that took everything their men threw at them and stubbornly hit back hard. Fritz knew the American field leadership was effective; whoever was in charge of the Amerikanernest was tough, determined, and re-silient.

The faces of the miners he worked with in the Germania mine flashed through his mind, their grit and innate optimism. He concluded that the Amerikanernest was not just well-led; it was stocked with men who would not quit, men with nerves of steel. [153]

Looking across the table at a prisoner's helmet, he stared at the outline of the Statue of Liberty and thought of that cold February day when he sailed past the statue on his first voyage to America. He recalled how he never thought the Americans would enter a war in Europe. *How mistaken I was.*

These Amerikanernest soldiers were not perfect; they were, after all, surrounded—a fate they, themselves, were primarily responsible for.[154] Militarily, they were naïve and inexperienced, but in equal measure, they were tough and stubborn.[155] *More importantly*, Fritz thought, *they learned quickly and adapted their tactics. Both traits were bad omens for the Kaiser.*

Fritz focused on his immediate problem. He leaned forward on his elbows and studied the map of Charlevaux Ravine and Hill 198. He knew the root cause of the problem: the 76th Reserve and the 2nd Landwehr were undermanned and stretched too thin on the Giselher Stellung.

Fritz stood back from his table, looked at the bigger picture, and studied his flanks. The French on his western flank had hit Hill 205 hard; the American 307th Infantry had battered into his eastern flank on Hill 198. The simultaneous assaults required reinforcements, leaving a gap in the line on the west side of Hill 198. He had not anticipated small American units would probe gaps and exploit them so quickly, using tactics somewhat similar to shock troops' infiltration. The American force had done well, got lucky, and had augered in on Charlevaux Ravine.

His 76th and the 2nd Landwehr found and severed the communications relays between the Amerikanernest and their support troops.

They had effectively cut off the Americans with a line of machine guns facing north and south from the Giselher Stellung.[156] Trench mortars arrived quickly and ranged the surrounded men from all directions. Snipers found their positions on all sides and picked at the enemy incessantly. The 76th had given the Americans no rest for five days. *The American artillery alone must have killed half their number; food, water, and ammunition must be almost gone,* thought Fritz. *They have got to be desperate.*

He looked further east on his maps, tracing his finger along the pencil marked Giselher Stellung. The American 28th Division had broken through, past Chatel Chehery, and now wheeled west, threatening his rear. His finger traced west, where the French were also breaking through Binarville.

The irony of the scenario amused Fritz—the 28th Division and the French were converging in a pincer movement using the Amerikanernest as a pivot point. The Deutsches Heer would have to pull back or risk being encircled.[157] It was incredulous that by surviving the fight and refusing to quit, the scrappy American fighters had acted as a beacon for other units to rally to, landing a body blow on the entire Third Army.

Four years ago, his men would have had the strength and resolve to stop them, but now their numbers were thinned out, and their will to fight was fading.[158] The need to withdraw was clear; he would do that regardless of what happened. But first, they had to try something new. If that didn't work, they would unleash everything they had on the Amerikanernest before withdrawing to Grandpré and the Kriemhilde Stellung.

* * *

At about 1600, Private Lowell Hollingshead, captured earlier that day as he searched for supplies outside the pocket, limped along the Charlevaux Mill Road carrying a white flag. He called out as he approached the perimeter, tentatively made eye contact with gunners training their weapons on him, and walked into the pocket. Fritz watched through binoculars from Hill 198.

Whittlesey conferred with Hollingshead and read a note penned by Fritz.[159] The interlude was brief. Within minutes, the Americans resumed their defensive posture, and runners passed the update along the line. William watched the familiar frame of Sergeant Greally, stopping at each hole for two or three minutes. Nods from men along the line as the news progressed. Greally made it to Gust and William.

"Evening, lads. News flash: the Boche asked for our surrender. The boss is having none of it. He thinks it's a sign that they are getting desperate. My two cents, for what it's worth, is we are not going to leave those men down," he nodded towards the corpses that now numbered over one hundred, "by handing this place over to the Kaiser and his tools. We'll hold this place to the last man."

He looked into the eyes of his two men and put one hand on each of their shoulders. "Keep the Faith, lads. Our boys are not long from here."

With that, he crawled to the next hole to repeat his message.

William estimated that there were about a hundred dead, probably two hundred badly wounded, and less than two hundred still actively fighting. Rations were long gone; most men had not eaten for days. If the rain continued to fall, water was down to a few teacups a day. More critically, ammunition was almost gone. Perhaps there was enough for one more attack, but soon ammunition would decide the outcome.

Despite those harsh realities, William's mind latched onto one simple concept: solidarity with Sigurd and the other hundred dead men that had gone west—Greally's simple phrase "Keep the Faith."

The Sergeant's phrase made sense to him now. He would keep faith with his brothers on this hillside no matter what happened. William felt at peace in his wet funk hole with Gust and Dolan, his ten rounds of Enfield ammunition, and his four magazines of 8mm. The shale he had been holding appealed to him, so he mindlessly put it in his tunic pocket. He wanted to keep a piece of this hillside with him, something that would remind him of this place, this time, and these army brothers.

The firing that ceased during the white flag episode started again with a vengeance. Moaning minnies fell through the trees, and the machine guns, snipers, and rifle fire were more intense than ever. For now, William, Gust, and Dolan had only to survive; their time to fight back would come soon enough. The pounding continued until 1740, then the inevitable infantry attack began. Dauntless Germans pressed in on the pocket from all sides. William fired carefully. He knew he only had ten rounds left; there was no rush. Death was now familiar, part of the shared experience of all the men in the pocket, as close as the piled-up corpses of his brothers. He would keep the faith.

The enemy kept coming. William stayed on rhythm—bolt, grip, trigger. Gust faced east, firing steadily, shouting, cursing. Dolan fired in single-shot mode, faster than the Enfields but slow for the Chauchat, slower than Fitz's finger snap. Everything was as it should be. There was no panic, just resolute determination from the Americans and the Germans.

* * *

Fritz watched from the northern hillside, scanning the Amerikanernest through field glasses. His eyes were drawn to the closest funk hole, the Chauchat, and the two riflemen. They were composed, unrushed, rooted like trees. As he watched, he knew his final attack would not prevail; their spirit was still unbroken. He knew they would fight to the last round, the last grenade, and the last man. They would not surrender.

Dispassionately now, Fritz watched the battle unfold. His men on the right made progress. On the left, they were pressing hard but losing momentum. He saw the Chauchat gunner spin around as he got hit. The American fell backward into his hole. Both infantrymen to either side of the gunner swung around. One dropped his rifle, manned the automatic gun, and continued firing. *This is interesting*, thought Fritz, wondering if these Americans would survive the attack.

* * *

William saw Dolan fall. He was hit but was moving and alert.

"I'm okay, Will. Take the gun. I can load."

William took over the Chauchat, put the stock to his shoulder, made sure it was on semi-automatic and began firing. The attacking Germans swung toward the center of the pocket to William's left. He could not get a clean shot at them as they traversed his field of fire.

"Gust, I'm repositioning. Can you cover me?" Gust nodded.

Dolan looked up at William. "Let's go. I got the mags."

William nodded. The three men took off to the left, crouching low and running fast over the steep forest terrain.

William jumped the logs that protected the wounded. He veered up the steep, slippery slope. Scores of Germans spilled across the road just as William got into position. He fired rapidly, the Chauchat tucked tightly into his side, blasting into the Germans crossing the road, clearing a swath through them. The bolt on the automatic rifle slammed open, momentarily halting William's fire. He pushed the mag release button forward, and the empty mag sprang out. Dolan snapped another mag in place immediately. The German attack began to break up, and momentum in the middle began to turn to favor the defenders.

* * *

The 254th Infantry Regiment sniper that plagued the American advance for over a week adjusted his Voightlander scope. Leopold Kuchler had wrapped his Gewehr 98 with sacking and moss. He had not fired in three minutes and was confident his position was not compromised. He traversed the Amerikanernest looking for his next target—officers, leaders, automatic weapons. *There.* There was a Chauchat in the open. He put his crosshairs on the man with the gun, exhaled slowly till his lungs emptied, then applied slow, even pressure on his trigger. The Patrone S, 8.2mm bullet exploded out of Leopold's muzzle at 2,700 feet per second.

* * *

William tracked the impacts of his rounds on the retreating Germans. As had happened before in this ancient forest, William's body and mind were in perfect synchronization; he was acutely aware of each sight, sound, smell, touch, and movement. Dolan on his right, spare magazine; Gust, left, on one knee; grey fleeting uniforms; shouts; grenades; Chauchat bolt bouncing against his right side; decaying forest smell in the air.

In an instant, William felt the kick of an invisible horse to his chest. He never heard the sound of the Gewehr 98. He flipped backward, felt his center of gravity shifting, felt the weight of the Chauchat drop from his hands, felt the pressure of the earth on his boots disappear, and saw the trees against the sky. Noises faded to silence. Then, his world went black.

* * *

Fritz had seen all he needed. He put his binoculars down, backed off the hilltop, and headed to his dugout on Hill 198 to pack his kit. His men were energized, glad to leave this section of the line, and those hard-nosed Americans who would not submit. They focused on pulling further north away from the onslaught of the AEF First Army.

The 76th withdrew from Giselher Stellung, bypassed the Amerikanernest, crossed Charlevaux Mill Road, and began their long walk to Kriemhilde Stellung and Grandpré, sixteen kilometers north. They moved quickly, knowing the 28th Division on their eastern flank was trying to connect with the French and cut them off.

None could see a way to win this long war. They did not know how or where, but the soldiers of the 76th knew defeat was close; perhaps a day or a week, but close.

* * *

Whittlesey's men fell back into their holes, shattered; their nerves frayed to breaking point. Brothers moved the dead and wounded, providing what care they could. Some soldiers counted their ammunition; others knew there was no point. The beleaguered Americans awaited the next attack; most knew they would not withstand another.

Gust and Dolan ran to William's side and lifted him gently back into the pocket. The gaping gunshot wound to his chest bled profusely, but he was alive. In a panic, they cut open his tunic and realized there was nothing that they could do other than apply dirty bandages to stem the loss of blood. Osro, Oscar, Gust, and Dolan watched over him, making him as comfortable and warm as possible.

Sergeant Michael Joseph Greally had died leading his men in the counterattack. Fifteen other Americans lost their lives in the final German attack.

At 1915, just as twilight settled into the ravine, Lieutenant Richard Tillman from the 307th Infantry broke through to Charlevaux Mill Road, east of the pocket. He probed west toward the Mill, his squad moving cautiously behind him. The officer smelled the decaying bodies first, then saw the funk holes and the clearing left by concentrated bombardment. He called out, "307th Infantry, coming in," and walked into the pocket.

There were no cheers from Whittlesey's men, just shock to see other Americans, and relief. Hundreds of 307th men from Companies A, B, and M arrived in the pocket within an hour.

The Lost Battalion, a label the 307th shared with the men, sank into their holes and closed their eyes. They processed the thought that reinforcements had finally arrived, and they would not have to fight again, or die, or watch their friends die on that godforsaken hillside. They ate field rations, smoked, and exhaled for the first time in two weeks.

Private Baxter, flush with new medical supplies, dressed William's wound. Dolan rounded up 307th field coats and blankets to keep him warm and comfortable. Evacuation of the hundreds of wounded would be in a few hours at first light.

27

Argonne Forest Day 13

TUESDAY, 8 OCTOBER 1918

THE POCKET

U.S. Army Ambulance Service, Section No. 611, attached to the 77th Division Sanitary Train since June, arrived on the road above the pocket at first light. Private Joe Fagan and Captain Woodfin Grady Page jumped out of their Ford Model T ambulance (commonly called a Henry) and ran down the slope to where the wounded lay.[160] The medics quickly got the most seriously injured back to Field Hospital No. 308 in the Abbey at La Chalade; they sent the walking wounded to the regimental aid station. They worked frantically. Doctor Josiah Powless soon joined Page. Powless had treated William when he needed a tetanus shot almost a week previously. Both doctors stayed for over six hours until they triaged all the wounded in the pocket.

William was among the first Page examined; Gust and Dolan ensured that. He grimaced when he saw the wound, but infection had not yet set in. Page quickly concluded that William could survive if he were treated quickly. He scribbled "GSW chest, pulmonary laceration, broken/fractured ribs, fractured scapula" on William's diagnosis tag. He promptly moved on to the next case—given the enormity of the task he managed that morning, it was all he could do for William.

As soon as Doctor Page finished William's tag, Gust and Dolan carried his litter to one of the ambulances that now lined Charlevaux Mill Road. They loaded the litter, touched William's arm, and quickly said their goodbyes, wanting him to be evacuated immediately. The Model T and its three wounded men disappeared around the bend in the road to the mill. Gust and Dolan turned back to the pocket. There was still much to do for their other brothers.

Per Page's instructions, the driver, Private Ray Gibson, did not stop at the dressing stations; he headed straight for the field hospital. Gibson drove past the mill pond, into the tiny village of Binarville, and broke out onto the southbound roadway toward Vienne-le-Chateau. Ammunition, sanitary, and troop trains cluttered the road, slowing progress for the ambulance. In the back of the Henry, William and two other soldiers faded in and out of consciousness.

Gibson turned left at Vienne-de-Chateau, over La Biessme creek into La Harazée, and on past Four de Paris. Within ninety minutes, he pulled up to the Cistercian Abbey in La Chalade, home to the overcrowded Field Hospital No. 308.

The Abbey was home to hundreds of wounded men stacked in the church, courtyard, and throughout the ancient building. Gibson and an orderly carried William inside, where doctors read his tag, examined his wounds, and discussed their options.

They did what they could to address the immediate threats to William's life but recognized that the care needed was beyond what they could administer. They agreed that he would not survive the long trip back to an evacuation hospital. The unit that offered William the best chance of survival was twelve kilometers to the rear—Mobile Hospital No. 4 at La Grange-aux-Bois.[162] This facility specialized in non-transportable wounded, severe head, chest, and abdominal cases. It had the X-ray equipment and the staff to do the best for William.[163]

Figure 13: Field Hospital No. 308, La Chalade [161]

The doctors of Field Hospital No. 308 walked away, not confident that the young soldier would survive his injury but certain that they had made the best decision for him. The nurses administered morphine to keep him sedated, and William faded into a deep, comfortable place.

28

The Long Road Home

Orderlies from Ambulance Company 308, 302nd Sanitary Train carried William's litter from the ancient Abbey to Sergeant Arthur Featherstone's Ford ambulance. Featherstone knew the road to the Mobile Hospital; he'd driven it daily for ten days. He drove past endless lines of soldiers, artillery, supply trucks, and horse-drawn wagons, all moving north to pursue the German Army. The Henry passed through the small towns of le Claon and Florent-en-Argonne and on to La Grange-aux-Bois and Mobile Hospital No. 4.

The 250-bed hospital had moved just outside town on the Clermont-St. to Menehould road on September 29. The sixty hospital staff lived in wooden French barracks buildings but had to expand the wards using the unit's Bessonneau tents.[164]

Sergeant Featherstone helped carry the litter into the hospital, where Chief Nurse Ruth Morton oversaw staff collecting William's personal items and admission paperwork. Nurse Olive Wilcox got him a bed, where Doctor Malvern Clopton examined the new patient's wounds and immediately requested X-rays.[165]

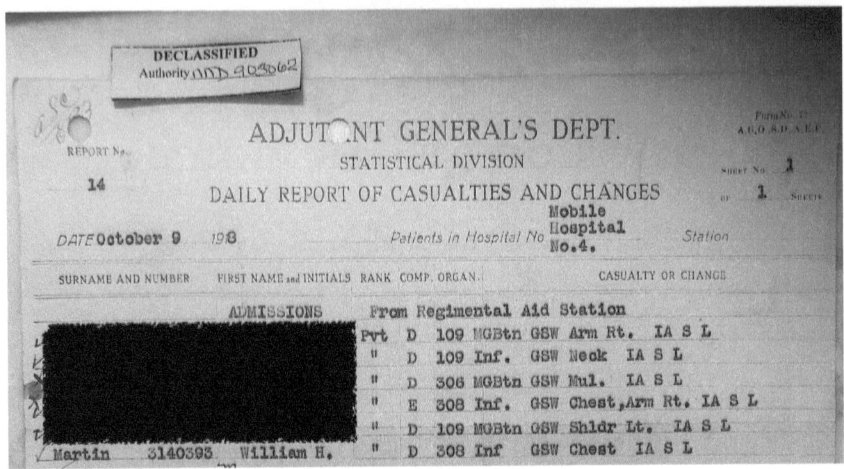

Figure 14: William's admission to Mobile Hospital No. 4 [166]

Over the coming two weeks, William was cared for by the dedicated doctors and nurses of Mobile Hospital No. 4. He succumbed to his wounds on October 24, 1918.

Orderlies removed William's body from the hospital to the morgue. The mortician removed the square identification tag from William's neck and attached it to a small wooden cross, on which he inscribed William's name and army number. He then tied the circular identification tag around William's ankle. The orderly sorted William's personal effects, noticed the odd stone among the other personal articles, and threw the stone outside the tent.

Early on October 25, soldiers moved the remains of Private Albert Madox Bryan and Private Delbert Sayers, both from the 312th Infantry, 78th Division, and William's remains into simple coffins made by the hospital carpentry shop. Chaplain Tom Sheedy arrived to bless the coffins while the soldiers loaded them onto a truck. The detail passed the village church, paused for a minute, and moved slowly to the American military cemetery, nestled in the woods opposite an orchard, three hundred meters south of the village.

The grave diggers waited patiently, smoked, and chatted quietly. All put out their cigarettes and stood silently while the truck slowly approached, wondering about the soldiers they were about to lower into the ground.

They buried William in grave number 182, at the end of a row of twenty-six deceased doughboys. Next to him lay Corporal Wallace J. Kaner, 326th Infantry, laid to rest the previous day. His new Army brothers were from across the United States, from New York and New Jersey, from Arizona, California, South Dakota, Wyoming, Minnesota, Oregon, Nebraska, and Wisconsin. Five of the twenty-six in his row were from Norway, Ireland, and Italy. [167]

The burial team hammered the wooden cross with William's identification tag in place. Chaplin Sheedy said a quiet prayer, touching William's cross as he prayed.

Private Bryan and Private Sayers were buried similarly at the start of the next row. When their work was done, the burial detail and the chaplain walked away and left the encased soldiers in peace in the tranquil French countryside.

Mobile Hospital No. 4 broke camp and moved to Cheppy two days later. By then, the American graveyard by the orchard had added fourteen new graves.

The Great War ended on November 11, 1918, just sixteen days after William's burial. The last artillery fired at the eleventh hour of the eleventh month. Their booms echoed over William's grave in La Grange aux Bois and faded into history forever.

* * *

The quiet graveyard remained untouched until April 7, 1921, when a small group gathered at the American Cemetery in La Grange aux Bois. GRS had pitched a tent and screening sheets for privacy. A work crew stood ready to exhume the fallen soldiers while officers prepared to document the process.

After over two years of darkness, GRS removed William's coffin from the Argonne earth into daylight. They placed his remains on a canvas sheet, then cleaned and saturated them with disinfectant and deodorant. Then, his body was carefully wrapped in a blanket and pinned closed. The work crew removed William's identification tag from the wooden cross and attached it carefully to the blanket over his chest. They then placed his blanket-wrapped body in a metal casket and covered it with a white sheet. The crew screwed the casket lid in place and used a hand pump to hermetically seal the casket. Finally, they encased the casket in a wooden shipping container and lifted it into a waiting truck.[168]

Selma requested the repatriation of her son's body back to Spokane rather than burial at the new Meuse-Argonne American Cemetery in France.

William's remains departed La Grange aux Bois by truck, then by train to the Port of Antwerp, arriving on May 1. His coffin, along with 5,823 others, was stored in a warehouse lined with American flags for a few days and then loaded on the US Army Transportation Corps (USAT) Wheaton on June 19. The troopship sailed into New York harbor and docked at Pier 4, Hoboken, New Jersey, on Saturday, July 2. The coffins remained on board until the following Tuesday due to an administrative error regarding the names of the fallen men aboard.

On Sunday, July 10, at 3 p.m. on Pier 4, Honor Guards, the Fort Hamilton Band from Brooklyn, Assistant Secretary of War Wainwright, and General Pershing stood before thousands of coffins brought home by the USAT Wheaton and the USAT Somme. There were 7,264 caskets in all, each draped with an American flag.[169] General Pershing spoke of the fallen advancing "weary of body, yet intrepid and resolute."[170]

While at Hoboken, soldiers checked all the caskets to ensure the remains and paperwork matched before shipping the soldiers on their final journeys. On July 23, William's body left New Jersey by train, traveling through the Oxford tunnel, over the Lackawanna Bridge, and through the Delaware Water Gap; through Chicago, Granger, over the Continental Divide, and onto the small towns of Granger and Pocatello.

On the morning of July 29, the train arrived in Spokane. William had left there three years and one month previously. Hazen and Jaeger undertakers received his remains at the station.

At 2:00 p.m., Selma, William's sisters Ella and Mary, brothers Jack and Freddie, his girlfriend Lizzie, and his childhood friends gathered at the Reorganized Church of Latter Day Saints at 3rd and Smith Street. William's casket awaited them at the altar.

William's family carried his casket down the aisle and into the bright afternoon sun after service. The Hazen and Jaeger hearse drove to Riverside Park Cemetery, a few miles west of town. Pallbearers from the American Legion carried William through the cemetery to the grave site, where flowers from the Women's Auxiliary and the Gold Star Mothers awaited. Members of the Modern Woodmen of America stood in respect for the fallen soldier, and a Guard of Honor from Fort Wright fired a volley over William's grave. Then William's family lowered his body into its final resting place overlooking his hometown.[171]

William's long journey and his Great War were finally over. His service to his country was short but with a distinction and intensity that few soldiers would match. He was one of 107 men killed on that hillside in the Argonne, one of 116,516 Americans who lost their lives in the Great War.[173] Many more would succumb to their physical and emotional wounds in the months and years that followed the armistice.

Figure 15: William's Grave, Riverside Memorial Park, Spokane [172]

On November 24, 1921, two weeks after he was a pallbearer at
the funeral of the Unknown Soldier in Arlington, Virginia, Colonel

Charles Whittlesey boarded the *S.S. Toloa*, en route to Havana, Cuba. On November 26, he retired for the night after dinner with the Captain and an extended visit to the smoking saloon. He was never seen again.

Whittlesey left a letter for the ship's captain with instructions on who to contact regarding his death. He also left letters to be mailed from Cuba. The US consulate in Havana determined that Whittlesey had "died of his own volition by drowning on the high seas."[174]

Oberleutnant Fritz Prinz returned to his home, family, and mining career after long and exemplary service to his country. His long war was finally over.

Endnotes

1. *Sunday Star.* (Washington, DC), May 1, 1927. Fritz Prinz's interview with James B. Wharton, Part 3, page 4.

2. On April 6, 1917, when the United States declared war against Germany, the nation had a standing army of 127,500 officers and soldiers. By the end of the war, four million had served in the United States Army, with an additional 800,000 in other military service branches.

   "The American Expeditionary Forces". U.S. Library of Congress, *Stars and Stripes*, https://www.loc.gov/collections/stars-and-stripes/articles-and-essays/a-world-at-war/american-expeditionary-forces/

3. Tungsten Ores, Hearings before the Committee on Ways and Means, a Bill to provide revenue for the Government, and to promote the production of tungsten ores and manufacture thereof in the United States, H.R. 4437. (Washington Government Printing Office, 1919). Page 6.

4. Ibid.

5. *The Emmett Index.* (Emmett, Gem County Idaho), 25 October 1917. Page 8.

6. The Lost Battalion was neither lost, nor a battalion. It had reached its objective at Charlevaux Mill in the Argonne. The unit consisted of Companies A, B, C of the 1st Battalion 308th Infantry Regiment; Companies E, G, H of the 2nd Battalion 308th Infantry; Company K of the 3rd Battalion of the 307th

Infantry Regiment; and C, D Companies of the 306th Machine Gun Battalion. All of these were part of the 77th Division. Total unit strength was approximately 545 men.

German units that confronted the Lost Battalion included the 254th Infantry Regiment and the 122nd Infantry Regiment.

The battle around Charlevaux Mill was heavily covered by the American press in 1918, and extensively documented by the US military. German coverage and interest of the battle was limited to standard military reporting.

7. "Great Power Competition involves rival nations with global interests, reach, and influence vying to be the preeminent actor in international politics. This means that great power competition occurs on a global scale. As such, competition between rival great powers unfolds in every domain–most recently in space—and across every area of responsibility. At the same time, most competition between rival powers occurs below the threshold of open hostilities. Day-to-day, great powers compete for influence and prestige."

Kaitlyn R. Johnson, *The Case for Change, Optimizing for Great Power Competition.* US Space Force, February 2024.

8. Weltpolitik ("world politics") was the imperialist foreign policy adopted by the German Empire during the reign of Emperor Wilhelm II. Its aim was to transform Germany into a global power through aggressive diplomacy, a strong military, and the acquisition of overseas colonies. It was a significant break with the Realpolitik policy of the Bismarck era. Realpolitik was the approach of conducting diplomatic or political policies based primarily on considerations of given circumstances and factors, rather than strictly following ideological, moral, or ethical premises.

9. T. S. Lovering and Ogden Tweto, *Geology and Ore Deposits of the Boulder County Tungsten District Colorado, Geological Survey Professinal Paper 245* (United States Government Prining Office, 1953). Page 74.

10.   Tungsten Ores, Hearings before the Committee on Ways and Means, a Bill to provide revenue for the Government, and to promote the production of tungsten ores and manufacture thereof in the United States, H.R. 4437. (Washington Government Printing Office, 1919).

"Germany... controlled completely this most essential of all war materials, which was so indispensable in speeding up our ship and gun program." (page 9) ↑

11.   77th Division Association, History of the Seventy Seventh Division August 25th, 1917- November 11th, 1918. Designed and Written in the Field, France. (New York: Wynkoop Hallenbeck Crawford Company). Page 150.

12.   *Sunday Star.* (Washington, DC), May 1, 1927. Fritz Prinz's interview with James B. Wharton, Part 3, page 4.

13.   Colonel Charles Whittlesey (Medal of Honor) (1884-1921) was born in Florence, Wisconsin. Whittlesey received a law degree from Harvard Law School in 1908. After graduating, he formed a law partnership with his Williams College classmate, J. Bayard Pruyn, in New York. He completed training in Plattsburg Officer's Training Program in 1916. In May 1917, Whittlesey took leave from his partnership and shipped to France with the 77th Division. He survived the battle in the pocket but not the effects of the war. He returned to work as a lawyer in New York, first with his own firm of Pruyn & Whittlesey, and subsequently in 1920 as an associate at White & Case. On Armistice Day in 1921, Whittlesey was at Arlington National Cemetery to serve as a pallbearer at the burial of the Unknown Soldier. On November 24, 1921, he boarded the S.S. Toloa, a steamship bound for Havana. On November 26, he took his own life at sea en route to Havana at age thirty-seven.

14.   *Sunday Star.* (Washington, DC), May 1, 1927. Fritz Prinz's interview with James B. Wharton, Part 3, page 4.

15.   National strategy orchestrates the instruments of national power in support of policy objectives and outlines a broad course of action or guidance statements adopted by the government at the national level in pursuit of national objectives. The 'DIME' acronym (diplomatic, informational, military, and economic) has been used for many years to describe the instruments of national power. Despite how long the DIME has been used for describing the instruments of national power, US policy makers and strategists have long understood that there are many more instruments involved in national security policy development and implementation. New acronyms such as MIDFIELD (military, informational, diplomatic, financial, intelligence, economic, law, and development) convey a much broader array of options for the strategic and policymaker to use.

US Department of Defense, Joint Doctrine Note 1-18, Strategy, 25 April 2018.

16.   A variety of German artillery shells, named for their visual effects or sounds.

17.   The Meuse Argonne offensive was also the deadliest campaign in American history, resulting in over 26,000 soldiers killed in action and over 120,000 total casualties-https://www.archives.gov/research/military/ww1/meuse-argonne

18.   Memo from Commanding General 6th Depot Division to Commanding General SOS, Subject: Replacement Drafts, 10 Sep 1918, 40th Division Records, AEF, Tours (National Archives at College Park, College Park, MD).

19.   Funk hole: Great War term for a hole used for safety and cover. In later wars this was referred to as a fox hole.

20.   Corporal James Dolan (Distinguished Service Cross) (1893-1927) was a native of Sweetwood Upper, Killargue, Dromahair, County Leitrim, Ireland. He immigrated in 1914 to New York and worked for the Morgan Steamship Line in Manhattan.

Following the outbreak of the war, James enlisted in the 77th Division on Sep 28, 1917. By July 1918, he was a Private First Class in the 308th Infantry, and by August 1918, he was promoted to Corporal in the field. He was a member of the "Lost Battalion." His Distinguished Service Cross citation (War Department, General Orders No. 32 (1919) reads:

The President of the United States of America, authorized by Act of Congress, July 9, 1918, takes pleasure in presenting the Distinguished Service Cross to Corporal James Dolan (ASN: 1709086), United States Army, for extraordinary heroism in action while serving with Company G, 308th Infantry Regiment, 77th Division, A.E.F., near Charlevaux, France, October 3 - 7, 1918. Corporal Dolan was very severely wounded while in charge of his automatic rifle section, which was a unit of a surrounded battalion. After receiving first aid, he resumed his post and remained in command of his section until the battalion was relieved.

James survived the war and returned to New York. He died at age thirty-three and is buried in Calvary Cemetery, Woodside, Queens, New York.

21.   In 1910 the German Army began using the new German Feldgrau (field-gray) uniform (formally, the M1907/10 Waffenrock). The Feldgrau uniform was for field use only; the Imperial Army continued to use Dunkelblau (dark blue) uniforms for non-field use.

22.   *Sunday Star.* (Washington, DC), May 1, 1927. Fritz Prinz's interview with James B. Wharton, Part 3, page 4.

23.   German Army, Supreme Army Command

24.   *Sunday Star.* (Washington, DC), May 1, 1927. Fritz Prinz's interview with James B. Wharton, Part 3, page 4.

25.   German for "front pig", reference a soldier serving at the front (slang).

26.   The official name of the German land forces or the Imperial German Army.

27.   *Evening Star.* (Washington, DC), May 1, 1927. Fritz Prinz's interview with James B. Wharton, Part 3, page 4.

28.   Tungsten Ores, Hearings before the Committee on Ways and Means, a Bill to provide revenue for the Government, and to promote the production of tungsten ores and manufacture thereof in the United States, H.R. 4437. (Washington Government Printing Office, 1919).

"It is a striking fact in the history of tungsten, that by far the greatest part of the world's tungsten ore was imported into Germany prior to the world war. The nations of the world were more or less taken by surprise, when with the advent of the war they suddenly realized that Germany completely controlled this vital essential of the war. Even the extensive British controlled deposits of Burma had been contributing to Germany's stores of tungsten.

Germany apparently was the only nation in the world that seed to realize fully the importance of tungsten during this period. (page 6)

There is no known substitute for tungsten, and it has been properly named the key war material. By the use of tungsten high-speed steel tools, one man and one machine can do the work of five men and five machines using carbon steel tools." (page 12)

29.   Ibid. Page 40.

30.   In 1897 German chancellor Bernhard von Bulow told the Reichstag, "We do not want to put anyone into the shade, but we demand a place for ourselves in the sun." The ensuing quest for a "place in the sun," connoting both new colonial holdings and a belt of naval stations ringing the world, inaugurated a vigorous, largely ahistorical pursuit of German sea power.

James Holmes (2004) Mahan, a "Place in the Sun," and Germany's Quest for Sea Power, Comparative Strategy, 23:1, 27-61, DOI: 10.1080/01495930490274490 ↑

31.   *"To deprive a nation of tungsten is to cripple its military power in time of war, and its industrial power in time of peace. Without high*

tungsten steels, machine tools could not be produced nor operated in sufficient quantities to make the "seventy-five" and its thousands of shells, the rifle and machine gun and its millions of cartridges, nor could automobiles, submarines nor engines be made fast enough to replace the wastage of war."

Prof. Colin G. Fink

President of the American Electro Chemical Society

The Emmett Index. (Emmett, Gem County Idaho), 25 October 1917. Page 8.

32.   Gun Shops, Krupp, Essen. United States Library of Congress's Prints and Photographs division [LC-DIG-ggbain-17887]. https://www.loc.gov/item/2014703497/.

33.   Rittmeister Wilhelm Scheck was born in 1877. He traveled to the United States in 1904. In 1906, he was President and General Manager of Germania Mine in Spokane, Washington. Wilhelm returned to Germany in August 1914 and served in Reserve Cavalry Division 51. Later, he served with the 51st Reserve Infantry Division and Corps Adjutant of the General Command for Special Use No. 62. According to Records of the War Department General and Special Staff, he was a prisoner of war in France in 1918. Wilhelm survived the war.

34.   Leutnant Rudolf Hacklander (1884-1914) lived in Kassel before moving to the United States in 1908 to work at Germania Mine in Spokane, Washington. Unverified reports in the Colville Examiner newspaper (December 1918) report he died in the first year of the war.

35.   Consul General Bopp was later tried and convicted of conspiracy acts of espionage and sabotage on American soil, January 1917.

"I have just learned to-day by telegram from the United States attorney that the jury in the Bopp neutrality cases in San Francisco has found all five defendants guilty on both indictments—that is, guilty of conspiracy to prepare a military expedition, and guilty of a con-

spiracy to restrain interstate and foreign trade by blowing up bridges and ships in violation of the Sherman Law. The five defendants were Consul General Bopp, the Vice Consul, Von Schack, the Attaché of the Consul, Von Brincken, the Consul General's spy, Charles C. Crowley, and another of his tools, Margaret Cornell."

Papers relating to the foreign relations of the United States, 1917, Supplement 1, The World War, File No.702.6211/325, The Assistant Attorney General (Warren) to the Counselor for the Department of State (Polk), Extract

36.	Name Index to Correspondence of the Military Intelligence Division of the War Department Staff, 1917-1941. Record Group 165, Records of the War Department General and Special Staffs, 1860 – 1952, M1194. Roll 203, image 457, Captain Scheck. National Archives microfilm publication.

37.	Carl von Clausewitz (1780-1831) was a Prussian general and military theorist. His seminal work is *Vom Kriege* (On War) was published in 1832.

38.	New York Passenger Arrival Lists, Ellis Island, 1892-1924. Washington: National Archives and Records Administration, publication T715 and M237, Roll 1625, vol 3578-3579, image 19 of 894. Microfilm.

39.	Fritz E. Wolff, Bryan T. Garcia, Donald T. McKay, David K. Norman, *Inactive and Abandoned Mine Lands – Germania Mine, Cedar Canyon Mining District, Stevens County, Washington* (Washington Division of Geology and Earth Sciences, Information Circular 117, February 2014).

40.	In October 1918, the Deucher Verein house was renamed Lafayette House, and served as a convalescent home for veteran soldiers and sailors at 112 West 59th Street (Central Park South), New York City.

41.	"It will be seen that out of 68 hours he gets 9 hours sleep, divided into three short periods of 3 hours a night."

Charles H. Walbourn. *Confessions of a Pullman conductor* (Original at University of Illinois at Urbana-Champaign, 1913). Page 46.

42.   "Spokane -- Stores -- Jones and Dillingham -- Oversize Box 2 (#2)," Spokane Public Library, accessed November 22, 2023, https://lange.spokanelibrary.org/items/show/1122. Courtesy of Spokane Library.

43.   National Archives and Records Administration Washington D.C. *New York Passenger Arrival Lists, Ellis Island, 1892-1924*, Roll 1398, vol 3074-3076, 6 Jan 1910, image 485 of 1282.

44.   *The Colville Examiner.* (Colville Washington). December 28, 1918, page 2. "German Officer Known in County".

45.   William Manchester, *The Arms of Krupp 1587-1968* (Little, Brown and Company, 1968). Page 356.

46.   *"Any improvement of efficiency in the field of metal cutting is to be valued in relation to the decisive importance of the mechanical workshops for military and economic armament. In this respect, we can, above all, point to our achievements in developing the manufacture cemented metal carbide (Widia) [Note: Widia was Krupp's trade name for Tungsten Carbide] and carbide-tipped tools and our leading position in this field. The use of these tools reduced the processing time to an extent never thought possible (for instance, during the was 1914-1918 the turning of a certain grenade with high-speed tool steel required approximately 220 minutes; the introduction of Widia enabled the construction of automatic machines which did that work in about 12 minutes). Modern production of grenades without Widia is, therefore, unthinkable."*

Trials of War Criminals before the Nuernberg Military Tribunals under Control Council Law No. 10, Nuernberg 1946-April 1949, Volume IX. Partial Translation of Document NI-764, Prosecution Exhibit 467, Extracts from a Krupp Memorandum, 16 July 1940 summarizing achievements in research and concerning production of war material and the necessity of increased prices (United States Government Printing Office, Washington, 1950).

47.   Howland Bancroft, *The Ore Deposits of Northeastern Washington* (Department of the Interior of the United States Geological Survey, Government Printing Office Washington, 1914). Page 114.

48.   Ibid. Page 118.

49.   Ibid. Page 119.

50.   Howland Bancroft, The Ore Deposits of Northeastern Washington (Department of the Interior of the United States Geological Survey, Government Printing Office Washington, 1914). Page 9.

51.   Ibid. Page 122.

52.   *The Colville Examiner. (Colville Washington).* December 28, 1918, Page 2.

53.   Mensur, or academic fencing was practiced by some German students notably of aristocratic class in the late 19th and early 20th centuries. Opponents stood at arm's length and did move flinch or more position while fencing with specially designed sabers called schlagers. Fencers attempted to hit unprotected areas of an opponent's face and head, oftentimes resulting in facial scars (a "smite") which was seen as a badge of honor amongst many student organizations.

54.   German plan to successfully fight both France and Russia in a two-front war. Developed by Chief of the German General Staff, Field Marshal Alfred Graf von Schlieffen.

55.   A schlager saber is a heavy weapon, three times the weight of the modern sport saber used in academic fencing (or Mensur).

56.   Telegram from the Imperial Chancellor, von Bethmann-Hollweg, to the German Ambassador at Vienna. Tschirschky, July 6, 1914. This would later be known as the "Blank cheque."

57.   *The Spokane Press.* (Spokane Washington), December 23, 1903, image 2, Santa Clause Sends Greeting to Little People of Spokane, Chronicling America, Library of Congress.

Image provided by Washington State Library, Olympia, WA

58.   Frank G. Odel was a performer and professional apiarist from Lincoln, Nebraska, who performed with a full colony of bees at shows around the country.

59.   "On April 6, 1917, when the United States declared war against Germany, the nation had a standing army of 127,500 officers and soldiers."

Library of Congress Digital Collections Stars and Stripes: The American Soldiers' Newspaper of World War I, 1918 to 1919, "The American Expeditionary Forces." https://www.loc.gov/collections/stars-and-stripes/articles-and-essays/a-world-at-war/american-expeditionary-forces/.

60.   Center of Military History (CHM), United States Army, CMH Pub 77–2. *The U.S. Army Campaigns of World War 1 Commemorative Series.* The U.S. Army in (Washington, D.C., 2017).

61.   District and Local Boards, prescribed by the President, under authority vested in him by the Selective Service Act of May 18, 1917 (Washington, U.S. Government Printing Office 1918). Page 67.

62.   Krupp's Paris Gun, first used in March 1918, was the world's longest range siege gun. It fired a 234 pound shell (216mm), 81 miles and had a maximum altitude of 26.3 miles.

63.   *Spokane Daily Chronicle*, June 29, 1918. Page 3.

64.   United States Army. American Expeditionary Forces. General Staff, G-2. Histories of two hundred and fifty-one divisions of the German army which participated in the war -1918. Washington: G.P.O, 1920. Pdf. https://www.loc.gov/item/45041080/.

65.   Frontline fighters.

66.   World War history: daily records and comments as appeared in American and foreign newspapers, -1926. (New York, NY), May. 10 1918. https://www.loc.gov/item/2004540423/1918-05-10/ed-1/.

67.   *History of the Two Hundred and Fifty Division of the German Army which Participated in the War (1914-1918).* War Department, Document No. 905. (U.S. Government Printing Office Washington, 1920). Pages 528-530.

68.   Known to the British and French as the Second Battle of the Marne.

69.   Dubbin was a wax product used to soften, condition, and waterproof leather and other materials. It consisted of natural wax, oil, and tallow.

70.   *Soldiers of the Great War, Volume III.* by W. M. Hauser, F. G. Howe, A. C. Doyle (Washington: Soldiers Record Publishing Association, 1920).

71.   "Each U.S. soldier in the field was also issued a first aid packet for individual use consisting of two bandages, two compresses, and two safety pins contained in a hermetically sealed metal case carried in a first aid pouch."

   Wever PC, Korst MB, Otte M. Historical Review: The U.S. Army Medical Belt for Front Line First Aid: A Well-Considered Design That Failed the Medical Department During the First World War. Mil Med. 2016 Oct;181(10):1187-1194. doi: 10.7205/MILMED-D-15-00390. PMID: 27753550.

72.   *Metric Manual for Soldiers,* Washington: Department of Commerce, Bureau of Standards, Miscellaneous Publication No. 21. (U.S. Government Printing Office Washington, 1918).

73.   Present day Marine Corps Air Station Miramar.

74.   Daniel Joseph Daly (November 11, 1873 – April 27, 1937), United States Marine Corps, was the recipient of two Medals of Honor: one during the Boxer Rebellion in 1900, and the second in Haiti in 1915. In the Great War, Daly fought at the Battle of Belleau Wood.

75.   Private Gustave Adolph "Gust" Dahlgren (1892-1947) was born in Frandefors, Dalsland, Sweden. In 1909, he immigrated to New York on the SS Adriatic. Gust moved to Michigan to work in lumber mills and later to Cuyuna, Minnesota, where

he worked in an iron mine. On May 25, 1918, he left for Camp Dodge, Iowa (163rd Depot Division).

76.   Private Oscar More Potter (1894-1984) was born in Cheney, Washington. In 1917, he worked as a farm laborer in Idaho. He left for Camp Lewis on 28 June 1918. Oscar survived the war and returned to Spokane, Washington.

77.   Private Sigurd Larssen Lima (1892-1918) was born in Gjesdal, Rogaland County, outside Stavanger, Norway. He immigrated to the US in 1911 and settled in Cooperstown, North Dakota, where he worked as a blacksmith. Sigurd was inducted in Cooperstown on May 24, 1918, and left for Camp Lewis, Washington. He served with the 25th Company, 7th Battalion, 166th Depot Brigade until July 16, when he transferred to Company H, 158th Infantry, 40th Division in Camp Kearny. Sigurd was a member of the "Lost Battalion." He was killed in action on Oct 3, 1918.

Following the fight in the pocket, Sigurd's remains were unidentified until 1932. He is buried in Grave 11, Row 4, Block G, in the Meuse-Argonne American Cemetery, France.

78.   General Order 83, Camp Kearny California, 18 June 1918. (National Archives at College Park, College Park, MD).

79.   Memorandum from Headquarters 40th Division, Camp Kearny, California to All Unit Commanders. Dated 8 July 1918. (National Archives at College Park, College Park, MD).

80.   James W. Rainey, "Ambivalent Warfare: The Tactical Doctrine of the AEF in World War I," *Parameters, Journal of the US Army War College*, Vol XIII No. 3, September (1983). Page 35.

81.   *"Close adherence is urged to the central idea that the essential principles of war have not changed, that the rifle and the bayonet remain the supreme weapons of the infantry soldier and that the ultimate success of the army depends upon their proper use in open warfare"*. Cable 228-S, General John Pershing to AG, 19 October 1917. ↑

82.   The law exempted them from having five years of U.S. residency, filing a declaration (or "first papers"), speaking English, and taking history and civics exams.

83.   USNA: U.S. National Army.

84.   The new San Bernardino train station opened on 15th July 1918. At the time, it was the largest train station depot west of the Mississippi River. The new station was designed in the Spanish Mission Revival style.

85.   Private Ralph Edmund John, *A Personal Memory of the Lost Battalion*, New York State Military Museum and Veterans Research Center. https://museum.dmna.ny.gov/application/files/4416/0521/1082/308th_article_John_Lost_Battalion.pdf.

86.   "Thank God", in Irish.

87.   A spiked helmet worn in the 19th and 20th Centuries by Prussian and German military, firefighters, and police. Beginning in 1916, the Army replaced the Pickelhaube with steel helmet (the Stahlhelm) intended to offer greater head protection from shell fragments.

88.   On 19 July 1918, the armored cruiser USS San Diego (Armored Cruiser No. 6—former USS California) hit a mine 10 miles southeast of Fire Island (Long Island) and sank quickly. German submarine U-156 had laid contact mines along the south shore of Long Island and the sinking of San Diego was attributed to her.

89.   Dazzle camouflage was used extensively in the Great War. It consisted of complex patterns of geometric shapes in contrasting colors interrupting and intersecting each other. Dazzle camouflage was not meant to conceal, rather to make it difficult to estimate a target's range, speed, and heading. ↑

90.   Benedict Crowell, *How America Went to War, an account from official sources of the Nation's War activities, 1917-1920* (New Haven: Yale University Press, 1921): Page 272.

91.   Shere Khan, and Baloo are characters from The Jungle Book (1894) by Rudyard Kipling.

92.   "Poilu" ("hairy one") was a common nickname for a French army infantryman in 1918.

93.   Memo from Commanding General to Commanding General S.O.S (Services of Supply, American Expeditionary Forces), Subject: Control of Troops Travelling on Troop Trains (National Archives at College Park, MD, 8 September 1918).

94.   Gievres stored the greater part of supplies sufficient to last the AEF for 30 days. At the Armistice there were completed about 4.500.000 square feet of covered storage space and about 10.000.000 square feet of open storage space. Gievres had approximately 700 officers and 25.000 soldiers.

The United States Army in the World War, 1917-1919: Reports of the Commander-in-Chief, Staff Sections and Services, Volume 15, (Washington, D.C., Center for Military History, 1991), page 40.

95.   Gièvres had the largest refrigeration and ice-making plant in the AEF. It also had a coffee roasting plant, field bakery, coal and gasoline storage; central baggage office; remount depot and a veterinary hospital.

American Armies and Battlefields In Europe: A History, Guide, and Reference Book (American Battle Monuments Commission, US Government Printing Office, 1938).

96.   Headquarters 6th Depot Division, Memorandum No. 6, 2 September, 1918.

97.   *"To my mind this system of replacements was a great mistake and one of the most unjust things of the war. It would have been better, in my judgment, to have had fewer divisions and to have trained the replacements in large central training camps instead of organizing these replacements into divisions and creating in their minds a division spirit and pride and then later scattering them for assignment, to go forth to battle under strange officers and in divisions with which they had no previous affiliation."*

Brig. Gen. W. P. Richardson, "World War Observations," *Infantry Journal*, Volume XVII, July 1920 to December 1920, page 2.

98.   Memo from Chief of Staff 6th Depot Division, to All Organization Commanders, Subject: Replacement Equipment, 30 Aug 1918, 40th Division Records, AEF, Tours (National Archives at College Park, College Park, MD).

99.   Civil Engineering records of Rifle Range at Mornay-Berry, 19 Sep 2918. 40th Division Records, AEF (National Archives at College Park, College Park, MD). ↑

100.   Memo from Commanding General 6th Depot Division, to Commanding General SOS, Subject: Replacement Drafts, 10 Sep 1918, 40th Division Records, AEF, Tours (National Archives at College Park, College Park, MD).

101.   Ibid.

102.   Drumfire describes a heavy continuous rapid artillery fire.

103.   *Sunday Star.* (Washington, DC), May 1, 1927. Fritz Prinz's interview with James B. Wharton, Part 3, page 4.

104.   Ibid.

105.   Palmer, Frederick. Our greatest battle, the Meuse-Argonne. New York, Dodd, Mead and Company, 1919. Pdf. https://www.loc.gov/item/19018745/.

106.   Ibid.

107.   40th Division Records, Headquarters 6th Dipot Division, AEF, APO 788, Special Orders, No. 26, September 20, 1918 (National Archives at College Park, College Park, MD).

108.   Ibid.

109.   Memo from Commander 158th Infantry Regiment to Commanding General 6th Depot Division, 25 October 1918.

110.   Whittlesey would later write of the new arrivals: "Their lack of training was as unquestioned as their valor. They were fine material...but were entirely unbroke to the matter of war."

L. Wardlaw Miles, Captain 308th Infantry, *A History of the 308th Infantry, 1917-1919* (New York and London: G.P. Putnam Sons 1927). Page 120.

111.   Sergeant Michael Joseph Greally (1888-1918) was born in Liverpool, son of Patrick and Ellen Grealy of Clonkeel townland, Killashee parish, County Longford, Ireland. The family returned from England to Clonkeel in the late 1800s. Michael emigrated to the United States in 1909 and became a naturalized US citizen in 1910. Before the war, he worked at the Army Quartermaster in Manhattan. He enlisted in the 308th Infantry, 77th Division in 1917 and was promoted to Sergeant in 1918. Michael was killed in action on October 8, 1918, as part of the Lost Battalion. He is buried in the Meuse-Argonne American Cemetery. His brother, James Greally, 467th Engineers, died in France one week after Michael was killed (James is buried in Suresnes American Cemetery, Paris). ↑

112.   308th Company G Monthly roster in August 1918 numbered 181 troops. Monthly roster in September 1918 numbered 223 troops. The September roster consisted of 23% replacements.

113.   French fighter aircraft made by Société Pour L'Aviation et ses Dérivés (SPAD).

114.   American Battle Monument Commissions, The Meuse-Argonne Offensive, a World War I Online Interactive, Released Wednesday, June 24, 2015. https://www.abmc.gov/news-events/news/meuse-argonne-offensive-world-war-i-online-interactive-released

115.   Members of the Field Artillery in the United States Army, from the red trouser stripe that was part of the their uniform.

116.   Stielhandgranate, literally German for "stick hand grenade"

117.   The Medical Department of the United States Army in the World War. Volume VIII Field Operations. Prepared under the direction of Maj. Gen. M.W. Ireland, the Surgeon General. Col

Charles Lynch, M.C. Col Joseph H. Ford, M.C. LtCol Frank W. Weed M.C. Government Printing Office 1925. Plate XXVI.

118.   308th movements and operations in the Argonne are based on multiple primary sources and official U.S. Army sources. These include:

77th Division Association, *History of the Seventy Seventh Division August 25th, 1917- November 11th, 1918. Designed and Written in the Field, France.* (New York: Wynkoop Hallenbeck Crawford Company, Printers, 1919).

American Battle Monuments Commission, *77th Division Summary of operations in the World War.* (US Government Printing Office, 1944).

L. Wardlaw Miles, Captain 308th Infantry, *A History of the 308th Infantry, 1917-1919* (New York and London: G.P. Putnam Sons 1927).

War Department. Army War College. Historical Section. World War I Branch. ca. 1918-ca. 1948, *The Operation of the So-Called "Lost Battalion", October 2 to 8, 1918.*

Alexander T. Hussey, Raymond M. Flynn, *The History of Company E, 308th Infantry, 1917-1919* (Knickerbocker Press, 1919).

History of Company D, 308th U.S. Infantry, 77th Division, American Expeditionary Force. 1919. Illustrations by Charles Costa, Pvt, Company D, 308th infantry. New York Public Library.

119.   Distinctive German steel helmet replaced the traditional boiled leather Pickelhaube ('spiked helmet') in 1916.

120.   First Lieutenant Arthur McKeogh, *The Victorious 77th Division (New York's Own), in the Argonne Fight.* (John H. Eggers Co. Inc. Times Building, Times Square New York, 1919). 5: German Machine Gun Tactics. 6: What is the Nature of the Gang.

121.   In August of 1917 the U.S. Government created the Graves Registration Service to provide assistance with handling and recording the growing number of soldiers killed in Europe. Soldiers were initially interred in temporary graves. Combat units typically undertook this duty; graves registration personnel pro-

vided assistance by locating, marking, maintaining, and registering the location of graves. In reality, however, soldiers were often buried along the front lines, near where they fell, which led to isolated or small groupings of graves spread over wide areas.

U.S. National Archives, Unwritten Records, Newly Digitized Series: Initial Burial Plats for World War I American Soldiers, November 6, 2018, Brandi K Oswald, posted in cartographic records, military, uncategorized, World War I.

122. L. Wardlaw Miles, Captain 308th Infantry, A History of the 308th Infantry, 1917-1919 (New York and London: G.P. Putnam Sons 1927). Page 120.

123. German field artillery shells, the 'whizz bang' was originally attributed to the noise made by shells from a German 77mm field gun, designed by Krupp.

124. 15 cm schwere Feldhaubitze 13 (15 cm sFH 13) was a heavy field howitzer. Shells and guns were referred to as 'five-nines' because the internal diameter of the barrel was 5.9 inches (150 mm). Designed by Krupp.

125. Minenwerfer ("mine launcher" or "mine thrower") is the German name for a class of short range mortars. Referred to as Moaning Minie by Allied troops.

126. 7.7 cm Feldkanone 96 neuer Art (7.7 cm FK 96) field gun. The gun's shells were commonly known as whiz-bangs.

127. Woolly Bear was a shell from a 15-cm Schwere Feldhaubitze 13 Howitzer. It was a type of the "Einbeitsgeschoss" (universal shell) developed by Krupps, that combined shrapnel with a high-explosive projectile.

128. Boyd Cable, *Between the Lines, WWI Centenary Series* (United Kingdom, Read Books Ltd, 2020)

129. Trench mortars

130. Dr. Josiah Alvin Powless (1871–1918) was the first Oneida Indian to graduate from a medical school in the United States. Dr.

Powless served as a first lieutenant in the Medical Department attached to the 308th Infantry in the Argonne. On 14 October 1918 at Chevieres he crossed an area of intense machine gun and artillery fire to aid Captain James McKibben. He dressed McKibben's wounds and carried him to the rear but was wounded in the process. He died on 6 November 1918 and was posthumously awarded the Distinguished Service Cross and the Silver Star.

131.   Captain George G. McMurtry (Congressional Medal of Honor) was a Harvard–educated Wall Street lawyer and served as a member of the Rough Riders during the Spanish American War.

132.   The German defense was Tranchée de la Palette, a well-fortified position on the high ground to the east of the Argonne Forest, north-east of Binarville. This was part of Giselher Stellung.

133.   Behind the front line in the Argonne, German defenses were layered. The second main defensive line was the Giselher Stellung which ran along Hill 198 to Hill 205 and la Palette and for miles to the east and west. This was the first major defensive line the 308th encountered. The third and fourth lines were called Kreimhilde and Freya after Wagner opera female characters. I Reserve Corps (German Third Army), 76th Reserve Division manned the Giselher Stellung.

134.   77th Division Association, *History of the Seventy Seventh Division August 25th, 1917- November 11th, 1918. Designed and Written in the Field, France.* (New York: Wynkoop Hallenbeck Crawford Company). Page 150.

135.   Orders from Pershing 27 September 1918: *"Division and Brigade commanders will place themselves as far up toward the front of the advance of their respective units as may be necessary to direct their movements with energy and rapidity in any attack. The enemy is in retreat or holding lightly in places, and advance elements of several divisions are already on First Army objectives and there should be no delay or hesitation in going forward. Detachments of sufficient*

size will be left behind to engage isolated strong points which will be turned and not be permitted to hold up or delay the advance of the entire brigade or division. All officers will push their units forward with all possible energy. Corps and Division Commanders will not hesitate to relieve on the spot any officer of whatever rank, who fails to show in this emergency those qualities of leadership required to accomplish the task which confronts us. This order will be published to all concerned by the quickest means possible. By command of General Pershing: H.A. DRUM, Colonel, Chief of Staff."

Col. Hugh A. Drum, "191-32.13: Letter (September 27, 1918)" in The United States Army in the World War, 1917-1919: Military Operations of the American Expeditionary Forces (vol. 9), (Washington, D.C., Center for Military History, 1990), pp. 138-40

136.	Walter J. Baldwin, Battalion Sergeant-Major, First Battalion, 308th Infantry, *Was there such a thing in the World's Great War as the Lost Battalion?* (Privately published, Thomas J. Baldwin, 2016). Page 43.

137.	L. Wardlaw Miles, Captain 308th Infantry, *A History of the 308th Infantry, 1917-1919* (New York and London: G.P. Putnam Sons 1927).

138.	Alexander T. Hussey, Raymond M. Flynn, *The History of Company E, 308th Infantry, 1917-1919* (Knickerbocker Press, 1919).

139.	Captain Nelson M. Holderman (Congressional Medal of Honor).

140.	Historical Section, Army War College, *The Operation of the So-Called "Lost Battalion", October 2 to 8, 1918*, Record Group 165: Records of the War Department General and Special Staffs, 1860 – 1952. (Washington: National Archives, August 1928) 13, Appendix B.

141.	Ibid.

142.   Positions of the Lost Battalion, Defense Visual Information Distribution Service (DVIDS), Photo ID 4682232, VIRIN: 180828-Z-A3538-1003.

Note: The appearance of U.S. Department of Defense (DoD) visual information does not imply or constitute DoD endorsement.

143.   "We concentrated 120 men with machine guns directly in rear of the Lost Battalion"

Sunday Star. (Washington, DC), May 1, 1927. Fritz Prinz's interview with James B. Wharton, Part 3, page 4. ↑

144.   "Our mission is to hold this position at all costs. No falling back! Have this understood by every man in your command." Order issued by Major Whittlesey in the Pocket, 12:00 p.m., 3 October 1918

L. Wardlaw Miles, Captain 308th Infantry, *A History of the 308th Infantry, 1917-1919* (New York and London: G.P. Putnam Sons 1927) 120.

145.   Historical Section, Army War College, *The Operation of the So-Called "Lost Battalion", October 2 to 8, 1918,* Record Group 165: Records of the War Department General and Special Staffs, 1860 – 1952. (Washington: National Archives, August 1928). 13, Appendix B.

146.   Cher Ami was the last bird released by the Lost Battalion. Today, Cher Ami can be seen in the Smithsonian, Washington, DC.

147.   L. Wardlaw Miles, Captain 308th Infantry, *A History of the 308th Infantry, 1917-1919* (New York and London: G.P. Putnam Sons 1927). Page 160.

148.   Pigeon Message from Capt. Whittlesey to the Commanding Officer of the 308th Infantry, 10/04/1918. National Archives, Records of the American Expeditionary Forces (World War I). (National Archives Identifier 595541)

149.   WWI slang for dead.

150.   The DH-4 Liberty was the only American-built airplane to be flown in combat by American crews.

151.   *Aviation Magazine*, (New York: Gardner Maffat Company) 1 January 1923. Both men would receive the Congressional Medal of Honor (posthumously).

152.   Cher Ami was a 2-year-old black and gray checkered English National Union Racing Pigeon Association cock #615, U. S. Army serial no. 43678 of the Signal Corps 1st Pigeon Division. Cher Ami was awarded the French Croix de Guerre with palm. He was returned to the United States and died at Fort Monmouth, N.J. on June 13, 1919, as a result of his wounds. Cher Ami is currently part of the Smithsonian.

153.   *"It was truly remarkable how your so-called Lost Battalion, hemmed in by our machine guns and cut off from food, ammunition or help from other American troops, was able to hold its dangerous position for five days.... I doubt very much if our own soldiers would have been capable of such a feat, although to be sure, their power for such resistance had been weakened by four weary years of war. You Americans, on the other hand, were fresh and absolutely nerveless."*

    Sunday Star. (Washington, DC), May 1, 1927. Fritz Prinz's interview with James B. Wharton, Part 3, page 4.

154.   *Sunday Star.* (Washington, DC), May 1, 1927. Fritz Prinz's interview with James B. Wharton, Part 3, page 4.

155.   German officer Hermann von Giehrl credited the AEF's victory in the Meuse-Argonne to the fact that the naïve and inexperienced American soldiers "willingly accepted the hardest losses as something quite natural," and their numbers made the campaign "a disproportioned struggle, which turned more and more to the disadvantage of the defender.

    Richard S. Faulkner, *The U.S. Army Campaigns of World War 1, Meuse-Argonne 26 September-11 November 1918* (Washington: Center of Military History, United States Army, 2018).

156.   Pratt, Fletcher and Johnson, Thomas M. "The Lost Battalion, As the Germans Saw It". The American Legion Magazine, Volume 24, No. 4 (April 1938). ↑

157.   *Sunday Star.* (Washington, DC), May 1, 1927. Fritz Prinz's interview with James B. Wharton, Part 3, page 4.

158.   Paul von Hindenburg, in his memoirs, wrote of this stage of the Meuse-Argonne offensive: *"It was plain that this situation could not last. Our armies were too weak and too tired. Moreover, the pressure which the American masses were putting on our most sensitive point in the region of the Meuse was too strong."*

Field Marshal Paul von Hindenburg, *Out Of My Life*, Volume 2, translated by F. A. Holt (Pickle Partners Publishing, 2012).

"I doubt very much if our own soldiers would have been capable of such a feat, although to be sure, their power for such resistance had been weakened by four weary years of war."

Sunday Star. (Washington, DC), May 1, 1927. Fritz Prinz's interview with James B. Wharton, Part 3, page 4.

159.   Private Lowell Hollingshead was captured and interrogated by Lt Fritz Prinz prior to releasing him back with the white flag and the handwritten note:

To the Commanding Officer of the 2nd Batl. J.R. 308 of the 77th American Division

Sir

The Bearer of the present, (here Hollingshead signed his name) has been taken prisoner by us on October (the date was left blank). He refused to the German Intelligence Officer every answer to his questions and is quite an honorable fellow, doing honor to his fatherland in the strictest sense of the word. He has been charged against his will, believing in doing wrong to his country, in carrying forward this present letter to the Officer in charge of the 2nd Batl.J.R.308 of the 77th Div. with the purpose to recommend this Commander to surrender with his forces as it would be quite useless to resist any more in view of the present conditions. The suffering of your wounded men can be heard over here in the German lines and we are appealing to your human senti-

ments. A white Flag shown by one of your man will tell us that you agree with these conditions. Please treat the (again, here Hollingshead had signed his name) as an honorable man. He is quite a soldier we envy you.

The German Commanding Officer.

160. *The Orlando Sentinel*, Orlando, Florida. 27 Jun 1974. 92.

161. Image from the National Library of Medicine, NLM Unique ID: 101400390, NLM Image ID:A07255

162. Mobile surgical hospitals treated the desperately wounded who could not tolerate further transportation. These patients were less than one percent of the total number of casualties.

Jaffin J. "Medical Support for the American Expeditionary Forces in France During the First World War" Master's Thesis, Command and General Staff College; 1991.

163. Borden S. Veeder, *Activities of Base Hospital 21, France May 1917 April 1919* (Saint Louis, Missouri: Washington University School of Medicine, Bernard Becker Medical Library Archives, 1919).

164. Mobile Hospital No. 4 mobilized in Paris under Base Hospital No. 21 in August 1918. The unit left Paris on 2 September, arriving in Trondes to support the St. Mihiel offensive. In late September 1918, the unit moved again to support the Meuse-Argonne offensive; it set up in a small French Camp on the outskirts of La Grange Aux Bois. While there it received four-hundred and sixty-four patients all of whom were classed as non-transportable cases of head, chest, abdominal, and large bone wounds. The unit performed three hundred and fifty-one operations at La Grange aux Bois with thirty percent mortality.

"Mobile Hospital No. 4," *The Rouen Post*, January 1938. The Rouen Post Base Hospital 21 Collection, 1-1938 (Saint Louis, Missouri: Washington University School of Medicine, Bernard Becker Medical Library Archives, 1938).

165. "The Rouen Post, January 1938" (1938). The Rouen Post. Paper 22.

https://digitalcommons.wustl.edu/rouen_post/22.

166. Adjutant Generals Dept, Statistical Division, *Daily Report of Casualties and Changes. October 9, 1918, Mobile Hospital No.4* (College Park, MD: National Archives at College Park, Record Group 120, Box Number 1316).

167. G.R.S. Plat D-220. Record Group 92, Records of the Office of the Quartermaster General, Series: Initial Burial Plats for World War I American Soldiers, 1920 – 1920, File Unit: Plat Book D.

168. Office of the Quartermaster General (OQMG), *History of the American Graves Registration Service: QMC in Europe, Volume 1* (Washington: Government Printing Office, 1920), 139.

169. *New York Tribune*, Sunday, June 10, 1921. 12.

170. *Army and Navy Journal*, July 16, 1921. 1225.

171. *Spokane Daily Chronicle*, July 30, 1921. 4.

172. William Martin Grave. Photo taken by Brian Maurice, 2019.

173. *American War and Military Operations Casualties: Lists and Statistics*, CRS Report No. RL32492, Version 25 (Washington, DC: Congressional Research Service, Sept. 14, 2018), 2.

174. U.S. Consulate General Havana to Department of State, Dispatch 417, November 30, 1921, file 337.113/415, 1910-29 Central Decimal File (NAID 302021), RG 59: General Records of the Department of State.